GRIEF STREET

Books by Thomas Adcock

Grief Street*
Thrown-Away Child*
Devil's Heaven*
Drown All the Dogs*
Dark Maze*
Sea of Green
Precinct 19

*Published by POCKET BOOKS

GRIEF STREET

A NEIL HOCKADAY MYSTERY

Thomas Adcock

POCKET BOOKS
New York London Toronto Sydney Tokyo Singapore

POCKET BOOKS, a division of Simon & Schuster Inc.
1230 Avenue of the Americas, New York, NY 10020

Adcock, Thomas, 1947–
Grief Street : a Neil Hockaday mystery / Thomas Adcock.
p. cm.
ISBN 0-671-51986-7
I. Title.
PS3551.D397G75 1997
813'.54—dc21 97-8279
CIP

ISBN: 978-1-4767-6303-3

First Pocket Books hardcover printing September 1997

10 9 8 7 6 5 4 3 2 1

Printed in the U.S.A.

At last, for Matt Kollasch

Acknowledgments

One fine day in New York I had lunch with a friend of mine from Berkeley by the name of Stan Lanier, a reader in the better precincts of crime literature and, by the way, a priest in the making. Concerned for the doubting soul of Detective Neil Hockaday, Stan suggested that our hero undergo a spiritual test in the line of duty. The author hopes that this book—a tale of Hock's holy cop trial—might win Stan's blessing. There is likewise hope for friendly verdicts from two others critical to the cause: Avery Brooke, oblate of the Order of the Holy Cross; and Fr. John Sheehan, SJ. Others deserving of thanks and free books are my daughter and son in-law, Anne and Chris Musella; the renowned Otto Penzler, whose story about another kind of bookman called Tony I have borrowed herein; my classiest friends, Roz and Jack Avrett, who have encouraged and sustained me over the years; and two pals who dependably suspect the best of me, Harold Gotha and Bob Leuci. Kisses to Sandi Franklin, Jennifer Wynn and Pam Widener for guiding me through Rikers Island, a world of the damned. And my continuing gratitude to Beth Dembitzer, a cool note in the hell of Hollywood. Readers may direct their gratitude to my editor, Peter J. Wolverton, who has once again taught me what I am trying to write. Above all, this: Hock and I are nothing without our indomitable Ruby Flagg and Kim Sykes.

—*Thomas Adcock*
New York

Maybe this world is
another planet's hell.

—Aldous Huxley

Prologue

BELOW, THE CLANKING FURNACE and the dripping ping of cold water, the buzz of flies . . .

. . . Its guttural wheezing.

Night-gray alley light fogged down through cellar windows, settling into its eyes: oval slits of gassy yellow, like an alligator's eyes reflecting the moon. The stench of excrement and rotting flesh was overwhelming.

I pulled a tin of Vicks chest rub from my coat pocket and slathered my nostrils with biting blue menthol. It hissed at me sharply as I blocked out the putrid odor. When I again breathed freely, its alligator eyes cut me a look that said it knew the one thing sure to scare me clean to the soul.

My head dropped.

I lifted a boot from a lump in the mushy dirt floor. A stone, I thought. But in the withered light striped across my toes I saw instead the remains of a forearm, a wrist, and a small white human hand. A plain gold band encircled the bone of a ring finger.

I bent to reach for the ring, and the possibility of its power. I tugged gold from a stiffened sliver of flesh, almost releasing it . . .

. . . A column of fat beetles marched past my feet, spooking me.

The ring fell. The beetles scuttled toward a sweating cement wall. Something that lay hidden there in the dark snatched them up. From shadows came the sound of tiny teeth crunching insect shells.

I straightened myself and looked back at it.

It was surrounded now by rats the size of rabbits, at least a dozen of the things. The biggest of them straddled its ragged lap, tail worming between thighs. It stroked the nape of the rat's grease-brown neck, as casually as somebody would scratch behind the ears of a collie dog.

"Do you know who I am?" it asked. Its breath plumed in the close, refrigerator-humid air, filling the space between us with a rank bowel smell.

Sunt lacrimae rerum et mentem mortalia tangunt. This now echoed in my frightened head, a Latin drill from Holy Cross schoolboy days; this, the greatest of all Virgil's lines: *These are the tears of things, and the stuff of our mortality cuts us to the heart.*

"Yes," I answered. "I know you."

"Understand, then—you mustn't say my name. Not 'til you're one of mine, and I swallow you."

"That I can wait on." When I am supposed to be as brave as the city of New York pays me to be, I take my sweet time. Also I try to crack wise. There is more percentage having a smart mouth than a dumb mouth.

"Aye, there's time enough for you," it said, in a voice now with the overlapping echoes of New York and Dublin. It said, "For me there's all eternity."

"And time enough for the truth at last?"

"The truth of me, you'd be asking?"

"Yes."

"There are truths that go 'round so dressed up that people take them for lies—but which are pure truths nonetheless." It paused, rasping. "You're after such purity?"

"I think so."

"Then ask me what you will."

"When you say *name,* you mean O'Shaughnessy, for instance. Or Brady, or Harrigan, or—"

"You know exactly what I mean."

"The mortal name people call you?"

"Come now, Detective Hockaday. Not people—*our* people."

"How do you mean?"

"It's said I'm the *fiandiu,* the *shooskie,* the *fule tief.* Isn't that so? The *auld sheeld*—the *muckle maister.* Which do you fancy?"

"I'll go with your favorite."

"You can be a king or a street sweeper, but everybody dances with the grim reaper!" Its bellowing laughter frightened the rats. They skittered off in a dozen directions.

Another smog-cloud of its foul breath stung my eyes. I wiped a sleeve over my face and crouched low, feeling around on the gummy floor for the ring.

"Leave the cursed thing be!" it shouted, knowing what I sought. "Leave it lie!"

"Why?"

For a split second, it hesitated, then said, "For the luck of it, lad!"

"What are you talking about?"

"The muck you're kneeling in's like my altar is what. My *memento mori.* It's so nicely shat through-and-through with blood and bone chunks and man-meat and vermin dung. Ah—where there's muck, there's luck!"

I yanked my hand from the floor. Again it laughed, loudly, sourly. I shut my tearing eyes for relief. My feet shifted, my boot heels sank an inch into muck. And suddenly my head was weaving, as if my neck was a toy spring; this jogged the helpless memory of a thousand nights of my drunkard past: swaying on a raft in a nauseous sea, looking hard at some fixed object, praying to God to make the wobbles go away.

When I managed to settle myself, I rose and started toward it—semiblindly, for all I could see were its vaporous outline and sulfurous eyes. As I moved, I patted my waist, where the nine-millimeter automatic should have been strapped to my belt, and under my arm, where my big piece should have been holstered. Here in the valley of the shadow of death—part of my beat—what was the sense of a mere policeman's bullets?

Closer and closer now in the dark gray light, and its face grew clearer. I allowed myself a heartbeat of surprise, though I was unsurprised. Then I began keening the prayer of Irish forebears, a prayer that blows away all horrors.

"God to enfold me, God to surround me, God in my speaking, God in my thinking . . . God in my sleeping, God in my waking, God in my watching, God in my hoping . . . God in my life, God in my lips, God in my soul, God in my heart—"

"Shut up, shut up!" Its voice rose again to bellowing. "You think I'm impressed by your mumbling the English of the *Carmina Gaedelica?* Oh my, yes—and I know the proper name of the bloody old Paddy's supplication. Ha! You thought perhaps I didn't speak Irish? I'm really quite erudite, and near dead tongues give me particular pleasure. Do think twice of me, Detective Hockaday."

"God in my sufficing—"

"Shut up, I tell you! Shut up and think! Did your priests never learn you I'm only that which Holy God allows me to be? That I've no powers but those that Holy God gave to me, including the jurisdiction of life and death—including, in this very instant, *your* life and death?"

"God in my slumber—"

"Shut up! Shut up!"

"God in mine ever-living soul—"

"Fook God!" With the blasphemy, spittle flew from its scabby lips.

It stood, flapping its great rat-catcher arms, swooping

them down toward the crawling vermin. Then it raised up a swollen-bellied rat overhead, stretching the she-creature until it shrieked from the pain to her womb.

"Fook your God—and fook your saints! The holy fookers all be damned!"

Sunt lacrimae rerum et mentem mortalia tangunt . . .

One

SOMEDAY IN THE NEAR FUTURE, the little bundle of joy en route to Ruby and me will take notice of the neighborhood and ask, "Pop, what in God's name is this place?"

As I have been asking this same question most of my life, it naturally follows that my baby should be likewise curious. So what answer will Pop provide?

How do I give meaning beyond the usual wicked, two-word label by which the neighborhood is known? And in light of the crimes of the past several days—which surely will creep my dreams for years to come—who am I to say the wicked name does not fit? For that matter, who is God himself to say?

In fostering my earliest notions of neighborhood, the nuns, priests, and brothers of my youth—God's mortal faculty of Holy Cross School—were the same as teachers anywhere else in America. They filled my schoolboy head with a lovely lie: order and brightness imposed by crayons on paper is an acceptable reality of life in the streets where I live.

But pretty blue Crayolas do not dependably portray the color of my sky. Nor of the viscous Hudson River, final resting place for hundreds of unlamented gangsters—not to mention a drainage ditch for thousands upon thousands of gallons of blood from the old West Side slaughterhouse days. Trees are rare here, and for most of the year look like skinny old ladies losing their hair; the sidewalks are not pleasantly dappled by sunshine and shade. The light that falls in my streets is thick with soot and is purely hot, like ashes from the sun.

Just the same, and for better or for worse, Ruby and I will raise our child here. Here, where all the goodness and all the evil of the world dwell; where the only impossible experience is complacency.

Our child will be a Kitchen kid, the same as me. I mean Kitchen as in Hell's Kitchen—my briar patch, my haven, the place that carved my soul, my home.

When I was a kid, the classrooms of Holy Cross were hardly the only places of learning. All the Kitchen was a school—a tuition-free college that taught us about poverty, booze, needle panic, switchblade fights, immigrant struggles, hoodlums, clay-footed priests, weary whores, politicians and their brethren pimps. Also it was a neighborhood with at least a hundred Irish pubs like the one where my mother worked herself to death; where the owner welcomed crooked cops with an obliging bargain, "Hear, see, and say nothin'—eat, drink, and pay nothin.' "

That is but one side of my two-faced neighborhood. Sometimes people have to leave the Kitchen to appreciate a place that is at once criminal and tender. On returning, we may then see how courage and misery pave the streets, as surely as concrete and cobblestone. When we have truly come home again, we feel this in our feet with every step.

There are wonderful old smokes hanging about the neighborhood to this day, the same as a generation ago: men and women who have become odd socks in a dusty drawer, pensioners sitting on stoops all day telling wide-eyed kids the amazing tall tales of their lives. They tell Kitchen kids the terrible and beautiful things that have happened in their streets: acts of brutality and heroism and nobility alike. And all these things are evident in the faces of our old smokes, each crease and wrinkle a page in the story of Hell's Kitchen.

An odd sock taught me long ago, "Teach yourself and test yourself, that's the way." I have forgotten his name but not his advice, which has brought me comfort, and which is not nearly as dangerous as shaving. Everybody should be educated the same, for fear of one day becoming the victim of an ill-guided razor.

It was on the stoops and in the streets of Hell's Kitchen where I learned as much as I ever learned in a classroom. For instance, I learned to value charity. Now today—after the dream-creeping crimes—I know this to be the most powerful of all my lessons.

Even in these vicious nowadays there are simple acts of mercy in my neighborhood, committed by people who do not care if anybody ever knows their names. I especially remember an unsung hero who collected woolen gloves and mittens all year long until Christmastime, when he roamed the streets giving warmth to people who had somehow lost their way. Nobody knew him by any name but Mitten Man. A few years ago, he died.

Certain other things are different about today's Kitchen. Uzis and TEC-9s have replaced the zip guns and switchblades of quainter years. Also, we are currently graced by a whole new class of immigrants: the type who walk Akita dogs, yap on cellular phones, and buy plastic bottles of Evian, which I recently learned is designer water from France. I like to think that Evian spelled backward is the French designer's joke on his American clientele.

In my boyhood, practically everybody in the neighborhood lived on the margins, much like Mother and me—taking in laundry, rolling up pennies, steering clear of the hard guys, mopping the hallway linoleum for a break in the rent. Everybody dreamed of leaving. We wanted to put the Kitchen and its ghosts behind us—the nagging ghosts of the potato famine. We wanted to forget, if not forgive. How I envied those who managed the great escape.

Back about midway through Ike, the big mustard yellow

Cirker moving vans would come around nearly every weekend and cart off the belongings of the upwardly mobile for the relative calm of the Bronx. In my sleep, I imagined some perfect Saturday morning in October when the Cirker van would pull up right in front of our own tenement. With all my heart I wanted to be like those lucky Kitchen kids, the ones on their way out: sitting in the cab next to the driver as the van pulled away forever, big grins on their faces, thinking crayon-picture thoughts of leafy Bronx neighborhoods like Riverdale or Woodlawn or Parkchester, waving at us suckers left behind.

I was eighteen when I temporarily escaped the neighborhood for the first time. This was a two-year hitch in Vietnam, a country I never heard of until Sam sent me over to kill commies. After that came a year of City College up in Harlem until I washed out.

Then I joined the department. Imagine: another Irish cop in the Emerald City. At this same time I married a Kitchen girl after she herself washed out as a novitiate—Judy McKelvey, aka Sister Maria of the Franciscan Order of Perpetual Adoration. I served a six-year stretch of domestic unbliss with the ex-nun. We lived in a cute little house over in Ridgewood until a Queens Civil Court judge awarded the place to her and otherwise instructed me in the meaning of divorce: from the Greek *divorcicus,* to pull one's testicles through one's wallet.

With experiences like that, who needs escape? So I returned to my briar patch for good.

Actually, for a number of years the homecoming was not so good. I thought I was doing all right by earning my gold shield early on, with assignment to an elite plainclothes squad that does not actually sound all that elite: the SCUM patrol, for Street Crimes Unit–Manhattan. But somewhere during those years I fell deep into the black well of being a cop boozer. If it was oblivion I was after in those self-pitying days, I might have reached my objective quicker by eating my gun.

Grief Street

†

It was an overly warm Thursday afternoon in April, the day before Good Friday, when I was walking along thinking about the neighborhood and ghosts and hardships and drinking, and some other things, too—including the luck of Ruby coming into my life, including our incipient bundle of joy. My reverie was interrupted by a guy in a black fedora tearing down Seventh Avenue on foot after a taxicab, which he finally nailed at the Forty-second Street light. I stopped to watch the guy attack the taxi with his feet and fists, smashing out a window.

The driver was wearing a turban and he hollered a lot of Punjabi threats through the broken window before roaring off. After which, the guy in the fedora ducked down into a subway hole and was gone himself. Case closed, I figured.

This incident occurred about halfway into the rush hour when I was crossing from the east side of the avenue and innocently walking along the remarkable street where I live. Since it was my day off, technically speaking, I classified what had happened right in front of my cop face as a low-priority case of tit for tat.

Meanwhile, Ruby was back at the apartment—three floors up over West Forty-third at Tenth Avenue—reading the script of a way-off-Broadway play that somebody had sent her in a plain brown wrapper.

On account of her needing peace and quiet from me, as my wife the actress expressed it, I had to go find something to occupy myself for a while. As I obliged her by walking out the door around noon, she shot me one of those looks I still get, even though I am no longer on speaking terms with Mr. Johnnie Walker. One of those *And-don't-be-going-to-the-bar-across-the-way* looks.

I had spent the early part of the afternoon in an air-conditioned cinema in Times Square that specializes in movies the way I like them: old, and full of grown-up words instead of car crashes and teenage twaddle. The

Royal Bijou was running a double feature: *The Illustrated Man,* with Rod Steiger and Claire Bloom, and *The Hairy Ape,* with William Bendix. How could I resist?

By the way, about my remarkable street:

At the epicenter of Forty-third is an ugly gray slab twenty-five storeys high, which since 1975 has been called One Times Square. This building—where the lighted apple drops every New Years's Eve, incidentally—is situated at the so-called Crossroads of the World, otherwise known as the intersection of Broadway and Seventh Avenue. East of this are a number of polite attractions, including the rarefied offices of the *New Yorker* magazine, Grand Central Station, and the United Nations Assembly Building. I keep mostly to the West Side.

The slab at Number One is girdled by the world-renowned neon news zipper that has given decades of no-nonsense crawling headlines such as HITLER DEAD! and ROSENBERGS FRIED! and NIXON DUMPED! A very long time ago, the *New York Times* was housed here, in what was then called the Times Tower—which was then a very fine Italianate stone building. In 1964 a gang of architectural morons skinned Times Tower down to its steel skeleton and globbed dull marble panels all over it and christened it the Allied Chemical Tower. These morons pronounced the resultant handiwork "sleek." Sleek like a Soviet high-rise. Years before this crime, sometime back in the 1930s, I believe, the *Times* itself had moved catty-corner to the block between Broadway and Eighth Avenue, into a nondescript building with bad ventilation and a lot of rodents.

When I passed by the mousy *Times* building at 229 West Forty-third that particular afternoon, a legless loon was holding forth across the street in the doorway of an old haunt of mine called Gough's. This used to be a pressmen's watering hole before computers stole away all the typesetting jobs, and also a snug for cops from the Midtown South station house. Reporters and editors wearing suits would sometimes drink at Gough's. If the suits sported the pressmen to some rounds, they were taught how to fold newsprint into square caps—toppers that protect hair from flying ink. Gough's is dead now, due halfway to employment attrition thanks to the thieving computers and halfway to the fact that so many of us former clients are currently on the wagon.

But the house loon of Gough's, bless his crazed heart, is still at his post in the trash-strewn doorway.

There he was now: perched on a slab of plywood with skate wheels bolted to the bottom, his means of transport. His greasy pants were hiked up over thigh stumps, to encourage the sympathies of passers-by.

He looked up at me sternly. For some reason he said, "God's really pissed off at you!"

He shook a paper cup that had a couple of suggestive quarters rattling inside. A thin woman bustling by in clicky high heels dimed him. I thought the tiny gift might agitate the loon, but instead it changed his tone from stern to singsong plaintive. He sang out something I do not believe has been routinely heard since the days of Charles Dickens prowling the tubercular streets of London: "Alms for the poor . . . alms for the poor . . ."

So I gave the loon all the change I had in my pocket, two quarters, two dimes, and a nickel. I kept back a subway token, though. He stared back and forth between his cup and my face. I asked, "Got enough to make it tonight, friend?"

"Shot of this golden stuff and I'll make it through whatever fate's in store," said Gough's loon. He took a flat-bottled pint of Duggan's Dew from his belt and nipped at it. "Me and God Almighty—him being in charge of fate and all—we're drinking buddies."

"How's that?"

"Don't you expect God takes himself a snootful now and again?"

A fair answer, I thought, and deserving of the token I had held back. I forked it over, as a sort of tip. The loon smiled calmly. I moved on.

The Times Square Hotel, twelve storeys of stout brick, stands at the corner of Eighth Avenue, which is the westerly edge of my own Hell's Kitchen. A few years ago the city rescued the place from disintegration by making it over as second-chance housing for the formerly hopeless. Ben & Jerry's leased part of the ground level and hired the tenants to run one of their ice cream parlors—at very decent wages. Washington politicians ignore a project like this because they get much better whoops from the money crowd by talking about how they want to get government off our backs.

Across the way from the Ben & Jerry's, I noticed a commotion going on between a pair of bearded merchants in yarmulkes and black coats over tallith fringes and a wired-up skell in a dirty tan windbreaker. Surrounding them was a small mob of Japanese tourists snapping pictures. "You can't redeem for this!" one of the yarmulkes shouted, over and over. He was holding a bouquet of Yankees pennants in one hand and some sort of store coupon in the other. "I swear to God," the skell responded each time. "I paid, I swear to God."

I crossed the street, and one of the Japanese turned to ask me, "Excuse, sir, please—what happening here?"

"A religious dispute," I said, trying to be entertaining. This seemed to make the Japanese guy's day. He gleefully translated for his countrymen, who became likewise pleased.

I crossed Eighth Avenue.

There is a battleship gray tenement on the north side of the next block, number 309, where a Kitchen kid called Alphonse Capone was born in the year 1899. His family escaped to Chicago, where young Alphonse earned the street name of Scarface and eventually distinguished himself in the beverage industry. Next door to Capone's birthplace is now a Christian bookshop. And next door to that is a squatty warehouse belonging to Charles Scribner & Sons, a publisher of less consecrated works. One of Scribner's authors, Ernest Hemingway, was allowed to stash crates of ammuni-

tion for his famous African safaris in an upper floor of the warehouse. One crate remains up there. Nobody has seen fit to disturb this bit of Papa's estate.

Across the way from Scribner's is my alma mater: Holy Cross School, with its west entry arch for boys, east for girls. Inside, in the basement dining hall, there is to this day something called the dead table.

I thought of my mother, Mairead, in heaven, and how years ago the two of us would shop the dead table on the second Wednesday of each month. Mother with her dollar bills, wet and greasy from the pub and held tight in a thick rubber band, me lugging a cloth bag of rolled pennies. This was how people like us purchased clothes whenever possible: by pawing through garments on the dead table, donations from the families of the parish deceased.

We never knew what extraordinary bargains might be found, save for the time that a family friend by the name of Father Tim broke the rules and tipped Mother to a fine boy's winter jacket—maroon and gray plaid wool, with a stand-up mouton collar and a belt that crossed over the front with a chrome buckle.

Until the blessing of a dead boy's coat, I walked to school in the winter with the Hudson River wind blowing at my back so hard it felt like whips. Mother would cook extra pancakes on the coldest mornings—not for my eating, but for stuffing under the arms of the six flannel men's shirts she had jerry-stitched into a boy's coat. *Hold them hotcakes tight with your hands, son, and you'll nae be minding cold. Quick like the fox, you'll be where you're going with no discomfort on arriving there. Warm hands and proper school, these be things to free my young Irishman from the crimes of ignorance and poverty and the raw-boned cold of America.*

The only brand-new thing my mother ever wore was a dress I bought her from Sak's Fifth Avenue so she could have something nice on the day the mayor swore me in as Patrolman Neil Hockaday of the New York Police Department. She wore it that once, to please me, then never again. When she passed, I gave her dress to the dead table.

I crossed Ninth Avenue.

Uptown from Forty-third, the blocks used to be full of hardware shops and saloons specializing in forty-cent draughts. Some of the hardwares have turned into the type of restaurants where customers have to specify radicchio, Bibb, or Belgian endive if they want to eat a salad. The sole surviving low-rent saloon has no identification to it, save for a sign on the door that reads NO DRUGS, NO THUGS.

Downtown, there was once the open-air Paddy's Market of pushcart fruits and vegetables—and swag of the day. Mother did not go to Macy's or Gimbel's when I needed things not easily available from the dead table—sneakers, khakis, polo shirts. Instead, she went to Paddy's Market and gave her list to a hobble-legged man called Gimp Higgins who sold tomatoes on the sidewalk. A couple of days later Gimp Higgins would happen to come into the possession of the very merchandise Mother wanted, at cut-rate prices.

There is still a market of fruit, vegetables, and swag down along Ninth Avenue. But the pushcarts are long gone. And the vendors of what is now called the International Market tend to be from Greece, the Philippines, Korea, the West Indies, or the remnants of Yugoslavia. Times do change. Which explains the modern additions of a gay bar, and a drop-in center for homeless old folks so they can sit around and drink coffee someplace warm instead of getting themselves mugged on a snowy day.

Also there is the addition of Covenant House, a sanctuary for runaway teens from Middle America. The priest who founded the place—relieved of duty for being overly fond of freckle-faced boys (though never defrocked)—once invited a fortunate guy from Texas by way of Connecticut to drop around and inspire the unfortunate youngsters of Hell's Kitchen. Which is how it was that George Herbert

Walker Bush came calling during the election year of 1992.

Maybe this seemed like a good idea to somebody on the president's campaign staff. But what the White House will never understand—no matter who lives there—is the impertinent wisdom of a Kitchen kid, native-born or naturalized. Being a Kitchen kid is a state of mind, a whole different level beyond White House mentality.

Picture the photo op:

A flock of sullen youths crowded around the feet of a president in a pinstripe suit and a society lady accent. George Bush lectures the assembled Kitchen kids on the pride and glory of a weekly paycheck at minimum wage. There comes the moment when these youths can no longer bear the crapola. So one of them gives the president some practical socioeconomic advice on the state of the union: "Get real, man. That chump Mickey D paycheck? Shit, I made that in twenty minutes selling powdered milk to ignorant frat boys from Connecticut come to the city after heroin." Meanwhile, just outside the photo-op set, one of the TV reporter's cars is stolen from where it is parked next to a fleet of NYPD and Secret Service vehicles.

The heist and the unscripted reality check delivered to the president of the United States were the only actually newsworthy things that occurred during George Bush's historic visit to Covenant House. But not a word was said about any of it in the next day's papers, nor on TV or radio. So after all these years, you are reading it here first.

I now approached the corner of West Forty-third and Tenth Avenue, which is personally landmarked to the northeast by a guy called Eddie the Ear. As usual, he was sitting in his folding lawn chair, puffing a cigar stub, fingers laced across his little pot belly, chair tilted back against the painted brick wall of the bar across the street from my place.

The bar is called Dinny's Lounge, incidentally. It is famous in particular circles for being the site of another

Hell's Kitchen event that never made the news. Here again, the scoop:

Back on the seventeenth of November, 1972, a legendary group of Irish-American gents who are now mostly guests of the federal witness protection program tossed a birthday party for the late Arnold "Rosie" Rosenbaum. In his day, Rosie was the biggest loan shark on the West Side—big in every way except brains. The boyos who sported him to birthday cake and so forth were members of the bygone Westies gang, which mainly capitalized itself by hiring out to perform acts of permanent violence on behalf of Mulberry Street mafiosi.

In kind moments, however, the Westies could be altruistic, as they considered themselves guardian angels of Hell's Kitchen. Good and bad angels were heard in equal measure that time when the Westies convinced dim-witted Rosie Rosenbaum that he, a loan shark, was a beloved figure in the Kitchen. And further, that Rosie's many debtors would be delighted to fête him at Dinny's Lounge on his natal day.

So, Rosie showed up and ate a lot of good food that November seventeenth. Big portions. Also he drank many big drinks. And much to his surprise and teary gratitude, he opened many nicely wrapped presents. Everybody wore party hats and felt pretty good and fuzzy when the big cake was wheeled in. Rosie blew out a half-century's worth of candles, after which he did the honors by cutting off the first slice—a slab roughly twice the size of his bowling hand.

Then came the second slice. This being in the person of a quick-stepping boyo who sidled up behind Rosie, pulled a machete out from under his coat, and whacked off Rosie's plump head with the party hat on top of it. The head mushed into the birthday cake and bloodied it up so badly it could only be half-eaten by the celebrants.

After cake and coffee, Rosie's hosts transported the remains of his body down to what used to be a kosher abattoir on Eleventh Avenue and West Thirty-eighth. The late

Arnold Rosenbaum was dumped into the sausage mash along with a lot of cow and lamb carcasses, and eventually became breakfast in homes from coast to coast.

A young flunky of Rosie's in those years and therefore a party guest (although he says he was among the first to scram out of Dinny's Lounge when the birthday boy was whacked), Eddie the Ear told me all this at the time. I was a cop then as now and therefore required to snoop around a little bit. But since the private death of a shylock is a departmental low priority in the first place, and since there was no trace of the shylock's corpus delicti in the second place, the matter was informally written off as a public service homicide.

He is not much to look at, Eddie the Ear: pink faced and maybe forty, but older looking because of his bald head, sturdy but growing a little rubbery around the middle. He is soft-spoken and wears spectacles that slip down over a bumpy snout. He dresses practically year-round in checked polyester pants, ripple-soled shoes, and a nylon bomber jacket with the breast patch of his union, Theatrical Stage Employees Local One.

Edward Michael Mallow's peculiarity appears only at close range. This is when a person can see how the left side of Eddie's head is a stretch of flat skin, including where a second ear should have grown but never did. There is not so much as a pucker to mark the spot.

When I was growing up, the nuns used to whisper how Eddie's peculiar head was the result of something unholy about the Mallow family—here in New York, and over on the other side, too. We boys at Holy Cross suspected the whispering had something to do with sex, a topic sure to set nuns to low and secret talking. Even the bravest among us had no stomach for listening close to the details of a sister's true sex concerns, the tales they invented having terrified us so.

Eddie maintains a sense of humor about his deformity. With one hand cupped to his lone ear and a finger of the other pointing to the flat side of his head, he says, "I must be the smartest guy in the world. What goes in one ear, it don't got nowhere to come out."

He enjoys thinking of himself as one of my snitches, even though I have never paid him a dollar out of the department's squeak budget. So the least I can do for Eddie the Ear when I see him is to indulge him with his favorite conversational gambit. Which is what I did now, by asking, "What do you hear lately, Eddie?"

Eddie pushed up his spectacles with a thumb. "Besides a kid being on the way to you and your missus," he said, "I hear Ruby's planning a return into show biz."

"I guess, maybe . . ."

I meant *I guess* about Ruby and show biz. There was little doubt as to the meaning of Ruby's belly. I looked at my wristwatch. It was time for me to be sitting around the apartment agitating about dinner and otherwise talking with my wife, after which I would nap and read; after which I would have reason to slip into a troubled sleep, with a sweaty dream about crimes against memory. As for right now, I had been gone plenty long enough to please Ruby.

"Anyhow," I said to Eddie, who was now wearing a look of anticipation, "a script came in the mail."

"Yeah, I heard that. Heard it's a real inter-restin' play."

"You know more about it than me, Eddie. Ruby was raving about the writing—and the politics of the piece, whatever they are. She never told me the title."

"I hear it's called *Grief Street.* I hear it's about the Kitchen."

Two

LATER INTO THE NIGHT, as I lay sweating and dreaming, others in Hell's Kitchen were wide awake. These were fourteen elderly congregants of Congregation Ezrath Israel, called the Actors Temple since it is near so many Broadway theaters. Their heads were bowed as they sat stiffly in the pews, listening intently to a friend of mine by the name of Rabbi Marvin Paznik read . . .

. . . After which they were horrified by something they would all describe as a "shadow."

Can a shadow have a smell? Fourteen old men and women agreed it could. They said the shadow reeked like something that thrives on death, something like maggots. They said the shadow that smelled was just "suddenly there."

They said the shadow covered their rabbi in darkness, like a black cloak. They said this shadow, whatever it was, smothered my friend; and with some unseen blade, slashed and hacked at him. And when the attack was over, the shadow vanished into the Hell's Kitchen night.

Rabbi Marvin Paznik had been celebrating a midnight observance of Yom Hashoah—the Day of Remembrance for the victims of the Holocaust, which happens to coincide with my own holiday of Good Friday. My friend Marv was leading a Kaddish, in respect for the millions of slaughtered souls, known and unknown.

From a page in his prayer book—marked with bloody whorls of his right index finger, which Marv likely used to follow the ritual reading—I know the last words he uttered:

"Man is feeble and perishable; many of his devices and efforts are vain. Like a shadow he appears and passes away, and no trace is left of his footprints. From the hour of his birth, he begins a journey fraught with pain and disappointment, and hourly hastens on toward the night of his grave. . . . The closed eye is only then satisfied with seeing . . ."

Three

AT TWILIGHT, the eve of midnight's holiday murder, I stood at the west window of my apartment. Thanks to the gauzy scrim of pollution that colors the air over New Jersey, with glassy particulates serving as thousands of prisms, sunsets can be spectacular.

Right now, in fact, I was absorbing an inspirational view of a flattening sun bleeding to death over the Jersey horizon. Closing in was the darkening color of a Hell's Kitchen night: black and blue, like bruises. Hanging just over the steeple of the Croatian church at West Forty-first was the trace of a full moon, its cheese yellow light growing stronger as the sun exhausted itself.

"So what do you think, Irish?"

Ruby asked me this from the couch. She was sitting there under the south window, shoes and socks on the floor, bare feet tucked beneath her thighs. In pregnancy, she was not entirely comfortable in such a position, but it was her long-established reading habit. In her lap was a script that must have been banged out on a very old typewriter with an even older two-tone ribbon. The text was faint black, the headings were typed in red.

Ruby was wearing the thick wire-rimmed spectacles she

never takes outside the apartment, preferring contact lenses over glasses, which she thinks make her look froggy-eyed. She explains away the vanity for reasons of business: *I have to look gorgeous, it's my job.* Specs or no, Ruby is certifiably gorgeous. Her skin is creamed coffee colored; her eyes are hazel, with an olive cast in evening's light; her ink black hair is what she calls nappy. She has a dimple in her chin. Below that is a décolletage that after I first laid eyes on it caused me a week of thinking little else besides the usual punchline from my childhood storybooks: *And then the little boy lived happily ever after.*

Whatever Ruby happens to be wearing—shorts and sneakers to the gym, a red dress on a Saturday night, one of my blue chambray shirts hanging down to her slim knees on our way to bed—I want to go bite something when I look at her. Even now after we have been together for a number of years, this is true, which does not surprise me because of what happens when I walk into someplace like a restaurant with Ruby: there is the inevitable lonesome guy with a face that seems to be asking, How come a hump like him gets a babe like her?

"What I think is, it's a perfect night for the shouters and the howlers at the moon," I said, looking up at the bruised sky, trying to be funny and diverting because I did not want to talk about that script of hers. Why, I did not quite know—not yet. "This is some night for the lobotomites."

"No, I mean what do you think about *Grief Street?*"

"Snappy title."

"That's all?"

"What can I tell you? It's not like I've read it for myself. All I know is what you were saying when I left, how it's brilliant and political and all. Eddie out there on the corner, he says it's about the neighborhood." Suddenly I began realizing what bothered me about this play Ruby loved so much. I asked, "Where does this thing come from?"

"You know what I wonder?"

"What?"

"Where Mr. Mallow heard about it."

"That's it. Eddie's your bashful playwright."

"That I doubt."

"Maybe you mentioned it someplace around the neighborhood. It's the kind of thing Eddie the Ear picks up on. It's his life."

"Whatever." Ruby waved fingers in front of her face, dismissing unnecessary details. "Anyway, do you think I should do it?"

Dispensing advice to an actor is tricky. I paced around in front of the window for a couple of seconds, playing for time, calculating an answer. Actors are not logical human beings. But then who is? On top of that, here I was talking to a pregnant actor. Ruby's motherly hormones were giving her the emotional loop-the-loop. How many months before the blessed event? I counted five. So how was Ruby supposed to commit to a rehearsal schedule, not to mention regular performances? But maybe she was talking about staging the piece at her failed theater on South Street, the Downtown Playhouse.

"How can you?" I reasoned, finally. "I thought you and some real estate agent were supposed to be closing on the theater building next month."

"The sale's definitely on. Then like I told you, we use the money to shop around for someplace nice and big for Mommy and Daddy and Baby makes three—someplace we're not going to leave until they carry us out sideways. All right?" Ruby sounded like the kind of schoolteacher you want to thwack with a spit wad. "And don't worry, Hock, like we agreed—it's going to be someplace in the neighborhood."

"I'm not worried."

"Then what's eating you?"

"Procedure. I mean, don't playwrights usually mail off their scripts to theaters?"

"Usually."

"You've got a theater. For a while anyway. So how come it wasn't mailed there?"

"Writers. Go figure."

"I've tried. I've been reading them for years."

"All I know is, this writer is tuned into my kind of politics. Not to mention there's a great part for me, the best I've ever been offered, to tell you the truth." Ruby touched the script in her lap. Onionskin pages were held in place with brass pins along the left margins. The padded envelope the script had come in—postmarked from the Times Square station, no return address—was on the floor next to Ruby's shoes and socks. There was also an unsigned cover letter on pale red paper. "On the first level, this is a murder mystery. You like murder mysteries, right?"

"The real ones are my business. Of the made-up kind, I don't go for those dopey beach books."

"Oh, but there's meat and potatoes with this story. Like I say, it's political. It's history, too. And it's about ideals." A tease of a smile played in Ruby's face. "And some people, Irish, they're going to find it personal. You—especially—have got to read this."

"Okay already."

"Anyway, I'd be playing this woman called Annie. She runs a saloon and a brothel out of a house on West Fortieth Street, around the turn of the century."

"Back then the street was mostly Irish."

"Nontraditional casting. My favorite."

"I thought you had a rule about your parts. No maids, no whores."

"Nobody's invited me to be onstage in a whole lot of years, my dear. I can afford to make an exception."

I should explain about Ruby. She left her hometown of New Orleans as an eighteen-year-old kid under the impression that Broadway was the place where an African American actress who did not happen to sing or dance might have a chance, especially if she was pretty. Everybody has to learn the hard way. So Ruby wound up taking a survival job on Madison Avenue. She did more than survive. She parlayed an entry-level job in the advertising dodge into something with a salary brisk enough to underwrite her dream of a New York theater where audiences could come to see African American actors who did not happen to sing or dance, and who were not necessarily good-looking. At least the real estate appreciated.

"Besides, this character is my kind of woman," Ruby said. "I'm talking capital-*W* Woman." She riffled the crisp pages of her script. "Annie Meath's her name. She mostly sits drinking at the parlor bar, tossing out sweet, subversive lines. When her girls aren't working the beds upstairs, she hires them out as thugs for labor disputes—strictly on the union side. Annie is many things, but she's no angel. One thing everybody calls her, though—the mother of Hell's Kitchen."

"This somehow sounds familiar."

"It should, it's street history. There really was a gang of strong-arm prostitutes. Annie's Goons they were called. Guess what makes Annie Meath's place history?"

"I don't like guessing. Tell me."

"This is one of my favorite scenes." Ruby fingered through some pages until she found what she was looking for, the pertinent stage directions and dialogue. "It's a blistering hot summer's night, and outside of Annie's brothel there's a small riot going on. There's a cop standing around watching. Annie Meath is sitting on her stoop observing the battle. First the cop shakes his head and says, 'This place is hell itself.' Then Annie says, 'Hell's a mild climate. This here is hell's kitchen, no less.' "

"I know that place," I said. Which was unwise of me, since it only made Ruby more excited about the prospects of taking on the play. "What street again?"

"West Fortieth."

"Sure—that decrepit brownstone between Ninth and Tenth. Next door there's a shelter for battered women. The shelter's run by an old teacher of mine from Holy Cross, Sister Roberta, one of the better ones as nuns go. Anyhow—as for the house next door that was run by another kind of woman, nobody ever marked it with a historical plaque or anything. But the old place is still there and standing, for those who care about neighborhood myths."

"This playwright cares." Ruby straightened her legs and put the script down. She picked up the cover letter and handed it to me. "Here, read this. Then like I asked before, tell me what you think."

The paper was a heavy bond, in contrast to the onionskin typescript. The handwritten message was brief and cryptic. Large, carefully wrought letters in black fountain pen ink had been applied to stationery the color of blanched cherries. The ink was fuzzy in most spots, as if the author had written on wet paper. It read:

> Dearest Ms. Flagg:
>
> I've taken the liberty of entrusting to you the enclosed script of *Grief Street.* As it is a life's work, I shan't offer it as doorstop matter for some cretinous producer's offices until such time as a bona fide artist such as your fine self has had opportunity to evaluate its potential. Thus, the play is submitted for your approval, with my attendant high hopes. Naturally, you will see yourself in the principal rôle of Annie Meath. I shall take the further liberty of telephoning one day soon, at which time we may enjoy proper discussion of our future—including a reading of the piece I have arranged for Monday evening next. Until then, my special blessings upon you & yrs.

There was no signature.

"Exactly what stage of development is the guy talking about?" I asked. I was now standing by the couch where Ruby sat, her face uptilted and enthusiastic. I gave the letter back to her and tried to muster something positive to say. "The guy writes a letter like he's living back in the time of his characters."

"We're talking about a backer's audition on Monday night, the day after Easter. A staged reading for potential angels is what I mean." Ruby talked like a teacher addressing a dunce. "And even at this early point in a long process—which is longer than I'm planning on being pregnant—*the guy* actually cares about artistic judgment."

Ruby grabbed the letter out of my hands. She was irritated with me, probably because I was not saying what she wanted to hear. Which is what I mean by actors being tricky when they ask for advice. "By the way, what makes you think the playwright's a man?"

"I don't know—"

"You don't know much else about it either. You should read the play."

"When do I get a chance? It came in the morning mail. You looked it over while I made coffee, you glommed onto it all to yourself, then you shooed me out of the house for the day—"

"Read it now. Who's stopping you?"

"Could a guy get his dinner first?"

"Stop worrying about your stomach all the time. People are going to start thinking you're the preg-o."

Another thing about Ruby: the bigger she grows these days, the more she tries to convince me how I should slim down by going to one of those gyms full of painful contraptions left over from the Middle Ages. Maybe some of my ancestors were tortured on such contraptions. This is how she nags me: *You should be fit, you're going to be a daddy. Don't even think of dropping dead on me when the tuition bills come rolling in.* I tell her I probably have a finite number of heartbeats and so I should not be wasting any of them sweating through exercises on torture racks.

"I'll look at it tonight," I promised.

"Fat chance. First you'll eat dinner, then you'll put on the radio while you're reading some novel. Not the beach kind. Then you'll fall asleep in your chair with your mouth open and your belly pooching over your belt. After which I'll have to drag you into bed and you'll fall dead asleep."

"Okay then, tomorrow. It's Good Friday tomorrow. I'm off in the afternoon."

†

So all right, Ruby knew my habits. I fell asleep somewhere in the middle of Robertson Davies's final novel—

The Cunning Man, about a police surgeon and the mysterious death of an Anglican priest, on Good Friday yet—and somewhere toward the end of Rich Conady's *Big Broadcast* program on WQEW. The radio show had just started when Ollie's Noodle Shop & Grille over on West Forty-fourth delivered our order of *mu shu* pork, shredded chicken with yellow leeks, and curry-flavored Singapore *mai fun.* When I nodded off, I remember Conady was playing a medley of Bix Beiderbecke.

Maybe it was the food that put the pictures in my head. I have vivid dreams when I eat from the Ollie's menu. Or maybe it was the nagging thought of Ruby's play, set in the very darkest of the Kitchen's dark days, which I knew without having to read some mysterious playwright's script.

I remember drifting off to those Bix tunes, to dark neighborhood memories, and to a dream about memory itself.

Thomas Adcock

Murals spray-painted on scarred walls of Kitchen buildings, portraits surrounded by images and symbols and people's names. What was this art? Memorials to the ones slaughtered in our streets. Paintings by survivors, telling us that the murdered must not be forgotten.

When we forget, memory is corroded. That is devastating.

Memory makes it possible for people to be responsive, and responsible: to learn, to plan, to choose, to create, to love. Memory civilizes us. Memory is the power to make connections, which is the whole idea of being a detective.

When people forget and cannot remember, they lose themselves and they are alone. That is a crime.

Some people can't help forgetting. Some choose to forget, some simply let it happen. Certain others make us want to forget. If we are not careful of them, they can steal our memories.

When people forget, lives are ravaged. What happens when a whole society forgets?

Four

"You don't look like no Jew-boy I ever seen."

"No, I suppose not."

Becker was the name of the tiresome muster sergeant I had to be in the same room with. His first name I do not know, or care to know. Becker is the kind of cop with shiny pants from a career of mostly sitting at a desk. He wears flag patches sewn to the sleeves of his size XXL uniform shirt, with U.S.A. embroidered in redundant gold under the stars and stripes. Cops like him all over the country sprouted these little flags back when Nixon was warming up to his final disgrace. If Becker was to have a stroke anytime during his tour, odds were that he would freeze up just the way he was now: jelly doughnut in one hand, clipboard in the other.

"So if you ain't Hebe," Becker wondered, pouring on the charm, "what's it to you?"

"It happened in my neighborhood, that's what. While I was sleeping." I was looking over the detail sheet from the abbreviated special incidents report Becker had read off to everybody during the morning roll call. It was bad enough I had heard it cold—the news about my friend's murder—from a slob like Becker. It was worse now, reading it black on white, every word whapping me in the chest. Sweat ran down my back and trickled into my shorts. I put a hand over my heart, thinking somehow that would stop the banging. "Five blocks from where I live . . ."

Victim DOA at Roosevelt Hospital . . . Facial region butchered beyond recognition . . . Print positive ID pending . . . Tentative ID as . . .

Whap? My friend's name again.

I am no stranger to dead names, mainly due to the hazards of my occupation. In my time I have seen hundreds of dead bodies, read hundreds more toe tags and newspaper obituaries and funeral programs—and homicide write-ups, like the one now rattling in my hands. But seeing the words PAZNIK, RABBI MARVIN in the familiar typeface of the Royal standard manual from the station house papering room that I myself have used to write a mile of anonymous dead names—this was personal, a violation. And a hollowing sadness, the kind that overwhelms me when I visit my mother's grave, when I brush my fingers across the letters of her name chiseled in a marble headstone. Sadder yet, I realized—too late to tell him—how much affection I had for my friend, a neighborhood good guy.

"Oh, that's right, you live in the city, in Hell's Kitchen yet—that slum." Becker was missing the point all over the place. Also he was chewing on a doughnut. Sugar crumbs bounced on soggy lips as he talked. "For crying out loud, Hockaday, you never heard of the Island?"

Becker lives in the Long Island cop ghetto of Massapequa. Other than driving back and forth between the suburban tract house where he sleeps and the precinct station house where he sits, he does not get around much. Consequently, he has no clue about the Evian gulpers crowding my neighborhood; how they would take one look at his face blotchy from crullers and his shiny pants and make him for something that goes to bed at night inside a cardboard box propped up in a doorway.

Any other day, I might have given Becker my low opinion of Massapequa and the Island in general. I would have asked, How'd you like an army of Island-hating cops like me—worse than me, cops with dark complexions—commuting out to Massapequa every day with guns and bad attitudes? But today it would give me no such pleasure to make Becker's neck bulge.

Besides which, I had no time. I needed clearance from my inspector—not an easy man to reach on the phone—and then I wanted to hurry over to Temple Ezrath Israel before a killer's trail went cool. *A shadow?* So I let it go with Becker by telling him, "Do all the decent folks a big favor, Sergeant. Shut your hole."

Becker bellied up to me, so close I could smell cinnamon on his breath. "You should watch your mouth, Hockaday. Maybe your back, too. You don't want it that somebody decorates you with a couple more nice wreaths. Follow?"

I turned, and slowly walked away from Becker. Also I followed him, so to speak. Meaning I know a threat when I hear one.

Of the various NYPD fraternal customs down through the years, "wreathing" is among the unloveliest. Cops employ this threatening custom to deter officers from ratting out their own kind, which is to say lodging a misconduct complaint against another cop with the Internal Affairs Division down at One-Pee-Pee. Last year, I was twice wreathed—a double commemoration of my filing brutality charges against one Joseph Kowalski, a desk sergeant at the Manhattan Sex Crimes Squad. What is it with these desk sergeants?

First it was in the station house basement, with a garland of thirteen dead sewer rats nailed anonymously to my locker door. The day after, another baker's dozen of the expired sweeties were strung over the outside doorknob of my apartment. This was all on account of my being uncharmed by what a number of my brethren either ignore or take as comedy, to wit: the "dickprint," meaning a ritual torturing of homosexual perpetrators in the custody of Sergeant "King Kong" Kowalski, as he is called on account of his size.

A couple of years ago when I was working a case that overlapped with the Sex Crimes Squad, I got wind of the dickprint routine. Two years and no resolution on my complaint of a drill that goes like this:

Some gay perp gets himself collared and is hauled into Kowalski's bailiwick. The perp is nervous, maybe this is his first time. Seeing the chance of squad room merriment, Kowalski feigns a sort of fatherly concern for the tenderfoot. He volunteers to personally take the guy's fingerprints. Kowalski escorts the perp into an airless, unused janitor's closet below the stairs at the Sex Crimes Squad, where stands a small battered desk, an immense chair, and an overhead naked light bulb. Kowalski takes the chair and rummages through the desk drawer, removing a standard FBI fingerprint form and an ink pad. He takes the perp's trembly hands and rolls them nice and gentle over the ink, splotching all ten imprints into the appropriate squares on the form. Kowalski then searches the drawer again, this time removing a pair of hospital gloves. He snaps the latex over his big mitts and announces, "Okay, now for your dickprint." The perp says, "My *what?*" Kowalski explains sympathetically, "Son, I don't like this any more than you do, but it's regulation in this here age of AIDS. Anybody arrested, we got to keep records of their fingertips, right? Now we got to also do the same with their johnsons. Understand? So now, drop your pants and flop it proud up here on the ink pad. Go ahead, son, close your eyes. Won't take but a few seconds." The perp, who is grateful to close his eyes during this indignity, does what he has to do, though not proudly. Kowalski makes some more rummaging sounds in the desk drawer, muttering, "Now, where's that dickprint form?" Of which there is no such thing, of course. Instead of gently inking down the perp's johnson, Kowalski takes a braided sap from his belt, raises it high over his head with both meaty paws, then whomps it down across the guy's vegetables.

So I did what I had to do: I complained. I make no claim to being a perfect cop and I carry no particular brief for homosexual gentlemen. But this Kowalski violates my code, such as it is. If I myself should for instance break somebody's thumb in the line of duty, which I have done, I will make certain of two things that to me seem only sporting: the perp should be guilty as hell, and his eyes should be open so he can see me coming at him.

So, two years ago I filed against Sergeant Kowalski. The only thing that has happened to date is my being wreathed twice, and now told by this sergeant with the shiny pants from Massapequa I should watch my back.

As I walked away from Becker and the latest threat, I was thinking with a cringe not only of cops who think the greatest sin—the only sin—is blowing a whistle, but of Ruby in her delicate condition. It was only luck, my finding the wreath on the apartment door before Ruby. It pains me to say so, but cops who make threats are like rabid dogs; they will bite, and they are not choosy about their victims. What if my luck ran out?

I headed for the stairs that would take me up to the squad room that Midtown South has seen fit to assign my sector of the SCUM patrol. My steps fell into the rhythm of Becker's wetly gnashing jaws. He chewed like a dog, open-mouthed, the sound of him echoing through the station house lobby.

†

The squad room is painted government green—windows included, which does not matter, since there is only an airshaft view of soot-crusted brick. Whatever time of year it is, and whatever the outdoor temperature and wind patterns, it is always about eighty-five degrees and humid in this room. There are a half-dozen steel desks and a like number of steel filing cabinets, all of them beige and dented; a hot plate for making coffee; a miniature refrigerator with cans of soda inside, along with cockroaches and mold; an oscillating fan, usually on the fritz; fluorescent lights buzzing overhead; a rogue's gallery of wanted posters taped to cement walls; and a lieutenant by the name of Rankin who is in charge of the daily assignments. Rankin sweats a lot, accounting for a share of squad room humidity. He does not wear deodorant.

"What do you know, Hock?" Rankin greeted me as I walked through the door, panting from the six-flight climb. The squad room was empty. My colleagues and I prefer clearing out fast and working the streets over hanging out in a close room with a ripe lieutenant. Rankin was breaking the law by smoking a Winston. Also he was pawing through a stack of complaint sheets. Stains under his armpits arced clear down to his gunbelt. When I had reached his desk, he said, "I hate to give you this two-bit job, Hock. But as you can see plain, I'm shorthanded."

"What is it?" I took the sheets Rankin handed me.

"Over to West Forty-sixth, Restaurant Row. Some con's running the coronary scam. The guy is old, could be eighty. But he's spry, and smooth. Get this—he wears kid gloves. He can make any regular-looking cop—in a suit or wearing the bag, don't matter. Talks like an Irishman who read some books." Rankin looked me over, nodding his approval of my own low-profile ensemble: khakis, gray sweatshirt, Yankees cap, worn-out tennis shoes, a face in need of a shave. I could be some ordinary neighborhood idler—a guy on his way to the OTB parlor or a blocked novelist, say. "The restaurant owners, they're squawking. You know how they got the mayor's ear. So we got orders. Somebody's got to pull a stake."

I knew the grift without having to read through the complaints: Cauc male, neat dresser, distinguished type with silver wings in his hair, a charming accent from the other side, and just enough in his spiel to give the reassuring impression of old money and an old boy school. He takes a good table at Barbetta's, say, and after a fine meal with all the proper wines he drops over in his chair and his face pinches up and he claws at his chest and somebody calls 911 and then the EMS unit comes and carts off the poor gasping heart attack victim. In all the commotion, the check for the guy's meal is the last thing anybody thinks about. And by the time the gasper reaches the emergency room at Roosevelt or St. Claire Hospital, he is miraculously recovered. A guy can get away with murder if he wears the right color skin and his breath smells like cash when he wants something.

"I can't be working a Mickey Mouse today," I told Rankin.

"How's that?"

"You heard about the rabbi who got it at the temple on the overnight?"

"Sure."

"Friend of mine."

"You ain't Jewish."

"So I'm told." I stepped over to my desk. Like static cling, some of the lieutenant's dampness followed me. "Sorry, Looey, but I'm putting in for a waiver on this one."

Rankin fumed and pawed through more paper. Nobody likes being overruled. A spark from his cigarette fell, landing on his shirt. It sizzled out in a circle of sweat. I sat down at my desk, picked up the telephone, and dialed Inspector Tomasino Neglio's office downtown.

For months, I had not spoken to Neglio on the subject of my beef with Kowalski. This was on purpose for two good reasons. First, whenever I run up against a lot of bureaucratic twaddle about the slow-grinding wheels of justice, I remember about Scotch whisky, which I do not want to think about. Second, reminding the boss at just the right time about something he was duty-bound to perform was a good tactic for getting something I might need in the short-term.

"What do you want now, Hock?" This was Neglio's usual hello to me. Today was no different from any other.

"You have to give me clearance for special assignment. By the way, what's happening with King Kong?"

"For your information, I just gave Kowalski the word. He's going to charm school, starting tomorrow." Neglio's tone had finality to it, as if the two of us were even; as if he owed me no special favors. "And don't be telling me what I got to give you or anybody else."

I thought, For what that hump Kowalski has done, he gets classes at charm school—that's it? I decided for the moment against squawking. Instead, I shifted to new grounds of negotiation. I said, "Maybe I'll be filing a whole new complaint."

"You want more trouble in your life?"

"How would you mean that, Inspector?"

"You know what I'm talking about. Anyhow, skip it. Kowalski hasn't done the dickprint number since you filed on him—and you know it, Hock."

"It's not Kowalski I'm talking about now. I'd be filing against a Sergeant Becker, up here at Midtown South."

"So what's he done to give you the hard-on?"

"Interesting. Becker asked the same as you asked—if I want more trouble." I heard some huffing on Neglio's end and figured the time was right to bring up the short-term matter of clearance again. "This morning, a rabbi from the neighborhood was murdered, right in his synagogue no less. The name was Marvin Paznik. He was a friend of mine, so I don't want to see the job going nine-to-five."

"Man of the cloth get canceled out, you better believe it's priority. Central Homicide's already on it."

"Try to persuade me that's a comfort."

"Now you got a beef with Central Homicide?"

"The squad mainly works nine to five, like I said." Sometimes when I am talking, the inspector does not listen well. Which is typical. The bureau types believe they have heard it all, which is the department's main qualification for indoor work. Street cops know the day we can't hear anymore is the day we get run over. "Regular murder, that's all right for Central Homicide. But not when murder gets complicated."

"What's complicated?"

"According to the report, there were fourteen eyewitnesses. That would be twenty-eight eyes saw the killer doing the rabbi. And everybody says this killer's only a shadow."

"What are you talking about—*shadow?*"

"That's what I want to know."

"All right. I give you today for a snoop."

"It's a start."

"Tell me something, Hock—and I don't mean in writing. What's this Sergeant Becker trying to hand you?"

"He reminds me I got wreathed. Then he tells me I should watch my back."

"Station house crap. You can't take it seriously."

"Yes I can."

"Look, maybe the sergeant only—"

"No—*you* look. You got wrong cops running around all over the place these days. Rabid cops like Kowalski and his fans. Here's a flash, Inspector: the department's full of these thugs, and anybody who reads the newspapers knows it." I was on a tear now. "But there's not so much to read about cop thugs going to Rikers Island with the regular thugs, is there? No. Instead you just blow off the problem by sending the likes of Kowalski to charm school. That's some fine inspiration for all the other rabid cops. Maybe there's one of them out there wants to give me a dirt nap someday instead of a wreath."

What could Neglio say to all that?

"Maybe since you're so quiet I should lay all this out for my friend Slattery at the *Post,*" I finally said.

"You shouldn't be talking about going to the newspapers." Neglio thought for a long moment before saying this. Then he added, "Not even to me."

"Why not?"

"Sometimes a confidence can be reckless."

"You're saying I can't trust you?"

"I'm saying don't push dangerous buttons."

"Kowalski and all the other rabid cops, I'm right about them—and you know it."

"Sure. You're morally right, Hock. Ever since you went on the wagon, you've been a regular Dudley Do-Right. You should relax your tight ass and think on this: when you get even with cops, it only leaves them with the impression that they owe you something."

Before hanging up the phone on me, the inspector wished me good luck and Godspeed. I would need it, he said, especially the Godspeed.

So I left the station house and tried concentrating on other things. For one, I actually considered starting up with a gym sometime like Ruby was nagging me to do. Maybe some jumping up and down would take the pressure off. The way things were rushing at me lately—fatherhood, Kowalski, department politics, dead rats, my friend's murder—I felt like a guy trying to drink water from a fire hose.

I legged it up Ninth Avenue to West Forty-seventh Street. Along the way, I thought about Becker's threat. I thought about how a rabid cop gunning for me would know how to keep his hands clean.

When I turned the corner and saw the synagogue, I thought about the last time I saw my friend . . .

. . . and what he told me that day, what he called me.

All the more reason for watching my back?

Five

Joseph Kowalski was spread out across most of the backseat. He was reading the "Strictly for Laughs" column by Joey Adams in the *Post,* and actually laughing. Or at least it seemed that way to the rookie officer driving the squad car. Who could tell? A laugh out of Kowalski was the same as a snarl out of anybody else, this being one of the reasons cops had tagged him King Kong.

The sergeant had a wide face, moist and white like pizza dough and too full of flesh to wrinkle. Kowalski's dough face concealed his age—maybe fifty, then again maybe sixty-five—and also his mood. The rest of him was clearly evident; he was just plain all-around fat. His legs and arms were like boiler room pipes. His gut was hard-bloated. His fingers were unbending and uniformly thick, like ten stiff salamis. Everything he held in his hands appeared to be too small, including the tabloid newspaper with the chunky headlines.

When he was finished laughing (or whatever), Kowalski tossed the *Post* to the sticky floor of the squad car. The newspaper thudded into place with all the other refuse Kowalski had generated in fifteen minutes of heading back uptown from One Police Plaza after a disagreeable appointment with Inspector Tomasino Neglio: an empty can of Yoo-Hoo chocolate soda, cellophane from a twin pack of Hostess cupcakes, a trio of Snickers candy bar wrappers. He lit up a Te-Amo cigar and looked out a dusty side window at the traffic crawling up Washington Street.

"I ought to phone up that Joey Adams someday," Kowalski said, turning to address the back of the driver's head. "I got this joke I made up. You want to hear, Matson?"

"Okay."

"How many New York cops does it take to throw a perp down a flight of stairs?"

"I don't know, Sarge. How many?"

"Fuck you. He fell."

"Very choice material."

"Sure it is." Sergeant Kowalski did not laugh at the choice material. Neither did the rookie Matson. "Good as anything Joey Adams thinks is hilarious," Kowalski said. "That freaking guy, he don't know what time it is. He's writing in a whole different age. Know what I'm saying?"

"No."

"Reading the guy nowadays, it's like stabbing myself in my heart for the old once-upon-a-times. Like when there was black-and-white sodas at Schrafft's and Miss Rheingold and the Automat and the Polo Grounds. And those columnists writing swifties in the tabs, which used to carry genuine comics like *Moon Mullins* and *Alley Oop*—not this lefty garbage like *Doonesbury.*" Kowalski sighed. He turned again to the side window. His breath made little fog circles on the glass. "Like they say, gone with the wind. Except for Joey Adams, who's getting lame from the memory. In other words I'm saying Joey ain't funny. He's a sad freaking mastodon tramping through a jungle he don't recognize anymore." Kowalski puffed, reflectively. "Maybe that's what I am, too."

"A mastodon?"

Officer Matson was sorry he said that; sorrier yet for the way he said it, with a stifled smirk. It was an easy thing for a young cop to see the sergeant as an old joke, to call him King Kong behind his back. But God help it if a rookie let on about the joke directly—especially a good-looking, young *black* rookie out of college like Ty Matson.

"Mastodons, they all supposedly went and died a long time ago." The way he said this, Kowalski sounded like a mourner at his best friend's wake. He had turned forward and taken the cigar from his lips. He now stared off into some gray, unseen horizon. Matson considered the surprisingly humble face reflected in the rearview mirror: was the fat sergeant remembering something sad or having a stroke?

"We all right, Sarge?"

"I was just thinking . . ." Kowalski's voice trailed off to some private, hushed place.

So far as Matson or most anybody else at Sex Crimes knew, contemplation was not the sergeant's style. Yet there he was, King Kong Kowalski with his big mouth full of opinions shut tight for once, his pig blue eyes empty of the usual contempt for all they saw.

Kowalski suddenly returned from wherever he had gone visiting. He asked, "How old are you, Matson?"

"Twenty-two."

"I got hemorrhoids that old."

Matson laughed this time. His voice was deep and creamy, like a bass in a gospel choir. Maybe the beauty of it irritated the sergeant. That was just the sort of thing that could set him off, as everybody at the squad knew only too well.

"What's so funny?" Kowalski spat flecks of tobacco leaf from his lips. "I got hemorrhoids? That's freaking hilarious to you?"

"No, Sarge, I only—"

"Back when things was still right, a cop like you, he wouldn't be getting in the face of a cop like me. Know what I'm saying?"

"I think so." Being a black cop and having to deal with his share of a certain type of white cop, Officer Matson knew to keep his responses cursory. This path of least resistance was bad for the digestion maybe, but good for the record.

"Sure you do. For instance—you'd hear on your radio up there a CFN call and you'd know to keep your mouth shut about how we used to have a what-do-you-call it . . ." Kowalski paused to resume smoking his cigar. "A shorthand way of saying stuff."

"What's a CFN?"

"Car full of niggers. I don't mean that personal."

"You people never do."

"One of my people says *nigger* nowadays, it's like some kind of a sin. We got persuaded to talk different. But guess what? I look around, I see the world ain't any better off for us being so freaking politically correct. I ask you, Officer Twenty-two Years Old—how come?"

"I'd be too young to answer that, Sarge." Matson cranked down the driver side window, which gave him something to do with his hands besides grab King Kong Kowalski by the neck. A pall of blue-gray Te-Amo smoke whooshed out from the car.

"Yeah, way too young. Any chance of you being a religious man?"

"I call myself God-fearing."

"Good answer. Me, I belong to the Holy Name Society of the Church of the Blessed Agony. That's out in Queens. It's Catholic." Kowalski pronounced it *cat-lick*. "Which you could say's ironic."

"How so?"

"Because of my personal take on this philosophical question we're discussing. Which is how come it ain't all sunshine and lollipops now that white cops for instance ain't allowed to be saying sinful things in public. Want to hear what I think?"

"Do I ever."

"The world goes stone evil when there's no sin."

"I'll bear that in mind."

"Yeah, do that!" Kowalski laugh-barked.

Having worked himself into a minor rage, Kowalski

sucked furiously on his cigar. The car filled with more smoke clouds, and Kowalski coughed. He searched his coat pockets for candy bars, but came up empty-handed. He sighed and shifted on hips as wide as a rowboat until he sat sideways, his boiler pipe legs flopped up in front of him, crossed at the ankles. Ashes curled off his cigar, dropping to his round lap and rolling down to the littered floor.

"Understand, Officer Matson, I'm the what-do-you-call ecumenical type." The sergeant had grown reasonably calm. "Meaning if I go saying nigger and sheeny and wop, then likewise I don't mind hearing po-lock."

"These ideas you got from reading your paper?"

"People don't like hearing what they are, it ain't my fault," Kowalski said, ignoring the question. "Take your queers. I ain't even allowed to say that—and you ain't neither, brother. It's like they passed some law up in Albany, you got to call them gay. The inspector, he says if I want I can say homosexual. But that don't feel right in my mouth. Feels like my mouth's gone to someplace unholy."

"You and the inspector, you talked about temperate language?"

"Can you believe it? Neglio calls me on the carpet, says I have to quote *Get your ass to charm school* unquote."

"Where?"

"Jesus H. Christ. Charm school, Matson! That's over to Diagnostic and Counseling Services, where they run you through the freaking squirrel cage."

"Oh."

"Like I'm foaming from rabies."

"Why would anybody think that?"

"All I know, it's on account of this official beef filed against me by one Detective Neil Hockaday of the SCUM patrol. Just because I do that little number of mine on the ballerinas."

"Oh, the dickprint?"

"Yeah, that." Kowalski's gaze fell on the crumpled *Post.*

"You seen this Hockaday in the papers probably. Freaking reporters!"

"Hockaday files a complaint on you. How about that?"

"Can you believe it? Who's this guy to be talking? Not so long ago they took him over to this Jersey tank. Took the pissbum six months to dry out."

"A cop filing on a cop." Matson whistled in admiration.

"Never would've happened when Joey Adams was still funny."

They drove through heavy traffic for another ten minutes without saying anything.

Kowalski threw down his cigar, thoughtfully aiming for a shallow puddle of spilled Yoo-Hoo. He made it, and the cigar guttered out. Matson attempted to ignore what he saw out the right side of the windshield: a suspicious man on top of a building. If Matson stopped, it meant spending even more time with Kowalski. On the other hand, Kowalski might be seeing the same thing he was; if Matson failed to stop, then Kowalski had grounds for writing him up on a neglect citation.

"Sorry, Sarge, looks like we got us a mope," Matson said, deciding ultimately against the risk of a citation. He slowed up the car, stopping parallel to a florist's panel truck parked on West Street on the uptown side of Canal. He twisted around for a look out the rear window. Kowalski turned as well. Matson said, "Up on that roof, see him?"

The mope was holding on to a bicycle and poised near the edge of a six-floor loft building fronting on Canal Street. He peered down over the lanes of Holland Tunnel traffic, then retreated backward about twenty feet with the bicycle. He looped one leg over the bike seat and then half-rolled and half-walked to the roof edge again, where he stopped. He went back and forth several times in this manner, as if he were dry-running a mighty cycle leap clear off the roof.

"You make anything in the way of physical ID?" Kowalski asked, squinting. He reached for glasses in a pocked leather case in the breast pocket of his coat.

"White guy. Thirties. Dark hair, real greasy. Some kind of lines smeared on his forehead."

"Freaking strung-out bedbug," Kowalski said, a groan somewhere in his voice. He held black horn-rimmed glasses in place. One of the stems was broken. "Some of your bedbugs, they like soaking their heads in Vaseline or some other kind of goo. Don't ask me why. Once I seen a guy do up his hair in duck fat. Some of them, they like schmutzing up their faces, too. Burnt cork, axle grease—or else plain old-fashioned turds. Don't ask me why."

"What do you think this guy's up to?"

"Trying to get his balls up for a swan, I'd say." Kowalski turned forward. He pointed one of his salami fingers at the shortwave on the dashboard. "You want to call it in, Officer Matson?"

"Oh, yeah . . ."

"Tell them we need the net boys." Kowalski turned back for another look out the rear window. "Aw, Jesus—forget it!"

"What's the matter?" Matson asked, dropping the mike.

"Guy ain't a swanny after all. Get a load of what he's doing. The freaking psycho, better he should splatter."

The man with the painted face and shiny hair had dropped the bicycle somewhere back at the middle of the rooftop. Standing now at the loft's precipice, hands at his crotch, he sent a long arc of urine six storeys down onto the Jersey-bound entrance lanes to the tunnel.

"Neglio, he calls me too hard-assed!" Kowalski barked. He turned and motioned for Matson to head onward uptown. After a few blocks, he said, "Let me tell you something, Matson my young friend. Deal with the wackos of this freaking city as long as me . . ."

Then, once again, Kowalski went off somewhere by himself.

"Sarge?"

"What?"

"Deal with the wackos for a long time—and what?"

"Some days, your own black ass'll turn into cement." Kowalski snorted. Then he looked blankly out a side window. "Other days, you come across some bedbug and you think, the terrible things of the world come on from little stuff we overlook. After a while, you see how the little stuff freaking accumulates."

Six

THE OLD MAN IN THE BLACK SUIT with a yarmulke somehow riding the crown of his bare, bony head stood at the front wall, rocking stiffly from the waist like he was a toy duck bobbing into a water glass. I could hear him chanting clear back where I was: *"Rodef shalom . . . Rodef shalom . . . Rodef shalom . . ."* His voice was parched.

"Old fellow's been standing there like that ever since the rabbi got the business," a uniform told me. The nameplate under his badge read R. CARAS. "He's been gibbering like that since just after midnight, over and over."

"It's not gibber," I said. "It's Hebrew."

"Whatever. Nobody got nothing out of the geezer. Somebody says he's the caretaker around here." Caras raised a blue serge arm and pointed up the aisle cutting through the center of the temple sanctuary. A couple of plainclothes officers were crawling on their hands and knees between the altar and a front pew roped off in yellow crime scene tape. "See—everybody's gone except the forensics boys. The detectives from Central Homicide, they took down all the statements they could. I'm on security post, to keep out the gawkers and the lawyers. Also I'm waiting on the geezer to fall over."

"I know him," I said. "If you don't mind, I'm going to help him."

I started up the aisle. One of the forensics cops lifted his head and grunted at me suspiciously. I held up my gold shield, the one I carry on a chain around my neck inside of whatever I'm wearing. Also I pointed to my navy blue Yankees baseball cap and said, "Color of the day." The forensics cop grunted again and resumed with his tweezers, picking through the tightly fibered altar carpet—the parts not soaked in blood anyway. I sidled through a row of pews and turned up a side aisle toward the old man at the wall.

"Mr. Glick?"

He kept on chanting, oblivious of me. His voice was dry and soft, like a tired hand scratching against a screen door.

I put my hand to his shoulder. "Come on, Mr. Glick." He made no response, so I tugged at him. The old man tilted backward and collapsed against me, as thin and weightless as brooms falling out of a closet. He trembled. I turned him around so he could see my face.

"You . . . ?" His dry throat closed, it was all he could say for the moment.

"Neil Hockaday. You remember, Mr. Glick. I was here last week, talking with the rabbi." I took the old man by the elbow and steered him to a pew. "Come on now, let's sit down."

Glick settled on the edge of a pew. I asked if he would like some water. He motioned—yes—with a papery white hand full of blue veins.

"Rodef shalom," he said, looking up at me. There was delirium in his disappearing voice, relief in his flinty face. He nodded his head. His eyes fluttered with exhaustion. He started chanting again, even as I managed to arrange him so that he was lying out flat on the pew. His knees cracked. *"Rodef shalom . . . Rodef shalom . . . Rodef shalom . . ."*

Officer Caras galloped up the side aisle. I knew this

without turning around for a look. I knew from the sound of patrolman's gear jouncing on his belt: revolver, flashlight, whistle, leather-bound violations book. When he reached me, he asked, "You make out anything your gibbering buddy says?"

Last week—there in the synagogue, in the rabbi's study, after my friend and I had finished soup kitchen duty, pouring minestrone into a few hundred cardboard cartons and wrapping up as many sandwiches in waxed paper—Marvin Paznik told me I was a *rodef shalom.* A pursuer of peace in a troubled, violent world.

Marv thought it was a big deal how I was the only cop serving as a volunteer at the soup kitchen he had started up in an old candy store on Ninth Avenue. An Irish Catholic cop at that. I reminded him more than once that in the religious sense the soup kitchen was nonpartisan. Also that volunteer work was a chore I got stuck with on account of my AA sponsor, Father Declan Byrne, who was very big on volunteerism. He thought it would be good for me to serve the public without a gun for a change, just like he thought it was good for him to be running the Holy Cross dead table on top of his priestly duties. So I had to go along, which I did not consider a big deal. But which Marv did, like I said. Whenever I turned up for soup kitchen duty, for instance, he had me walk back to the synagogue with him afterward for lunch.

Food was not the main thing. Glick, the temple caretaker, would call out to Kam-Wei down at Ninth and Forty-fourth for Chinese. When it came he would dish it up for us in the study so that Marv and I could have a meal "like a couple of gentlemen," as old Glick put it. During lunch, but especially afterward, Marv would talk about whatever was on his mind. Which for me was the main thing, because the late Rabbi Marvin Paznik was one of the best talkers I have ever enjoyed hearing.

"When it really comes down to the barbed wire and you need somebody to fight for you—and believe me, blood will run in the streets one day soon—who do you want on your side? Who can you trust when your back is turned?" Marvin tossed out these rhetorical questions the last time I saw him. He was sitting behind his desk in the study, hands folded in his lap, a half-empty plate of noodles and chicken in tea sauce in front of him. I was finishing off a fortune cookie that advised, A POLITE BOY IS A POPULAR BOY. Which is exactly what all the nuns at Holy Cross used to tell me as a kid, only none of them were Chinese. "How about you, Neil? Could you trust a priest? The president? The mayor with that demented smile of his? A captain of industry?"

"No."

"God help us, though, you could trust a cop."

"A certain kind of cop, maybe."

Marv lifted a hand and rubbed his beard. It was a short black beard, flecked with the same shade of gray as the bristly, thinning hair on his head. "A certain kind of cop," he said, reflecting on what I had said by repeating it. "I like that. I don't suppose you ever heard of Shabbatai Sevi."

"Sorry, no."

"Don't be sorry. Not so many Jews ever heard of him either."

"Who was he?"

"A mystic during the Ottoman Empire, latter part of the seventeenth century. Shabbatai Sevi was obsessed by a certain Talmudic saying: the *mashiah* will arrive when all men are holy, or else when all men are sinners. That sounds contradictory, I know, but we're talking Talmud. By the way, that's messiah to you."

"How did Sevi figure? Good guys or bad guys?"

"He decided on the preponderance of evidence around him."

"Meaning, you're saying he was a bad guy?"

"More like a pragmatist in a bad mood all the time. A psychopath maybe, which in the rabbinate is entirely possible. But Sevi was not an evil man—well, not exactly. He had a cult, like anybody else who isn't exactly evil.

Hundreds of thousands of people, actually—a surprising thing, since practically nobody today ever heard of Sevi. Anyway, he married one of his many female admirers, a Christian prostitute. So maybe he wasn't so crazy? Never mind about his sex life. He taught something he called the Doctrine of Universal Sin."

"Which is?"

"Shabbatai Sevi had a big idea how the world then was even more of a godforsaken sinkhole than it is today. He asked himself, So where the hell is God when you need him?" Marv laughed. "I'm not saying those were the exact words, but you get the picture."

I said I did.

"Sevi figures the world's an armpit because God is sick as a dog, too weak to do anything about plagues and locusts and raining toads and all the rest of it. God needs a doctor, you see. He's wounded bad. Hell's bells—God needs surgery already! So who's going to be God's physician?"

"That I don't know," I said. "But it reminds me of a joke."

"So knock-knock already."

"What's the difference between a surgeon and God?"

"What?"

"God knows he's not a surgeon."

Marv laughed and said, "My brother the cardiologist, I got to tell him that one." He actually wrote down my joke on a notepad. After which he returned to the matter of Shabbatai Sevi, a psycho-mystic evaporated in time.

"Who can heal a wounded God?" Marv asked. "Who can heal the world?" Rabbis and Jesuit priests, I have noticed, enjoy telling us things by posing riddles. "A holy man? An army of holy men? But even holy men are mortals, and aren't mortals weaker than supernatural beings? What is man but a hemophiliac?"

"You're saying if God is a patient, he needs a doctor stronger than he is."

"But, can there be such a doctor?"

I said something about this being altogether too Talmudic for an ex-choirboy such as myself.

"Like I mentioned, though, Sevi had a theory—the Doctrine of Universal Sin." Marvin picked open his own fortune cookie. He read the slip of paper inside, shrugged, dropped it to his desk for me to see. "Here's the way he saw it: there is nobody more powerful than God, but there is something equal to His power. What would that be?"

Anybody who ever crossed the threshold of Holy Cross School knows the answer to that one, especially if they ever sat in Sister Bertice's classroom. "Evil," I promptly said. Whichever pole of the hereafter was now her home, I felt the late Sister B. smiling at me.

"Bingo! So, let's say God's ass is in a sling. What are Shabbatai Sevi and his cult supposed to do about it?"

"I don't know. What?"

"Find a way—through the practice of evil, the only power equal to God—to perform a great *tikkun olam.*"

"Sevi might have had a blasphemy problem with that."

"To be sure."

"By the way, what's a *tikkun olam?*"

"A healing of the world, for the benefit of all people. In the specific case of Sevi and his cause, it means the rectification of a shattered God."

"I'm getting the idea here that Sevi wanted Satan to make a house call."

"Well—like I said, the guy was pragmatic."

"Also you said he was nuts. Is it possible to be both?"

"Maybe not. Maybe Shabbatai Sevi was only a prophet. That would explain why he died a forgotten man. We either forget our prophets or we kill them, often both."

"What did the prophet foresee?"

"That holiness is impossible."

"So life is what—hopeless?"

"I wouldn't say that. What I would say is that we need to be sure of whom we can trust at the time when everything comes down on our heads. A certain kind of cop, as you put it. A *rodef shalom*. That's you, Neil."

And how would I explain all this to Officer Caras standing next to me with his revolver and his belt utilities clattering back into place on his hips? Officer Caras waiting for a coherent answer to a reasonable question, asked in a synagogue where an unholy thing had happened.

"Mr. Glick?" I said, ignoring Caras, since I had no coherent answer for him—or for that matter, me. I placed my hand on Glick's head. He was fevered, his hair felt like baby's down. I slipped a finger under his jaw, feeling for a pulse, finding one. "I know you're tired, Mr. Glick. But before you rest, can you help me with something?"

"Rodef shalom . . . Rodef shalom . . ."

"Come on, Hockaday, what's he saying?" Caras was growing impatient. So were the forensics cops, who both stood now, staring at me with my hand across the head of the old man lying on the pew.

"Never mind," I said. I asked Glick, "What happened here? Tell me—in English."

Glick waggled a thin hand over his throat. I knelt, so he could whisper into my ear. His voice was a dead man's cough. "Reb Paznik's face . . . Och, his face! His face! Thanks be to God, you've come to slay the beast."

Seven

THE NIGHT BEFORE, King Kong Kowalski had driven his candy-apple red '71 Buick Roadmaster (a bulky and problematical car, though one with ample front-seat gut room) from his house in Queens over to Jersey. There he attended a strictly word-of-mouth sporting event in the warehouse district of Newark.

Now he was sitting in a storefront basement on West Thirteenth Street in Manhattan, haunches straddled over two folding chairs, tilting perilously into the ear of a corrections officer by the name of Harry Darcy. He was telling Darcy about Newark and last evening's card of "ultimate fighting," a type of blood struggle where ex-jocks and bar bouncers and kick-boxing refugees take the place of pit bull dogs, a sporting event where a mere ring will not do. Ultimate fighting, Kowalski was explaining confidentially, was performed in a thirty-foot octagonal span of chain-link fencing—without benefit of referee.

Harry Darcy—big, middle-aged, close-cropped blond hair, a red face shot full of booze—was likewise a rabid public servant of the city of New York. Likewise, he had been induced by his superior—in this case, the warden of Rikers Island—to enroll in a sensitivity training course sanctioned by the city and state of New York. He was drinking creamed coffee from a paper cup and seemed about half-interested in what Kowalski was saying out of the side of his mouth.

"The thing you got to love about it—" Kowalski, too, was having coffee. Also a waxed-paper bag full of custard-packed crullers. He interrupted himself to tongue sticky sugar off his fingers. "They don't pay attention to the rules of that dead fop over in Scotland. Know what I'm saying?"

"Marquess of Queensberry?"

"Him, yeah."

Darcy's eyes blinked heavily. He was headachy with the walking flu and queasy from last night's whisky. All the way in from Parkchester in the Bronx, where he lived, he had had to stand up in the subway car. The only thing he had to read was *The Chief*, a newspaper for civil service employees. An irritating little guy had got on the train at Tremont station, pulled out a plastic saxophone-piano thing and started playing for handouts, right next to hung-over Harry Darcy. Darcy had considered killing him—he had an off-duty revolver concealed in a belt clip, after all—but thought better of it. Instead, he had said to Little Guy, "Shut up, you runt fuck, I don't want to deal with that shit noise." Little Guy was terrified. With a squeak, he stopped playing and said, hopefully, "I know some other tunes." Harry Darcy had leaned his back against the door of the subway car, closed his eyes, sighed deeply.

Now again, Darcy sighed a deep sigh. He wondered if anybody in the world felt lousier than he felt. And further, for what grim reason had he freely chosen a seat right next to King Kong Kowalski? To invite increased discomfort on himself, in the theory that agony would have its way with him all the more swiftly? Even in the worst of times at Rikers—when rioting mentals were flinging their feces all over the place—Harry Darcy had not in many years thought so perversely. For perversity, there was the nostalgia of Holy Cross School back in Hell's Kitchen, which he had escaped so many years back . . .

. . . Now today sat Corrections Officer Darcy, in charm school, his rabid ears filled with the scraw of a long-ago nun:

There was once a wicked little boy in the grip of the devil. When he went to Communion, he did not swallow the Host, but deliberately concealed it in the corner of his mouth. He went to his hideout with his gang, put the Host on the ground and hammered a nail through it. The Host spurted blood.

Darcy closed his throbbing eyes and smacked himself on the forehead. Maybe that would blast away the sudden awfulness of a Hell's Kitchen remembrance. Religion class, a nun's *exemplum vérité* as prelude to the lesson of the day from old Father Gerald Morrison—a treatise on one of only two subjects of interest to him: agony and memory. "Creepy" Morrison, he and his classmates called the priest.

He opened his eyes and forced himself to divert his attention to the rabid cop from Manhattan Sex Crimes sitting next to him who had been all on about the night before over in Newark. Only not now. King Kong Kowalski tipped back his head and poured straggling crumbs and custard globs from the cruller bag into his open maw.

Darcy asked, manfully, "So in this ultimate fighting deal—what, anything goes?"

"Gouge the eyes. Bite the neck . . ." A puff of crumbs from Kowalski's lips, then he went on. "Elbows. Whatever."

"Knees? Butt heads?"

"Yeah, sure."

"Kick a guy in the nuts?" Darcy decided, Yes—a boot in the groin, that would feel lousier than I'm feeling.

"Whatever," Kowalski affirmed. "Last night, for example, I seen this one guy beef-jerky another guy's lips."

"Beef-jerky?"

"Means he bit the guy's lips right off his freaking face."

Definitely—that would feel lousier.

Kowalski belched, crumpled his empty bag, dropped it to a tile floor as bubbled and beige as vomit. Darcy felt two things: a case of the whirlies coming on, and an equally powerful need to get away from the sight and sound of Kowalski. He cast his eyes around the room for a vacant chair. Too late. It was nine o'clock now, and the place was filled to capacity. A hundred sullen men, some as whirly in the head as Darcy himself, waited for the headmaster of charm school to show up.

Darcy turned from Kowalski and pretended to be absorbed in something from a back page of *The Chief* newspaper he was still carrying around. He reread an advertisement his warden had circled for him in red grease pencil:

Diagnostic & Counseling Services
851 W. 13th St. NYC 10011
phone 212.904-9202 or 516.765-5922

APPEAL! Attention: police, fire, corrections, courts, teachers, transit authority, state employees, sanitation. APPEAL a psychological or character disqualification that may affect you for life. FIGHT BACK! Clear your name & Establish your Eligibility. (Professional staff has over 75 years combined experience in the evaluation, assessment, and treatment of mental health problems for law enforcement officers & their families. Free consultation.)

"Listen," Kowalski said, butting Darcy's ribs with a pillowy elbow, "I heard this great freaking joke at ringside."

"I bet you did. I bet you're going to repeat it."

"What goes ha-ha-ha-ha-ha-ha-ha-ha-THUMP?"

"I don't know."

"A leper laughing his head off."

Harry Darcy sighed and thought again about the small revolver riding his hip. Lucky for Kowalski, a trim gentleman of about sixty years wearing a navy blazer, bow tie, buck shoes, and a cloud of cotton white hair took his place up front at a lectern.

The white-haired gent pulled some papers from a briefcase and smoothed them out on the lectern. Then he took a pair of black horn-rims from his blazer pocket, put them on his suntanned face, and surveyed his bleary-eyed class. He shook his head, after which he turned around to a blackboard on the wall and chalked up the lesson of the day: MANNERS ARE WHAT WE USE TO GET WHAT WE WANT WITHOUT APPEARING TO BE SWINE.

"Freaking beautyful," Kowalski said in a brushy laugh-snarl-whisper, audible enough to reach the front of the room. "The professor there, he must of took a wrong turn somewheres on his way to poetry class at some rich girls' college up in Vermont."

Fump, fump, fump. The professor whacked a microphone clipped to the plywood lectern. "Testing . . . testing." Then he did it again. *Fump, fump, fump.* Darcy felt explosions inside his head. So did many other queasers in the crowd. Sound test completed, the professor looked out over the crowd of aching heads to Kowalski. "Do you wish to address the class, my good sir?"

"Hey . . . !" King Kong Kowalski on the defensive. "I ain't your good *nothing.*"

"No?" The professor smiled. "Do you mean to say you're good for nothing?"

"What's the freaking—?"

"Incidentally, my name is Thornton. You can call me Mr. Thornton."

"You can kiss my hairy butt!"

"For the benefit of those without your own knowledge of such intimacy, sir, do tell: why on earth should one gentleman wish to place his lips against another gentleman's hirsute buttocks?"

The mood of the class brightened. Sullen queasers and otherwise unwilling students of charm school changed heart, Harry Darcy included. Here suddenly—for a change, and what a change—was a joke at the expense of Kowalski. Here stood Professor Thornton, waiting for an answer, as cool and controlled as an undertaker's handshake. And over there sat lobster-faced King Kong

Kowalski, that legendary mass of distemper, sputtering and jabbing an impotent finger in the air.

The more Kowalski jabbed and sputtered, the more mirth he provoked. Quiet laughs at first, the kind that noses make. Then in waves the laughs grew loud and helpless and wide-mouthed enough to see back teeth.

Darcy leaned toward Kowalski and smirked. "So that's it, King Kong? You got a shine for the boys? I never figured you to be with a woman, but—"

"Shut your trap," Kowalski interrupted, all rage and tremble. Laughing faces from the row in front agitated him all the more. "Don't be calling me that name, Darcy. And don't be talking about my woman."

"What woman would that be, King Kong?"

"Freaking smart-ass, I'm warning you."

"You are?" Darcy stood up, raising his voice to address Thornton. "You got King Kong Kowalski here so upset he's making threats."

"Is that so?" Thornton stepped around from behind the lectern, his eyes still on Kowalski, whose name he finally knew. "Threats are impolite, Mr. Kowalski. They are also unintelligent. Perhaps this is why you've been tagged with the gorilla sobriquet."

The class stamped feet and roared happily. Kowalski jabbed and sputtered. Darcy took his chair again, the storm in his head lifted courtesy of the fat sergeant's discomfort.

"Come, Mr. Kowalski, speak up," Thornton said as the men quieted. "You seem to have so very much on your mind."

Silence from Kowalski, who decided to ignore the professor. Instead, he trained the heat of a malignant glare on Darcy—a glare known to Neil Hockaday, the rat cop responsible for the humiliation of his being at charm school, and to perpetrators Kowalski deemed worthy of dickprinting.

"As our colleague Mr. King Kong Kowalski is temporarily at a loss for words," Thornton continued evenly, "might any of you other gentlemen explain what we've learned from this contretemps?"

There was dull mumbling around the room. *What's contretemps? . . . Hell if I know . . . What's sobriquet?* But nobody raised his hand.

Thornton stepped to the blackboard. He tapped fingers to the slogan he had chalked up and explained, "I wanted our disagreeable colleague to be quiet, yes? Accordingly, I simply employed good manners, which flummoxed poor Mr. Kowalski. You see that I've obtained my goal. In other words, I got what I was after. Now then, everything we'll be discussing here in the ensuing days revolves around this elementary principle of courtesy in exchange for desire."

With no further interruption, the professor spoke for another hour.

Privately, Kowalski snarled at Darcy, "I make conversation with you, Darcy, I try to be nice. But you turn on me. Like a rat. Maybe you don't know, but we got a custom in the department for dealing with rat bastards. After that if the rat bastard don't give in we got a process of elimination, let's call it. You could ask a certain rat bastard out of Street Crimes, name of Hockaday."

Hockaday. Again, Darcy traveled back in time to the Hell's Kitchen of his youth, to the Saturday morning he took leave: him sitting up front in the mover's truck, looking down at a sad sack kid from the old block standing beside his Irish mother with her russet hair going gray and old-lady stiff; the two of them, mother and son, staring and thirsty-eyed as the yellow Cirker van pulled away, taking forever with it young Harry Darcy.

Eight

TWO MEN TALK IN A PARLOR of lush decay:

Double windows flanking a broken stoop, shrouded inside with the remains of moth-pecked velvet. A spoonful of light strains into the room through grime-encrusted panes, a cinder black hole in the ceiling marks the spot where a chandelier banished shadows of another age. Cracked and fallen-away plaster moldings are trace evidence of a salon once ornate with cherubs and rosettas, oak clusters and braids of grape leaves. Crumbled walls lay bare wooden lathing supports beneath, like the exposed ribs of some partly consumed animal carcass.

Outdoors, in the cool sun, a dented ice cream truck is parked in front of the house. One of the men inside—the older, elegant one wearing a satin robe over a waistcoat and kid gloves—turns back a scrap of drapery for a look at the musical truck, and its driver. A scratchy recording of "The Farmer in the Dell" attracts no buyers from a childless block. The driver sits, idle, slurping something red from an aqua blue plastic bowl. Indoors, the parlor is as close and darkly moist as the icebox in the truck; indoors, the air seems water-painted in shades of gray.

"Fool," sniffs the man in the waistcoat. He steps back from the window, crosses the room, joins his companion.

The men now sit before a useless fireplace—mantel collapsed, bricks fallen to powder ash in the hearth. They face each other in opposite antique divans covered in threadworn silk brocade. Between them: a mahogany table stained by rings of wet glasses, a half-gone fifth of Black Bush on the table, a silver box of perfumed cigarettes. They smoke, and drink their Irish whisky from scarred crystal.

"I take it you're completely decided?"

"You take it right."

"Well, I suppose none of us goes on forever. Not you, not me . . . not them."

"Them two, they're ripe for change. Here's just the place they'll believe is forever, the place where all their tomorrows belong."

"As I said, nothing is forever."

"That there's a pseudo-conclusion, old man."

"Why?"

"I got to spell it out? Okay. A leg of lamb is better than nothing. Nothing is better than heaven. Therefore, a leg of lamb is better than heaven. You buy that?"

"Of course not."

"How come?"

"The reasoning is fallacious."

"No, that don't explain it."

"It *don't?*" the elegant one says in a mocking way. "Then you'll spell it out for me."

"Sure. It's the word *nothing,* that's your problem. People say it all the time, but it ain't lucid."

"Good God, he says *ain't,* yet presumes to speak on the efficacy of language." The elegant one, thumb cinched in waistcoat, says, "Here now—you and I, man, we hail from the grandest land of speech. Show some respect and please drop the crudities."

"Fair play, if you'll likewise drop the subject of God."

"Ho-ho, you don't fancy hearing the Lord's name!"

"Another pseudo-conclusion. I'm not at all sure why I tolerate you. Perhaps it's only that I'm amused by this playwright conceit of yours, this lie of your soul."

"I've used the last of my life to write down the grieving truth. As well you know, since you're guiding the tale to an audience."

"But for all your writing, do you know what's the truth and what's the lie?"

"My answer's not likely the same as yours, please God."

"Please, that name!"

"Oh, very well. Go on—say what you wish."

"Truth has a thousand obstacles to overcome before it's got safely black on white. The liar is the least of its foes."

"A mere variation of his tongue, and see how he changes the shape of all else around him. My, but aren't you the subtle bugger of a Paddy ghost, the old shape-shifter himself."

"Yes, old man. See how I've adapted to your subtle world above."

"Stop, or I'll start believing your malarkey."

"A world grown so subtle that it's as ludicrous to believe in a god as it is to believe in ghosts."

"On that much we agree. But on the ambiguity of this word *nothing*—"

"A ridiculous concept! I become quite impatient when people accept it senselessly."

"If a person says, for instance: see no evil, hear no evil, speak no evil?"

"The very height of absurdity. To suggest that evil may be ignored, that evil may thus be rendered into nothingness. Ridiculous! Of *nothing,* it may only be truly said there is no such thing as nothing."

"I see. A leg of lamb—"

"Aye, there's the perfect example of circular thought. My first usage of the word *nothing* excluded all things in the world that are worse than a leg of lamb, among which *nothing* itself is of course included. Then I claimed that there was nothing better than heaven, so-called. Here now, *nothing* excludes everything in the world, great and small, which again includes nothing itself."

"To quote your beard, it ain't lucid."

"No, it ain't. Twice I used that dreadful term—*nothing.* To what end? The word *nothing* is but a stepchild. Applied to anything, no conclusion may be drawn regarding the genus of nothing."

"Yet we hear *nothing* every day. It sounds so definite, so clear."

"Aye, and every mortal fool swears there is meaning when he hears it."

"But in reality—as you've shown—*nothing* is an expression of confusion."

"Confusion's an excellent hiding place. Your own bloody God's a confusion and a mystery, same as me."

"God, did you say?"

"The holiest of holy buggers is up in heaven watching the store. Fair play then, here am I—down to earth in Hell's Kitchen, tending to business."

"What business would you be calling your nasty talk?"

"To make certain the world knows what truly happened

in this place. To make certain people take a fine, long look—and see what they'd sooner forget."

"Madness!"

"Nae, come now. I'll be recruiting the finest sorts for this crusade—the sane and the saintly. Aye, and a certain detective, with only the slightest of these two afflictions. Him and his swollen missus."

Nine

"ACCORDING TO THE POLICE REPORT, you saw what—a shadow?" I asked. Only shadow? Shadow, and some putrid odor? "There must have been more. Please, Mr. Glick, think carefully."

I waited for an answer.

The old man was calm. He had stopped repeating himself. *His face . . . His face.* He had taken water. Color had begun creeping back into his pale skin. I thought he was up to answering a few questions. But a long moment had passed and he was only blinking, as if he had felt himself near mortal end.

"That's it, the geezer claims he seen nothing but a shadow," Officer Caras said. Maybe he was trying to be helpful. "All fourteen of them here—same story."

"Mr. Glick . . . ?" I ignored Caras. "Are you sure?"

"As sure as I breathe." Words at last. He laid a paper hand across his chest. "To tell you the truth, I'm a little surprised I'm drawing air. The others . . . ?" Sad eyes swept over both of us cops. "How are the others?"

I had to say I did not know myself.

"Some of them poor old folks, they went over to Roosevelt," Caras said. "You know, on account of shock. Nobody croaked, so far as I know."

"Thanks very much, Officer, that's enough," I said to Caras. I turned to Glick. "I'll see you home myself. You should have a meal if you can, then sleep. But first help me out, all right?"

"Certainly, yes. I have waited all these hours to help."

"You were saying—about some beast, about a face?"

"I mean Rabbi's face, God bless."

"Tell me . . ."

"You ask me for careful thought, and it's what I have prayed through the dark of night to give you—what I prayed to God I should tell a *rodef shalom.* You understand what I'm saying here? No, of course not. Who can understand but an old Jew?

"The rabbi, maybe he already mentioned—I was with my father and two brothers in the camps. My mother and sister, they took to another camp. Anyway, so much for my family. My sister and I lived, that's all.

"So, I have seen many hateful, horrible things . . . Och, but it sounds so puny what I tell you! In English I don't know the words strong enough. In Yiddish I don't know the words even. All right, never mind. But please, allow me to say this about all I have seen: even you, a policeman in New York City—you should not have such a life.

"Enough!

"The horrible thing I must tell you is something I know from my experience, which you must take on faith. But I warn you: what I say is not something a detective would call a proper clue, it is not something seen. A shadow, what is that? A destroyer of light, yes? Light we need to see. Therefore, we do not actually *see* a shadow. Maybe you think it's crazy what I'm saying, but this is the only way I have to tell you of the shadow that was here. Right here, at midnight, in this temple.

"I have known shadow in my life. The others who were here for the Kaddish of Yom Hashoah—they, too, know the shadow. We know what to fear in the dark: the terror of imagination.

"What I'm telling you, Mr. Detective, I don't bother saying to your colleagues. An ordinary policeman is like any other simpleton, he has no respect for what he cannot understand . . ."

Glick's pale eyes passed over Caras, then focused again on me.

"There was a great Flemish artist by the name Petrus Christus, a heretical Christian of the fifteenth century. One of his paintings hangs at the Metropolitan Museum—a very Christian scene, the assumption into heaven of the Virgin Mary. You would think that the Christian mother of God could have herself an easy journey, yes, Mr. Detective?"

"Offhand, yes."

"Don't forget, Petrus Christus was a heretic. There on the canvas is a death's head—Och, so much like the ones I would see on the sleeves of the camp commandants!—and huge, huge bat wings. Beneath those wings, the bodies of men and women and children are dropping downward, into hell. And there is an animal head—bloody and severed, with sharp teeth and spiny quills—that hangs from a thread. The animal's limbs are pressed together in its terrible descent. Anybody looking at this picture sees himself: falling, all of us falling, in spite of the beautiful Virgin Mary, mother of God. Petrus Christus never actually saw such a thing as he painted, of course. But this Christian artist, he looked into shadow sometime during his life, and imagined—and was terrified. He knows what we old Jews know."

"Knows what?" The old man's story was absorbing; I was growing slightly impatient. But he had waited all night to say his piece, and he would say it in his own due time. "Exactly what was in the shadow that came here, Mr. Glick?"

"The things I have seen in my time have not left me a brave man. It shames me to say I looked away from the shadow, for fear of my imagination. Ask the others, they'll say the same. But this is my belief: if seeing is not believing, then it must also be true that believing is not seeing. The shadow killed our rabbi, I am telling you. It scalped off his face and like a thief ran away with it. This thief . . ."

Glick's voice failed him momentarily. He raised a hand to his throat. His veiny eyelids drooped, and finally shut.

"Its name is Bá'al zbub."

Glick's eyes opened then, and he was quiet for several seconds. He seemed greatly relieved. He asked, "You'll take me home now?"

†

I had Glick on my arm and we were standing next to a maple tree at the curb outside the synagogue. The maple was struggling to bloom leaves in tenement-shadowed West Forty-seventh Street, I was struggling for a taxicab. Officer Caras had offered to run the old fellow down to his place near Herald Square in a sector car, but I declined the pleasure on Glick's behalf. A little of Caras goes a long way, especially for a man confused about what he saw . . .

. . . Or did not see.

I was certainly confused.

A yellow cab swooped around from behind a van, cutting across its path and almost scoring a direct hit on a speeding bicycle messenger in black Lycra and visored helmet. There was the usual ruckus of horns and death threats, after which the aggrieved parties went their separate fist-shaking ways. The cabby was calm as a corpse as he braked to a stop in front of us.

I opened the back door of the taxi for Glick to slide in ahead of me. As I started to climb in behind him, there was a tap on my shoulder. I turned.

"Say there, Detective—I couldn't help hearing what the caretaker told you . . ." This was the voice of one of the forensics cops, the one who had been crawling around the carpet, picking through the fiber nap with tweezers. He was a buttery guy in a machine-wash and tumble-dry tan suit. "About the rabbi's face, I mean."

"What about his face?"

"It's gone—missing. Just like the caretaker says. Only the old guy didn't elaborate. Well, not in the usual way."

"You have some useful elaboration?"

"What's your interest?"

"Personal."

The buttery guy shrugged in a friendly way. He seemed helpful. He told me his name was Bilkiss. I told him mine again. Also I told him that Marv Paznik was a friend, but I left out the part about the AA connection.

"Whoever did your buddy the rabbi," Bilkiss explained, "here's how it plays: first he jabs him three times quick in the chest. Pop goes the heart. Pop-pop go the lungs. Happened so quick the rabbi never had air to holler."

"Then?"

"It's probably true nobody saw it happen. No mystery about the results, though. The rabbi's face was skinned clean off the skull. I'm not talking a scalp job like in a cowboy-and-Indian flick. This killer—what these old folks are calling a shadow—he made a deep incision sideways across the crown of the head, then he sliced down the sides and under the chin. After that he just tore off the face, like it was sealing wax on a head of cheese."

"Sounds almost surgical. Like this shadow knew exactly what he was doing."

"He knows from scalpels all right."

"Any weapons recovered?"

"No."

The cabby tapped his horn. Time to go.

"Thanks, Bilkiss."

†

I have affection for Glick, and for my elders in general, but I can live without ever having to see the old guy eat again.

His apartment was two stifling rooms on the airshaft side of a loft building. The place smelled of soiled laundry and bad breath. And kasha, which besides matzoh and ice cream was the only thing Glick ate at home. So I boiled water and made him a bowl of kasha. Half of it wound up dribbled all over his shirt. When he finished the mush and put down his spoon, his face wore a bad-dog look that said, Okay—so I know I made a revolting mess for you, but I don't know how I did it exactly, and I don't know where I stand on the issue of giving a crap.

So I helped him out of his wet shirt. Then I sponged off his bad-dog chin and put him to bed.

"That Hebrew word you said?" I asked, covering him with a light blanket.

"Rodef shalom?"

"No, the other one. Starts with a *B.*"

"Bá'al zbub. The beast is here." The way Glick said this, it was like a whisper in a cemetery. "The same as Beelzebub. It means lord of the flies. It's the name of Satan."

Then old Glick fell into sleep as quick as a child flattened by a day at the seashore. His belly full and his imaginings now duly relayed to me, he snored contentedly, white fingers laced atop his chest as if waiting for a nosegay of lilies. I left him resting in peace and walked back uptown along Broadway.

Satan?

Besides this from Glick, I had the troubling thought of my own future dotage: old, sagging, slobbering Neil Hockaday making a revolting mess for poor Ruby to clean up.

†

I stopped feeling sorry for myself when I hit Forty-second Street and caught the eye of an acquaintance of mine by the name of Pauly Kerwin. He is a scrawny old carnival orphan with round, beaten-in features on a salmon pink face, and the forever sweet and wind-tossed look of a genuine old-fashioned skell. Pauly is a midget.

Anybody who calls him a "little person" should—and these are Pauly's own words—drop dead with flies on his face. When I last saw him—the other week it was, when he was wearing the same hostile paper sign around his neck he was wearing now—Pauly explained his sentiments on height: "When they called us midgets, at least there was a place for us to live that we could afford. Outside of carnivals, I'm talking, right here in Times Square. But now we're evicted in the name of progress and fresh money. Now we're a bunch of short refugees in a war on anybody who's anyways different from Mr. and Mrs. Purple Mountain Majesty. Yeah, and all of a sudden the citizens got to be calling us *little people.* Feh! Call me a midget and give me back my goddamn room!"

By room, Pauly meant his longtime domicile at the demolished Percival Apartments, a casualty of Times Square gone to the Disney dogs. The late Percival—in its final years, the notorious Percival—was the oldest building on Forty-second between Seventh and Eighth Avenues, that celebrated block known as the Deuce. Before long, I expect, even the term *Deuce* will vanish, as surely as wounded horses are shot, as surely as the wrecking balls knocked down the Percival, killing my boyhood memories and dumping Pauly Kerwin on the street.

The Percival was born in 1872 as a Catholic school for rich boys. Ten years later it was redesigned—by no less than the legendary firm of McKim, Mead & White—as an elegant hotel for rich bachelors. At the eve of the twentieth century it went through a series of grand restaurant incarnations, the last of which was Murray's Roman Gardens, with private upstairs dining rooms and pied-à-terres.

Murray's gave way to my own 1950s vintage memory of the Percival: Hubert's Museum by then, a heavenly sprawl of adolescent bad taste for gawking sailors and hooky-playing schoolboys. There was a rumpus room of Skee-Ball and pinball machines, a freak show run by a barker called Karoy *("I'm the man with the i-run tongue!"),* and, for the sailors, the French Academy of Medicine–Paris, France. Professor Ray Heckler operated his famous flea circus in a corner of Hubert's *("If a dog was to walk by, I'd lose my act!").* Once, I saw the legendary world's champion heavyweight boxer Jack Johnson at Hubert's, sitting in a chair behind a curtain that lifted for the holders of twenty-five-cent tickets. By the middle 1960s, my own heaven was gone to peep shows (live and video) and the Barracks, a homosexual brothel popular with the military.

In my truant days, I had no idea that the cramped top floor of the Percival was known to a certain mordantly humored crowd as the Midget Arms. Because the ceilings were quite low up on six, management had always found it difficult to rent out the rooms to normal-size persons—even on an hourly basis to the hot sheet trade. But the sizable community of midgets in the entertainment business in and around old Times Square found these same rooms cozy; quite desirable, too, since life presented them little opportunity of otherwise looking down over people.

Pauly Kerwin knows where the Percival was, as do some of the other wee troupers declining here and there in the streets, not so we should see them. To all others, the Percival has disappeared. It is now Madame Tussaud's Wax Museum. Wide-hipped tourists flock to the place, after which they grab something to eat a few doors to the east at what in the language of the new Deuce is called a brew parlor. There, the golf polos and madras pants and beaded T-shirts mix with Armani-clad male yuppies well under

five foot ten sucking on tall cigars. More casualties: the cigar boys work in the glass-and-chrome office silos of the new Times Square.

Pauly's own claim to the show business fraternity, by the way, was his tough-guy supporting role in a movie called *Terror in Tinytown,* the all-midget cult classic released in 1949. He plays the heavy to this day, not by choice. He scowls, and has taken to wearing a sign on his neck that reads: THERE'S SIXTY MILLION WAYS TO DIE, PICK ONE AND I'LL KILL YOU, ROTTEN MOTHER-FUCKING AMERICA. Considering the personal security needs of a homeless midget, the tough-guy act makes sense; it scares people off by making them believe he is barking nuts. On the other hand, Pauly's beggar proceeds have taken a resultant nosedive, along with his value to me as a street informer, since people generally do not talk to him anymore.

"Hock, boyo, how's it hanging?" Pauly had been scowling and moping outside a freshly opened tourist boutique, shaking his cup for spare change. Calling out to me in that wheezing, catarrh-rustling, old-time skelly voice scattered his prospects. Pauly only sighed. Then he hopped up and down, waving his stubby arms, and called again, "Hock, hey—*hey!*" Like anybody else, I wanted to avoid Pauly. He sensed as much. "Don't be passing me up! *Hey!* For the love of God, Hock—talk to me!"

There was no avoiding the summons. So I had to stop in front of this new shop full of tchotchkes, which stands on the very place I used to have my shoes shined and repaired; where there used to be a neighborly slogan in the window that made me smile: WE SHINE & SEAL & FIX THE HEELS, WE LACE THE HOLES & SAVE YOUR SOLES. Standing there now with Pauly Kerwin and his own not-so-neighborly slogan, I was unsmiling.

"Why do you want to be out here with that sour thing around your neck, Pauly? For the love of God yourself—it's Good Friday."

"No shit? I must not of checked my Filofax."

"You want to talk about anything in particular?"

"I as't you, how's it hanging?"

"Don't worry about me. How about yourself, Pauly? Found a place to stay?"

"Well, you know—Bob's. If you call that a right place for sleeping."

Pauly was referring to an oasis down on Thirty-seventh Street off Eleventh Avenue: Bob's Park, so-called in honor of a junkie-turned-social worker named Bob Smith. I know Smith only by reputation, as a neighborhood good guy, like Marv Paznik used to be. He had somehow straightened out under his own steam and was now working for a regular paycheck. He had chased his old gang of heroin shooters and crackheads out from the weedy vacant lot next to the tenement house where he lived; where he lives still, even though he draws enough salary in his reformed life to move someplace better, maybe even out of the Kitchen. After rousting the junkies, Smith had spent a bundle of his own money for the gate and equipment and landscaping necessary to create a quiet, decent retreat. Sometimes on weekends, he would personally hire a band so his neighbors could sing and dance; sometimes salsa, sometimes jazz, sometimes an Irish group that made the aging Hibernians in the block weep for green meadow memories of the other side.

All this about Bob Smith was fresh in my mind from a big profile about him in last week's *New York* magazine, which is a publication of no use to me unless I happen to see that a writer named Peter Benjaminson has something in it. Over the years, I have noticed that this particular writer shares my own regards, high and low, on civic matters. In the magazine profile that this Benjaminson wrote, Bob Smith had the good grace to credit the late, great Fiorello La Guardia as the inspiration for the park he gave to our neighborhood: "Every Fourth of July, Mayor La Guardia would get on the radio to remind everybody that Americans have the right to happiness—the *right!* He said we ought to look it up in the Declaration of Independence once a year, along with the parts about life and liberty. That's why the Little Flower built parks and bandshells during the Great Depression. Because happiness was in short supply. Which is the case with Hell's Kitchen today, which is why I spent my money like I did."

By day, Bob's Park is full of children who would otherwise not be listening to their better angels. By night, Smith permits an informal encampment of harmless old ancient mariners with nowhere else to go—people such as Pauly Kerwin, a midget who lost his home in favor of madras pants and corporate shrimps with *pricey* smokes.

"You're safe there at least," I said.

"About as safe as Christ'd feel about now."

"What's that mean?"

"Today's Good Friday, right?"

"Yes."

"The anniversary of when they invented giving the shaft to a guy."

"In a manner of speaking."

"So—you think if Jesus Christ was to come back here today he'd actually want to see all the goddamn crosses you citizens are always putting up all over?"

"I'm missing your point, Pauly."

"Naturally. You're a man with a roof. What do I got? I don't got my room anymore. Instead I got Bob's Park where I got to do the lay-me-down-to-sleep-and-pray-the-Lord-my-soul-to-keep. You and me, Hock, we can't help but see things different."

"I'm still missing."

"One guy's cross is another guy's shaft."

"I'll think about that."

"Yeah, think about it tonight. In the bed you got, with the wifey all pretty and warm beside you."

"I have to be going, Pauly."

"And nobody's even telling you. Must be nice."

Pauly said this to my back as I walked west through the sanitized Deuce toward the Kitchen, no less unsettled than I was from leaving old Glick behind. Besides all that was agitating inside me—the unfinished business of King Kong

Kowalski, a cop threat *("You should watch your mouth, Hockaday . . . Maybe your back, too"),* fatherhood looming, an old man in a stifling room napping like a corpse, a midget sleeping in a park, a murderous shadow—I had this on my mind, too: the Good Friday communion mass at Holy Cross Church, and whether I was in the mood for a stroll down the memory lane of crucifixion, and looking in on Ruby before I headed back to the station house, where who knows but another sweet wreath awaited me.

I stopped in front of the church. I just stood there on the sidewalk at the bottom of the stairs for a while, staring. Set into the round window over the big blue entrance doors was the crucifix I have known throughout my life, all the way from short pants to police blues.

Yet here was I now, looking at that glass cross as if I had never seen it before. And struggling with the deepest mystery I know as a Catholic, half fallen-away though I may be: how are ultimate mercy and ultimate vengeance known by this single sign?

The mystic Shabbatai Sevi, three hundred years ago—had not he been crazed by a matter very nearly the same? How had Marv put it . . . ?

How strangely do we remember the small things of a dead friend.

Again I pictured the day Marv told me the Sevi legend: Lunch in his office at Temple Ezrath Israel. Chinese take-out. Marv opens his fortune cookie, reads the slip of paper inside, shrugs, drops it to his desk . . .

Marv explaining, *There is nobody more powerful than God, but there is something equal to his power.* As I listen to him, I glance at a strange message wrapped in a cookie: THE INFLICTION OF CRUELTY WITH A GOOD CONSCIENCE IS A DELIGHT TO MORALISTS.

I turned away from the glass cross.

I glanced to the other side of Forty-second Street:

A swirl of orange neon letters in a smoky window, spelling out some old favorite pastimes. A gray steel door I promised myself and God and Father Declan—and Ruby, and our baby inside her—that I shall not enter again.

One day at a time. Tomorrow would be another day, another time . . .

. . . Time was when I and my colleagues relaxed on the other side of that gray door over there. And sometimes the relaxing had a way of erupting into a large general fistfight. A colleague clubbed me over the head one night with a shoe, and called me a dumb mick. I saw myself again, roaring around the place like an angry bear until I found him, knocked him down, thinking how I sure did show him I was no dumb mick.

God help me, I needed a drink.

I made my way, weaving and staggering, through a ruckus of horns and shouting and fists shaking at me from car windows—toward the doorway of my fondly recollected oblivion from agitating thought.

Ten

"THIS ONE, you got to love . . ."

"Somehow I doubt it."

"Come on now—ain't I trying to be nice?"

"Goodness, yes, it's practically the mountain come to Mohammed. You in this little old Hell's Kitchen dive for gentlemen of a certain persuasion—well, it's hardly your mise-en-scène now, is it?"

"Cut it. Alls I'm saying is . . . ! Oh, goddammit! You could listen at least!"

"Don't raise your voice. It's embarrassing."

"Embarrassing? You want to talk freaking embarrassing—?"

"Just go ahead and tell the joke."

"Okay, there's—"

"No, wait. I have to take care of my regular."

"Regular my ass!"

"Hush, sweety."

"Don't be calling me that!"

The bartender—young and blond and blue-eyed, with earrings, sleeveless black T-shirt, black Speedo swim trunks, and construction boots; skin tan as toast, muscles taut enough to bounce coins—glided off to attend to a well-tailored, middle-aged gent perched on the end stool. The two men kissed. The bartender pulled up a draught of beer and set it down for his friend the regular customer. A quiet laugh was shared. After which the bartender returned to the fat man in the bad suit with his hand grazing through a wooden bowl of trail mix.

"You really must stop eating like that, sweety. Gluttony is one of the seven deadly sins. You're opposed to sin, aren't you?"

"Quit busting my chops."

"What then? You'll see me to paradise? As Jesus did for Dismas?"

"What in the . . . ?"

"Dismas, the penitent thief in Luke, chapter twenty-three? There were two thieves crucified along with Jesus on Good Friday—Dismas, and Gemas. Dismas was the one who did not mock Christ, but accepted him. And for this, Jesus promised him everlasting life in heaven."

"Forget about it. You, I don't got to be hearing Bible stories from."

"God knows I've tried to forget them myself. Which reminds me, how goes it at dear Mother's sodality?"

"Never mind about the church lady stuff. Pour me out another one."

"That would be four by my count."

"So I had a rotten day, all right?"

"All right by me."

"You want to hear the freaking joke or not?"

"Why not?"

"Couple of lah-di-dah tycoons, they're all dressed up and having some belts at this exclusive joint in the Chrysler Building. They're sitting at a table in the Cloud Club on the seventy-first floor, right next to this huge window with a breathtaking view of Manhattan. Man Number One, he's wearing black horn-rims. He says to the other guy, 'This here building, the aerodynamics are unique in the world . . .' "

"The tycoon said *this here?*"

"Shut up. So Man Number Two, he asks how come about

the unique aerodynamics. Guy in the specs says, 'It's the wind patterns, the updrafts to be specific.' Then he puts his hand on the window and says, 'See, if I was to jump out, I'd fall thirty, forty, maybe fifty feet. Then, amazingly enough, the updraft, it'd blow me right back inside this here window.' The second guy laughs and says, 'Pal, you had one too many . . .' "

"What were they drinking?"

"Martinis. The first guy says, 'Sure, I had a few, but it don't mean I ain't telling the truth. I know what I'm talking about, I jumped many times myself.' The second guy says he don't believe it. So, the first guy whips off his specs and his necktie and his suitcoat and he opens up the window and takes a dive . . ."

"And the second guy?"

"He's watching, he's horrified. His pal starts falling—thirty feet, forty feet, fifty feet, sixty feet, seventy feet. And then—a miracle! He floats straight back up and inside the window. Incredible. He puts the glasses back on and his suit and tie, and says to the other guy, 'Go on, try it, it's a freaking blast . . .' "

"Naturally, the second guy jumps."

"Yeah. And he falls—thirty feet, forty feet, fifty, sixty, seventy, eighty, ninety . . ."

"No updraft?"

"Splat! Guy hits the sidewalk. Turns into the world's biggest pizza pie . . ."

"Big surprise."

"Meanwhile, back up in the Cloud Club, this waiter comes over to the table and tells the guy in the specs, 'Hey, Clark Kent—you know what? You're a real asshole when you get drunk.' "

"That's actually . . ." The bartender paused and laughed, much to his surprise. "It's not bad."

"Like I say, you got to love it."

"I just might."

"Well," said the fat man, smiling, "it's a start for me and you then, ain't it?"

Eleven

"YOU'RE NOT GOING TO LIKE what's in there."

"The hell I won't, you should pardon the expression."

"I'm coming in with you."

"Suit yourself, Father. But I'm not treating."

Which is how it came to pass that on Good Friday I was bellied up to the bar with the swirly orange neon window instead of kneeling at the altar across the way, consuming the flesh and blood of Jesus with the transubstantiating assistance of Father Declan Byrne, my link to bittersweet remembrance of an immigrant Irish Hell's Kitchen. As for himself, perched upon the barstool next to my own instead of relaxing between his masses:

Moments ago, Father Declan had stepped out from the sanctuary of Holy Cross for some air, some springtime sun, and a few quick coughs on a cigarette. What should he see but myself, staggering through the honking traffic of Forty-second Street, headed straightaway for trouble in a bottle. Being largely responsible for having me hauled away for various drying-out sessions in my past, and my elder in overfamiliarity with Mr. Johnnie Walker, Father Declan was naturally inspired to hot pursuit. And so he dropped a half-smoked Pall Mall and came galloping after me, arms akimbo, black hair flying, cassock flapping, rosary beads clacking.

"So—didn't I tell you?" said my sidekick, smug as could be. He rolled billowy priest sleeves up past dimpled elbows so as not to shmutz his holiday purple cassock on the moist mahogany of a bar. Meanwhile, I took in the alien scene of the place: lousy with potted palms and mirrors and salmon pink walls with cool recessed lighting, and more of those short guys with the big cigars. One of them yapped on a cell phone; the subject was money, not the kind that could be folded into a wallet. There were three television sets suspended over the long curving bar, each the size of an icebox from my tenement youth, each tuned to a professional golf tournament. (As nearly as I understand it, golf is the same as playing marbles, only more expensive.) Underneath the TV golfers and their rainbow Coogi sweaters was a crawling line of video letters and numbers: the daily stock quotations. The meaning of *You're not going to like what's in there* was slowly but surely dawning on me. Father Declan rubbed more salt. "All this you see, it's only the first phase of destruction," he said. "Wait until they get around to ruining the outside. With a canopy, with velvet ropes—"

"Here? In the Kitchen?"

"I'd not lie to you, Neil. It's what they're talking about. Besides the canopy and such, there's to be a doorman, too."

"What? Some guy wearing a black suit and a thick neck, deciding whether you're hip enough to get inside?"

"Exactly the type."

"This bar, it was a neighborhood treasure—the last of the Hell's Kitchen forty-cent draught joints. And now here they're killing it." Even as I spoke, a couple of workmen were busy dismantling the window fixtures, which were covered in layers of grease and smoke thick enough to please an archaeologist. The bartender coming our way was a brisk young guy who looked like he ought to be serving double lattes instead of liquor. I found the sight of him sobering. So I ordered a seltzer and fruit, and the same for the Roman collar next to me. I asked Father Declan, with a long-lost sigh that set the mood for a moment of nostalgia between an odd couple of ex-boozer harps, "Where did all the old beer boyos go?"

"God only knows, the poor sods." Father Declan wiped dry lips with the back of his hand. Some drinker's habits never die. I suppose it was strange for the coffee latte bartender and the tiny yuppies to see us sitting there: Father Declan, sixtysomething, plump, and purple-clad; wiping his lips Bowery-style and chatting with his brogue to another one, younger and with a New York–born tongue, yet also wearing the map of Ireland for a face; stranger yet, two harps drinking charged water in place of whisky. "And poor, poor Forty-second Street," my homeboy lamented. "It seems only yesterday how all these pubs stretching from Hudson docks to the Deuce were meant for our crowd."

"Well, but, Father—that whole waterfront life, it's all gone, all of it. And the Deuce is under new ownership."

"When I think how many times I prayed for cleanliness and godliness to take root in these sorry old blocks . . ." Father Declan looked heavenward and shook his head, then entertained a second thought. "On the other hand, is it possible the Holy Father never answered my earnest prayers? After all, what we see now of these changes is sterility and eviction. Which are different things than clean and holy."

"Or else he did answer, and here we are again, faced with an act of God resulting in unintended consequences."

"Hear you, son, you're talking like one of them double-dome Jesuits. Well, but it's better than how I'm sounding . . ." Father Declan paused, and wiped his lips again. It was easy to read his mind, since the same idea crowded my own head: the want of a real drink. His hand trembled. Poor Declan Byrne, here he had come to rescue me. I touched his shoulder, and it calmed him. "Forgive me," he said, sighing as I had sighed. "I'm like a codger moaning for a past gone rosy-colored in the crust of his brain."

"We have our soft spots for the old days, that's all," I said. Me—forgive a priest?

"That—and appreciation for such streets that provide the justice of common ground," said Father Declan, chuckling at his own remark.

I asked him what he meant.

"The finest of all the many revelries on the used-to-be Deuce came upon a blue and sunny day of June, better than fifty years ago," he said. "It was mostly a good-hearted mob filling Times Square that day, cheered up and larky by the news of the Japanese surrender—meaning an end to the long war. Among the celebrants was a darkly smiling sailor from California with wiry black hair, a swoop nose, and—this pains me to say—an Irish name."

I had an idea who the priest was talking about.

"The young sailor, a lieutenant he was, had come to spend the thousands he'd cheated off his mates in tricky shipboard poker games," Father Declan continued. "But he never got his chance at the fleshpots, for the lieutenant cheater's disgrace was there properly avenged on Forty-second Street: his pockets were picked clean. Alas for the young crook from California, this lesson was ignored. He became a politician and otherwise continued his opprobrious ways. Not thirty years later, his sins were so avenged as to force him to a surrender as sure and humiliating as Tojo's own."

"And your story," I said, smiling, as warmly amused as if I had heard it with a glass of Scotch, at least in hand, "it's as sure a morality tale as any ever told by the sisters of Holy Cross School."

"But then it's no mere nun's fable, it's all quite true." Father Declan consulted his wristwatch, pawed at his lips. "Look now, I've got to be getting back. There's another mass to come. Will you leave with me, son?"

"Yes. I'll pay up for us, too."

The tab turned out to be approximately five times the

price of two sodas out of a delicatessen cooler. Plus tip. Being the son of a hard-working Hell's Kitchen barmaid, I am ordinarily generous about tipping. Not this time. I left nothing extra, my own small avenging act for the vandalism done to a neighborhood treasure.

I was steady on my feet on the way back across Forty-second. Walking along with a priest, I had no bother of dodging cars and trucks. Father Declan, stoutly marching along in collar and cassock, puffing on a cigarette, parted traffic as if he were Moses cutting through the sea.

"You'll be coming in with me for the mass?" asked Father Declan. We had reached the broad steps of the church. He tossed down his cigarette, stepped on it. I looked up at the cross over the doorway, then glanced at my own wristwatch. The priest asked, "Pressed for time, are we then?"

"It's just that—"

"Don't even say it, Neil, it'd be a fib. You haven't been to a mass since Christmas last. You don't think I keep track of you and the other just-in-case Catholics of this parish?"

"Sunday I'll be here."

"Will you now? Easter being soon enough to be getting right with Our Lord and Savior?"

I thought, This is the fundamental of us being Catholic-born: we are guilty before taking our first breath. Then came a question, in the street below that contrarian cross, "Father, help me . . . ?" It was me who asked this, odd as the voice sounded within my head, as if someone else were speaking. I welcome such unsettling sensations in my life as a detective, which is more art than science, and I have learned to value the artistic moment.

"What's this torment now?" The scolding tone of Father Declan's voice was replaced by a catch, as if he was sorrier than even myself to have sensed trouble. "Tell me."

"I'm looking for a murderer."

"Good luck for us survivors you're a copper then."

"But this time . . ."

A shadow of death this time. The smell of maggots and a shadow that slayed a friend. How could fourteen people see only a shadow? A shadow that mutilated my friend as he read ancient words: *The closed eye is only then satisfied with seeing.* And how had Glick put it? *He looked into shadow and imagined—and he was terrified . . . Bá'al zbub . . . Do you understand?*

"What are your troubles, son?"

Did Father Declan yet know it was Marv—Rabbi Paznik, a fellow cleric in the neighborhood—who was murdered on his holy day? If not, how could I deliver such news on this, his own holy day? I answered with, "You could say I'm having a crisis of faith."

"Keep faith that God never fails us."

"That's what I'm lacking."

"I'll not like hearing blasphemy." Father Declan rubbed

his head, as if it were suddenly hammering with pain. "Answer me this: what would a religious crisis be having to do with a policeman's job of work?"

"Ordinarily, little or nothing. But this time . . ." How could I say what I thought? *Maybe you think it's crazy what I'm saying.* "Put it this way, there's something unholy about the murder."

Father Declan rubbed his pained head more vigorously. He was trying to respond, but could only repeat what I had said. "Unholy . . . ?"

"As a cop, let's say, I just don't get it."

"I imagine there are such crimes as tax the limits of a policeman. Neither badge nor gun means a fiddler's fart to the intelligent sinner." Father Declan stroked his chin. "And this is what you feel you're up against, Neil? A force of especially intelligent evil?"

"That's it, yes."

"And it's the help of the church you've forsaken that you're now asking?"

"I—"

"Never mind, save to rejoice you've come to the right place. But I've not the proper guidance for you myself, Neil. Nor the time. Tell me true, though, are you afraid?"

Was I?

"By your silence, I take it you're afraid indeed, son. 'Tis no shame, even for a policeman. Can you remember the *Carmina Gaedelica?* The ancient prayer of preservation given to God by Irish fishermen caught in their boats in hurricanes, and crofters in their fields as the cyclones blew?"

Again I was silent, in the shamed way only a shamrock Catholic who has forgot a sacred boyhood lesson can be.

"God to enfold me, God to surround me, God in my speaking, God in my thinking . . ."

Father Declan intoned the old words quickly. I remembered the rest, as if reciting the Baltimore catechism itself. *God in my sleeping, God in my waking, God in my watching, God in my hoping, God in my life, God in my lips, God in my soul, God in my heart, God in my sufficing, God in my slumber, God in mine ever-living soul.*

When he was through keening aloud that which drummed through my own memory, Father Declan consulted his wristwatch. "Now I've got my next mass, and after that the preparing to do for the march in the street tonight. The Way of the Cross, you know. Meanwhile, son, remember the *Carmina Gaedelica* and you'll be safe from Satan himself."

"I've got more questions."

"Do you remember Father Gerald Morrison?"

"He's still alive?"

"Yes, and I know what you little shits called him—Creepy Morrison. That I keep track of, too."

"We were only kids—"

"Hellions you were, it's truer said. Anyway—Father Gerald, that's your man, not I. The kind of priest I am's good for the usual sins, such as getting drunk and cursing and idling. But Father Gerald, now there's a man studious in the ways of keenest perfidy. It's because he's Society of Jesus, of course. The Jesuits know even the sins of the popes."

"Where do I find him?"

"Father Gerald serves in hermitage."

"Creepy Morrison's a hermit?"

"Aye. He's living upstate in the Catskill mountains, studying and praying for the sins of the world. There's a way of seeing him if you like. I can arrange it. It's not far, but the journey's no easy one."

†

Anybody in New York with access to a radio or television set had heard about the murder of Rabbi Paznik. Not really *all* about it, but certainly as much as the department wanted the public informed for the time being.

I stopped at Alps Pharmacy on the corner of Ninth Avenue for some aspirin and caught the public line on WINS radio. People were not being told about Marv's face being stolen away, nor about fourteen eyewitnesses claiming the killer was a "shadow." These details were omitted for the purposes of fact-checking against a perp, a necessary withholding tactic in high-profile homicide cases likely to attract a parade of remorseful wackos wanting to be locked up on account of what their demons supposedly did. The Paznik murder was such a likely case.

Ruby had heard the news, such as it was, and by the sight of me understood something beyond the headlines: namely that this was a job with my name written all over it. One look at my troubled face coming through the door and she knew I was on a case requiring a detective possessed of that special quality Inspector Neglio once praised in me. "Hock," he said one grand, boozy night back in my drinking days, the night he presented me with my gold shield, "you've got an imagination just this side of being a lunatic."

Again, I found Ruby curled up on the couch below the parlor window reading the script of *Grief Street* through her froggy wire-rims. And again, the sky through the window behind her was turning black and blue with the approach of another Hell's Kitchen night.

She took off the glasses. Ordinarily, Ruby's hazel chocolate eyes are bright and eager. But not now. They had gone vacant and gray-brown, like a street in a driver education film waiting for some terrible accident to happen.

"Don't cry," I said, knowing Ruby's own considerable imagination. I sat down beside her, kissed her brown cheeks, which smelled of blueberry-scented soap, put a hand over hers. I might well have been touching marble. "Don't cry, it's bad for the baby."

"There are worse things in the life of a child than his mother's tears."

"What's this mood of yours?"

"Another case full of dread is about to consume a part of you, a part of us."

"Ruby, don't—"

"Don't pat my hand and say, There-there, little gal,

you're pregnant. I wouldn't be the first woman in history to know that all by herself. This case—it's about your rabbi friend, isn't it?"

"I wouldn't be the first cop working a job that's close to home."

"You always manage somehow to make it personal. Which is boneheaded. Not to mention that it goes against lesson number one at police academy."

"I don't need you to be calling me stupid."

"Correction. I called you a bonehead."

This is where Ruby might have laughed at me, and made me like it. Instead she cried. The tears came abruptly, and it was a few seconds before she realized them. Then again, that apprehensive look in her uptilted face. This was disconcerting to me, and it struck me how much—how selfishly—I relied on Ruby for my own sense of balance.

"I see you've been studying the bashful playwright's script." I thought a change of subject was in order. How could I then know I had done no such thing? "Still high on your role?"

Ruby's hands clenched, then relaxed. The pages of the script, which she had unclipped to look at one by one, spilled to the floor. I leaned forward and gathered up the onionskin papers, among them the title page and the page immediately following—on which a poetic inscription had been penned, with ink the same pale cherry color as the handwritten letter from the anonymous author.

"Go ahead, read at least the epigraph if nothing else," Ruby said. Even without her glasses, she saw which page I held.

I first read the epigraph to myself, nodding my head in agreement. Then I recited the line from Pablo Neruda: " 'Out of every dead child comes a rifle with eyes, every crime breeds bullets that will one day find their way to your heart.' "

"Disturbing, wouldn't you agree?" Ruby said.

"Also beautiful in a way."

"Isn't that just like your precious Hell's Kitchen?" Apprehension remained in Ruby's face. "I heard on the radio that it was not beautiful today in your briar patch."

"No, it wasn't."

"Tell me. Don't skip anything just because I'm a pregnant lady."

I told her everything, or practically: about the crime scene at Temple Ezrath Israel, a remembrance of Marv telling me about Shabbatai Sevi and his notion of a wounded God; about old Mr. Glick and his confusion about a "shadow," and his apartment that smelled of kasha; about Pauly Kerwin sleeping in Bob's Park because the Midget Arms and just about everything else on the Deuce was going Disney; about my brief temptation on seeing the swirly orange windows, a bar chat with Father Declan Byrne, my confession to him of feeling out of my depth in an unholy case, his suggestion that I make an uneasy journey to consult a hermit.

"All very interesting, especially the unlikely part about your leaving the city to go talk to some lonesome priest up in the Catskills," Ruby said. "But you edited, didn't you, dear? You left out something nasty, didn't you? Something with a tail—?"

There was a lot of sudden noise from the street below, interrupting Ruby. We both looked out the window, and Ruby asked, "Speaking of holy questions, what's with the mob down there?"

Striding righteously down Tenth Avenue in sandals and raggedy caftans—against the snarl of theater-rush traffic—was a pack of earnest-looking pillars of Catholic laity. Seven good men and true, engaged in a passion play straight from devoutest Eire: sullen-faced marchers, shoulders high, sharing the burden of a wooden cross the length of a city bus. As kids, I pegged these guys as the type who irritated me and my own crowd with their unseemly eagerness to know by heart all the prayers—the Hail Mary, the Our Father, the Confiteor, the Apostles' Creed, the Act of Contrition, the Litany of the Blessed

Virgin Mary—equally as well in Irish, English, and Latin. They preferred Latin, of course, this being the language of Christian martyrs; so attested Creepy Morrison and all others of the Holy Cross School faculty, including even the otherwise dear and reasonable Sister Roberta, who were horrified by the official scrapping of the Latin mass. Creepy Morrison lived to regale these irritatingly pious lads with tales of martyrs screaming out Latin supplications as barbarians ripped out their fingernails, or skinned them alive—or as they quaked in the catacombs before jeering centurions booted them into the blood-soaked arenas of ancient Rome, there to perish in foaming lion jaws for the savage amusement of the emperor.

Deprived of glorious sufferings from such ancient cruelties and decadence, the present-day martyrs of Tenth Avenue proudly made do on this Good Friday night with the casual taunts of modern-day heathens.

Yo, Pontius Pilate, how come you want to whack the good dude with that big old cross? . . . Ain't you the assholes that was waving around the plastic fetus in everybody's face a couple weeks back there? . . . Yo, god boy, your fly's open!

O Lord, how the new martyrs hungered for words to break their bones as surely as sticks and stones.

Ruby looked to me for an explanation of all this. The phrase I was thinking of was *holy codswallop*, but I said nothing. So she asked again, "What's with them?"

"You're observing a holy rite known as the Way of the Cross, a reenactment of the crucifixion," I said, finally. "It's one of our little Catholic embarrassments. Like exorcism. The cross boys will be turning east on Forty-second to pass by the church. Father Declan will bless the bunch of them, without a blush."

"Talk about religious embarrassment. Nothing's more embarrassing than a bug-eyed Southern Baptist preacher waist-deep in a tub of water."

"Maybe." I shrugged and turned away from the window. "How do you mean I edited something?"

"A friend of yours called today."

"Who?"

"Harry Darcy."

I could not place the name, I told Ruby.

"From a long time ago. He mentioned short pants and classroom nuns."

"Where did he get my number?"

"He's got access. Harry Darcy's in the system, he's a corrections officer at Rikers Island."

This was not helping me compute a face behind a forgotten name.

"He mentioned something besides school days," Ruby said. "He mentioned rats."

"What are you talking about?"

Ruby cut me a look that said I should knock it off because she was on to me.

"Same thing I asked Harry. He said to me, 'Well, I'm very surprised, Mrs. Hockaday. You really don't know?' No, I don't, I said. So I made him tell."

"About what?"

"About wreathing. Another one of your little embarrassments."

"That is a sick thing done by rabid cops." I might have raised my voice. "But it's nothing you need to know about."

"Rabid cops string up rats on my husband's locker at the station house—and that's nothing I need to know? Then somebody who doesn't belong here comes sneaking down the hallway outside our apartment and spikes rats on the front door—and that's none of my business either?"

"You shouldn't be intimidated." This was a lie to myself as much as it was to Ruby. First thing tomorrow, I decided, I would make a surprise visit to Rikers and find this friend of mine, so-called. Maybe I would punch out his face for upsetting my pregnant wife. "Besides spilling to you about the wreathing, what did this Darcy want?"

"What did you do with the rats on our front door?"

"Took them down. I didn't want you seeing that crap."

"Speaking of which, this Harry Darcy wants to see you."

"Did he say why?"

"Something about King Kong Kowalski. Harry Darcy says—"

The rest of it would have to wait. Just then I was distracted by the *crack-crack-crack* of automatic rifle fire, people screaming, tires screeching, horns blasting . . .

. . . seven martyrs and their cross, fallen and bloody down below my window on Forty-second Street.

Twelve

MY APARTMENT WINDOW WAS A MOVIE SCREEN. This was the picture:

A small army of cops in helmets and bulletproof shields and knee-high leather boots—waving their big, ugly AK-47s and otherwise scaring the stuffings out of scrambling motorists and pedestrians—galloped across Forty-second Street from the riot squad station house a block east of the pandemonium. A posse of Mounted Division officers was already on scene. Horses skittered in tight circles; cops with scope-sighted rifles drawn, cocked for killing on sight, scanned surrounding rooftops for snipers.

I pulled Ruby from the couch to the floor, shoved her down, and made her lie as flat out as her belly permitted. I tilted the couch over her, making a sort of tent. Ruby, clutching the script of *Grief Street* to her chest, shouted at me as I hopped toward the bedroom, "Come back in one piece, damn you, Irish!"

From the bedroom closet, I grabbed my shoulder holster with the big piece inside of it—a .44 caliber Charter Arms Bulldog, capable of blowing a hole the size of a baseball in a man's chest. It was the perfect complement of the Glock nine-millimeter already clipped to my belt. I pulled on a denim jacket, ran out the door and down the stairway, to the fading sounds of Ruby's admonitions.

"Damn you, Irish! Be careful! Come back in one piece, you hear me? Come back to us! Come back . . . !"

A squad car from the Manhattan North station house careened into the Plexiglas bus shelter on Tenth Avenue, almost flattening me in the process. Four uniforms piled out and ignored me. They ran into the clogged avenue and started assaulting vehicles, banging on windows and fenders with their nightsticks, shouting at the drivers: *Let's clear the fucking fire lane! Come on, come on—move it!*

The distant wail of ambulance sirens.

Crack-crack-crack.

Again, the sound of automatic rifle fire. Bullets thudding into the enormous cross fallen to the street, splintering wood; bullets ripping into the thrashing bodies of its seven martyred bearers.

Someone in a clump of gawkers pointed upward, to the top of the five-storey white brick building on the south side of Forty-second—the National Video Center, housing New York's all-news television station, Channel 1. Then everybody started pointing, including some cops. There was nothing to see up there but blackness, then spits of yellow fire . . .

Crack-crack-crack.

Then someone screamed and the crowd panicked, stampeding toward the shelter of a coffee shop across the way. People did not bother about the door, they simply crashed through the windows.

Then: blade-whomping sounds of NYPD helicopters, low in the sky, speeding uptown from the police chopper pad in Chelsea.

Seconds later: a tidal wave of blazing white light from overhead, turning the Hell's Kitchen night into mazda day.

I ran around the stampede outside the coffee shop, down Tenth Avenue, gold shield held high in my left hand, the nina ready in my shooting hand.

And just who was it I expected to shoot?

I stopped at the corner, pressed myself against the white brick, and peered around into the gritty bleakness of Forty-first Street. This street and Fortieth are dead blocks, bounded by gas stations and warehouses west of Tenth Avenue, the Lincoln Tunnel to Jersey on the south where Thirty-ninth Street used to be, and the long back shadows of the Port Authority Bus Terminal to the east on Ninth Avenue.

Here, in this dead patch of Hell's Kitchen, are only the sheltering arms of Covenant House, some nickel-and-dime drug trade, an ever-changing cast of skells, and enough strolling pross to account for a morning-after litter of used condoms.

An old smoke once told me of a much different street in the days when he was young: a street of lime kilns and stone masons' yards, where brownstone slabs quarried from across the river at Weehawken and Guttenberg arrived in skiffs each morning, to be properly cut and shaped in the Kitchen for rich men's homes. For a suspended second, I indulged the thought of this ironic past. Then, down toward the end of Forty-first, nearly to Ninth Avenue, I saw a man; that is, I saw a silhouette.

The silhouette appeared to have a pistol. It moved toward a car—a station wagon half-illuminated by the yellow plume of a streetlamp, clear enough for me to see Jersey plates. The silhouette raised a foot, kicked the driver side door.

"Police!" it shouted. "Get the fuck out of the car!"

No response. The car door was kicked several more times, the window bashed with the gun butt.

"Let's go, let's go! Police! Get the fuck out!"

Another figure approached from behind the car, slowly. When he stepped into light I could see he wore the bag, the navy blue NYPD uniform. Also that he was African American, and young enough to be a rookie. And by now I saw fully his silhouetted partner—a white plainclothes cop in his thirties, wearing jeans and construction boots and a denim jacket like the one I was wearing myself.

The white cop stepped back from the car, raised a foot, and rammed it against the driver window, smashing it. Then he pulled open the door, and yanked a guy out from behind the wheel.

"You're under arrest, you horny fucking mutt," the white cop said to the john, a guy who looked like he was born middle-aged and suburban. To his black uniformed partner on the other side of the car, "Haul out dolly, too, Matson. Let's have us a look at the sweetheart of Sigma Chi."

John wore a white shirt, a necktie, and a striped suitcoat. Striped trousers and plaid boxer shorts were drooped down around his ankles. John looked like he would not mind it so much if he should suddenly drop dead.

Officer Matson, meanwhile, did what he was told. He opened the passenger door and let out a tall, broad-shouldered, dark-skinned number with a bouffant of strawberry blond hair and a shimmery green dress showing lots of thigh. She was the type who had been through the drill more than once, and so she should have been taking the bust in stride. But she was not. She was as jumpy as her client—both looking up at the sky and trying to make sense of the helicopter commotion.

I started walking toward the car, sticking to the shadows, keeping a watch on the rooflines as I made my way.

"What's wrong—you fucking go deaf on me, John?" the white cop asked. John bent down to pull up his pants. The cop grabbed his suitcoat lapels, jerking him back up, and barked, "I say you can do that?"

"Sorry . . ."

The next thing out of John's mouth reflected neither arrogance nor resistance, merely his ignorance of the departmental reference for a male of the species on the inside of a prostitution collar. As a matter of fact, he was trying to be helpful about something more important than the rented company he kept. But the cop, being that he was ignorant by a different style and uncurious about the helicopters and what had brought them, read John all wrong.

"My name isn't John." The guy with his pants down was out of breath, although not from whatever it was that Sweetheart had earlier been doing to him. "Look, I want to explain, Officer. See, I was scared to get out of the car. I mean, after what I saw coming down off that roof—"

The cop rammed his fist into John's breastbone. This would hurt like hell for at least a week, but would leave John with no bruises to show a lawyer, not to mention the Civilian Complaint Review Board. The guy's knees crumpled and he started bawling and snotting.

I happened to know this cop who had hammered John's chest: Larry Webster, one of the charmers out of Manhattan Sex Crimes.

"John's got something to say. Let him talk, Webster." I said this after calling out my name and the color of the day, and making certain the two cops saw my ranking gold shield.

"So you're Hockaday." Matson the rookie said this matter-of-factly.

"Sure, you're looking at the famous Detective Hockaday that ratted out Sergeant Kowalski," Webster said. "Watch he don't try crowding our collar, Matson."

"You've got no problem from me," I said to Webster. There was a snarl on his face. Matson's face was neutral, the kind I could talk to. So I did. I motioned toward the roof of the National Video Center. "There was a sniper up there. He took out seven down on Forty-second Street while you were putting the drop on John and Sweetheart back here. It sounds to me like John saw something."

"My advice, don't say nothing more until you lawyer up," Webster counseled John.

"Looking who's crowding," I said. "I should say interfering."

Webster ignored my threat. He turned to the tall bouffant number and asked, "What do they call you, Sweetheart?"

"Trixie."

"Ain't that pretty. Matson, come on over here with Miss Trixie. Let's see if she's got one."

Matson rounded the front of the station wagon. He gave me a little salute off the brim of his hat, and presented Trixie to Webster.

"It's showtime, Trixie," Webster said. "Let's have a look at what you're peddling."

Trixie was return business, all right. No sense in being difficult. She tossed her head and sighed theatrically, after which she hiked up the front of her shimmery green dress. Underneath, she was outfitted with the same equipment as were the rest of us standing there under the streetlamp. John tried looking away. Webster removed a leather sap from the back of his belt and persuaded him otherwise, after which John attempted to appear surprised. Only Matson was surprised, though, his smooth brown face going somewhat bilious.

"Oh, the first time's a real shock, ain't it?" Webster said, taunting John.

"Well, yeah, it—"

"Pull up your pants, you lying mutt." Webster whapped him gently on the buttocks with his sap when he bent over. "We take you downtown and pull up your rap sheet, I bet a thousand bucks it turns out you're a recidivist."

"Sure he is, so what?" I said, trying to place myself between Webster and John. Webster was not having it. Matson moved in. He put a calming hand on his partner's sap arm, but Webster shook it off. So I laid it out for both officers. "Here's how it goes down, men: you've got your Mickey Mouse collar; plus, if I'm the type who would rat out a fellow cop, then there's the matter of interfering with a detective's investigation of a homicide."

"He's the type," Matson said to Webster, defusing the situation. I liked the way the rookie handled himself.

"Good." I turned to John. "You were saying, about something coming down off a roof?"

"This big shadowy thing, smelly as shit—"

Webster cut in and again reminded John, "I told you, can it until you're lawyered up."

"All right, we'll do it the long way." I said to Matson, "Go on and get the unit, I'll be riding with you to the party."

†

I had not laid eyes on Sergeant Joseph Kowalski since shortly before I filed the brutality complaint against him. His appearance had not improved with time. The man was well beyond the upper limits of the departmental weight rule. King Kong was a table set for two. No doubt this was why the overnight trick was Kowalski's shift of choice. Snap inspectors from IAD rarely work such hours themselves.

There he sat now: up behind the massive booking desk, with a commanding view of the squad room, his steel half-frame glasses glinting under fluorescent lights as he pored over a pile of muster reports; a necktie full of stains stretched between a collar that could not be closed; his great mastiff hound jaws pulverized the contents of a box of Russell Stover chocolates at his elbow. I felt sorry for the chocolates.

Our party entered, noisily. First Trixie and John, linked

with NYPD bracelets. Then Webster and Matson, with me trailing along behind.

Trixie and John were arguing back and forth on the equity of partial payment for personal services not fully rendered. Webster prodded them with his sap and yelled at them. Matson saw opportunity in the distraction. He turned to me and whispered urgently, "Step light here, Detective. I'm warning you, the sergeant's out for your ass. Told me so himself yesterday when I was driving him back from where you know you got him sent. You have one ally in this station house, that's namely me. And I'm not enough."

"Thanks." Mine was a thin response, not at all to an ally's satisfaction.

"You'd best listen close. I'm not kidding around with you. I admire what you did, understand? My whole life I been familiar with cops like the ones on this detail. They soon as kill you, and nobody's going to see justice done if they get riled enough to do you. These boys, they're the established injustice."

"What are you doing here among the rabid, Matson?"

"Me . . . ?" Matson turned and glanced up at the booking desk Buddha. "The sarge, he'd say I'm the nigger in the woodpile." He put a finger to his lips, and I also quickly shut up.

Kowalski's head swiveled on his neck at our approach. He looked like a toad hoping the buzz he heard was a nice, fat fly. Looking straight past the familiar faces of the quarrelsome Trixie and John, and Officers Webster and Matson, Kowalski trained his fly-roving eyes on mine.

"Well, well—if it ain't freaking Neil Hockaday," he said. "Rat bastard newspaper pinup boy. What's keeping you out so late?"

Webster snorted, "The detective here, he was prowling rubber alley back of the bus terminal, right when we're picking up these couple of lovebirds." Webster planted a knee in the small of John's back and slammed him up against the booking desk. John's nose went red and runny.

Kowalski picked a chocolate from his box and casually lifted it to his mouth. "Jesus H. Christ, Hockaday. You want a piece of Trixie here, you ought to be discreet. For one thing, you don't want that pretty wife of yours knowing about your filthy-hearted sins . . ." Kowalski paused, then smiled and asked Matson, "You know Hockaday here went and married one of your kind?"

"He did, sir?" Matson's face remained carefully composed. "The detective married a man?"

"Oh, Jeez—that's a good one!" Kowalski's face reddened with laughter, and a gob of chocolate spit flew from his mouth. Webster laughed, too, and sent Trixie smashing nose-first against the desk. Kowalski said, "You're okay, Matson."

I took a pen and my case notebook from my jacket pocket and started writing.

"What do you think you're doing?" Kowalski barked.

"Making contemporaneous notes on what goes on at your house, Sergeant. Go ahead, think of something else stupid to say. I take shorthand."

"Stop it, Hock. You're scaring me so freaking bad it's making my panties bunch."

"You think this is funny?"

"I'll tell you funny. Guy comes in here earlier tonight, I got to print him. No problem with the left hand. But then I pick up his right hand and the freaking guy's only got stubs. So I as't him, 'One question, brother—how in hell do you whack off?' "

Everybody laughed, including the nose-bleeding John and Trixie.

"See, that's funny," Kowalski said. "But you, Hockaday—you ain't funny at all."

"I'm not in a funny mood, being that it's a sacred day."

"Tell me something I don't know."

"Okay. You're familiar with the Way of the Cross parade they have every year up at Holy Cross parish?"

"Sure I am."

"Somebody blasphemed tonight's pageant. And your

boys here, Webster and Matson—they went for this cheap collar they brought you instead of attending to a sin right in God's face." I was sorry I had to include Matson, but it was for the greater good in every way. Matson cut me a look that said he understood the game play. A game it was. Finally I had Kowalski—fellow Catholic, staunch member of the Holy Name Society of his own parish out in Queens—exactly where I wanted him: steaming mad. Not only that, by this time the back-and-forth between Kowalski and me had attracted a fair audience of the established unjust, as Matson saw it. "I'd better make a note of this failing. Inspector Neglio's a Catholic, too, you know."

Kowalski's moon face shook as he put an accusatory question to Webster. "What freaking happened out there?"

I spoke up before Webster could open his mouth.

"Somebody murdered the seven guys carrying the cross, Sergeant. Sniper on a rooftop. The victims were good Catholic men, like you and me. I tried telling your boys all about it. Actually, so did John here. Isn't that right, John?"

"Well now, I did see somebody come rushing down off that roof with a rifle," said John, patting his soggy nose. Good for John, he realized without my having to tell him that his best course now was to blurt out everything he had seen. "Somebody in black, I couldn't see his face, he ran by the front of the car and I looked up—and there he was, staring at me, and puffing really putrid breath. Oh my Lord, I thought he was going to shoot us! I closed my eyes and prayed. Next thing I knew, the whole car was shaking. Somebody was kicking at it. I was so afraid . . . !"

John had himself very worked up. He was hyperventilating, in fact, and inhaling blood that glistened on his upper lip. Trixie, on the other hand, seemed bored. I spotted a paper napkin up on the rim of Kowalski's desk, grabbed it, and gave it to John. John wiped himself, and said to Kowalski, as if the sergeant were a judge, "My name's Ralph Irvine, your honor, and I'm head of the New Jersey chapter of the Christian Coalition." I could not have prayed for more.

Webster protested, "He's a mutt faggot's what he is."

"You're all witnesses," I said, turning my back on Kowalski, addressing the audience of idle station house cops. I counted ten of them. "You have just heard a Christian gentleman say he witnessed a suspected killer in flight. All right now, Mr. Irvine, tell us who was kicking your car."

John fingered Webster.

"And tell us, please, how did Officer Webster respond when you tried explaining about the killer you saw."

"He punched me in the chest—real hard—and I fell down."

"You noticed me at the scene of your arrest, on West Forty-first Street. Isn't that right, Mr. Irvine?"

"Yes, and I—"

Webster shoved past John and moved in close to me. Close enough so I could tell that his dinner included something in tomato sauce and onions. Just in case, I made a quick physical assessment: Webster was solid and compact, so I would give him the edge on strength; but he was half a head shorter than me, giving me the fine advantage of reach. I pocketed my notebook and pen.

"That's about enough yap out of you," Webster growled.

"If you say so."

Whereupon I grabbed the front of Webster's neck with my right hand, squeezing his esophagus like it was a plastic mustard bottle and dancing him backward, fast. The impact of his skull on the oak booking desk made a sound like a dropped crate. This had a calming effect on Webster. The only cop trick older than this would be the one Webster had pulled on John, the stiff jab to the sternum. I now demonstrated the same on Webster. He, too, went down, huffing and spitting.

I looked up at Kowalski. The sergeant, knowing when he was stymied fair and square, grunted. The ten witness cops were looking around at anything besides the sprawl of Webster. Matson stayed cool, except for a slight upturn at the corners of his mouth, which could only be seen if a person was looking close. Trixie attended to a hangnail, as best she could in handcuffs. I resumed my interrogation of John from the Christian Coalition.

"After Officer Webster assaulted you, Mr. Irvine—the first time, I mean, out in the street—didn't I question you about what you might have seen in connection with a murder that had just occurred nearby? And wasn't that questioning done in the presence of Officer Webster?"

"Yes. I told you I saw something shadowy."

"What, exactly?"

"Some guy, I guess. Wearing like a big baggy robe with a hood over his head. Gray and raggedy. His face was like a shadow. I think he was surprised I was there in my car. He had this rifle . . . Don't ask me what kind, I don't know guns . . . He aimed it at me . . . But he didn't shoot, and then—poof!—he was gone."

"And Officer Webster wasn't interested in any of this?"

"No. He cut me off. This is the first I've been able to say anything." John turned and pointed with his foot to Webster, who was still on the floor trying to catch his breath. "The only thing he cared about was insulting you, Detective, and humiliating my friend and me."

"Who you calling *friend?*" Trixie said, raising her cuffs to waggle an indignant finger at John. "You was a damn friend, you'd pony up with my fee."

"Missy, you got some freaking pair of *babalones* to be asking John to pay his fare," Kowalski said. He was becoming amused again. "Ain't you got respect for the right time and place?"

"Speaking of which," I said, addressing my witnesses, reclaiming the floor, "you men have been shown, here and now, that a fellow officer wantonly obstructed justice. If it was a few of you, it could be deniable. But it's a whole lot of us, isn't it? Ten of you men, two civilian witnesses, the sergeant, myself—and Officers Matson and Webster, neither of whom are disputing the facts presented."

Nobody said anything. Webster picked himself up from

the floor. He was in no position to look anybody in the eye.

"Funny enough for you, Kowalski?" The sergeant gave me no answer, not in so many words. The look on his face was cooperative, though, unless he looked that way when he had not been fed in a while. "All right, here's how it goes: there's no show tonight. Get it? None of your dick-prints. You're going to release Trixie and John. So do it—now."

"All right already." Kowalski peered down at Matson. "Take the bracelets off the ballerinas and toss them out the door."

Matson took John and Trixie through the lobby full of mumbling cops and out to the street. The party was over.

"Get out of my sight, you freaking hump," Kowalski said to Webster. Then to me, "It's unwise of you being in my face again, Hockaday."

"So I hear. Also I've been told I should watch my back. Which I'm doing. If I should turn around in the dark and see you, Sergeant, I swear to God—I'll do you like Webster. Only I'll do it so you won't be able to get up anymore."

I left Manhattan Sex Crimes feeling dirty and frightened and wondering why. In fact, had I not been feeling dirty and frightened ever since filing against Kowalski? The answer now finally came. I had abandoned my tribe: the tribe of all tribes, the New York cop tribe.

Matson was loitering at the curb, half sitting on the hood of a squad car. "You need to, Detective, you can count on me," he said as I passed him by.

"Thanks again," I said. But I thought, Can I?

On the subway uptown I reflected on Neglio's warning me about the price of getting even with cops. Also I reflected on the morning's likely tabloid headlines. What a story! Flash: upon one single, sacred day, the blasphemous murders of a rabbi observing Yom Hashoah and seven devout Catholics carrying out a Good Friday pageant. I could see the streamers: HOLY HORRORS! maybe, or SATAN STALKS MID-

TOWN? or even GOD TO HELL'S KITCHEN: DROP DEAD! Anyway, something worthy of punctuation.

But I did not then know the half of it.

Nor did I know of a gathering that would soon take place near my apartment house—in the dark and tiny hours of the Saturday morning before Easter, when finally Ruby and I were able to drift into troubled sleep.

Thirteen

"FOR FIGHTING BACK, this is what cops need. What's right there in this room: friends."

"And what are friends for?"

"Percentage."

"By which you mean to speak not of friends, but of the most powerful ally of all . . ."

"Oh Jeez, there he goes again. For the love of God, pal, take a fucking drink."

"I tell you what friends ain't for. Friends ain't for sitting around here gawking like babes watching Oprah."

"Yeah, we ought to move!"

"Hang another wreath?"

"Doesn't cut it anymore."

"How about this: my old lady was pregnant last time, she was real clumsy. Follow me?"

"Pregnant ladies, they get into accidents."

"Real cute—"

"Gentlemen, gentlemen—!"

"You're supposed to be drinking. Who as't you?"

"Yeah!"

"All of you—*think!* Think of the alternatives."

"Fuck you!"

"Yeah, fuck you real good!"

"Hold on . . . He's saying there's maybe another way."

"That's what you're saying?"

"If you imbeciles will listen—"

"Fuck you!"

"Shut up and let him talk."

"At personal peril, you ignore sublime brutality."

"Talk fucking English!"

"By which I mean, the powers of simple persuasion."

"What the fuck's he saying?"

"There is the old power of storytelling, genuine to this day, even as multitudes no longer wish to hear. But there is the modern power of manufactured myth—the press, you see. The journalists have constructed for themselves a chapel, a temple of fame, if you will, in which they put up and take down portraits all the day long and make such a hammering you can scarcely hear yourself speak . . . By the way, you've arranged it with that reporter?"

"He bought it big time."

"Excellent . . . Now there is, of course, the one true power—"

"All right, we all been listening polite to this crapola—"

"Shut up, I said . . . Go on, say what you want."

"I speak of power here and now—a power beyond the dominion of heaven and earth."

"Oh, Jeez . . ."

Fourteen

"CONGRATULATIONS, DUDLEY, I'm looking at your Irish mug all over the cover of the *Post* . . ."

It was a scolding voice to rouse me from dreaming about a nun, of all fevered and troubling things. There was Sister Roberta, lingering in my muzzy view like an image in the after-burn of a switched-off television screen, a big-hipped woman with tuxedo black eyes and cloistered white skin; hovering in the dusty air of Father Creepy Morrison's religion class, hotly warning us incorrigible boys against touching ourselves lest we cause the saints to weep.

Truth to tell, I admired Sister Roberta's *exemplae vérité*. She owned an imagination Hitchcock would have admired.

There was a boy whose father, a diplomat, was transferred from Washington to a hardship post in the tropics. The boy had been taught to say three Hail Marys before he went to sleep. But one night, he was very tired and got into bed before he remembered. He forced himself to get out, and just as he knelt down beside the bed, a snake slithered out from under the pillow—where his head had been a moment earlier.

Screaming against the side of my sweating head was the telephone. I picked up the receiver to silence the scream, only to hear some ranting voice on a mobile phone unmercifully scolding somebody named Dudley.

I yawned noisily into the phone, at the same time touching Ruby's warm bare shoulder. Slumbering, she still smelled faintly of her blueberry soap. My eyes dropped shut again. I thought of Ruby and me making love under palm trees. (And also I thought, Here's the difference between man and nun: only a nun would associate the tropical with hardship.) Mightily, I tried blocking out the awful voice going on and on with the sight of Ruby and me behind my eyelids: green palms, blue sea, Ruby's cinnamon skin.

But here now, this pleasantness was rudely overtaken. Suddenly, here was the nag-dreaming sight of myself walking through an Irish cemetery, with jackdaws perched on tombstones. And somewhere, the sound of sirens. From somewhere else, the hot black eyes of Sister Roberta—warning us.

There was a boy who knew he was supposed to make the sign of the cross whenever he heard a siren. But one day he heard a siren and defiantly refused to bless himself. When he got home, his house had burned to the ground.

"Oh, boy, Hock—this ought to really impress all your newfound pals at Manhattan Sex Crimes. Hah! Think I didn't hear about that star chamber of yours last night? You hump, you're stirring up nothing but ugly. You know what I'm saying? Let me tell you—Hizzoner himself, he's always thinking he's the police commissioner . . . Christ, he's got me on the blower before the sun—"

"What time is it?"

"Look out a window, why don't you? See what I mean? For you I wait until the sun's up before calling. What *time* is it? Time you showed respect. In the whole department, who loves you?"

"You, Inspector. Only you."

"Remember the other day, tight-ass—I warned you about pushing dangerous buttons? You should listen when I tell you. Today I'm saying your big mouth's got your teats in the wringer."

"Enough already." I was sitting straight up in bed, and so was Ruby. Whoever was pounding out in the hallway—just now as the siren stopped, somewhere close—was likewise alert. I had a fair idea who that might be. "Much as I'm enjoying the wake-up call, Inspector, I have to ring off. Somebody's at the door."

"The toast of the morning *Post,* he should have an escort. I give you five minutes to get decent, Hock. Then you're coming downtown this morning, where your butt's officially on the carpet—along with mine."

"Who's in a twist?"

"Read the goddamn paper and you figure it out!"

"Anything else?"

"Don't forget about brushing your teeth. I like the air around me sweet."

I hung up the telephone.

"Neglio?" Ruby asked.

"From his car phone yet." Tin wife perception sometimes gives a cop more guilt than comfort, this being one of those times.

"How about the guy battering down the house out there in the hallway?" Ruby asked.

"They want to make sure I get downtown fast."

"I'm used to your being a cop, Irish. I'm even proud of it sometimes. But I'm not willing to get used to the department."

"That makes two of us."

"You're in deep, aren't you?"

"Maybe deeper than I know." I stepped out of bed and headed for my toothbrush. Ruby followed and I told her, "As far as the here and now of this morning, all I know is Neglio's on about something in the *Post.*"

"Deeper than you know," Ruby said, drawing out her words thoughtfully. "Yes, and didn't I tell you?"

"Tell me what?"

"You should read the play."

Grief Street

†

A white-haired man somewhere in his sixties wearing a blue parka over a plaid shirt brought the Jeep Cherokee to a stop at the end of a narrow road, a small patch of gravel on an incline. "Ought to be a proper parking place," he muttered, as he always did. "Road ought to be wider, too." He cut the engine, turned the wheels inward, and pulled up the emergency brake. He patted his shirt pocket, making certain the slippery piece of folded paper was still there. Then he climbed from the Jeep and started hiking uphill through the forest pathway, which made his knees ache, on top of which the blossoming spring plants were inspiring his hay fever.

Twenty minutes later—was it so long ago that he made the trip from the road in half the time?—he spotted the priest in the clearing, sitting on a great oak stump in front of the house, feet just nicely grazing the ground, smoking a morning pipe. He recognized the priest's shabby pants—gray worsted wool, in the pattern of corrugated iron—as those from a sturdy suit he had donated to the church at least ten years ago.

"Hallo, Father—I've brung a fax!"

The messenger, sneezing from a snoot full of forest pollen, hastened toward the priest.

Fax machines! Bad, bad invention—sure to be the death of philately!

Father Gerald Morrison merely thought this, for he was mindful of the occupational hazard of hermits talking to themselves. If allowed to fester, he further believed, such vain and useless chatter would interfere with his thrice daily implorations to God on behalf of the world's sinners. And so he kept his mouth on a regimen: beyond the regular holy implorations, Father Morrison spoke only the minimum necessary in periodic exchanges with villagers, though a bit more freely in the company of official visitors, who were rare. Whenever possible, of course, nods and hand motions should suffice.

When offering a purely personal prayer, this, too, was silent communication. He thought of it as analogous to humble writers insisting their names be lowercased. Humility was an important quality to keep earnestly in mind, Father Morrison would remind himself—especially for a man living atop a mountain in a tidy house surrounded by forest greenery and brook and garden; a man whose days were spent in consultation with God as mortal spokesman for all his glorious and wicked children, a man whose worldly debts were the responsibility of some faceless diocesan bookkeeper.

Thus did Father Morrison feel obliged to pray mutely for his own close needs. Beyond entreating the saints for comfort during occasional sickness or frightful weather, he had but one other selfish prayer: a plea for strength in coping with the irony of a role God had assigned to a naturally garrulous man.

O Lord, soothe my Irish lips and tongue and teeth, for they all do ache to speak, the hermit would often pray. Or else, if in a sarcastic mood, *Provide me courageous and mournful eyes to see such time in my life as I hath offended Thee.* Or even perhaps, when petulant, *Then it's true what the scurrilous heathen say—You're a rum joker, are You?*

Being human, how could he not sometimes resent such a role? From head to toe, after all, Gerald Morrison was God's very model of a gabber. Every one of his thoughts, from lightest to darkest, animated a face in that one crucial instant prior to their bursting into words, a characteristic that never failed to command his listeners' attention. He had the stout build and ruddy skin of an outdoors worker—his chest was quite prominent, housing strong lungs—and he was glad for the garden labor of the nearly self-sufficient hermitage; and, too, for the job of tending four goats, two pigs, one cow, and a beehive. Work begat hunger—he was an excellent and bountiful cook—and when he ate, he missed talking most of all. He was, of course, a Jesuit. Like Talmudists of all persuasions he loved books, all the better if they were crammed full of wild and conflicting notions; when he read, or talked about his reading, time was of no consequence. His hips were wide, providing him cushion and ballast for sitting anywhere at all for long periods of time in perfect contentment. Otherwise, too, he had the bottom parts of a natural sitter: short legs and small feet.

Those who had heard him speak—such witnesses were dying out, for Father Morrison was himself aged, and had been in solitary hermitage now nearly thirty years—would never forget the timbre of his voice. Villagers down the mountain, who had only heard a word here and there over the years, spoke of it in awed musical terms. "Such a common-looking fellow," seemed the consensus of these privileged few, mostly old men entrusted to bring him mail and assorted supplies once per month, "and yet he has the most elegant voice, smooth and rich as a cello." In his teaching days at Holy Cross School back in the city, children were convinced that his voice was an echo of God. To be sure, the nuns and brothers knew this reaction verged on a sacrilege. But they knew as well that Father Morrison possessed a terrible, swift wit and heaven-sent intelligence. As for himself, on the silent mountain all these years, the hermit looked skyward once each year and asked an unanswerable question, *Certainly my voice, at the least, is cast by You—and, it's said by young and old, so much in Your own image . . . What, then, is the design of Your wisdom in closing my mouth, in setting me apart from my fellows?*

The hermit raised a hand and waved greeting at the white-haired messenger.

What's old Charlie on about? He isn't due with the load from his store for another week.

"Father . . ." Poor Charlie was out of breath and had to wait a second or two before he could speak. He sneezed several times during the interim.

Next year, it's got to be a younger man fetches my things. I don't fancy having Charlie up here gasping and keeling over. A new man . . . Well, it'll be interesting to see who they scrounge up.

Charlie wiped his forehead with a handkerchief, after which he blew his nose. Then he took the folded fax paper from his shirt pocket and held it out to the silent priest.

"See at the top there, in big bold letters it says 'Urgent, Reply Requested,'" Charlie said. Another spasm of sneezes, as much from excitement now as from the pollen. My, oh my—this urgency from New York City was likely to keep Charlie and his cronies down at the village store thrilled for weeks. Naturally, Charlie had read the full text. Anyone could tell just by looking at the cat-that-ate-the-canary look on his face. Snooping was ever so much easier in the fax age. Charlie said, "It come over the fax wire right while I'm opening up. I figure it's best I run up here straightaway, Father. So I jump right in the Jeep, don't even think twice. Store's just going to have to stay closed 'til I get back."

The giddy old bugger's trying to make me talk. Always torturing me, he is—always!

The hermit nodded thankfully, and smiled. He took off his glasses, steaming up each lens with a puff of hot air, then wiping them with a handkerchief. Then he took the fax from Charlie's eager hand. He opened it—ever so slowly, just to increase Charlie's anxiety—and finally read the transcript:

> URGENT—REPLY REQUESTED.
>
> Dearest Father Morrison:
>
> Peace of Christ! Begging your indulgence, I wish to send a policeman your way as an official visitor. There have been terrible crimes here of late—horrible, unspeakably evil crimes. Upon arrival of Detective Neil Hockaday, you'll learn the exact horror—and I trust you will understand at once why your good counsel is critical to justice. By the way, you'll

remember Neil Hockaday from years ago, when he was a boy in your religion class here at Holy Cross. He's made quite a reputation for himself. It distresses me to say, however, that Neil's grown a bit fallen away from the church, though I do sense that he's now finally prepared to make a firm purpose of amendment. After all, you see, Neil's discovered by this terrible evil it has fallen to him to battle that it behooves a good Catholic to live the church each moment of the day, particularly when the good Catholic happens to be a policeman. Kindly respond with immediacy.

—Yrs in Christ's Love,
Fr. Declan Byrne

The hermit looked up at Charlie, who had begun to shake. Not because he was cold.

Small wonder old Charlie's all of a twitter. The bugger's probably read this fax letter twenty times over. And probably, too, he's already rung up most of his pals before driving up to me. Jaysus, don't Declan have the talent for sounding all mystic like. Just like an Irish parish priest. Never forgetting about business. Firm purpose of amendment—oh, please!

"Have you a pen, Charlie?"

"Father—!"

The sound of Father Gerald Morrison's voice stunned Charlie into more sneezes. No, not the sound alone this time; it was more the casual phrasing that overwhelmed. Charlie searched his pockets and produced a blue ink Bic.

Filthy things, these ballpoint pens. Bad, bad invention!

The hermit smiled as he took the pen.

Yes, I do remember young Neil Hockaday. He called me "Creepy" behind my back, like all the others with their short pants and snotty faces. Lovely mother the boy had, though—Mairead, God rest her.

The hermit turned over Father Declan's fax and wrote

on the clean back: *By all means, send me your policeman right away—Rev. Fr. Gerald Morrison, SJ.* He placed this return message into Charlie's hand.

"Immediately on this now," said Father Morrison. Wide-eyed, Charlie turned and trotted off, and was chased by a cello voice that spoke more words than he had ever known the hermit to speak at one time. "A safe and careful journey to you, Charlie—but please, be your fleetest."

The hermit puffed on his pipe as he watched Charlie disappear down the forest path.

My haste is not what Charlie's thinking has got so many words from me—though I don't begrudge him or his mates the tales to be made of horrid crime reports and how they've got me stirred. There's really no sense in getting riled about gossip and evil. Both these things are forever in bountiful supply. But this news Charlie brings—an official visit, and from someone outside the church! No yap of liturgy, no tired gossip from Rome. Comes now at last the answer to my prayers—a policeman with urgent questions, which I am duty-bound to answer.

Aye, here now's my chance to loose a long-suffering tongue!

†

"Just tell me one thing, Detective—how much you got to pay your press agent?"

This was asked as I settled into the backseat of a black Chrysler with a discreet red flasher in the windshield and a convenient copy of the morning *New York Post* for me to read. Until the question, put to me with a sneery laugh, I felt I ought to be sitting up front with the uniform sent to fetch me; after all, I am not the type of cop meant for the black Chrysler fleet. But now I was glad enough for the divide.

"Shut up and drive," I growled at the uniform. He shut up.

I spotted Eddie the Ear, early at his post, sitting in his chair against the wall of Dinny's Lounge. He waved at me.

I waved back, and then when the car pulled off from the curb and headed toward the West Side Highway, I picked up the newspaper.

The photograph splashed all over the tabloid cover was from a few years back, a grainy, nighttime shot of myself standing around in the Kitchen at the scene of slaughter on Tenth Avenue. I remembered that night: the bloody mess of a bodega owner, Benito Riestra, his neck gashed open by the deadly swing of a box cutter, his wife, Carolena, rocking him in her arms, keening—"*¡Han matado a mi esposo!*" . . . "*¡Dios, guardar a mi esposo!*"

Slattery was there that night. I remember his taking my picture with that huge old flashing Speed-Graphic he hauls around in a ripped leather box. The camera and the box used to belong to Weegee, the legendary New York crime photographer back when FDR and the Little Flower were in office. Such is the claim of its current owner, himself a legend in his own time and the world's last card-in-the-hatband newspaperman, in journalistic if not technological spirit. Weegee's clunky camera aside, Slattery also hauls around an up-to-date attaché containing an impressive assortment of electronic spying contraptions and a cell phone that tucks inside his shirt pocket.

Ordinarily, I have a warm spot for Slats, as I call him because if he turns sideways he is thin to the point of disappearance. He is one of the few people I know outside the department who can appreciate its dicey internal politics, and how this can chew at a cop's life. As a reporter, Slats has had his uses over the years. And in my drinking days I could do a lot worse than palling around with a guy who was able to cadge free drinks at the better quality bars. But this morning was no day deserving of my warmth. Slattery had sandbagged me with his exclusive.

There on the cover of his paper was my sweating face in a crime scene photo, beneath a block-lettered streamer offering up no less than: THE ONLY COP WHO CAN SAVE AMERICA? In smaller letters teased along the bottom margin: *Life Imitates Art: Mystery Playwright Predicts Murder! . . . Post Exclusive, with photos, Pages 4–5.*

I groaned and turned pages as instructed. The photo layout was dominated by Speed-Graphic prints of a shuttered Temple Ezrath Israel, fitted out with black mourning ribbons, the steps of Holy Cross Church, the roof of the National Video Center, and last night's bloody pandemonium on West Forty-second Street. There were assembled portraits of the murdered: the late Rabbi Paznik, and all seven of the Good Friday crossbearers. There was my own NYPD file photo . . . and also Ruby's show biz head shot, the one her agent has mailed off to every newspaper and magazine in town at one time or another.

Slats was good, very good. I had to admit it. His Weegee photos were straight out of film noir. He had hustled for portraits and dead accurate details, and had provoked a secret source into serving up one truly strange tale.

And, oh brother—how it had paid off. He must have worked all through the night writing his piece. And I had to admit, Slats had himself one honey of a card-in-the-hatband scoop:

Hell's Kitchen Slay Orgy
Echoed in "Grief Street"

By William Slattery

This is the true story of eight good men slain yesterday in gritty Hell's Kitchen—eight devoutly religious men. It is also the story of eerie similarities between art and life in Hell's Kitchen, parallels between the very real homicides of yesterday and the events of "Grief Street"—the title of a murder mystery for the stage. The playwright, who wishes to remain anonymous, has spoken by telephone exclusively to the *New York Post*.

Dead—for real—are a popular young rabbi who ran a neighborhood soup kitchen, and seven parishioners of the Roman Catholic Church of the Holy Cross. The end came on yesterday's separate but equally sobering holy observances for Jews and Christians—an overlapping day of religious meaning that began with murder in the morning blackness, and ended in an evening sniper attack.

First to die was Rabbi Marvin Paznik, 36, of Temple Ezrath Israel on West 48th Street. Shortly after midnight, during prayer services for the Day of Remembrance for the victims of the Holocaust, an unknown assailant rose from a pew to attack the rabbi. Police reports state the killer used a large knife, mortally wounding Rabbi Paznik, then escaped the synagogue in the presence of horrified worshipers. From confidential sources, the *Post* has further learned that the rabbi was mutilated during the attack. Specifically, the killer cut away a substantial portion of skin covering the rabbi's head and neck—apparently fleeing with the grisly prize.

Later, during a Catholic street pageant, seven men bearing a large crucifix were shot dead by sniper fire from the rooftop of the National Video Center building on West 42nd Street. The victims were: Ronald Barron, 58, Daniel McLendon, 31, Charles Haley, 50, Lester Knightly, 49, J. C. Turner, 33, Frank Esser, 38, and Kim Behm, 47.

While the plot of "Grief Street" broadly hints at the real-life murders, even more ironic are certain facts obtained by the *Post* from sources within the police department and elsewhere:

- On Thursday, less than 24 hours prior to the first murder, an anonymously mailed copy of the "Grief Street" script was received by Ruby Flagg, the actress-wife of hero NYPD Detective Neil Hockaday.
- Hockaday—familiar to *Post* readers for solving many of the city's most notorious serial murder cases—was a friend of Rabbi Paznik. The ace detective had spent all day Friday investigating his friend's slaying.

• Hockaday and Ms. Flagg reside in a Hell's Kitchen apartment that overlooks the block of West Forty-second Street where the seven marchers were slain.

Earlier last night, the playwright—or his agent—sent pages of the script of "Grief Street" to the Post offices. The pages came in a plain manila envelope, marked to the attention of this reporter. Likewise, in his phone call, the playwright asked for this reporter. His voice was so muffled it was clear only that he was male.

In the partial script, a charitable rabbi is murdered, as are several ardent Catholics. However, the action and themes of the play occur in Hell's Kitchen of some 100 years ago. Among the main characters is a policeman of Irish extraction.

"The script has been sent to actors around town, including Ruby Flagg," said the playwright by phone. "We're currently looking for financial backers, and to that end we have contacted several parties who will very soon be treated to a staged reading of the play."

The playwright declined to provide any further details. When asked why he had singled out Ruby Flagg for his cast, he abruptly hung up the telephone.

I abruptly stopped reading at this point. The rest of Slattery's story was the same compilation of spooned-out facts as I had heard on the radio. The part about Marv Paznik being mutilated, though—that had taken some solid digging. Another reason I stopped reading Slattery was because my driver was acting up again.

"Didn't mean to bust your chops, Detective," he said over his shoulder. "I'm only saying—publicity like that, it can really help a guy in your position."

"You didn't mention your name, friendly."

"Baize."

"What position would you be talking about, Officer Baize?"

"You know."

"I'm afraid not."

"Come on . . . A cop who needs buffers, you know?"

"No I don't."

"All right. Skip it."

"I'm writing down your name, Officer Baize."

Of course I knew what he was talking about. A cop bringing up a tribal brother on charges is serious aggravation for the department—for the city, too. Cops tend to take sides as firm as granite cliffs in such matters. And when thirty thousand persons with guns are squared off in a city that never sleeps, nobody hears the lullaby of old Broadway.

In the edgy process of pressing the bureau for a disciplinary hearing into King Kong Kowalski and his savage circus on the overnight shift, wreathings were maybe only tribulations. Maybe the real trouble lay ahead. It was anybody's guess if I was eventually going to be hammered by some rabid cop of the street, who would at least be mercifully quick to the point, or by some inconvenienced bureau type who could do serious damage to the brass ring in the merry-go-round of a cop career: retirement benefits, should I live to collect.

Somebody in my position, therefore, needed buffers. Such as hero status in the press. Or so Officer Baize apparently believed. I put his name down on a list I had started, the one with King Kong Kowalski at the top.

"What for?" Baize asked. He seemed more nervous than hostile. But one never knows.

"These days it pays to remember anybody who looks at me funny," I told him.

"I'm only saying—"

"Skip it, Baize. You make the list."

He skipped it the rest of the way downtown to One-Pee-Pee, where trouble waited in pinstripes. Not the kind the Yankees wear.

Fifteen

THE FAT MAN AT THE BAR finished off a glass of beer and shoved away a greasy plate with the leavings of bone and gristle and catsup in it. Then he sucked at his teeth, making squeaky noises, and said, "Nothing like a couple-a-pound sirloin to put away a lousy stinking morning." He pronounced it *sir-uh-loin.*

The blond bartender looked up from the newspaper laid out between his elbows. He brushed lazily at an earring, and asked, "More tough lessons at charm school, sweety?"

"Like I said, don't be calling me that in here."

"It's just the two of us. Loosen up."

"Loose, that's your brand. I ain't the type."

"Whatever. We're both children of God."

"Don't start. We were getting along good."

"Sorry." The bartender closed his paper. He smiled brightly. "I'll make it up to you."

"A free drink?"

"Better."

"Nothing's finer than booze you don't got to pay for."

"Have we read today's crime blotter?"

"You mean in the *Post* about them murders and some cockamamie mystery play?"

"Let's not forget your friend—that cute Mr. Hockaday."

"The rat bastard. Him and his wife with their freaking mug shots, they went and spoiled the whole paper for me, including Joey Adams. Give me a drink."

"Remember my regular?" The bartender picked up the fat man's glass and filled it with another draught of beer, and set it back down. He poured a shot of white label and set that down, too. "The chaser's on the house."

"Thanks. See, we're getting along grand. What are you talking, your *regular?*"

"My friend. You know, he was here the other day when you dropped by. Stuart. He's such a sophisticate—"

"Stuart? The one you kissed on the button? Jesus!"

"Let's behave ourselves."

"Yeah, let's do."

"Anyway—my friend is in the theater, you see."

"I bet he said *thespian* before *mama* or *dada.*"

"Stuart Godwin is no mere actor! He's an impresario."

"That mean he's rich?"

"Very. Stuart has a town house on the Upper East Side. He bought it from Nixon."

"Freaking Nixon. So, your rich squeeze—he does his slumming here?"

"Don't be evil."

"Tell that to your friends."

"Knock it off, sweety. I'm trying to be helpful."

"Say what you got to say."

The bartender opened the paper again, to a page full of photos surrounding a story by William Slattery. He pointed to a paragraph.

"It says here the script of this play, *Grief Street,* has been sent around town to a cast of actors—your cute friend's wife being one."

"Yeah . . . ?" The fat man was suddenly interested.

"It says there's going to be a reading of the play. But we don't know when, or where."

"And you do?"

"Oh, sure. Stuart mentioned it . . ."

Sixteen

THE MAYOR OF THE CITY of New York nowadays—as the inspector says, *Hizzoner himself, he's always thinking he's the police commissioner*—is called Dick Tracy behind his back. This is because he is forever rushing to crime scenes where nobody needs him.

I myself do not call the mayor Dick Tracy behind his back. I call him Fearless Fosdick.

Hizzoner's résumé includes being a United States district attorney in New York at a fortuitous time when a lot of city detectives happened to be making righteous cases against a lot of elderly mafiosi, cases that were bumped up to the feds for prosecution. Hizzoner had a crack public relations man on his staff, the best that government could buy, and put him to work making sure that his name made the headlines, warranted or otherwise. In the stories that went with the headlines, the detectives who had done the scut work were usually not mentioned. If this is Dick Tracy, then I myself am Wonder Woman.

Dick Tracy of the comic strips has big shoulders, a square jaw, a lot of friends, few words, real hair, and a sharp wardrobe. Hizzoner is built like a thin pear. His face is creased and pointy. He spends much of the day telling people how they should do their jobs, a habit that has not endeared him to civil servants. Hizzoner's "hair" looks like a Brillo pad run over by a truck and then pasted to his head. He is windy and wears the kind of suits junior accountants buy off the rack.

It is Saturday morning, and here I am at City Hall—in the office of the mayor—standing on the rug with Inspector Neglio. Neglio is looking good, if shaky, in Gucci loafers, gabardine trousers, and a suede jacket. I am the one in blue: jeans and a denim shirt. Fosdick is wearing shiny wingtip shoes and gray pinstripes. Which might have been all right if the suit was flannel and charcoal gray with narrow stripes. Instead, it was aluminum gray sharkskin with chalk stripes.

Hizzoner—standing in front of his desk with his hands in his pants pockets, watching me walk through the door and cross the room—was not smiling. The newspaper with my face on the cover lay on the floor, torn and crumpled at the mayor's feet, like he had recently danced on it. The inspector was sweating, and I almost felt sorry for him. Neglio could not help it, he considered politicians to be serious people.

"Here comes the cop who's going to save America." The mayor's pointy face curled, and he glared at me like I was something that belonged in a landfill over in Staten Island. I did not bother about sticking my hand out for a shake. "Inspector," he asked, his head swiveling around on a pencil neck toward Neglio, "what are you going to do about this publicity hog?"

So that was it? The mayor was twisted because the press was not touting Hizzoner as the leading character in this murder investigation?

"We think you've gone too far, Hock," the inspector said. I no longer felt sorry for him. In fact, I wanted to punch him. From the pained look on his face, I would say that Neglio knew he had it coming. "We think what's been published here compromises the integrity of a high-profile case, and the official chain of command."

"You want to know what I think?"

"No."

I took a quick body count of the mayor's office because maybe later—in a court of law, say—it could prove useful to reassemble the audience. Besides the inspector and Hizzoner, there was a City Hall flunky whose name I could get easily enough, two cops of my acquaintance from the mayoral bodyguard detail, and the inspector's aide. My witnesses, for better or for worse.

"Then I'll be happy to tell you," I said. "I don't have time for this, there's police work to do."

"Cut the crap," Neglio said. "You're borderline insubordinate in front of all the wrong people. I can kick your emerald ass clean off the force here and now, after which you can kiss your pension good-bye. *Capice?*"

I understood, all right. The inspector and I took a long beat and glowered at each other.

"So much for the luck of the Irish," said Fosdick. He turned on the demented smile.

I might have shut my mouth like a good boy, but Neglio and his pal were irritating. Besides which I had been dragged out of bed from a dream about Ruby and palm trees. And besides that, there were these savage tribesmen after me.

"Now if I lost my job, I wonder what I'd do," I said, talking like the choirboy I used to be. "Say, here's an idea. I could apply for a police reporter's job over at the *Post*. My first story could be about a serious brutality complaint that's being sugared off to charm school."

Nobody said anything.

"By the way, Inspector, would this be a good time to discuss Kowalski and what he's been up to at Manhattan Sex Crimes?"

"No."

"Has the mayor been fully briefed?"

"I'll tell you one more time," Neglio snarled. "Cut the goddamn crap."

But it was no time to be cutting the crap. Crap and chutzpah were about all I had going for me.

"So maybe I could write a follow-up on how some rabid cops broke into my apartment house and hung dead rats on my door to scare my pregnant wife." I paused for a look at Fosdick. The arrogance had disappeared from his face, and he was otherwise having a hard time trying to appear relevant. I asked him, "You know about wreathing, sir?"

The mayor said nothing. Neglio said, "Here's what I know, Hock: I warned you before about talking to reporters."

"You think I'm after buffers here?"

"Could be."

"And it could be some of your rabid cops went from hanging wreaths to bumping friends of mine."

"You're talking real wild now."

"Am I?"

Fosdick and the witnesses looked like they all wanted to be somewhere else. They would have welcomed a fire drill.

"Let's say it wasn't you who went yapping to Slattery," Neglio said, reasoning. Finally he started sounding like a cop instead of some City Hall hack. "Who did, then? Who told him about that little item we held back?"

"The rabbi getting scalped, you mean?" Good question, I thought. Mumbling Mr. Glick? The old synagogue members? No, not them; they only saw a shadow. The forensics cops? Officer Caras? All I could think to say was, "Reporters have snitches. Just like cops. Only they call them sources."

"Also reporters hold back, just like cops."

"Hold back?"

"You're forgetting the playwright. The guy Slattery says in his story called him up. Maybe he said lots more than Slattery let on. Maybe we've got a real hungry playwright off his nut. A failed writer living in some crib. He gets it in his head he should murder somebody—for art, for a murder mystery. Christ, that'd be some Broadway ballyhoo for the record books."

"Now you're the one talking wild, Inspector."

"No—I'm talking about desperate. There's a difference."

"That being?"

"Motive. Desperation has a motive behind it, wild doesn't. A desperate killer is somebody you can catch, Hock. You've done it before."

"Wait a minute. What's this all about? First you chew me out for all the excitement. Now you want to put me in charge of it?"

"Mr. Mayor, would you like to take that one?"

A fine pass-off for a man of the bureau. I had to admire it. The inspector kept his backside covered by deferring to mayoral rank.

Fosdick fingered his necktie like he was a kid on his first communion day. Probably he would have preferred no witnesses in the room after all. He said, "Detective Hockaday, in the name of the people of New York, I'm asking you to apprehend the person or persons—"

"In the name of myself, I accept."

"Whatever you need, Detective Hockaday," the mayor said. "I mean it—anything at all."

"Thanks. For right now, just let me have Officer Baize and the shiny black car. Also I might need your help on a phone call."

"You got it."

"Me, too—anything you want," Neglio added. "Including exceptional clearance."

Exceptional clearance. License to kill.

"You think it's that desperate, Tommy?"

"A guy goes scalping a rabbi, climbs a roof and blasts seven men to kingdom come, he disappears like a shadow each time—I call that desperate. Don't you?"

"I have a feeling we're going to be calling it wild."

†

Before leaving City Hall, I rang up the warden at Rikers Island. I told the lady who answered the phone that it was Detective Neil Hockaday calling, which got me connected with the deputy warden. I asked this deputy when Corrections Officer Harry Darcy was next docketed for work.

"You're in luck," he said. "He's pulling early afternoon at the bing."

The bing—as in *bing-bing* to the neck with a screw's baton, and a troublesome inmate's manners improve—is part of the House of Detention for Men, a cell block for the especially violent and mentally disturbed. Lucky me.

"I want to see him," I said. "But he shouldn't know I'm coming."

"What for?"

"Let's not argue. I'll put the mayor on the line. He'll explain."

Fosdick proceeded to tell a rattled deputy warden how to do his job. After which I collected Baize from a nap in the outer office and told him how to do his, by driving me over to a building catty-corner from Ruby's Downtown Playhouse on South Street—the editorial offices of the *New York Post*—so I could press my luck some more.

Seventeen

"WHO'S YOUR SOURCE?"

"Don't ask."

So it went for half an hour at his desk: Slattery and myself in the eternal back-and-forth.

He was relatively unsurprised that I had badged my way into the building and then the city room, where I found him in a fedora, feet propped up on his desk next to his trusty Speed-Graphic, and smoking a Camel under a bilingual sign on the office wall: NO SMOKING/PROHIBIDO FUMAR. In a room full of hatless, obedient nonsmokers who never heard of a Speed-Graphic and who looked more like insurance agents who belonged to health clubs than newspaper reporters, Slats was a refreshing sight. I had to give him that.

"Kind of early for interrogations, isn't it, Hock?" Slattery did not gloat—not too much at least. Also I had to give him that. He looked as if he had been up all night and through the tiny hours, which of course he probably had, feeding facts into his story from early edition to this morning's latest. "Being the crack-of-noon type, you must have hated the rousting you got this morning."

"Until now I thought I was the low-profile type, too. Thanks for nothing."

"Hungry?"

"That's one of the things bothering me."

We left the city room for the cafeteria on the fourth floor. Which has always been a dump, though never so bad as it is now that it has been modernized—by means of a lot of employee downsizing, as they say. Slattery made his usual bleak joke about an eventual outbreak of cholera in the place. The steam tables were full of pre-cooked mush best identified by color: a brown thing, a green thing, a gray thing, and so forth. Nobody was there to actually serve any mush. Instead there were cracked plates and ladles under a plastic sneeze guard, over which a cheery cardboard sign declared: WE PUT THE SERVICE BACK IN SELF-SERVICE. A cashier sat on a stool down the end of the line, offering no cheer whatever.

Since he had sandbagged me with the cover story, and even seemed a little embarrassed by it, Slats treated. He had Pepsi, which he perked up with rye whisky from a pocket flask, along with no food. I had a brown thing that looked like a hot roast beef sandwich drenched in gravy and a Dr. Brown's celery soda, unperked.

"How come you never called me for comment in your story?" I asked him. "Or my wife for that matter?"

"Sorry about that. I really am. You know how it goes, sometimes your source lays down conditions."

"Conditions. I see. What you did, Slats, it's not smart."

"Get over it."

"Oh, that's what I'm supposed to do? For years, I'm tipping you good stories. Now you blow me off for a two-day wonder."

"I'm not going to debate the merits of an exclusive with you."

"You disappoint me, Slats."

"How? I make you out an ace cop, I publicize Ruby—"

"You got no idea, do you?"

"About what?

"Cop egos and cop resentments. Cops are no better than

actors when it comes to gracious reaction to good press notices about somebody else they know in the trade."

"So?"

"So I have this IAD complaint going against a big cop. I guess you didn't know that. The resentment from all over the department is about all I can handle. This story of yours, it can push everything over the top. Ego, resentment, and a certain know-how for making a crime of passion neat instead of sloppy. Which is the difference between unsolvable and solvable. So thanks loads, good buddy."

"Who are you beefing about to IAD?"

"You'll find out, Slats, in due time. Only you won't find out from me, and you won't be getting my side of the story."

"Why not?"

"You don't bother calling up Ruby or me about today's headlines and you're asking why not? You got some brass knockers, Slats. But just remember, you're not the only reporter in New York."

"Come on, Hock, that's not your style." For just a moment, it looked as if Slattery was worried I would cut him off. But then he cooled down, which irritated me.

"Just tell me if your source is a cop," I said.

"Did you read the paper or not?" Slattery drank down half his spiked Pepsi. "The story says 'sources within the police department and elsewhere.' "

"Elsewhere? Meaning your playwright caller?"

"Elsewhere means elsewhere."

"How many people are you talking to on this, Slats? One, two, three—more than that?"

"Sources is plural. Plural means plural."

"By the way, what do you mean *not my style?*"

"What's with all the straight-out questions? You always go at things sideways, you always make people spill things they don't realize they're spilling. It's what makes you a great detective." Slattery put back the rest of his Pepsi. He thought about mixing another drink but instead poured straight from his flask, draining it. I thought about whisky going down my own insides, and that fine old softness and warmth I miss so much. I fought off a shudder. Slattery said, "Back when you and I were still out there drinking together, we used to talk about detectives all the time. And—oh boy, the great stories you'd tell me when you'd had some jars! So what's wrong with you now, Hock? Why would you want to keep stories all to yourself?"

Slats was right. Asking blunt questions was out of character, and counterproductive. I might have worried about that—haste makes waste, especially in hot pursuit—except for the fact that it suddenly hit me that Slattery had confirmed at least one of his sources, without realizing it.

"Back when was back when," I said. "You keep on drinking, Slats. Me, I have to move on. Where I'm going, there's a wild story. When I'm ready with it, I'll call you up and tell you where you can read it."

Eighteen

ONCE UPON A TIME in the borough of Queens, there was a green and quiet island at the edge of Bowery Bay in the East River. The island was home to a Dutch farming family by the name of Ryhen, which over a few hundred years somehow came to be called Rikers. The Rikers clan grew rich raising potatoes and tomatoes and sunflowers in the sandy earth of their sunny island.

Then along about the time that Annie Meath named my neighborhood during a summer's night riot, the Rikers family sold their farm to the city of New York for a hundred and eighty thousand bucks, which in those days was a fortune. The city, having no use for vegetables or big yellow flowers, converted the farm to a dump site for three things: subway excavations, garbage, criminals.

Rikers Island quickly grew from eighty-seven natural acres to four hundred mostly man-made junk acres. The city's criminals were dealt with in a campus of ten different jails. This included the notorious House of Detention for Men, which is classically famous for its role in the movie *The Public Enemy,* the one starring Jimmy Cagney and the grapefruit, which I have enjoyed a number of times at the Royal Bijou cinema.

When the war was over in 1945, the city was able to attend to a problem that understandably worried law-abiding citizens of the Queens mainland: namely, a rat population on Rikers Island that greatly outnumbered the eight million human beings of New York City. These were not ordinary rats, they were a breed that became known as "Rikers Island rats." There were regular panics in the streets when members of the breed were spotted swimming through the greasy waters of the East River en route to Queens proper. Many of these swimmers, buoyant and quite strong from life in the city's enormous open-air garbage dump, were the size of cocker spaniels. The city responded with two actions: closure of the garbage dump, and installation of steel nets ringing the island waters. When the hungry rats fled they were successfully snared in the nets, where they either drowned or starved to death.

There are still rats on Rikers Island, and because of their genetic lines they are significantly larger than rats living elsewhere in New York. People have mostly forgotten about the underwater nets, and the City Corrections Department likes to keep it that way, which is why the occasional inmate who attempts a water escape is never heard from again.

Each year, a hundred forty thousand men and women (mostly men) pass through Rikers Island, giving it the distinction of being the world's largest penal institution—by far. At any one time, Rikers houses twenty thousand of America's despised class; ninety percent of the inmates are black or Latino and lack a high school diploma, one of four is mentally ill, the HIV-positive ratio is well on its way toward fifty percent of the prisoner population.

Everybody works a job on Rikers, the eight thousand COs and the inmates alike. Some details are better than others. Corrections officers do not like pulling bing duty, for instance, because it gives them tremendous headaches by the end of the tour, from inmate howling alone.

Prisoners particularly enjoy farm work, farms having been reestablished on the island during the Reagan years, when a tide of homeless people began washing up in New York's streets and food had to be found for them someplace. There are now thirteen cultivated fields on the island. Lettuce, cabbage, and broccoli grow in the spring; tomatoes, eggplant, watermelon, zucchini, and pumpkin in the summer; collard greens and bell peppers in autumn.

Inmates especially prize the Hart Island detail. Not only is this outdoors work, it is off-island work. Men who can be trusted with shovels—and the sturdier women—are loaded into a boat each morning at the eastern edge of Rikers Island, where they set off for another city-owned property in Bowery Bay. This is called Hart Island, where the unclaimed dead are buried in New York's version of potter's field.

I was this Saturday en route to Rikers Island to get the drop on the guy who telephoned Ruby last Thursday and upset her about the wreathings. I could be thankful the wreaths were not made of Rikers Island rats.

The black Chrysler with its specially coded NYPD license plates took me across the Francis Buono Memorial Bridge between Queens and Rikers Island, the only public access. Ahead of us was a blue and orange New York City Corrections Department bus, a shuttle that runs between Rikers and the Twin Donut Shop near the Queens Plaza subway station.

At the first guard station on the island, beyond which is a cluster of Quonset dormitories that look like airport hangars for the damned, family members piled out of the bus for ID processing, which in several cases involved body searches. Baize and I badged the man on duty and were waved onto a roadway taking us to the farthest end of the island, and the bing.

Baize pulled up in front of the bing, where he parked and waited with the car. I walked up to the CO posted at the weapons bin and was given a receipt for my nina. I could not help notice the CO's name plate: PANYAGUA.

"That name—in Spanish it means bread and water," I said, immediately regretting the remark. Panyagua nodded and smiled, like maybe he had heard this a thousand times before, which of course he had.

I was then double-doored through the main entrance of the bing, into an airless central corridor flanked by three tiers of steel cages. A young CO by the name of Musella was my escort to D-unit, where Harry Darcy was supposed to be working.

"It's relatively quiet now," Musella said as we walked over the rippled steel floor. There was a lot of thrash music playing—the kind of noise that many people on the outside listen to because they have never heard of melody, and they have been trained to believe that silence or thought, God forbid, should never be experienced during waking hours—and only the occasional scream. One or two inmates were singing, I could not hear what. I heard our steps echo, though. So this was relative quiet. Musella explained, "We just ran everybody through the monkey juice line."

"Methadone?" I guessed.

"Yeah, calms them down for hours." Musella motioned toward the overhead cells. "Look at these guys, they'll be starting up the show pretty soon. Always a show after the monkey juice line. Some guys go through these exercise routines they invent and they grunt and groan a lot, other guys start dancing or singing songs."

We turned a corner, walked another fifty yards to D-unit, and there he was: Fat Buns.

He was sitting at a little desk next to a double door, wearing his navy blue twill uniform and his CO badge and his gunbelt. There were four empty cardboard coffee cups on the desk, one of them half full of damp cigarette butts. Today's *New York Post* was on the desk, too, spread open to Slattery's story and the photo layout.

"Fat Buns" I remembered, but not the man's real name: Harry Darcy. After all this time, though, I recognized the pudgy kid I once swatted twenty times on the butt with a wooden paddle in Brother Earl's gym class at Holy Cross. This was because of a little game the brother enjoyed.

Brother Earl lived for the day when two boys acted up in his class. He would have the offenders grip an overhead ladder bar, facing each other, suspended there for as long as it took. The longer the better. The first one to fall was the loser and had to absorb his own ten swats of punishment plus the other guy's—pants down. The winner had to do the swatting. Brother Earl, of course, would have to make certain the swats were properly delivered. If he judged them insufficiently painful—that is, too soft to leave welts on bared thighs and buttocks, which Brother Earl always carefully inspected—then the loser was made to return the favor.

The day Fat Buns and I were hanging on the ladder was no contest. I won. Nonetheless, forty swats were exchanged.

Here I had come all this way up to Rikers to punch out a guy named Darcy for upsetting my wife with a telephone call—telling her about rats, and something about King Kong Kowalski. But now, all I could see was this kid that all the rest of us little shits called Fat Buns, and that day . . .

Those awful minutes the two of us were nose to nose, hands looped over a bar, a ribby boy and a chubby boy hanging like meat on hooks for the amusement of a sadist in a cassock; Harry sweating, and me as well, and the tendons in our young arms bursting just about; and the whole gym class dancing around, some boys looking away because they had known themselves this torture, the other ones jeering at Fat Buns; Brother Earl hopping around and clapping his hands and grinning like a future mayor, his crucifix swinging in an arc, visions of Harry Darcy's pink fanny no doubt dancing in his head; then Fat Buns looking down, and crying, his thick fingers slipping one by one, his plump body dropping to the gym floor; and finally me crying, and giving Fat Buns twenty swats that grievously disappointed Brother Earl; and me taking my twenty in return, getting far more than I gave. I cannot remember what classroom infraction Harry and I committed that called for these swats, in the way that I have no memory of bad weather on a summer's day of my youth. . . .

Harry Darcy wore his hair the exact same way as when he was a kid. Butch cuts at the Three Aces Barber Shop on Ninth Avenue ran forty cents on weekdays back then, a half-dollar on Saturday. Today it runs eight dollars, and

only Tony on the third chair knows how to do it right. Darcy's hair was still mostly blond, but if a person looked close he would see some gray. He moved the same as always, rolling from side to side on wide feet. His face was redder than I remembered. I knew what that was from. Only a couple of years ago, people could have said the same of me.

"You shouldn't have told my wife about the wreathings. She's pregnant. You made her cry." That was the first thing I said to Harry Darcy. He might have been able to read what else was on my mind: *If it was the two of us hanging on that ladder bar right now, and you were the one to drop first—this time I'd give it to you good enough to save my own ass, that's for sure, Fat Buns.* But the next thing I actually said was, "How are you, Harry?"

Harry was flustered.

"Okay. I guess. Got a little trouble on my hands right now, but generally okay. Jeez, Neil, it's been a hell of a long time."

"What kind of trouble?"

"Aw, they got me going to charm school. You know."

"How about Darcy and I have a private talk?" I asked Musella. He grunted and wandered off, leaving Darcy and me alone. "What's the charge on you, Harry?"

"I crack heads too much. Not here. Nobody pays attention when you clobber big guys in the bing. They got it coming anyways—and more besides. Me, I'm always going after the herbs in the dormitories."

"Whose Herb?"

"Herb's not a guy. It's a type of a guy. The schmucks doing life six months at a time. You know? Petty types, guys who can't hack the chaos on the outside. So they do what it takes to get back inside, only nothing violent, since they don't have the intelligence to be mad as hell. To these herbs, I'm telling you—Rikers Island is home sweet home. It makes me crazy." Darcy paused in his rant. He lit up a Pall Mall and offered me one. I passed.

Then Darcy started talking at me as if it was only last Tuesday we were both wearing short pants and neckties at Holy Cross, as if we had been best of pals back in those days. But I only knew him casually then, that was all. Maybe Darcy was hyper from the cigarettes and coffee. Maybe in the bing he was starved for sane conversation. Or maybe it was another one of those unaccountable times when people just start talking at me.

I remembered a time . . . some foggy night of drinking with Slattery . . . when I bragged about how people talked at me, with no rhyme nor reason. "You have one of those listening kinds of Irish faces," Slattery said. I said, "No—

it's yet another thing that makes me the grandest detective in New York." Such a fathead I have been in my time. A nun should be thwacking me now. For penance I decided to continue tipping stories to Slattery, to whom I had been such a shitheel only a little while ago because I was disgusted he was still boozing and therefore not as magnificent as myself the nonboozer one day at a time.

"You ought to see the goddamn herbs on a homecoming day, Neil. They'd drive you barking nuts." Harry Darcy rolled his eyes. "It's like they can't wait to pull on the throw-up green jumpsuit and the Air Patakis, like they're going to sit around of an evening in the comfort of their own parlor. Jee-zus!"

"Air Pataki? Governor Pataki's got a private plane up in Albany?"

"No, it's what the inmates call those cheap sneakers the state corrections department issues out."

"I see."

We stood looking at each other for a long moment. There were shouted threats echoing through the cell block from somewhere. A *bing-bing,* followed by the sound of a falling body, ended it.

"Neil—if I'd of known, I never would of told your wife what those cops done. She was the one asked me. She tell you that? Jeez, I'm sorry, man." Darcy was now looking down at his wide feet. "The wreaths, that's not all I called about. She tell you what else I said?"

"Something about King Kong Kowalski. He's a problem, but I've got some other troubles, too."

"Yeah, I seen in the paper."

"Harry, you have something you want to tell me?"

"Remember that day in gym?"

"I think about Holy Cross sometimes."

"Oh man, I been thinking about it a lot these days. How I went through all that hell with my eyes closed. Brother Earl and all that Holy Cross batshit. And how it's so nuts I'm as old as I am and reliving it—*seeing* it, like I'm watching a movie."

A picture of Marv flashed in my mind. He was reading Kaddish, and about to die in a vicious shadow. I heard him speak. *A journey fraught with pain and disappointment, and hourly hastens on toward the night of his grave . . . The closed eye is only then satisfied with seeing.*

"Not everything's clear to us at the time it happens." I was proud of myself for saying that. It sounded smart, like something Marv would say.

"How come you went easy on me that day?"

"I don't know. It just seemed so unfair. I never thought about it."

"No—you don't have to think about it."

"About what?"

"Working with people who have power over you, even if they shouldn't have. That's a real talent. Which somehow comes natural to you, like it's a blessing."

"People with power over you. You're talking about Brother Earl?"

"Yeah, I been thinking about that particular bastard, and all the creep bastards I've known like him. And how it's only now I'm learning to hate them the right way. Charm school makes you think, you know?"

"And teaches how to hate?"

"Not exactly. Here's all I'm saying—if you don't hate violent creeps enough, you wind up being just another violent creep. My own formula from what I get out of charm school, okay?"

"If you say so."

"Another thing. I look around me, I see how us screws and the prisoners, we could change places today—and how tomorrow nobody'd notice anything different. Same with cops and crooks, right?"

"Different teams, same game."

"That's right. Hell, we're all nothing but fish swimming around inside of a pet shop aquarium. Us fish are real stupid, you ever notice? We invent this funny idea that we're big fish and little fish. Which is bullshit. We're nothing but clowns going around in stupid circles, and the only fish that matter are the guys buying and selling the aquariums. When the lights go out at night, and we're still turning circles in water inside of a bowl up on somebody's shelf, guess what?"

"I don't like to guess."

"Clowns aren't funny in the dark."

"Very illuminating, Harry."

"I'm getting mad about it. In fact, I'm hating it real good. That's what I get out of charm school. I hate the bullshit so bad that guess what?"

"Harry—"

"Oh yeah, sorry. I hate bullshit so bad that the *last* thing I want to do is go crack some herb skulls for relief. Because you know why? That'd make me the same as Brother Earl getting his brand of relief in a boy's gym class, the creep. See what I mean?"

"This is like a confession I'm hearing."

"*Like* a confession—that's the problem. I'm thinking all this, I'm saying all this, but I get no absolution."

"You should see a priest."

"Maybe. If I should ever go to church again. Meanwhile, there's something I want to know. You ever hold it against me I gave you twenty that day you went easy on me?"

I could have said no, but that would have been a truth from a forgotten yesterday. Today when I saw Harry Darcy for the first time in all these years, I felt an irresistible resentment. *This time I'd give it to you good enough to save my own ass, that's for sure, Fat Buns.*

I told Harry Darcy today's truth.

He took it well, then told me what he had to say.

"What I called your house about, it's something this Sergeant Joe Kowalski said to me. I hear this creep's the cop answer to Brother Earl."

"Something like that."

"Anyhow, Kowalski's got it out for you. It's way beyond wreathing." Darcy squeezed a last drag out of his

Pall Mall and then dropped it into the coffee cup ashtray, where it sizzled out in something wet and brown like the roast beef brown thing I had eaten with Slattery. He lit up another one. "This guy's getting up his balls to cancel you out, Hockaday. I seen it before with violence freaks, of which there's plenty of specimens around me every day. They talk violent, they breathe violent, they'd eat violent if they could. Kowalski, he's become a big fan of ultimate fighting. You know what that is? Forget it, you don't want to know. Anyways, I'm telling you—he's coming to get you. You understand? He told me himself, flat out."

"What did he say exactly?"

"He says, quote unquote, If the rat bastard don't give in we got a process of elimination, let's call it."

"I'm going to need you one day soon, Harry."

"For what?"

"It's not enough your casually telling me like this about Kowalski's threat."

"Doesn't seem so casual to me. There's the code with screws, too. You don't rat."

"I don't care what anybody calls it. You'll have to testify downtown, Harry—at an Internal Affairs hearing. That's how we put away a creep like Kowalski."

"Jeez, I don't know."

"There's something in it for you, Harry. Unofficial, but it's something."

"What's that?"

"Absolution, let's call it. Can I count on you?"

"Yeah, I guess so."

"All right then, no hard feelings about that day."

It was not hard to forgive the likes of Harry Darcy, for I, too, have been a slow learner in my time. It was touching to behold him in the painful throes of discovering a big, rude fact of life: in prison it hardly matters who occupies the cells. There was poor Fat Buns Darcy where I have spent some time: all grown up and jeering at himself for being the late-blooming type, trying to figure out what it means to be a man while he still has the time and energy, trying to slip off his clown clothes, trying to figure his way out of being a prisoner in charge of a prison full of prisoners.

But in the case of the next guy on my list of people to see—try as I might, I could not feel so charitably.

Nineteen

By the time he got me from Rikers Island back over to Manhattan and then to Hell's Kitchen where he had started out so early in the morning, the rookie Baize was feeling very put upon for all his troubles of driving and waiting. Also he had a savage headache from fighting crosstown holiday traffic against a setting sun so piercing bright I could see it shining through his thumb on the steering wheel.

"This goddamn assignment—they can shove it," he complained. "I'm a cop, you know."

"Here's five hundred bucks' worth of advice," I offered. "Don't be whining around anybody else."

"I got the right to beef."

"The point is, a cop doesn't have to tell another cop that he's a cop."

"Well," he whined again, missing the point again, "I sure didn't join the department to wind up being a taxi driver."

"Good for you, kid. I don't like taking cabs myself."

"How come?"

"When I know the driver's story—and I always do, they never fail to talk at me—suddenly I'd rather walk."

But when it comes to snitches, I thought to myself, the

opposite is generally true: a man full of troubles is an attractive stool pigeon; his information is as reliable as his motives are dark.

In New York, there are two types of confidential informants, as snitches are officially called: registered and unregistered. Detectives are officially required to deal only with the registered variety of CI, unless a supervisor approves an exception for some special reason, of which there are not too many. Naturally, there is a gray area the size of a small ocean.

The most trustworthy CI is somebody in the sporting life with a specific grudge against somebody else in the life, which is to say a crook who wants to jackpot a rival crook for some personal or professional reason. Detectives should always be looking to cultivate trustworthy people of this sporting sort: a little fish with disparaging information about a big fish. Harry Darcy could appreciate this. Ideally, the little fish should have an outstanding criminal charge that can be reasonably dropped in the interest of greater social good, or else a charge that can at least be reduced. Ninety-five percent of a detective's caseload is solved by information rather than investigation that requires actual work, mental or physical—especially physical. As I am myself notoriously unfond of physical exertion, I hold that a detective is only as good as his snitches.

Once I have converted a little fish into a snitch—the best snitches are not volunteers—I am obliged to inform my supervisor. Supposedly, my man (sometimes woman, although sporting women are far less talky) has not committed a crime lately, although here is another gray area. The snitch is fingerprinted and photographed, and classified by criminal specialty. His CI file is then available to everybody else in the ranks.

A crook in New York can make a handsome sideline out of snitching. It is not uncommon, for instance, for a CI specializing in narcotics to earn a thousand dollars a week, plus a percentage of the take on property confiscation.

There is a saying in the department: a good snitch never has to do time—ever. This is the main perquisite in the total benefits package of a nonviolent career criminal. All such a careerist must do is maintain a good CI file—one with numerous "assist" citations for his information—and he presents a good picture of himself in the eyes of a judge. A crook with a productive record of snitching—and who is smart enough to pursue his trade without benefit of a gun—will usually walk. The benevolence of the real-world criminal justice system of New York City begins before the snitch goes up in front of a judge, even before he calls his lawyer; when he needs bail, a friendly cop will always come running.

Nobody likes talking about the biggest and grayest area between registered and unregistered snitches, namely the wannabe CI—the crook who shops around for a detective who can sponsor him to registration, in return, of course, for some long money. The conflict of interest is as obvious and flagrant today as it was before the Knapp Commission back in the 1970s allegedly put an end to it once and for all. It happened then, it happens now.

If there is one certain principle in the unprincipled world of snitching, it is this: no matter what—white, black, or gray—a detective should never trust a cop buff. Buffs tend to believe what they read in the newspapers and what they see on the tube, and otherwise dwell in fantasy land. Even worse, their agendas are unknown.

Meaning in particular that Eddie the Ear—never mind his tipping me about Rosie Rosenbaum's unfortunate birthday party all those years ago, never mind all the times since then he has proffered assistance in my line of duty—is definitely not a recruitable CI. Eddie loves hanging around cops the way a jock loves a locker room, which to my way of thinking is strange romance. Worse yet, Eddie loves cops-and-robbers stories in all the places they are imperfectly told: the tabloids, the crime novels, the movies, and the bar at Dinny's Lounge, where a lot of cops have taken up boozy self-glorifications where I left off.

So, on at least two counts, Eddie is not snitch material: he is a buff, and so far as I know he has never been a player in the sporting life. Either way, by my lights this means Eddie has no business trading in information about my business. Which is why he was next on my list of persons I had to confront.

Baize dropped me at square one: my own unfashionable apartment house, across the way from the landmark of Edward Michael Mallow propped up in a folding chair against the brick wall of Dinny's Lounge, wearing his checkered pants and union jacket, puffing a cigar stub, fingers laced over his small belly. He was scratching pink skin on the closed side of his head as I walked up to him. He looked like he had been up all night, which figured. His expression was sour.

"What do you hear, Eddie?"

"Not much since after I seen this morning's *Post.*"

"That's a disappointing answer."

"So what do you want out of me anyways?"

"You and me—we're friends for a long time, right?"

"Sure, whatever you say." Eddie the Ear held up a couple of crossed fingers. "We're just like that. Got us a Damon and Pythias thing going here."

"What's with the sarcasm?"

"Friends, they look out for each other. Like since I am a guy with confidential knowledge about what's going down in the Kitchen, maybe my friend ought to be tossing business my way sometimes—especially when my friend's a cop who needs to know what's going on."

"You're angry at me that I don't cut you into the department squeak budget?" Here I had planned a mild confrontation with Eddie the Ear and he was turning the tables on me. "So you want to cause me trouble, you go whispering to Slattery?"

"The *Post* splashes ink, what's it got to do with me?"

"I can think of three things, any one of which tells me

it's your big mouth. One—you're the guy who told Slattery the play was sent to Ruby. How you know, that's another question." I paused for a moment to see how Eddie would take this. Like a poker player he took it. "Two—you're Slattery's source on Marv being a friend of mine. Three—you get it to Slattery just before the final edition that I'm rousted downtown. This was either before Baize came into my house and nearly busted down my door, or else when you were waving at me as I drove off."

Before responding to all this, Eddie slid the horn-rims down off his bumpy nose and cleaned the lenses. Then he put his glasses back on and puffed his cigar a few times.

"There's flaws in your thinking," he finally said. "The writer himself, he could of told Slattery about sending Ruby that play—what-do-you-call-it, *Grief Street.* Plenty of cops in the department know you was friends with Marv—on account of you doing that alkie penance at his soup kitchen. And that cop who picked you up in the Chrysler? What'd you call him—Baize? He could of told Slattery lots sooner than me."

"Are you denying you talked to Slattery?"

"I ain't confirming, I ain't denying."

"As long as I've known you, Eddie, you're always looking to sell what you know. And you haven't been subtle about it."

"A guy's got to keep himself in walking-around money." Eddie the Ear's face wrinkled into a gloat. "One way or another, you know?"

"A friend doesn't sell out a friend."

"Yeah? Let me ask you, is a friend supposed to have enough respect to be interested in his pal's life?"

"What are you talking about?"

"You and me, Hock. Only whenever we talk, it's all about you—and nothing about me. You notice I got respect enough to listen? When do you ever listen? Tell me something you know about Eddie Mallow."

"Well, I don't know, there's . . ."

I stopped myself from telling Eddie that he and his

missing ear were the stuff of long-ago secret nun talk, urgent sex whisperings we boys were afraid to know.

"Tell me one thing about Eddie Mallow besides he is a guy with one ear missing, which you don't even bother to know how that happened. Start simple, Hock. Where does Eddie Mallow live?"

Many years ago at Police Academy, just before graduation and assignment to my first foot post, I was taught Lesson Number One in surviving the streets as a rookie beat cop. I recollected the face of my instructor on this point, if not the name. I have remembered the words, if not the importance of applying the meaning to my own circumstances: *Know the people on your beat—where they live, what they do, when they do it.* Some big-time gold shield detective I turned out to be. I cannot even keep to Lesson Number One. So who am I to have bullied the rookie Baize?

"Eddie, I'm sorry. I see you just about every day, but I don't know where you live."

"What cops don't know could fill a jail."

"Be that as it may—"

"To you, I'm just funny-looking wallpaper . . ."

"For crying out loud—mea culpa."

"I'm like some gabby old broad underneath a hair dryer."

"Look, I promise—we'll have a heart-to-heart someday soon. Right now I'm dog tired. Before I go home, though, I have to know something." I reached for my wallet. "You want money? I'm taking it out of my own pocket."

"It ain't the dough. Jesus, Hock—you think it was about the dough?"

In a heat of embarrassment I did not completely understand, I put away my wallet and left Eddie's question unanswered. I looked at him carefully. For the first time in my life I tried to picture him someplace besides in a chair leaned up against the outside wall of a cop bar. I drew a blank. Which was pathetic for a cop once praised for having a near lunatic imagination. I tried to cover up my further embarrassment by putting a sideways question to Eddie, which he answered in a sideways fashion of his own.

"By the way, Eddie—what did you think of the play?"

"What makes you think I read it?"

"Interest in the Kitchen, in the people who live here. Besides which you told me yourself what it was generally about."

"Yeah, I got interest in people. All kinds. Ain't it ironical some people don't got any interest in me?"

"What about the playwright? Do you find him interesting, too?"

"Only interest I got in a writer is if he's any good."

"What's good by your lights?"

"A writer worth reading makes a riddle out of an answer."

†

I have learned to know when something is seriously troubling Ruby. She stays home for the day and conducts a certain domestic ritual.

First, she hauls out a packing box from under the bed. This is a clumsy square thing that could just as well be stored in some dusty corner of her theater, but which instead she insists on having close by. She brings this box out to the kitchen, opens it up, and pulls out an electric contraption: an Oster bread-making machine, which takes over the single, foot-square kitchen counter.

By the way, ours is a kitchen in name only. The bare minimum of appliances are crammed Pullman-style against an alcove wall: two-burner range, tiny sink, half-size refrigerator, two overhead cupboards. There are no drawers. Dishes and cutlery and so forth are kept a few steps away in the parlor sideboard.

So this is what confronted me on returning home from a day that for me had begun with a rousting and ended in a serpentine conversation with Eddie the Ear: Ruby standing at the kitchen alcove, flour spots on her cheeks, tapping her foot; bread machine steaming and gurgling; wooden cutting board balanced on the stove top, covered in flour; half the sofa taken over by finished loaves cooling down, each one neatly covered with a checkered dish towel. All this bread is too much for us, of course, and so Ruby mostly gives it away; I myself have delivered loaves to Holy Cross and the soup kitchen, too.

I kissed Ruby hello and sank into my easy chair, a big fringed green upholstered number, circa 1935, that came to me via Salvation Army. It is always after such a disquieting day as today when I sit in that chair wishing I had a dog.

"Maybe after the theater is sold, and when we move to someplace bigger, I can go up to the pound in East Harlem and find myself a nice mutt," I said to Ruby's back. She opened the Oster and popped out a fresh brown loaf with a nutty aroma.

"Another mutt. That's all we need around here."

"You have a bread machine, I should have a dog."

"Why?"

"So I can come home and make a fool of myself on the floor with a dog. The dog won't scold me. Not only that, he'll make a fool of himself, too."

"Don't you think you're doing just fine alone?"

"I love you, too."

"Incidentally, are you saying I'm making a fool of myself baking all this bread?"

"You're nobody's fool, Ruby."

She turned. Somewhere in the short space of time between my walking through the door and plopping myself down in the green chair Ruby had begun to cry. We are both learning about pregnancy and hormones and roller-coaster mood swings.

"I'm your fool, Irish."

She swept over to me and sat in my lap, eyes streaming tears. I wondered what on earth I should say.

"The story in the paper," Ruby said, before I had the

chance of anything myself. Her shoulders heaved. "I'm so sorry."

"Sorry for what?"

"If I wasn't in theater . . ." Ruby paused. Her shoulders trembled. I pulled her closer. "After I read the *Post* this morning, I couldn't help thinking I'm . . . well, responsible."

"You should know better."

"But I'm a fool."

"No, you're not. You're in the dark. People are afraid of the dark. Why shouldn't they be? When it's dark, people have to think. Thinking is scarier than knowing."

"I wish there was some way out of the dark."

"There is—looking."

As quickly as Ruby's tears had come, they were now gone. She sat up and asked, "Is that why you became a detective? Because you're afraid of the dark?"

"Maybe it is. I don't know—I never thought about it." But I thought now about poor Fat Buns, and our remembrances of darkest school days at Holy Cross. "That's the second time today I said that."

"What was the first time?"

"When I went to see Harry Darcy, up at Rikers. He warned me that King Kong Kowalski doesn't wish me all the best."

"Big surprise. What else did you talk about?"

"We go a long way back, Harry and me. I think he was glad to see somebody from the old neighborhood." I thought, Harry Darcy had been one of the lucky kids who left the Kitchen, but where had it got him? "Darcy got something off his chest about when we were kids in school together."

"You can take the boy out of Holy Cross, but you can't take the Holy Cross out of the boy." Ruby slid off me and stepped over to the couch. She uncovered a loaf and tapped the top of it with a finger. "This one I baked with olives and sun-dried tomatoes. We'll have it with dinner."

"Tomorrow's Easter. I'll be going to mass. I can take a few loaves with me. You want to come?"

"Ask me in the morning."

For the rest of the evening, we talked about other things—anything besides the case. I was grateful for the rest. We talked of dogs, and bread, and the idea of a big new apartment—one with a proper kitchen to it—and whether the newest Hockaday would be boy or girl.

Toward the very end of the night—after a fine dinner of salmon, boiled new potatoes, fresh asparagus, and Ben & Jerry's kiwi-strawberry sorbet for dessert; after I had done my duty and cleaned up the dishes; then, as we were lying together in the dark—Ruby again raised the subject of being a detective.

She asked, "What's the toughest thing about your job?"

I thought for a long moment. "Sometimes I feel like I'm blind," I said. "A blind man born with sight, but who lost it, then lost even the memory of seeing."

"Too much to think about?"

"Always—and with the added trouble that I'm not too bright. Maybe that's why I drank."

"Go easy on yourself."

"How do I do that?"

"You made a baby for us. Wasn't that nice and easy?" Ruby pushed close against me. She lifted my arm around her waist, and tucked a leg between my own. "Mama used to tell me another way of being easy."

"What was that?"

"Try not to hold all your thoughts in one hand, or else you'll be afraid to ever open it."

"One thought at a time?"

Ruby slipped herself beneath me, circled her arms around my back, and pulled me down into her warmth and softness.

"Tell me what you're thinking now, Irish."

†

And then later, after Ruby had drifted into sleep, I sat up and looked out the window to a moon so bright I could feel its light on my face.

I thought about the play, too. And how with all that was happening, maybe this was the only time I had to read it. So I crept out from bed, put on my robe, and went to the parlor. The manuscript—with Ruby's lines, in the character of Annie Meath, highlighted in yellow—lay on the end of the sofa without the bread.

For the next two hours, I read, searching for clues in a made-up story of grief and violence from years ago that could help me in the present murderous day. As if the play was a blueprint, written by a simple author. *A writer worth reading makes a riddle out of an answer.* I found no answers in the fluent pages of *Grief Street.* Nor clues, nor even foreshadowings of conceivable things to come, notwithstanding Slattery's breathless suggestion of all this help in the simple pages of the *Post.*

I found instead a drama of immigrant sorrows, told by someone who knew what he was talking about; I saw the early texture of a neighborhood that came to shape souls, for better or for worse; I met eloquent characters variously disappointed by the myth of an American dream. The least eloquent of the cast—a brooding cop, stumbling around toward resolution of double murder at Easter time—indeed seemed somewhat like myself. These parallels Slattery pointed out in his piece, a job as uncomplicated as pointing out himself in a mirror. But the rest was quite beyond him, or myself this late at night, for all the rest was a riddle.

Exhausted by the mystery of fine writing with no answers, I took to bed a riddle that especially haunted me, a man waiting for his child to be born. The riddle was a poem, composed by a character never seen in the play—a girl dying from tuberculosis. If I understood the playwright's meaning, the purpose of the girl's poem was in speaking to generations across the divides of time and culture, and in speaking of the history that unites and dignifies us all—memory:

When you are outside playing ball,
please toss one for me.
Let the grownups mourn and cry,
and give their hearts some ease.
But you, please listen, please:
Live each one of you for one of us.

I fell asleep dreaming the girl's poem, and remember dreaming it again as I woke; and thinking, It seems insane to be dreaming such things at once.

Riddles, and murder, and eloquence . . .

But then, dreaming permits each and every one of us to be quietly and safely insane every night of our lives.

Twenty

"REMEMBER THE EASTER WE WERE WALKING to church with them in the sunny morning like this? My-oh-my, but weren't we the pride of the parish? Oh, I remember that Easter best of all. My little men—one nestled in your arms, so quiet and cooing, so beautiful. The other toddling along."

"Yeah, yeah. They was freaking angels."

"I'll thank you not to cuss today."

"What'll you have, then? An amen face like your own?"

"Calm yourself, dear."

"*Dear,* she says. *Calm yourself,* she says. Here's what I got to say to you—don't be always living in that past you made up for yourself."

"But my dear, we all live in the past. There is nowhere else to live."

"Yeah? What do you call the here and now?"

"Unbearable."

"When you're right," he said, with a shrug, "you're freaking right."

The fat man in the tight blue suit and the woman in the pink feathered bonnet walked in silence for another block of Queens Boulevard. When their hands touched as they moved along, one or the other of them would draw back, as if intimacy was the most irritating factor of an unbearable married life. Occasionally some passerby would greet them. She would smile, seeming to mean it, and say, "God bless you this morning, the day of the Resurrection of Christ the Lord." The fat man would wheeze and look away.

"So," he asked, snorting, "what do you call the future?"

"The future is heaven."

"Think again, old babe. Maybe the future's dead."

"Don't say such a horrid thing."

"Your precious past—that's dead for a fact."

"It's not!"

"You think I wouldn't give my left nut to turn the clock back?" The fat man had become excited by this. He had to stop a moment to catch his breath, pulling loose a necktie that gagged him as he did so. "But changing time, that ain't in my ability. No man's rich enough to buy back his past."

"I see him in my sleep—"

"Jesus H. Christ, here we go again."

"Not the one who left us to be with God. I mean the one still out there someplace . . . someplace. You know who he looks like?"

The fat man did not answer immediately. His doughy face revealed nothing.

"I don't know," he finally said. "Who?"

"Like you, Joe. Like a dream of you—from years ago, when the world was right."

Twenty-one

Sister Roberta Lowther herself being right next to me as I knelt at the altar to take into my mouth my Easter communion host—the Body of Christ, soon to be followed by His Blood—I naturally felt my head pounding at the sternest of all her many warnings. *No teeth, boys! Let the host melt in your mouth, else you'll risk biting the Son of God in two. For that, you're sure to roast in hell for eternity.* To this day, I am extra mindful of my teeth at Christmas and Easter masses.

I stole a number of sidelong glances at Sister. Her own eyes remained devoutly shut as the priest, aided by two altar boys in charge of the host tray and wine chalice, moved us through the rite—mumbling the ancient pledge on behalf of Jesus, "This is my Body" and "This is my Blood"—and thereby converting symbol to Lordly tissue and life fluid. Transubstantiation seemed a mystery more easily understood than another: how was it that Sister Roberta Lowther had not changed in appearance in all these years?

Many nuns I have known, Sister Roberta included, simply do not age. If they are young when we first come to know them, they remain forever so; if old, then they looked that way their whole lives. Sister Roberta was a nun of the first category.

Back when I was wearing short pants in her classroom, her face was oval and fair, as unlined as a dish of sweet cream. She was remarkably pretty for a nun so capable of unpretty tales calculated to terrify us boys.

Every day, of course, she wore the same ensemble: ankle-length black habit, purple rosary dangling down her hip, mannish steel-frame convent glasses, black shoes with chunky heels, a plain gold band denoting that she was a bride of Christ. Sister Roberta was the first nun I mocked by calling her Mrs. Christ behind her back. She was never without the veil, which concealed any hair that might be graying on Sister's head, and which also gentled her face in soft shadows. My own mother, Mairead, might look like this, were she a nun. To this day I have no idea what color Sister's hair is, though I imagine it to be as darkly red as Mother's own when she herself was young and strong.

Sister wore all of this today, with one addition. She and many others—the young priest celebrating communion, old Father Declan waiting to deliver the Easter homily, the altar boys, the singers in the choir—wore black armbands, symbol of interfaith mourning for the victims of the Yom Hashoah and Good Friday murders.

"Peace be with you, Sister," I whispered to her. Our group had finished its wafers and wine, and had cleared the altar. We were now on our way back to pews, walking slowly to the stiff cadence of liturgical organ music, hands locked in front of us to preserve the blessings—to keep them from slipping out from our fingers and accidentally falling into hell, this according to Creepy Morrison, though I thought at the time he was only having a joke during a bad mood. "Have you ever met my wife?"

"Why, yes—that lovely McKelvey girl. A Franciscan novitiate, wasn't she? My own order."

"No, Sister. I mean—yes, she was a novitiate. But that and our marriage, it was all some time ago . . ."

The formerly lovely Judy McKelvey and I had the usual wedding ceremony at Holy Cross. I remember thinking at the time that the processional music seemed very much the same as the sound of soldiers going to war.

"I'm afraid neither of these things worked out."

"Dear God!" Sister said. Her hand flew to her throat when she realized the full horror of my meaning. "I'm so sorry!"

Sister Roberta turned, faced the altar, and crossed herself, then took her place in a pew near the back of the sanctuary. Ruby was waiting for me in the one just behind, as she is much more just-in-case about religious matters than myself. Also because she was tending a shopping bag full of wrapped bread. Before turning into my own pew, I leaned down and spoke to Sister. "I'll look for you after the mass. I want you to meet Ruby. We're expecting, you know."

"Expecting? A baby you mean? You?"

"Yes."

"Dear God!"

Sister turned and watched as I sidled through my row, bumping over a line of knees and padded kneelers. When I sat down next to Ruby, she grabbed my thigh and squeezed. I caught Sister's sternly amused look, and wondered what to make of it.

Ruby put her lips to my ear. "Who is that?" I told her, and then she asked, "The one who runs the shelter?" Yes, I said. "Should we give the bread to her?" A good idea, I agreed.

I looked up toward the altar, past communion celebrants crowding the aisle, flocking back to their seats. Father Declan had a few more hosts to drop on sinners' tongues. As he finished up his priestly task, I stared at his tired face, and reflected on the Easter homily he had earlier delivered.

Ordinarily, Father Declan owns the darkly complexioned type of Irish face, carrying in it a hint of the Spanish Armada and its aftermath of breeding. But today he was ashen; I saw this all the way from the back of the church, as I had seen moments earlier while taking communion. His weariness looked like Slattery's own of yesterday, as if Father Declan, too, had been up all night writing—in his case a homily. Ordinarily, Father Declan's homilies are notoriously restful; many a wife's elbow has thumped the ribs of a snoring husband during such orations. But today, Father Declan was filled with the sorrow of knowing Friday's crimes; filled, too, with an eloquent rage created through his long night.

I wondered, Did he weaken during the raging night? Did he drink?

"Sometimes when men are killed, the murder is done by no single hand," Father Declan began, his voice more somber than I had ever known it. "Sometimes man is killed by the impotence and silence of many. And do we not see this in our criminal age, this time of scoundrels and cynics and intoxicating moral mediocrity and willful ignorance?

"Yes, my friends, ours is an age of great crime. I am suspicious of rosy romanticism, but still I must tell you that I remember a day when we knew hunger, yet hope as well; when we were uncertain, yet trusted in the unknown future; when there was in these teeming immigrant streets of ours privation, yet spiritual plenitude. It is true, it is true.

"I knew myself of a young girl called Brigid, whose ancestors preceded my own in the same difficult journey—from County Donegal in Ireland to New York. Brigid was called to join her family already arrived from the other side. In Brigid's case, an aunt and uncle who had earlier made their way to this very neighborhood of ours, poor and rough at the time as ever. But upon arrival, young Brigid only discovered her family'd been murdered in their sleep, by someone in ferocious want of their meager possessions.

"Knowing not what to do, except that she had no desire of returning to Donegal, Brigid trudged all over town. In a short time, she found the better streets of the strange city of New York, where she looked for work as a scullery maid in some great home. For days, she knew an unsuccessful time of it, sleeping shamefully where she could, in doorways and such hidden places.

"Tired from roaming, and hungry and near delirium, she stopped one afternoon at a church. And there spent her last coins offering up a prayer of hope for her own lost cause to St. Jude, and another for the soul of purgatory closest to heaven. Afterward, in the street outside, a handsome young man came up to her and said, 'I understand you need a job.' The young man handed her a calling card, with a fancy address embossed on it. 'Go to this place at once,' he said, 'and the lady of the house will take care of you.' Well, and that's just what Brigid did.

"She rang the bell of a great house in Madison Avenue, and a sad-faced woman came downstairs to admit her. Though Brigid had presented the calling card, the woman expressed surprise that anyone had directed her to the house—for she lived alone in but two rooms of the place, without family or friend, and hardly needed help. Disappointed again, Brigid was turning to leave when she noticed a huge oil painting over the fireplace. 'But, that is the very man who gave me the card,' she said, pointing.

"Quite startled, the woman murmured, 'That is my son who died some years ago.' She took Brigid to her heart then, and raised her as her own daughter.

"Now Brigid, you see, had in her an acute hope. She had—despite grief and desperation, despite the murders of all she had in this world of family—a way of seeing herself through fear and hunger and cold. She had her faith and its teachings, her Catholic religion—which is, above all, a method of seeing.

"If we—now, in this criminal age of scoundrels and mediocrities—lose *our* faith, then how may we see?

"My friends, we know that murderous grief will surely have its say. As indeed it has, on this day we celebrate the triumph of regeneration over death. But will we listen to what this grief tells us . . . ?

"Will we listen to our Catholic hearts? And practice what has been put there by the Holy Church? Will we accept that all humanity makes one family, one generation to the next, and that each of us is an equal child of God? Will we live each day in strivance toward such civilization?

"I offer two thoughts. The first from St. Patrick, who warns that civilization may pass in a moment, like a cloud, or like smoke scattered by the wind. The second thought from myself: if we are to be saved from this criminal age, it will not be the work of policemen, but of saints that dwell within policemen's hearts."

†

Declan Byrne stood in a patch of shade at the top of the outside stairs, greeting parishioners as they poured out from the church dressed in their holiday finery, squinting gladly in the bright Easter morning sun beginning to warm the chill air. He hardly had time to swipe a few puffs on his Pall Mall, what with so many congregants circled around him, pumping his hand in congratulations for a homily that had been above and beyond.

"Nobody dozing on you today, hey, Father?" I heard someone say. And, "Bless you, it was real inspiring." As well as, "Your masterpiece, I should say" and "The Lord surely blew his breath into your lungs this morning, Father."

We were squinting ourselves, Ruby and Sister Roberta and I, as we stepped out from the church. I heard Father Declan's voice before I saw him motioning for me to join him.

"Neil—a word, please . . . Neil!"

"Go ahead, son," Sister Roberta said. She hooked an arm over Ruby's and the two of them started downstairs to the street, where parishioners mingled, chatting with one another before returning home for the holiday dinner or strolling across town to the parade on Fifth Avenue.

"Father B's a fine ham, and he's got himself an admiring crowd this morning. We'll just take a few minutes to get acquainted, your pretty wife and me."

I had to wait awhile for Father Declan's fan club to break up before we could talk. A man said, "You look peaked, Father. Feeling all right?" Father Declan took a handkerchief from somewhere inside his cassock and wiped his perspiring forehead. "Oh yes, fine, fine," he assured the man. It sounded like a lie to me. That, or else Father was having the shakes. I wondered about his drinking again.

"Well, are you?" I asked when I finally reached him.

"Am I what?"

"Feeling well."

"I've all my fingers, if it's what you mean."

"No, it's not. Level with me."

"I've not had a drink." Father Declan sighed. "The Friday horrors have taken over my mind, possessing me like. I'd no time for the sweet good-bye of whisky with the possession driving me so to conclusion."

"What conclusion?"

"Remember when last we spoke?" The priest lighted another Pall Mall and gave a glance to the bar across the street. "Remember your saying this violent wickedness was beyond your depth?"

I said I remembered.

"But I don't think it's the case, you see. And that's what I tried getting across in my homily."

"With all due respect, Father, I don't—"

"Don't be a doubter, son. At least not before you spend some time upstate with Father Morrison—Creepy Morrison to you."

"You called him?"

"It's not so easy as that. I sent Father a fax message, in care of an old fellow named Charlie who runs the village store. Quicker than I'd thought came the reply, courtesy of Charlie. Anyway, Father Morrison's expecting you anytime."

"Thanks. I'll see about checking out a car from the department."

"Ah—it sounds so fine, a drive in the mountains. How I wish I could be going with you, Neil. But I've got Wednesday's dead table to prepare."

"I could wait until—"

"Please no, not on my account. Go soon. It'd do you worlds of good. As a cop and as a Catholic, too."

†

Which was it, Ruby wanted to know—the house to the east, or the one to the west?

"And what makes you ask?" said Sister Roberta, her face as inscrutable as it was ageless.

We were in a tiny parlor at the front of a gray brick house on West Fortieth Street, having walked there after the mass. Half the parlor, actually. The other side of the room was taken over by a neat row of three cots and

nightstands. All the rooms in the house, downstairs and up, were similarly cut and divided into such impersonal spheres, with only this one half-space as a sitting room. The outside of the old house itself was unremarkable in appearance, although better maintained than others of the block.

Sister had just finished explaining the reason for anonymity: vengeful husbands and boyfriends—fathers, even—were known to stalk the neighborhood of known shelters. This, she said, was among the saddest facts of modern violent life she knew. I certainly agreed.

Sister and Ruby had struck an immediate affinity during my brief talk with Father Declan about traveling up to the Catskills. Such an affinity that Ruby had promptly accepted Sister's invitation to Easter dinner at the shelter. Which seemed only appropriate, since there she was with all that bread on her hands. The two of them now sipped Bloody Marys as we sat in the parlor. I struggled with tea. Four of the twenty-six guests of the house were busy preparing dinner out in the kitchen, the others variously attending to daily chores around the place.

"I'm an actress," Ruby said, "and I have a part in a new play that—"

"So I've been reading in the paper," Sister interrupted.

I tried to picture Sister Roberta reading crime stories in the tabloids. *Dear God!* I might as well have tried tuning in a picture of a nun buying condoms.

"Annie Meath, that's the name of my character," Ruby said. "She was a real-life woman, but not what you'd call a church lady. Maybe you know the legend of a Hell's Kitchen gang called Annie's Goons?"

Sister seemed lost. I explained, "Annie Meath's house was the place that gave the neighborhood its name."

"Oh yes, yes," Sister said, nodding. "The Hell's Kitchen house. That story I remember. The poor people, so hot in there."

"Forgive me, Sister," Ruby said. "It was—well, a bawdy house that Annie Meath ran next door."

"A whorehouse? Yes, I suppose it was. Dear me."

"But was it the house to your east, or west?"

"It's the one with the two double windows," Sister said. "A rather fancy house in its day, especially for the neighborhood." She turned her veiled face my way. "Unless I'm very much mistaken."

"It's what I've always heard myself," I agreed.

"What about these days?" Ruby asked. "Who lives there now?"

"The place is officially closed down. Nobody lives there, so to speak."

"So to speak?"

"Well, there's the squatter."

"Oh?"

"It's what he calls himself, a wee joke between us couple of aging immigrants." Sister's voice filled with affection. "Mr. Monaghan is a fine gentleman, really, an old-fashioned charmer. Ruby, dear, do you know what is said of Irish charmers?"

"What's that?"

"No siren did ever so charm the ear of the listener as the listening ear of a fine Irishman has charmed the soul of the siren. That's my Mr. Monaghan, bless him. We have great long chats. That's what he calls them—chats. The truth is, it's me doing nearly all the talking."

"A charming squatter?" I asked. Like a cop I asked.

"You'd never know by the looks of him. He's clean, and beautifully dressed. Squatters don't often grow silvery haired like my Mr. Monaghan." Sister Roberta cut me a look that said she did not care for the suspicion in my tone. "And he's beautifully spoken, when I give him the chance at speaking."

I suddenly remembered Lieutenant Rankin and how he wanted me on that Mickey Mouse stake up on Restaurant Row, duty which I escaped courtesy of Neglio's clearance. *Over to West Forty-sixth . . . Some con's running the coronary scam. . . . Old but spry, and smooth . . . Talks like an Irishman who read some books.*

"Just how long has this Monaghan lived next to you, Sister?" I asked.

"Your police department's forever running poor squatters out from their digs. Now why are you wanting to be such brutes?"

"What I do on my own, and what's policy in the department—very often, Sister, that's two different things."

"All the same, Neil. If it should happen you coppers make trouble for my gentleman neighbor, I'll know it's you was the snake in the grass that informed."

"Sister, please, give me a break."

"I'll give you this warning fair: make trouble for my Mr. Monaghan and I'll reconsider including your soul in my evening prayers."

So I dropped any further inquiry about Monaghan the squatter, though I made a mental note to ask a Midtown South cruiser to make some surreptitious pass-bys during the night, when squatters tend to come and go, and report back to me. Sister Roberta, meanwhile, amused Ruby by scolding me as a generally troublemaking schoolboy grown up to become a stranger to the old priests and nuns who loved him in spite of himself. She had lost nothing of her guilt-making skills.

The three of us spent another half hour talking over small things. Then Sister and Ruby joined the crew in the kitchen. I was put into service lugging card tables upstairs from a storage bin down in the cellar and setting them into a long row together so everybody could sit around to a fine Easter dinner of ham and goose and carrots and string beans and Irish cockley pie and Ruby's bread. There was wine, except for me, and ginger cake with whipped cream and coffee for dessert.

It was near dusk as we stood at the top of the stoop, saying good night to Sister Roberta and the others at the shelter. Another sun—a scumbled soft blaze of orange and yellow—was dying over the Hudson sky. A tinkling ice cream truck passed us by, turning up Tenth Avenue and out of sight.

Down on the street, we headed for Tenth Avenue ourselves. But first, Ruby stopped in front of the house next door, the one with the double windows and crumbled stoop. The entrance door—at the top, where the stairs used to end—was boarded over. Most of the windows were as well, except for ones in the front. The glass was crusted with grime, but intact. There appeared to be dark red curtains on the parlor side.

"Wouldn't you love to go in?"

I could forgo the pleasure of rooting around in a squatter's mess, I said.

Ruby turned from the house, and looked up and down the tired street. "Tell me what was it like here."

"This block wasn't much like the rest of the neighborhood. It was brownstone houses instead of tenements. Shabby elegant, that's how my mother described it. There was even some honest money in a few of the houses. But if I remember right . . ." I pointed to Annie Meath's place, where the squatter was maybe inside, and looking out at us now. "This one had a doctor in it, right up to the time I was a rookie in the department. I forget the name. He was the kind of doctor girls in trouble had to go to then. Or gangsters in trouble."

"And the rest of the block?"

"I remember old Greek gents sitting around all day in coffeehouses. At night the second-floor anisette parlors would open, and there would be sad music. That's about all I can tell you, really."

"I can see how it was grand years and years ago."

"Maybe so."

"It could be again."

Sunlight faded off, and we moved on. Walking up the avenue to Forty-third Street, I caught Ruby staring at my stomach. Which I admit was pooching out over my belt slightly.

I was anxious to talk about anything besides what Ruby obviously had on her mind. So I told her how I had to drive upstate to see a hermit priest by the name of Creepy

Morrison; how Father Declan had made arrangements, no doubt looking upon the excursion as a means of bringing me back into the fold.

"Do you realize you're waddling?" Ruby asked, ignoring everything I said.

"So I ate a big dinner. So I'm walking heavy."

"No, you're waddling. Tomorrow morning, let's find you a gym."

"Don't start."

"If you drop dead from a heart attack, I'll never forgive you."

"So she starts."

"Tomorrow, Hock, I mean it. You're joining up at a gym."

"I told you, I'm going to the mountains tomorrow."

"On Monday? Aren't you forgetting something?"

"Forgetting what?"

"The staged reading. It's supposed to be Monday night. You're not sticking around for that?"

"Well—"

"Good, Monday night's settled. As for the day, you've got time for the gym."

"And so, Your Honor," I said, speaking to the imaginary judge I address when Ruby nags me, "I had to kill her."

As usual, Ruby changed the subject.

"I like Sister Roberta," she said. By now we were climbing the stairway to our apartment. "She'd make a good neighbor."

"Neighbor . . . ?"

The telephone started ringing on the other side of our door. I put the key in the lock and hurried inside, thinking it might be Neglio. Instead it was a man asking for Ruby.

"Yes?" she said when I handed her the receiver. Then, the rest of Ruby's end of the line: "Yes, I see . . . No, that's quite convenient . . . Oh, how interesting!"

"Well?" I asked.

"Half-past seven tomorrow night, East Sixty-fourth Street off Park. And talk about shabby elegant."

"Meaning?"

"The reading's at Stuart Godwin's house."

"You know him?"

"By reputation. He's a producer with a couple of good credits—some bad ones, too. But that's not what I mean by shabby."

"No?"

"Godwin owns the town house where Dick Nixon lived after he was run out of Washington."

Twenty-two

"BUT WHAT'S TO BECOME OF ME, and my home?" The old man in the handsome silk robe and waistcoat cups his face with soft gloved hands as he says this. He refills his glass with Black Bush. His voice is slurry from whisky. "Oh, me—oh, me!"

"Shut up already," the other man says. "You sound like that pansy Godwin."

"I never bargained for all this rushy stuff! A year I thought it was I had left."

"Ain't you heard babies only take nine months?"

"*Ain't?* Must you?"

"Mostly, yes, I must maintain character."

"Gawd—really!"

"Must *you?*"

"Oh, tosh!" The man in the robe rolls his eyes and takes a pull at his whisky glass. "She's some ways from nine months full, isn't she? Why is it you're dragging them in so early on?"

"The whorl . . . !" The other man savors the word, as if it was rare steak juicing in his mouth. He draws out the letters—*whooorrrl*—and trills them in the old country way. "The whorl must be fed."

"Cod your talk of the *whorl!* Tell me clear and true, why do you lure them here?"

"They own more sensitivity than most ignoramuses. They've got the ears for hearing these walls talk. They'll come here, and they'll know. Them two, at least, will know."

"But it's why I wrote the bleeding play! Imagine—whole audiences knowing your fury."

"It's not near enough. The whorl must also take them two in time." He stopped, to again savor his words. "Ignoramuses don't trouble to remember their own history unless they see the blood of it on a regular basis."

"God, you're daft!"

"Fook your god! His furies are as wicked as often as good, same as me."

"Have a respectful tongue. There's friends of ours to take offense at your blaspheming sentiments."

"Our friends in blue? They been around?"

"None today. Decent Christians have hallowed places to be going."

"Fools!"

"They're nae fools!" He barks this out, and waves an arm over his head, an attempt at moral punctuation. But in his drunkenness, the gesture is merely comical. His companion laughs heartily, and in doing so fills the close air between them with sick-smelling breath. The man in the robe winces at the odor, and declares, "This is the Sabbath of our Lord's Resurrection, after all."

"Speak for yourself."

"Piffle and tosh! Our friends are hardly the only ones weary of your folderol." He drains his glass, pours another. He offers the bottle to his now scowling companion, who shakes his head no. "Don't be misled by my own gentlemanly sufferance. I'm simply as indulgent of you as I am dependent. Therefore, I seldom speak out."

"Excepting when you've gone potty-headed."

"Aye."

"At no time do you believe I am who I profess to be?"

"I have no respect for the wicked."

"Come with me, I'll show you what's worthy of your respect." He rises from his chair, steps past the broken hearthstones to a door behind the staircase. "Come?"

"Down below?"

"Unless you're frightened of learning truth."

"Liar!"

"You think so?"

"Aye, you're a bloody damn liar!"

"High compliment indeed. Do you know what a liar is?"

"Charlatan!"

"More flattery! Yes, I am all that you say: a man who begins by making falsehood appear as truth, and ends with making truth itself appear as falsehood."

"I'll not listen to filthy riddles!" He claps his hands to his ears, repeating the unintended comical pose. He sits writhing in his chair. His drink crashes to the floor, a gray-black thicket of layered dust absorbs the gold whisky. "I'll not!"

"Here now, I thought you were going below with me." He laughs again, befouling more air. "I thought you were unafraid."

"I never said . . . What I mean—"

"At least come a few steps down the stairs. Come, see what I've to show of the proud craft of perjury."

He rises from the chair, wraps his robe tightly around his thin frame, stumbles toward the staircase door. He follows behind his companion as the two clump slowly down into darkness.

A match is lit, and touched to a candle.

"Can you see it?" His breath is vile at this close range. He points to a stone slab. "Can you make out the lettering?"

"I see it's a tombstone you've drug down here to your black mess. Damn you!"

"Yes, damned I am."

"I can't make out . . ." He steadies himself on the rail,

feels knees tremoring, heart thrashing. "Am I to read an elegy in the stone? Is that your point?"

"Step closer."

"What trick is this?"

"Here—take my candle if you lack trust. I'll just wait on the step while you go ahead. Come straight back if you wish."

Accepting the challenge, he descends slowly. Two risers from the bottom of the stair is close enough to make out the chiseled words:

Here lie
Two grandparents with their two grandchildren
Two husbands with their two wives
Two fathers with their four children
Two mothers each with daughter and son
One maiden with her mother and father
Sister and brother times two.
Yet but six corpses all lie buried here,
Though how this number, 'tis unclear.

He sees how the tombstone is well sunk into the oily earthen floor, as would be so in a proper graveyard. He hears beetles and worms making way through close-packed dampness, and things with claws darting in shadows, and the *click-click-click* of unseen bats swooping through the velvet dark.

He sees the crucifix, burnt crisp to black and suspended upside down above the stone. He rushes back up the steps.

"God in heaven!"

"Well, but now it's neither godly nor heavenly as you claim."

"The stink down here!"

"Like the sweet whiff of autopsy."

"And the meaning of the grave marker?"

"Hah!" Spit flies. "As if you didn't know. It's a fitting epitaph for what's buried there—and for what'll be buried yet."

"I don't understand . . ." His heart thrashes. He puts a hand to his chest.

"Of course you do, my fine old friend. The stone's no mystery to you or me—merely to all others. In due time, the grandest detective of New York shall come discover the grave, and know the honor of solving the riddle we share."

Twenty-three

WE HAD A WINDOW BOOTH at Kraft Restaurant, the neighborhood spoon. Wanda the waitress had greeted us with her usual "Hiya, honies" and sponged our table and set down coffee, and was now padding off to the kitchen to order up our scrambled eggs, bagels, and orange juice.

Spilling over the damp Formica between us were the *Daily News* and the *Post,* with cover-page follow-ups to Friday's murders. The reportage was mostly rehash and reaction—enough of both to keep the city frazzled—with only one new tidbit for public consumption: both tabloids had by now picked up on the connecting elements of the murders.

The *Post* cover declared MURDER MOST WEIRD. Slattery's account on page three was called "Cops Told of Shadow & Smell in Hell's Kitchen Murders." Not to be outdone in purple headline prose, the *Daily News* banner read THE SHADOW KNOWS! A double-page inside spread—synopses of uniform reports, lots of photographs, quotes from Fosdick in praise of myself, and also himself for putting me on the job—appeared under the block-lettered title SCENT OF A GHOST KILLER.

Ruby and I were old news for the moment, for which I

was grateful. And there was nothing further on the play or its slippery author.

I turned to the sports section in the *Daily News* and read a story about the Yankees spring training camp down in Florida and how Don Mattingly was not there this season. Which saddened me immensely. So I turned to the movie clock to check out the offerings.

When I was through with the paper, I pushed it aside. Ruby was still doing the crossword puzzle in the *Post.* She looked up at me and smiled.

"What's a five-letter slang word beginning with *f* and ending with *o* that means adipose?" she asked.

"Fatso."

"That's right."

Ruby just kept smiling at me, making no move to fill in the squares with *f-a-t-s-o.* I decided to change the subject fast.

"Today's my day for the scut work of being a detective—checking through the uniform reports myself, double-checking with the forensics lab, revisiting the crime scenes."

"Sounds like drudgery."

"Well, it is. Unavoidable, though. Even for a detective on special assignment from the mayor, no less, charged with the job of routing the unholy murdering scourge of Hell's Kitchen, and thereby soothing the raw nerves of all New York."

"That's nice, dear." Ruby folded up the newspaper in front of her. "Listen, I'm going to be making some telephone calls this morning. By this afternoon I'll have a gym lined up for you, like we were talking about."

"I don't remember talking about that."

"Oh? Well anyway, I'll see about having a personal trainer, too. He'll work out some exercise routines for you."

"Come on—what's this all about?"

"You're becoming larger than life, Irish. I don't mean in the heroic sense."

"A couple of pounds I might have put on, but—"

"Face it, dear. You're on your way to becoming a giant balloon floating over Broadway in Macy's Thanksgiving Day Parade."

"By the way—for God's sake, who needs a personal trainer?"

"You do. As long as you're going to sweat, you should have someone make you like it."

"How long have you been plotting this torture?"

"Don't think of it that way."

"What do you call exercise in a gym?"

"A simple pleasure. Good medicine for the strain of a complex life."

"Unless you're a thief, running around is unnatural." Besides which, I thought to myself, the closest thing I've ever known to a personal trainer is Brother Earl.

Wanda returned with breakfast. This did not make things any easier. Ruby watched my every bite, rolling her eyes whenever my knife went for the butter.

I ate with resentment. Going to this gym of Ruby's would interfere with plans I had for slipping into the Royal Bijou to catch Richard Basehart, Scott Brady, and Jack Webb in the 1948 semidocumentary cop flick *He*

Walked by Night. Watching other cops go through hell on a case sometimes helps, even if they are only movie cops.

"Don't forget, we're going to Stuart Godwin's house tonight," Ruby said.

"We are?"

"For the staged reading."

"But I can't do that and the gym, too." Aha! My way out. "I've got a whole lot of housekeeping on this case, and I have to get it done before I pick up the car and leave town tomorrow, and—"

"Where do you think you're going?"

"I told you, there's somebody I have to see."

"The hermit? A woman I could understand. But you can't be just an ordinary jerk husband, can you, Irish? You have to go off and see some wacko on a mountain."

"The name is Creepy Morrison."

"Of course. Only you would have an appointment with someone named Creepy."

"It's Father Gerald Morrison actually. I need his help."

"How come?"

"I'm just a cop. Cops know only so much about evil. Creepy Morrison's a Jesuit."

"I see." From the way she said that, it did not sound as if Ruby saw. At least not yet.

"Good, I'm glad you understand how I've got a lot on my mind. How I haven't got time for playing around in some gym this afternoon."

"Make time, belly boy. I'll be calling you at the station house with marching orders."

"Any percentage in my arguing the point?"

"In another life, I made the trains in Italy run on time."

"I always suspected something like that. So while I'm sweating today, what's your plan?"

"Wouldn't you like to know."

†

The six flights did me in. I collapsed at my desk and used a paper towel to wipe my face and neck. I suppose

Ruby was right about the gym, not that it made the idea any more acceptable to me.

Lieutenant Rankin's pungent aroma hung over the squad room—body odor mainly, but also the stink of a half-gone Winston left burning in a tin ashtray. Rankin himself was temporarily absent. It was not hard to guess his location, what with all the flushing going on in the hallway lavatory.

I picked up a pencil and made a list of housekeeping tasks on a fresh pad. This took a minute, after which I went to the top of the list and made my first phone call.

Officer Tyrone Matson was pulling a day shift. A piece of luck, I was able to talk with a friendly source. I caught him in the middle of running some nervous victims through mug shot albums. He was in a talkative mood. Talkative like King Kong Kowalski can get.

"You don't stay a rookie for long at Sex Crimes," Matson said. "A little birdy told me I'd get hard-assed on this job. Well, a great big birdy. Anyhow, he was right."

"What do you have?"

"Private party at a commuter bar."

"Usual suspects? Usual short-con?"

"Who else but a bunch of suits from Jersey?" This was a rhetorical question, requiring no response from me. "So anyhow, the suits are lured into the back room by working girls who nuzzled them for private drinkies away from the crowd. Pretty soon, the suits are blasted and the girls claim they're all of a sudden in love and start stripping."

"And the suits, so to speak, follow suit?"

"The old story, right. The working girls help the johns get comfortable by taking off their pants and hanging them up over chairs near the door. The suits are now prancing around in their boxers, and they're not watching the door."

"Frolic ensues, after which the suits go home to Jersey with big smiles on their faces."

"Right. Then they get undressed in their nice Jersey bedrooms with the wall-to-wall carpeting. They go to hang up their suits in the closet, and they are naturally outraged to discover their wallets were lifted out of their pants."

"The classic mistake," I said. "Johns are always ignoring the whereabouts of their pants."

"Jesus, men are stupid. I ask myself sometimes, Is there any hope? What do you think, Detective?"

"Men are idiots, and I notice women are making great strides toward equality."

"I guess that's something to think about."

"About these poor downtrodden victims you're showing the pictures to. Did they come to you on the rebound?"

"Of course. Central Robbery doesn't want to deal with the creeps. So they're bounced on over here. It makes the vics think the department gives a damn about their losses."

"Kowalski solicits the bounce?"

"The boss enjoys having dickprint candidates around."

"Short of that, what's your resolution?"

"Flipping through the mug files of known pross lets them vent. That's about as far as it ever goes. I tell them there might be a trial, that the opposing attorney will want to be asking a lot of public questions."

I wanted a drink. So I changed the subject.

"The other night, when I met up with you and Webster on West Forty-first . . ."

"After the Good Friday killings. Those guys marching with the cross?"

"That's it. At the same time, in the next block, you'd collared this John named Irvine."

"Another beauty from Jersey. Makes his living off the Fetus and Flag set."

"That's the one, the Christian Coalition guy."

"Naturally he was getting it on with a tranny."

"That I don't care about. This Irvine guy, he saw a gunman escape—"

"Sure, the one they're calling the Ghost Killer—the shadow. You know, I went back there to take a look at where Irvine said the guy came down off the roof of that recording studio."

"Good. Save me some time, Matson. Tell me how it played to you."

"Seems strange—they got all that high-priced hardware up on the roof, satellite dishes and like that, and yet it's nothing to scale the wall."

"How so?"

"Crates are stacked up near the loading docks, like a regular stairway. A man gets to the top of the pile, it's nothing to hop a little, grab hold of the parapet, and scramble on over the top by kicking his legs."

"Still, he'd have to be in pretty good shape."

"Oh, I don't know. I think even you could do it."

"Thanks a lot, Matson." So I could eliminate Superman from my list of suspects, I said to myself. Any schlub in need of gym sessions could scale that studio roof from the back end, do his shooting at the front, then drop back down to the dark emptiness of West Forty-first. "I'll be back to you later."

"Anytime."

Next, I called up Central Homicide. I expected little, which came in the form of Officer Caras.

"Naw, nobody's remembering seeing nothing but the shadow," he said. "I got all the reports right here in front of me. No weapon recovered, not to mention the rabbi's face."

"The killer just walked into the service like he belonged? Then did what he had to do?"

"That's the way it plays."

"Forensics recover anything at all?"

"Nothing spectacular. Some wool threads. Charcoal gray. Full of dirt and smelling funky, like the guy never heard of a dry cleaner. The blood, that all checks out to Rabbi Paznik. The usual kind of street schmutz from shoes tracking through the carpet. Of course, it's only a guess whose shoes made the prints, you know? Turns out the rabbi and the killer, they're about the same size."

"Did you background the witnesses?"

"Sure we did. Fourteen straight-arrow Jew retirees, except for this one broad's a notorious mah-jongg cheat and one of the old gents one time fed poison hamburger to a dog owned by an upstairs neighbor because the yapping was driving him nuts. Which in my personal book don't make him such a bad guy, since I hate dog owners."

"Why is that, Caras?"

"People who keep dogs, they don't have the guts to bite people themselves."

"I see. So you're telling me that none of what you've got so far is going anywhere."

"No, it ain't."

"Anything more out of Mr. Glick?"

"Oh yeah . . . he says he wants to be helpful. To you, Hockaday, since you're some kind of . . . Oh, I don't know, he starts in with that Hebe jabber and I don't follow. That's why I had to go and write down the message."

"Rodef shalom?"

"Whatever." I heard Caras rustle through paper. "Okay, I found it."

"The message?"

"Yeah, it's another Hebe word."

"Hebrew."

"Whatever. I got to spell it: *z-a-c-h-o-r.* I as't him what it means, he says maybe you'd know."

"I don't. But I can find out."

Lieutenant Rankin came clomping in, tucking his shirt and buckling his belt after his ablutions next door. I rang off with Caras.

"Well, well—I didn't know we'd be seeing your celebrated likes around our humble quarters so soon," Rankin said. He bent over the refrigerator and pulled out a can of Yoo-Hoo. Before sitting down behind his desk, he slammed the top of the oscillating fan, which brought some moving air to the squad room. Rankin picked the Winston from the ashtray and puffed at it. "I heard about the exceptional clearance order you got from Inspector

Neglio. Also I seen the papers, cover boy, and how the mayor's your number one fan. So what are you doing around here with us peasants?"

"Phone calls, like a cop has to make. By the way, I can give you a line on that coronary scam giving you trouble up on Restaurant Row."

"Oh, that? And just the other day you got no time for my troubles."

"You want to bust my chops or make a collar?"

"I don't mind both."

I wrote off the lieutenant's remark to the phenomenon of a man with a title too big for his general good.

"There's a squatter by the name of Monaghan living in a sealed brownstone three blocks from here. He's got to be sixty years old or better and he's no wacko, so you won't have trouble." I wrote down the number of the house on West Fortieth Street, the one next to Sister Roberta's shelter. "Sharp dresser, good talker."

"He sound like an old sod mick?"

"If I was the kind to be counting insults, Looey, that's twice now you would have been thrown out the window."

"Don't be minding my mouth, Hock. It's your own you should be watching."

"One of the things the mayor and I talked about was dealing with chickenshit bureau cops like you, the kind that really tire my ass." I started dialing the phone. "The mayor gave me a private number. He said to call him up when I was having problems with a real class-A chickenshit . . ."

"Give us a break, Hockaday. Hang it up."

"My mouth's suddenly all right with you?"

"Just give me the address you wrote out. I'll send over a crew."

"Much better, Looey, maybe we can be friends someday." I hung up the phone, putting an end to my bluff, knowing it would come to haunt me as yet another grievance by the wreathing types. I got up from my desk and walked over to Rankin to hand him the slip of paper. "This

Monaghan, he should profile all the way. Call in your restaurant managers and you ought to be able to make the guy on a lineup. Just do me one favor."

"What's that?"

"Next door to where you roust Monaghan, there's a mission run by a nun—Sister Roberta Lowther. Make her know I'm no part of this."

†

Two more calls. One to Inspector Neglio to clear an out-of-town date with a hermit, one to the sector garage to reserve an unmarked car.

It was early to be calling Ruby, but I rang her anyway. There was no use avoiding her on the subject of my afternoon. She would only track me down.

"Housekeeping went faster than I thought," I said. "I don't suppose you're ready with that gym date."

"You mean you're freed up right now?"

"I guess."

"Good. As it turns out, the trainer wasn't available this afternoon. But he can take you now."

My luck.

Ruby told me to go to the Chelsea Racquet and Fitness Club down on West Eighteenth Street off Sixth Avenue.

"Take the train down to Union Square and stop off at that sporting goods shop on the north side," she said. "You're going to need tennis shoes, shorts, and a T-shirt and a jockstrap. Can you remember all that?"

"Actually I can."

"I can't wait to see you in your little gym shorts."

"You're coming to the gym?"

"No, Irish, I told you—I've got things to do this afternoon."

"What?"

"Wait and see."

Twenty-four

By now, the class mostly treated Thornton with respect. One imperious glare from those intelligent blue eyes of his could translate into an incomplete evaluation and a man was back to square one at charm school. There was a greater reason for respecting Thornton, though, and everybody knew it, even if they could not necessarily articulate it: Thornton was smarter than anybody in the room.

So when he walked into class in his crisp linen blazer and creased chinos and buck shoes, nobody in the crowd of baggy pants and ripple-soled oxfords and sweat-stained shirts with clip-on neckties snorted or farted or belched, as had been the general greeting on day one. The hang-over ratio remained just as high, though.

Professor Thornton, as per custom, marched first to the blackboard and chalked up the day's lesson theme: IS IT PROGRESS IF A CANNIBAL USES KNIFE & FORK? He then stepped to the lectern and spread out some papers he lifted out from his attaché, after which he fumped the microphone several times.

King Kong Kowalski leaned over and whispered into Harry Darcy's ear, "Reminds me of these two cannibals eating a comedian for dinner one night; the one cannibal, he says to the other one, 'This taste funny to you?' "

"Very droll, Kowalski."

"I got a million."

"Swell."

"Two old pensioners in Miami Beach decide to shack up together. The woman, she asks the man, 'Vot about de sex?' The old guy shrugs, he says, 'Infrequently.' The old gal, she asks, 'Is dot von vord or two?' "

Fump . . . Fump . . . Fump . . .

"Testing, testing . . ."

"Joseph Kowalski?"

"Present."

There was a smattering of careful laughter.

"So I hear." Thornton stepped from behind the lectern and walked slowly down through an aisle between chairs. He stopped at two chairs in the last row occupied by one man. "You're a big fellow with big things on his mind, Sergeant King Kong Kowalski. Incidentally, I understand you don't like that handle."

"Says who?"

"Says you, Kowalski. You're a big man with a big mouth." Thornton pointed to Harry Darcy on the next chair while he said to Kowalski, "On the first day of our little seminar, I heard you object to Mr. Darcy here calling you 'King Kong.' From all the way up in the front of this room I heard you. That's how big your mouth is, King Kong."

Before anyone could enjoy a laugh at Kowalski's expense, even a careful one, Thornton whirled around and said, "Come on—speak up, men. Let's hear how many more big gobs there are in class today. With enough of you *present,* I'll know that I've failed to inspire the least appreciation for civility and that we'll all just have to muddle through this whole exercise—from the top."

There was no sound.

"Now then, Sergeant Kowalski . . . That is how you'd prefer to be addressed?"

"Yeah."

"That would be 'Yeah, *sir.*'"

"Yes, sir."

"Better than I could have expected. Now then, Sergeant, as it has been observed, you're fat. And, as I've noted, you've an oversized mouth, a truly tiresome feature. But sometimes—especially in fat men, I've found—a big mouth camouflages big ideas, or big problems. Which is it with you, Sergeant?"

"I don't know what you're talking about, *sir.*"

"Really?" Thornton turned from Kowalski to Darcy. "Officer Darcy, cast your mind back to our first day together, when Sergeant Kowalski threatened you after you called him King Kong."

"Well, sir, I don't know . . ."

"Please, don't be insulting." Thornton held up a hand, like a traffic cop. "I heard everything exchanged between you two. You thought it private, but I heard. About the departmental 'custom' of dealing with 'rat bastards' like this Detective Hockaday who's been in the newspapers lately. I would consider that a threat, Officer Darcy."

"Well . . ."

Thornton addressed the whole room again. "Wouldn't every last man of you hear that as a threat—to Officer Darcy, or Detective Hockaday, or possibly both gentlemen?"

A murmur of unanimous agreement.

"Now then—you understand I have a keen sense of hearing, and a keen sense of interpreting what I hear," Thornton said to Kowalski. "Should I go on talking about what I heard said between you and Officer Darcy?"

"Hey, it's your class."

"Yours as well, Sergeant. Now, you'll remember that Officer Darcy cast aspersions as to your sexual preference?"

"I don't have to put up with this freaking crap!"

"Sensitive on this point, are we—sweety?"

"It ain't like that!" Kowalski's massive face and neck were shaking. "I'm telling you, it ain't!"

"Nonetheless, here you are—quaking with anger simply because a man called you sweety."

"A guy don't say that to another guy."

"Oh, but I think they do."

"Yeah, well—you're wrong as two left feet."

"Am I, Sergeant? After our first session here, exactly where did you happen to go for lunch?"

"How should I know?" Kowalski laugh-snorted. His face turned storm purple. "I'm a big guy, I eat at so many freaking places I lose track."

"I'd be surprised if you ever lost track of a certain bar in Hell's Kitchen . . ." Thornton paused, knowing the effect he would create. Indeed, Kowalski was humiliated. Every man in the room sensed it. "You and the bartender talked about Good Friday, the day of all those murders. Do you remember now, Sergeant?"

Kowalski said nothing.

"Can you remember talking about the two thieves who were crucified with Jesus?" Thornton's tone was merciless. "Remember—Dismas, Gemas?"

Sweat flooded out of Kowalski. In the long, gruesome moment that Thornton let him flood before speaking again, Kowalski might have lost a pound.

"Sergeant," Thornton said, moving to Kowalski, touching his arm. "I want you to come up to the front of the class with me."

"No."

"Think about your pension, Sergeant, and my opinion about whether or not you should get it. Or how about a more immediate thought? Such as whether or not I'll contact this Detective Hockaday about the threatening things you've said in this room. I understand the detective is pushing for a disciplinary hearing against you."

"How do you freaking know?"

"I do my homework, Sergeant Kowalski. I suggest you attend to yours. You've a lot of catching up to do. In the meantime, I believe I've asked you to step to the front of the class."

Kowalski struggled up from his chairs. Thornton turned and walked back up the aisle. Kowalski lumbered along behind him. He did not look at the other men as he passed them by, and they did not look at him. There was a shared sense of looming disgrace in the room; no matter what, Joseph Kowalski was a member of the cop tribe, and no cop enjoys viewing the degradation of another.

Thornton stood to the side of the lectern.

"So where do you want me?" Kowalski asked him.

"At the microphone, of course."

Kowalski did as he was told. He gripped the edge of the lectern with his wet hands. He turned and said to Thornton, angrily, "The bartender, he's got nothing to do with nothing, and so I ain't about to discuss him here!"

"No, that would be trite," Thornton said. "Why don't you tell us about her?"

"Her who?"

"*Her* as in your telling Mr. Darcy, 'Don't be talking about my woman.' "

"How do you know—?"

"I told you before, Sergeant—homework."

Kowalski just stood there, glaring first at Thornton, then at the men sitting quietly out front in rows. Thornton stepped to the blackboard again, picked up chalk, and hesitated.

"Sergeant, so that you don't think ill of me, I want you to understand something." Thornton had turned from the blackboard to speak to Kowalski. What he said was meant for all to hear. "This isn't personal between us. I'm only doing my job, which is to transform you into a receptive student. You may be interested to know that in the teaching trade, we refer to this as the bust-down. Being the first bust-down of a class is an honor you'll want to thank me for sometime in the future.

As for now—you're a new man today, Sergeant. Congratulations."

Thornton smiled. Kowalski looked like a man who had just been hit in the face with a pie. Thornton returned to the blackboard. Beneath what he had earlier written, he chalked the second part of the day's lesson: WHERE THERE IS YET SHAME, THERE MAY IN TIME BE VIRTUE.

Twenty-five

"Go slack in the abdominals and your body invites every ache and pain that ever was . . .

"Ten, eleven, twelve, thirteen . . . Keep breathing, so long as you breathe the right way, out on the stress point, you can do it!

"That's it. The heart rate's high, and we're moving, moving . . . burning and burning, working on strength and flexibility at the same time . . . Keep it up . . . Having fun?

"Thirty, thirty-one, thirty-two . . ."

Quent is the name of the guy Ruby found for me at the gym. He is thirtysomething, hard-bodied, fair-skinned, and dark-haired. He wears tight white denims and cowboy boots and an olive green suede jacket over a cream-colored silk T-shirt. Naturally, he is also in theater—in a way.

A young blond lady with a bare midriff, wearing aqua blue tights and matching sports halter and pedaling away to nowhere on a StairMaster machine, has suddenly caught Quent's principal attention. I am meanwhile left lying in a growing pool of my own sweat on an adjacent rubbery black mat, hands locked behind my neck, knees bent, belly crunching up and down. I am feeling skin folds, and I am feeling old. *Forty-four, forty-five, forty-six, forty-seven, forty-eight . . .*

"Yeah, you saw me?" Quent says.

"Well, for just a second." Blue Tights flashed her capped teeth. "I mean, like it went so fast."

"Keep going," Quent said, turning to me. Then back to Blue Tights. "Was I convincing?"

"Like what do you mean?"

"Did you sense the angst?"

"Jeez, like it was only dandruff shampoo."

"But, I was playing a guy in real misery."

"Yeah . . . I guess so." Blue Tights stopped pedaling. She picked up a terry cloth towel and daubed sweat beads from her face. "Like I never knew there was so much to it."

"Sure. It's a commercial. But it's acting. Anyway, that's the way I look at it."

"Like, you're a true artist?"

"You like artists?"

"Artists are cool."

"I have to look over my new eight-by-tens after this. You want to help?"

"Cool."

Postgym arrangements settled, Quent returned to business. He had me get up off the mat, wipe up my sweat with a towel, and follow him to a contraption whereby I cinched myself into a leather belt attached to a weighted pulley and squatted up and down until the point of fainting. After that, it was back to the mat.

I strapped two-pound weights around my ankles and knelt on all fours. One leg I tucked into my chest and thrust straight back, then repeated for three sets of ten reps; after this, I had to pump the leg straight up over my hips for another thirty reps; then a final thirty reps of crisscrossing the leg over the opposite buttock, then arcing it ungainfully out to the side as far as possible. I thought I was dead. Quent thought otherwise and had me perform the same torture with the other leg.

A flurry of push-ups was next. In another life, army basic training at Fort Dix, I was pretty good at push-ups—the real kind, military style, with legs and elbows locked and haunches raised and the whole body pumping up and down like a diving board. Quent was marginally kinder than the drill sergeant. He put me in modified position, knees on the mat so that only my upper body was lowered and lifted. And thus I learned how time is the thief of virility. After twenty modified push-ups, I again thought I was dead. Quent commanded five more.

"Stick with me, Hockaday, I'll make you clean and lean." He laughed darkly and motioned for me to get up from the mat. I was directed to sop up more puddles of sweat as fast as I could, then hustle along behind him while my heart rate was still up in order to get maximum aerobic value from the next method of killing me. No problem about keeping the heart pounding. Gasping and wheezing like the trucks I hear in the streets outside my window, I plopped down on a stationary bicycle with a lot of dials and graphs on a glowing dashboard where there should have been handlebars. Quent grinned—luridly—as he set the dials. Then asked, "You love your wife, Ruby, right, Hockaday?"

I would have said yes, but the only sound from me then was a grunt.

"After two or three more of these pleasurable sessions, Ruby's going to love you back like never before. Start pedaling, try to keep this digital readout here at eighty revolutions or higher."

"Let me ask you . . ." I had to pause. "Where do you know Ruby?"

"Oh, from back when she was in the advertising business. She handled casting calls from her agency before she went and bought the theater."

"I see."

"Yeah, she's all right," Quent said. "She put me in my first commercial, actually. For a brand of scented shaving cream. Then later, I had some work at her theater, the Downtown Playhouse."

"I don't get it about the scented shaving cream. You shave, then you put on lotion. The lotion's got an aroma. Who needs scent in the shaving cream?"

"Americans like smelling good. What can I tell you?" Quent stepped close to my bike and read the dials. "You slipped down to seventy-two. Keep it at eighty or over."

"What did you do at Ruby's theater?"

"I played the white guy whenever one was needed. Did you see me?"

"Afraid not."

"Ruby tells me she's selling the theater."

"That's right. Money troubles. Lucky for her, the real estate's worth something."

"She tells me she's back into acting herself. Commercials, legit—anything she can get."

"That's right."

"In fact," Quent said, "I guess I'll see you two tonight."

"You got a call for the reading?"

"Oh yeah, that crazy play. Just keep pedaling, try pumping up to ninety revs."

Quent walked over to the television set that had been blasting out MTV junk since I arrived. He turned up the volume. Possibly there were slack-jawed creatures on Mars who could not quite hear the latest stylings of the latest forgettable band, composed of pimply faces with drug-heavy eyelids screaming in a vaguely southwestern dialect.

A guy about my own age—a guy after my own heart—comes walking into the gym. He flips on the radio next to the television set and finds WBGO-FM out of Newark. Young Jeanie Bryson, God bless her for being a golden exception to the rule, is singing a Patti Page tune—"Some Cats Know." Out of respect, the guy flips off the drug addict with the guitar currently sliding over the television screen for the slack-jaws on their StairMasters.

Somebody shouts, "Hey!" There is a silent chorus of

dirty looks. Quent plays arbiter. He douses the radio and returns the tyranny of the lowest common denominator.

The poor WBGO guy does not want trouble. Lucky for him, he brought his trusty Walkman. I made a note to do the same good thing for myself next time.

Meanwhile, for the next thirty minutes or so I died numerous times, as much from the music as from the exercise. Quent encouraged me by suggesting that fitness was next to godliness. I told him as a physical trainer he would make a great nun.

Just as it helped to think of nuns when I felt the urge to reintroduce myself to Mr. Johnnie Walker, it helped to think of them on the rowing machines and the tricep lifters and the over-the-shoulder pulls and all the other cold, black, steely machinery that was supposed to inspire godliness.

On the other hand, I turned to thoughts of Ruby waiting for the new and improved me to show up at home. I pictured her lying in the middle of a bed covered in white sheets, mocha skin soft and dark and smelling of blueberry, beneath something in ivory satin lace high up the thigh, her fingernails and toenails painted plum red.

Sheets!

"Girls, you must never let a boy take you to a restaurant with white tablecloths," Sister Roberta said. We boys of Holy Cross, suspecting the worst impulses thwarting our advances against our opposite numbers, recruited spies in the girls' hygiene class. And so we knew precisely what sinister things Sister was saying. "It might put the image of sheets in his head!"

When the interrupting nuns and the exercises finally did me in, I crawled upstairs to the men's locker room and sprawled on my back on top of a wooden bench for about twenty minutes. I was breathing like a racehorse, and damping down yet another surface with my sweat.

I then luxuriated for a quarter hour in a steam room, and topped this off with a shave (unscented) and a cold shower. I had to admit that I felt maybe fifteen pounds lighter, and maybe ten years younger. But I harbored the suspicion it would not be long before stiffness would have its way with me.

I left the gym and caught the IRT Broadway line uptown to Forty-second Street and stopped in one of the few recent additions to the new family-friendly Times Square I care to patronize: the Stardust Dine-O-Mat, where the waitresses wear khaki uniforms and peaked overseas caps like the Andrews Sisters on canteen duty at the U.S.O.; they look ever ready to burst into a few bars of "Boogie-Woogie Bugle Boy." Besides which, the Stardust knows from egg creams and tin roofs and extra-extra-thick chocolate malteds served with long spoons in stainless steel canisters—the latter of which was my revenge for an afternoon's torture conspired by Ruby, Quent, nuns on the mind, and MTV.

One booth over from mine sat a Middle American family—Mom and Dad, two boys aged about ten and twelve, a teenage daughter with braces on her teeth—chatting with one another in flat midwestern tones. They were there for the early-bird blue plate special. I enjoyed the thought of those kids somehow finding a way of becoming seduced by the Gotham beneath the suburban glitz of this generally awful new Times Square. Dad, bless his heart, shoved enough coins into the tabletop juke for a fine medley, the first tune of which came up as Vera Lynn singing " 'Til the Lights of London Shine Again."

I flashed on an old Lillian Ross story I read a number of years ago in *The New Yorker* magazine called "The Yellow Bus," in which a gang of high school kids from Kansas visits New York City on their senior class trip. All the kids decide the city with its winos and grifters and noise and dirty streets is totally horrid—*gross,* as kids today would put it—except for a boy who knows at once that New York is the city of his dreams and destiny; the place that will allow him to soar above and beyond the lowest common denominator. One taste of the Apple, and this boy is gloriously seduced and corrupted, thus promising new life to the old town for all the rest of us.

I imagined my own kid as that boy in the yellow bus. He was my kind of kid. Ruby's, too. Right then and there in the Stardust Dine-O-Mat, I promised our kid good music on a juke, and to otherwise insure him with the strength and grace of real melody.

My kid!

I sipped my extra-extra-thick malted and stared at that tourist family in the next booth and thought about the sea of changes I have known in New York; how some of it gladdens me, how some of it pains my middle-aged heart. I said a little prayer that at least one of this mom and dad's three wide-eyed kids would somehow be gloriously seduced and corrupted.

Dad quietly settled the bill, and the family rose from their booth, moving toward the door. The juke was playing the last of Dad's tunes, Coleman Hawkins's rendition of "Crazy Rhythm."

The girl with the braces on her teeth stopped in the doorway, entranced, her ears cocked to hear the last swinging chords of the Coleman Hawkins orchestra. She tugged at her daddy's sleeve and asked him, "Is that really the way it was?" And Dad said, "Yes, and it was great." The girl said "Wow!" and gave joy to my New York soul.

†

Walking toward home across Forty-third Street, with the malted milk a guilty lump in my stomach, I had less sanguine thoughts. Old Mr. Glick and his one-word message came to mind in a strangely urgent way. I stopped to use the public phone at Eighth Avenue, unable to wait until I was home and could call him from the comfort of my green chair. I dialed Glick's flat in Herald Square.

"Yes?" It was a pained, scratchy voice that answered, an old woman's voice.

"I'm calling for Mr. Glick, please. My name is Neil Hockaday."

"You're the nice policeman who brought my brother home from temple?"

"Oh, I'm speaking to his sister?"

"Minnie Katz. It's my married name."

"Is your brother there?"

"Sam's gone, Mr. Hockaday."

Did I ever know his name was Sam? No, and shame on me for that.

"What time will he be in?"

"He won't."

"Mrs. Katz—?"

"Sam's gone."

I waited a moment. I could hear old Sam Glick's sister using a tissue.

"Mrs. Katz, I have to ask you something. It's unpleasant. I'll make it quick."

"About how Sam died?"

"Yes."

"Don't worry, Mr. Hockaday. It wasn't like the rabbi. Nobody hurt Sam."

"Thank God."

"I should tell you, Sam loved the both of you young fellows. He was a plain man, from plain people in the old country. But you know, he had a welcome ear for the sound of intelligence. He told me all the smart talks you and Rabbi Paznik had. Oh, but he loved hearing them."

"Mrs. Katz, how did Sam die?"

"He was old, he went in his sleep. Nice and peaceful. The day before, I knew he was leaving. You know how?"

"How?"

"Sam forgot his English. It flew from his head. Only Yiddish he could talk. And Hebrew, of course. So I just knew he was going away."

"I understand."

Then I heard Sam Glick in my head, and felt strange urgency again:

A shadow, what is that? A destroyer of light, yes? Light we need to see. Therefore, we do not actually see a shadow, Maybe you think it's crazy what I'm saying . . . I have known shadow in my life. Please understand me . . . We old Jews know what to fear in the dark: the terror of imagination . . . Och! In English I don't know the words strong enough.

"Sam tried calling you, Mr. Hockaday. He left a message with another policeman. Did you ever get it, dear?"

"Yes—*zachor.*"

Twenty-six

SISTER ROBERTA HERSELF ANSWERED the frantic pounding at the back door. She had been enjoying a cup of tea at the kitchen table, and the one brief hour of the day when everybody in the house was gone—to work, or errands—and Sister had time for such things as crossword puzzles or novel reading or writing letters to family in Ireland.

At first, the pounding on the door had frightened her. She jumped in her chair and spilled the teapot, scalding a wrist in the process. But soon she would know better than to be frightened.

She took a cold, wet dishrag from the sink and wrapped her wrist—probably the wrong thing to do; probably she should apply salve, and a warm compress—and called out to whoever was banging so urgently, "We're coming, we're coming!" She had the presence of mind to say "we," reasoning that an intruder under the influence of darker angels might behave himself thinking it was not just one little old nun at home all by herself.

"Who is it?" Sister said, a hand resting atop the police bar braced against the back kitchen door.

"It's I, Sister—Eoin Monaghan. Please—oh please, let me in!"

There was no mistaking Mr. Monaghan's voice. Sister's stiff hands fumbled with the police bar, then the three dead bolts, then the chain locks.

"Hurry! Please!"

Finally, Sister opened the door.

"What is it, Mr. Monaghan?"

Her neighbor rushed past her, turned, and shut the door. He did not slam it.

"They're after me, Sister. It's all so embarrassing. Really, good God, I'm terribly ashamed. I don't know where to turn but to your own pure heart."

"After you? Whatever do you mean?"

"Coppers."

"Dear God!" Sister slapped a hand to her mouth. She clutched at Eoin Monaghan's cashmere woolen coat sleeve, pulling him across the kitchen floor, out through a pantry, and into the safety of a windowless dining room where she sat him down at a table. He always dressed so nicely, she thought, even frazzled as she was. The cashmere felt like butter. The gloves he wore—like the upper-class gents of Dublin, as she remembered from childhood—were even the creamy color of butter. "Now what's this all about, Mr. Monaghan?"

"I'd give anything to spare you this bother of mine, dear Sister Roberta . . ." Monaghan clasped his heaving chest with both hands. "But as I'm poor as the mice sharing my own quarters, I'm forced to appeal to your charitable view."

"The coppers are trying to run you out from your squat?" Suspicion unsweetened Sister Roberta's face. "Is that what you're saying?"

"Aye, you've put it just right by today's lexicon. Poverty's always been a crime, and the wrong people are forever being held responsible."

"Tell me—who's over there to your place now?"

"A pair of coppers suddenly come snooping up front. Of course, they can't get into the house that way. But they were making a racket on the door with their nightsticks all the same, and waked me from a fine nap I was having."

"They're still there?"

"So far as I know. When they crept 'round the side alley, I lit out from the back over to here. God, but I'm so embarrassed."

"Yes, you said that, Mr. Monaghan."

"Why do you never call me Eoin?"

"I don't know . . ." Sister was flustered. "You just seem so fine and all, like a right gent deserving of being called mister."

"I'm hardly so. Poor and idle, that's truly me. A double reproach on society. I try hiding the poverty from others, and the idleness from myself." Monaghan cupped his head in his hands. "Would you have any whisky in the house?"

"I would. It's good quality, nothing to be drowning self-pity."

"Your mercy will be appreciated. And you know better than I how you'll be rewarded in eternity."

Sister fetched him a glass and bottle of twelve-year-old Glenlivit Scotch. She set these down on the table and said, "Feel better, Mr. Monaghan, but no more. I'll be leaving you for a short time."

"Leaving . . . ?" Monaghan's voice became uneasy. "For where?"

"I'll just scoot over to have a word with these coppers."

Sister turned. Monaghan took her arm and stopped her, whirled her back around, took her hand and gave it a continental buss.

"Dear God!" Sister's face broke into a cherry flush. "There's a thrill I haven't known since girly days back on the other side!"

"Here now—where's your jar, Sister, and what's your hurry?" Monaghan pulled at the fingertips of a glove, as if by habit to remove it, then stopped. He took up the Glenlivit bottle and poured himself a finger of thick gold. "Won't you join me?"

"But the coppers?" How she wanted to stay, alone, with her fine gentleman friend. She crossed herself.

"Please—don't go."

"I must, I must."

He could have stopped her again, of course. But instead he put back his drink, and poured another.

Sister scurried through the pantry, crossing herself again, then on through the kitchen. She stopped for a moment at the sink, where she picked up the cool dishrag again and sponged her heated cheeks and forehead. Then she stepped out the back door into a garden patched with carrots and potatoes and peas and peppers and melons. The plants had only begun pushing leaves up through the rows of topsoil, bordered one from the other with rocks and cinders and marked with paper seedling packets speared to sticks. One of the guests had hosed the garden about a half-hour ago. The soil was still black and glistening wet.

A chill was coming with the early sundown. Sister rubbed her hands together. She looked to the house next door. Boarded windows, crumbled brownstone, and a garden full of urban bramble; a dung heap she often called it, through which her eyes moved uneasily; a morass of weeds and glass and shards and tin cans and odd bits of cloth and broken toys, and stiff dead birds with their eyes plucked out by the hungry things that fed upon the mess.

Mr. Monaghan—her poor countryman; dear Eoin, as she indeed thought of him in her lonely place—went in and out of his decrepit shelter through the dung heap. Sister Roberta shivered. In and out from this shameful old house of whores' ghosts, this house that birthed the unholy name of Hell's Kitchen. *Dear God!*

Sister's ears pricked beneath her veil. A rustling sound from the bramble. Coppers? She thought of Neil Hockaday, and how he might be the one who revealed poor Mr. Monaghan. *Oh, what betrayal! And here I was little Neil's own teacher!* Again, the sweetness fled from her face.

"Hallo!" she called, with a sharp edge to her voice; and

God help Neil Hockaday if he answered her call. "Hallo there!"

No answer.

Sister lifted her black skirts a few inches off the ground and sallied forth from her garden to the mess next door, prepared to boot a rat or starving cat to kingdom come if the creature should dare come close enough to her sturdy convent shoes. She walked this way, skirts raised and scowling, clear to the other side of the house full of whores' ghosts.

No coppers were there. But they had been, just as Eoin had said. For now Sister saw the second of two officers climbing back into the prowl car up in the street, and the first one sitting at the wheel. She ducked back and watched as the car moved off.

Sister started back toward her own house, first stopping for a moment at the open door her Eoin used to come and go from this dreadful squat she had never seen herself. It was a Dutch door, well built and intact after more than a hundred years, but ill-sized; with both halves open, a man would have to crouch to get through it. Sister was put in mind of a favorite Irish faerie book of her childhood, a pen-and-ink illustration of a black-hearted poem in which an ogress stands behind the Dutch door of a cottage, bristled arms spread over the half-sill, luring a curious boy in the lane with her singsong: "Cross patch, pull the latch, open my door, come in!"

Sister peered through the darkness of what she guessed to be a back kitchen, the layout being the same as her own house. There seemed to be light from some source up front, and after a few seconds, when her eyes had grown accustomed, Sister saw the outlines of walls and a corridor beyond the kitchen, and the remains of beautiful plaster mouldings.

A fine house this had been in its time, she thought. *What am I thinking? A fine house indeed!*

"Dear God!" she said aloud. She crossed herself and

turned away, shivering. The afternoon was growing as suddenly dark as it was growing cold.

Sister hustled past the old whorehouse to the comfort and safety and blessedness of her own sheltered quarters. *Well now, I might join Eoin in a few jars of whisky.*

At her own back door, she turned at a sound.

Another rustling from the putrid bramble across the way? A storm rising? A squirrel racing across utility wires?

Something closed over her throat, something from behind. Sister tried screaming, producing nothing but a hoarse puff. Something caught her flailing left hand at the wrist, yanked it behind her, pulling her arm so hard she heard bone break.

Then down she went, kicking and clawing through the struggling vegetable plants. Something dark, strong, and silent—and stinking—rode her back.

Her face went slamming into damp soil. Something straddled above her, something with overwhelming weight and power.

Sister Roberta used what breath she had to whisper prayers of self-preservation into the dirt. And prayers for the forgiveness of sin, even as she heard the tearing away of her skirts and knew, in clenching horror, the violation to come.

But before that, an unanticipated violence: the fierce stabbing pain in her broken arm; a swoon of dark colors behind her eyes; blood bursting from her wrist, slicking bared thighs and buttocks.

Twenty-seven

HERE NOW ARE RUBY AND I, stepping out of a taxicab in front of Nixon's place on East Sixty-fourth Street. Stuart Godwin's place, that is, he being the Broadway type who had a lot of answering to do about *Grief Street.* Ruby had her questions, I certainly had mine.

For the moment, Ruby and I were the only ones who arrived in a car that was yellow. The curb was lousy with BMWs and Jags. Everybody stepping out of the Beamers belonged to the same raffish contingent: young goombata from Bay Ridge or someplace who looked like and acted like the sons of don't-ask-who kind of men in the don't-ask-what kind of business. The Jags were transport for another class: men who were prettier than a lot of women I have seen in my life.

Also there was a parade of plain black cars with tinted windows. Liveried drivers would step out and open doors for the type of silver-templed, suntanned guys who have so much money they do not carry actual cash.

Some more regular taxicabs like ours started showing up. White women in their thirties piled out of these. They all wore black dresses and blond hair, and came in groups.

"You always see them at rich guys' houses, and they

always bring girlfriends," Ruby whispered as we walked up to the door, pointing at these groupings. "You're going to see squadrons of them tonight, looking for men and pretending not to."

There was a party going on inside the house, audible every time the butler opened up to admit somebody. As he was letting us in, a couple of hammered, sweaty-faced young guys with low-ball glasses in their hands stumbled out into the street to have themselves a puke break.

"So this is show biz?" I asked Ruby.

"It's the part we call Deep Backstage, it's not always pretty," she said. "Don't you know that all the wrong people own the money?"

Nixon's old salon—the big oblong room at the lower back end of the house, French doors leading out to a Japanese garden—was crawling with wrong people. Ruby and I snaked through a path of Armani suits and Donna Karan cocktail frocks in the general direction of the bar.

I managed to get us a pair of seltzers with lime. Myself because I am a drunk, and Ruby because she had to perform.

A squadron of black dresses gave me the once-over and moved on, unimpressed. They nibbled low-fat carrot cake covered in low-fat cream cheese frosting, poking at it with sterling forks that had prongs sharp enough to break skin. The goombata hovered over a long table full of shucked oysters fanned out on a bed of crushed ice. A couple of silver-templed guys were talking investments: derivatives, whatever they are. Two ladies who fill their days with shopping and starving themselves were having a lively discussion about a scandal at the neighborhood prep school where their boys Spencer and Porter were students.

Spencer? Porter?

"My son tells me they snort it for extra concentration just before a test."

"Has Porter actually used it?"

"Well of course not. But everybody knows it's going on. Porter says the snorters use Bic pen barrels."

"And Spencer says they cut the Ritalin into lines, just like coke. But where do they get it?"

"Porter says the bigger boys steal the pills from little dorks with A.D.D.—attention deficit disorder. Twenty milligrams goes for four dollars."

"Oh—and have you heard what the girls do?"

"No."

"They carry around the stash in those adorable black and yellow Carmex lip gloss tubs from Caswell-Massey."

We were spared anything further on the subject of upscale drug addicts in the person of Stuart Godwin, who came sweeping up beside Ruby and introduced himself—to her but not me, even though I was standing right there. He was dressed in loose black silk pants, a maroon velvet smoking jacket with black satin shawl and belt, wing-collar formal shirt, and speckled bow tie. His black hair was combed straight back and brilliantined. He looked like a movie cad, circa 1930. He was only fifty years old or so and would have had to study that 1930s look. His face was powdered and lightly pancaked, and he smelled like a guy who shops at Bijan of Fifth Avenue, by appointment only. Also he was waving around a perfumed cigarette in a tortoiseshell holder, like Noël Coward.

"Now, you would be our Annie Meath, isn't that right?" he asked Ruby.

"And you would be our producer?"

"Oh, that depends on so many little things."

I said to Godwin, "Let me ask you something . . ."

"By the way, Mr. Godwin," Ruby said, "this is my husband, Neil Hockaday."

"But of course, the police detective from the tabloids." Godwin gave me a once-over that lingered more appreciatively than what I got from the blondies in the black dresses. He turned to Ruby, and said, "Call me Stuart."

"Listen, Stuart," I asked, "where's the playwright?"

"I'm afraid that's one of the little things. For all I know, the author could be one of us here in the room. I'm as much in the dark about him as everybody else here.

Which of course can't last forever if I'm going to involve myself as producer."

"No, of course not," Ruby said.

"All I know is that I received this wonderful script in the mail," Godwin said. "And then a follow-up telephone call, asking if I'd care to host a backers' audition."

"I see you're happy to oblige," I said.

"And why not? I thought perhaps it might flush out our author. It's all very deliciously mysterious, don't you think, Detective Hockaday?"

"Especially the part about people getting murdered."

"Well, I don't know about that . . ." Godwin puffed furiously on his cigarette.

"The caller, what did he sound like?"

"Am I being interrogated, Detective?"

"If that's what you want to call it."

"Well . . . He was a mature man, not old but mature. Quite articulate. Elegant, I would say. I had the feeling he was speaking through some sort of material, as if he'd wrapped the telephone in wool, something like that."

"Did he have an accent of any sort?"

"I don't think so. I really don't remember. I was just so shocked to be dealing with someone like this."

"So, besides asking you to assemble the deep pockets, what else did he have to say?"

"He kept the conversation short. I don't think he spoke for more than half a minute. Just enough time to ask me the favor, you see."

"I see."

Godwin puffed some more. He turned to Ruby. "Do you like my house?"

"It's very beautiful, this room." Ruby took in the salon decor: hand-carved plaster walls painted in creamy yellow tones, black-and-white photo portraits of the New York theatrical world, ceiling rosettes and softly lighted chandeliers, Bokhara rugs, long couches covered in taupe suede, fresh flowers in tall vases everywhere, a regiment of potted palms, a mahogany bar fitted into a corner, and the meticulous garden just a few steps through the leaded-glass doors. There were folding chairs temporarily set up in the corner opposite the bar, grouped in front of stools and music stands; the stools were for the actors, each music stand held a script of *Grief Street*. Ruby said, "I understand the house was owned by the Nixons years ago."

"Yes, poor Pat and Dick were forced to buy."

"Forced?"

"Actually, they preferred the ease of an apartment. They made offers at a number of co-op buildings around town—Beekman Place, Sutton Place, Park Avenue, and so forth. One by one, the co-op boards rejected the Nixons as undesirable neighbors."

"Delicious," Ruby said.

"Yes. And so it's how they came to buy this house. It sat empty for nearly a year during the renovation work the Nixons wanted. As well as the Secret Service, I suppose." Godwin rolled his eyes. He cupped a hand to his mouth confidentially, and asked Ruby, "Would you like to know a little house secret?"

"Sure."

"For the renovations in the master bedroom, Nixon's contractor hired a Zen Buddhist bathroom designer."

"Only in New York."

"Naturally. The designer decided that Nixon's soul required extreme purification, and that the bathroom was of course the place where this could best occur. And so he had some co-religionists come by on the eve of the final design stage, the painting. Zen slogans were applied to all the walls, after which there was much chanting—then, an exorcism was performed for the benefit of the wicked president."

"And the next day it was all covered up?"

"Yes, with Dutch tiles and a glaze of royal blue. Nixon was never the wiser."

A young blond man with earrings and a deep suntan sidled up next to Godwin. He was maybe twenty-five years old and wore an open purple silk sports jacket, without benefit of a shirt underneath. The wavy golden hair covering his very impressive pectoral muscles was as carefully combed as my head.

"Oh!" Godwin said. He rose about an inch from the floor on the balls of his feet, as if he had been goosed from behind. He turned to the taller man at his side, smiled, and offered a cheek for a kiss. "Johnny, sweety—meet my new friends."

Godwin was kissed on the cheek. He turned and received a peck on the other. To Ruby and me, Johnny offered his shaking hand.

"Johnny Kay, this is Ruby Flagg, the actress . . ." Johnny and Ruby shook. "And her husband, Detective Neil Hockaday of the New York Police Department. Watch out, Detective Hockaday seems to be in the investigative mood."

"You look familiar," I said to Kay.

"Oh, really?" Ruby asked, curious and amused at once.

"I work in Hell's Kitchen," Kay complained. "Maybe

you've seen me around. I work at a little place behind the bus terminal. The Savoy Bar and Grill."

"Small world. I was near there last Friday night."

The Savoy was a mind-your-own-business after-five watering hole with two things in the window: dark curtains and a discreet sign that announced the inside as a place FOR A GAY OLD TIME. On the other side of Ninth Avenue from the Savoy is where a Christian Coalition john by the name of Ralph Irvine and Trixie the tranny were interrupted by the flight of my shadowy quarry.

"I'm so sorry you didn't stop in our establishment," Kay said. He had a smirk on his face, the kind I do not appreciate. "It would have been my pleasure to serve you."

"How do you know where I live, Johnny?"

"You're a community legend. What with that spread in the *New York Post* and all."

I wanted to go at Kay sideways for a while, to see what it was behind that smirk of his. But Godwin broke it up.

"Detective Hockaday—please, you mustn't give all my guests the third degree." Godwin said this with a reedy Noël Coward laugh. Then he took Kay's arm. "Come now, Johnny, let's toodle off and leave Ruby and her policeman to mingle with the others. Ruby, dear—we'll be starting up in about five minutes."

Ruby nodded. Godwin and Kay toodled.

"There's something about that guy," I said.

"Which one?" Ruby asked.

"Johnny Kay . . . Something familiar. But I can't get a fix on him." So I thought about things, including something I had been meaning to ask Ruby. "Speaking of mysterious, you've been close-mouthed about your day. What's up?"

"Oh, big news, Irish. Really big—"

"Girlfriend, how are you doing?" This was Quent interrupting, Ruby's actor friend and the guy at Chelsea Racquet and Fitness Club who was responsible for the wracking pain in my legs, ankles, hips, stomach, and shoulders. He was drinking beer from a bottle. Which he stopped doing while he and Ruby air-kissed like a couple of Hollywood stars. Then Quent asked, "Is your husband mad about my killing him today?"

"He's grateful, so am I," Ruby said, laughing. Quent was smart enough to read off of my face that he should keep his own straight.

"So," he asked Ruby, changing the subject, "do you think this play has a chance of actually going up?"

"Who knows?"

"It's a damn good story. And beautifully written."

"Not to mention the press it's getting from the weird connection to these murders . . ."

"The hell with weird." Quent finished his beer. "You know how long it's been since I've had stage work?"

"I've been out of it myself."

"And here you're selling your very own theater."

"I didn't want to, I had to."

"*Had* to?" I said, cutting in. "As in the past tense? You mean it's sold?"

"Today," Ruby answered, with no further elaboration besides the big smile on her face. That was her news? Really big news it was. She turned to Quent. "But what about you? Didn't I read in one of the trades about something you had going not too long ago?"

"Yeah, last winter I had a one-man show with three other guys," Quent said. I thought to myself, Only an actor could deliver a line like that. "Since then it's like I can't get arrested."

"Ever think of writing a play?" I asked.

"Why?"

"Just curious."

"Maybe I should write. It's not like I want to spend the rest of my life working in a gym with guys gone to flab, you should pardon the expression." Quent considered the empty beer bottle he was holding. "Maybe I ought to get another one before we start."

Quent loped off to the bar and I asked Ruby, "Can he write?"

"Everybody thinks they can write. Especially unemployed actors."

"Anyway—so you closed on the theater today?"

"That's not all."

Ruby started to tell me more, but then Godwin broke things up again. He ding-dinged one of the skin-breaking sterling forks against a wineglass until everybody in the room fell to quiet.

"Boys and girls—let's all mosey over this way now," he said. He was standing in a back corner of the room with the folding chairs. Johnny Kay stood there beside him, looking through the crowd toward something up front. Godwin said, "It's show time."

Ruby kissed my cheek and left me for her place behind the music stands. Quent was already sitting on his stool, turning over script pages, lips moving as he read.

I sat down in a folding chair in the back row and waited, trying to guess Ruby's additional news. I might have got it, too, if not for the smell of grilled beef in the air.

Also there was suddenly a tapping on my shoulder.

I swiveled around in my chair and looked up at King Kong Kowalski.

"Bad news," Kowalski said. He was chewing on a hamburger wrapped in a yellow sheet of McDonald's waxed paper. *And how did he know where to find me?* "I'm talking real freaking bad."

Twenty-eight

"You're saying nobody could of got through the front door?" Kowalski asked the group of women assembled in the dining room. Webster and Matson were out back, shining flashlights around the garden where the struggle had taken place. A forensics unit was dusting for prints in the kitchen, where they had also taken the Glenlivit bottle and glass from the dining room.

"This here's a shelter, Sergeant," one of the women said. "It's where we run to so we can get away from all this kind of violent man-type shit . . ." She stopped, and broke into weeping. Two women closed around her, patting her back.

"We all of us got three kind of keys to get in and out of the shelter," another woman said. She held up a jangling chain for Kowalski to see.

"Anybody try breaking through the door, there's supposed to be a silent alarm go off at the police station," someone else said. "So whyn't *you* be telling *us* if the guy come through the front or not."

"Back door's wired up, too," the first woman said. "So's all the windows. Sister Roberta, she had to open up that back door to somebody she know."

There was general agreement on this point.

"And you were all gone out of the house at the time?" Kowalski asked. He was reading questions from a list he had dashed off on a pad, checking them off as he asked them.

"Yeah, just like we say. Some got jobs, some got counseling downtown. All of us got errands to do, people to see. You know."

"Now, when everybody came home this afternoon—"

"Marie, she was the one who found her like that."

"Marie—?"

"I got to tell you again?"

"Please."

"All right, it's my night in the galley," Marie explained. "So I get home after working, and I go upstairs to my room like everybody else. Only I don't get the chance to lie down for a nap like everybody else. Only got time to wash my face, then I go down to the kitchen to start up the dinner."

"That's when you found Sister?"

"Not right off. I set the kettles to boil, and I take out the salad things and put them on the chopping block to prep. I don't know why, but I never thought nothing of that back door being swung open like it was."

"Anyway," Kowalski said, "the next thing you did, you walked out back in the garden?"

"First, I notice the cup and saucer on the table. That ain't right. Supposed to be everybody clean up after themselves right away—Sister's rule. I go look at the cup, and see it's tea gone cold. That's strange. And that's when it finally hits me the back door's standing open."

"The door's not ordinarily open?"

"It's open plenty. Just not when it's getting to sundown is all."

"So you go outside then?"

"I go to the door, poke my head out, and I call, 'Sister Roberta, you out here?' It's dark, I can't see nothing."

"No answer."

"No, sir. That's when I figure something's real wrong. So I shut the door in a hurry and I bolt it. Then I run upstairs for Sister, only she ain't around . . ."

"Nobody seen her since coming home," somebody else said.

"That's right," Marie said. "We're all right scared then."

"So you came back downstairs together?"

"And when we do, that's when Doris seen the liquor out."

"That's right," Doris said. "Highly unusual. Sister takes a drink now and again, but not all alone like that."

"All right," Kowalski said tiredly. "Thank you, ladies."

He left them there in the dining room and plodded through the kitchen. On the way out to the garden he stopped to ask the forensics officers if they had found anything useful.

"Find us the rapist, and it's nothing to make a DNA match to the semen we scraped out of the nun," said the unit leader. He was a forty-year-old stocky guy by the name of Baldwin. Kowalski found him at the kitchen table, bent over a portable microscope and looking at advance specimens on glass slides. "But we're not dealing here with the so-to-speak garden variety rapist, are we?"

"We sure ain't."

"In that case, we're not likely to find DNA patterns on federal profile. So we can't advance a suspect." Baldwin returned to his microscope and continued talking. "That leaves us nothing but old-fashioned fingerprints, of which I'd say offhand we've got only one set. We'll know something inside of twenty-four hours, Sarge, but I can tell you by experience that somebody was wearing gloves. And I don't imagine that was Sister."

"Like what do you mean—latex gloves?"

"No. I'd say a fine fabric of some sort."

"Okay, thanks," Kowalski said. He had to turn sideways to get through the door into the open air, to where Sister Roberta had been attacked. She had long since been taken by ambulance to Roosevelt Hospital. Webster and Matson were still walking up and down the garden rows with their torches. Kowalski called to them, "Find it yet?"

Both officers responded in the negative.

"Jesus Christ!" Kowalski quietly cursed. The air was just cool enough for his breath to hang for a second in the black-and-blue night, after which he crossed himself. "Jesus freaking Christ!"

†

Kowalski had now told me everything. Everything, that is, up to the point of his stopping by Roosevelt Hospital to check on Sister Roberta's condition and then knowing where to find me so he could tell me the story.

We were standing outside Godwin's house on East Sixty-fourth Street, at about the same spot where the plastered young guys had earlier stumbled out to relieve themselves of too much liquor. Kowalski was smoking one of his Te-Amos. My head and stomach were feeling about the same as the young pukers.

"Let me guess," I said, "they didn't find it."

"Naw, this mutt who done Sister every which way—"

"Spare me the details, Sergeant."

"Anyways, this mutt, he cuts off her hand and takes it with him. Like maybe it's some kind of sick-assed trophy."

I ached for a drink. I could have gone back inside the house, bellied up to the bar, told the man to line them up. Nobody could have blamed me, not Father Declan, not even Ruby.

"Was it the left hand? The one with the gold band?"

"You think I don't notice that? I'm in the freaking Holy Name Society."

"God bless you, Sergeant."

"Like I say, this is one freaking sick-assed pervo." Kowalski took a Three Musketeers candy bar from his coat pocket. I remembered an advertisement in the back of comic books from my youth: a picture of the mustachioed trio of D'Artagnan's comrades pausing from a daring deed for a snack, under the slogan THREE MUSKETEERS, A

CANDY BAR BIG ENOUGH TO SHARE WITH A PAL. Kowalski did not share. He said, "Mind if I ask you something hypothetical?"

"Yes. But will it keep you from asking?"

"Supposing I find this pervo," Kowalski said, licking his fingertips, ignoring my answer. "I take him into my little parlor downtown. You know the one I mean?"

"The janitor's closet."

"That's right. I take this one into my parlor, I do the number on this nun-raping pervo . . . Which by the way, I hear this nun, she was a teacher of yours when you were a little kid at Holy Cross."

"What's your point, Kowalski?"

"The point is, I torture the shit out of this particular mutt, like I have done before to some deserving others. So now—you going to rat me out to IAD I took care of a sick-ass who stuck it to this nun of your youth?"

"All right, so you hypothetically catch this mutt," I said after thinking for a long moment. At least Kowalski had me thinking of something besides whisky. "Let's suppose you dickprint him. Would your conscience be clear?"

"Damn straight."

"That's what makes you and me two different kinds of Catholics."

"How's that?"

"You, Kowalski, are the type that delights the moralists of the world. You've got a talent for inflicting cruelty with a clear conscience. That's how they invented hell."

"That's one smart freaking mouth you got on you, Hockaday, but it don't make you better than me. Want to know how come?"

I said nothing, which of course did not keep Kowalski from doing the same.

"I seen your Sister Roberta over to the Roosevelt emergency room, right? I seen her there in a bed with that bloody stump at the end of her arm the mutt left her after doing what he did. She's in freaking shock from all the blood she lost. Nobody can get nothing out of her—not me, not the croakers, not even this old priest they scare up to give her last rites, okay? All she does is talk delirium. You don't want to know details like what the pervo done to her when he jumped her and tore off her habit? Okay, you're the sensitive type. But you really ought to know what Sister's saying in her delirium, at least what we can make out."

"What?"

"She's calling you out, Hockaday. She's spitting on your name. All my life, I ain't ever heard a nun so pissed off. Over and over she keeps gasping out the same thing—*Oh, what betrayal! And here I was little Neil's own teacher!* How do you freaking like that? How's *your* freaking conscience, Hockaday? All clear on that?"

Betrayal? What could I say?

"You think my kind of a Catholic heart ain't about cut out of my chest when I got to hear that? But it don't end there, Hockaday, you arrogant mick. The priest that come, it turns out he's a friend of yours, too. Jesus, I feel sorry for him. I feel sorry for anybody's got you for a friend."

"What priest?"

"Another mick—Declan Byrne."

"He gave Sister Roberta last rites?"

"Not so far as he's concerned, on account of Sister's completely out of it. This priest, he's doing all he can, but she don't understand him. She can't respond. All she's doing is spitting on your name. The priest, he's all broken up. Maybe he thinks if Sister don't make it through the night she's going to wind up with all the unbaptized babies in limbo or something. You being a real good type of Catholic, you know what that means—don't you, Hockaday?"

How many times as a boy at Holy Cross had I heard it explained in religion class? I knew . . .

Limbo is worse than hell itself. It's packed with heathens and pagans flying around and crying for their mothers because they'll never be admitted to the ineffable presence of

Our Lord and the glorious company of saints, martyrs, and virgins.

. . . And vengeful Kowalski would now have me know that Sister's worst fate would be my fault.

But at that moment—a terrible moment—Johnny Kay walked past the butler in the doorway. Finally, I had a fix on him.

Finally, after three days in which I felt as if I were bumping around in total darkness, I saw in the stricken faces of Johnny Kay and Joseph Kowalski something that made sense; a terrible sense, but only the beginning of it.

"I'll be heading inside now, Sergeant," I said as Johnny Kay walked up, as King Kong Kowalski's mighty jowls trembled. "I have the feeling there's nothing better I could do now than hear that play."

†

I made it back in time for the final scene of *Grief Street* . . .

> SETTING: the parlor bar of Annie Meath's bawdy house on West Fortieth Street, circa 1880.
>
> DRAMATIS PERSONAE: Annie (Ruby); the offstage presence of Sweeney (Quent, with hand over mouth); and Malloy (also Quent), a customer awaiting his turn for a room and prostitute.
>
> DENOUEMENT: an exchange between Annie and Malloy underscores the themes of memory, immigrant community, and political ideals arising from within a mystery narrative, in which a simple policeman—somewhat dull, but tenderhearted—confronts pure evil in his hunt for the killer of an American dream.

. . . And there was now no mistaking the message. Nor the messenger I myself was after in the real life mystery of who was killing the dreamers of Hell's Kitchen:

SWEENEY

(Offstage) Come turn up the light here, will you, Annie darling? It's so dark I ain't finding me girl I bought and paid for.

ANNIE

(Shouting up the stairway) The bloody sun hasn't light enough to brighten your pecker, Mr. Sweeney.

SWEENEY

Aw, g'way with you!

ANNIE

(Addressing MALLOY, seated at the bar) Listen to himself, will you? Can't even find the lamp. Most people go all their lives like him—fool blind, too stupid to walk 'round and find the gas wick so's they can turn it up and see.

MALLOY

A man living in this godforsaken quarter of the city, I say he's got the right to the peace and quiet of the dark.

ANNIE

But there's no comfort in that either, fool man. Never no peace in turning a blind eye to the grief of these streets. And sure no comfort in fatuous slogans by the political hacks. They're the ones putting daft into your head, Malloy.

MALLOY

Just how's that?

ANNIE

Persuading you to believe there's somehow comfort in blindness. As if we'll not be trampling each other to death when we're all crowded up into one dark room.

MALLOY

Your mouth's making more of the moment than warrants. I come here for the plainest peace and comfort there is—Annie Meath's whisky and Annie Meath's girls.

ANNIE

Oh, another blind pig I'm entertaining, is it? Shame on you, Malloy, forgetting what you come for—deep down, I mean. The promises, I mean.

MALLOY

Oh, Gawd—what promises?

ANNIE

Life . . . liberty . . . the pursuit of happiness. Are you forgetting how it was back there in the starving fields of the other side of the ocean?

MALLOY

Well, I'll thank you not to be morbid! Jaysus, woman—who'd want to dwell on fear and hunger and dying? Sure now I remember it all. And sure I remember first hearing the promises. But you'd do well to remember this, Annie: promises are made to be broken, even American promises.

ANNIE

You're a cynical bastard, Malloy.

MALLOY

Nae, merely a man who wants no further trouble in his poor life.

ANNIE

But don't you see? You've troubles all the same. No matter, you've got to live with the results, whether or not you heed the warnings of failed promises.

MALLOY
Oh, Christ—what warnings are you meaning?

ANNIE
These here are the meanest streets of New York we're in. And the meanest thing about them's how we're only steps from other streets—where people are living like the kings of old Tara.

MALLOY
Wake up, Annie Meath. Always been the rich, always been the poor.

ANNIE
That's the curse of the other side. Here it's America—where they've pledged to us poor that we'll not suffer such brutality as we've fled. But I'll give you this, Malloy: you're right about broken promises.

MALLOY
Hah! So you see it plain, my way.

ANNIE
Not plain, Malloy. I see the divide of money increasing, all right—and no effort by the pols or the press to halt it, as both lying institutions profit by keeping us people down. I see the poor kept drugged and drunk, and ignorant. I see our own ignorance of one another breeding fear, and our fear becoming hatred; I see unintentional remarks and gestures read as attacks on respect, which is all that poor folk have left to them.

MALLOY
You're saying the old curse is coming back?

ANNIE
Aye. It's a senseless time we're living, ain't it? Shame on people finding comfort in being deaf, dumb, and blind

to the sorrows of folks kept down. But I tell you—the last straw's coming. And blood will run in the streets.

MALLOY

Ain't it strange—a bawd like you blowing the bugle?

ANNIE

I'd be happy to stand aside for some proper crier. Tell me where he is, Malloy. Can you see him, can you hear him? Is there anybody respectable telling us we're living the crime of lies gone to secrets if we don't remember? Anybody respectable telling us there's hell to pay?

MALLOY

Nae. You got me there.

ANNIE

If it takes the devil himself to make us remember where we come from, and the promises that brought us to this place—amen, I say, amen!

Twenty-nine

TWO THINGS WERE PRESSING on my mind Tuesday. I thought one and then the other during all eighty miles of the drive up Route 9-W—north out of Manhattan and through the Hudson Valley towns, rising ever more gradually to the high ground and greening forests of the Catskill Mountains.

First, poor Sister Roberta Lowther lying comatose under blankets in a hospital bed at Roosevelt. I had stopped to see her before heading off with the map and instructions prepared for me by Father Declan; Ruby had made up a box of sandwiches for me, and a bottle of coffee, and an overnight bag with a change of clothes.

Someone—a nurse maybe—had coiled Sister's rosary around the bandaged stump of her left arm. I brought the gift of flowers she could neither see nor smell, and set them down on a small table at her bedside.

Sister's breathing was shallow, sometimes to the point of nonexistent. She was attached to a web of medical contraptions. I watched dials slowly pulsing news in tiny red lights: grim news that a person remained alive, thanks only to machines. But mostly I looked at Sister's unveiled face.

For the first time, I saw her hair. It had gone thin and straight, and white. But what had it been? My mother's own curling dark auburn, as I had long imagined? Sister's face was neither smooth nor ageless now. Under fluorescent light, her forehead and cheeks and neck were laced with old woman wrinkles. Someone had pulled her eyelids shut. The skin was so delicate, so nearly transparent, I thought I saw Sister's blue eyes staring up at me.

Oh, what betrayal! And here I was little Neil's own teacher!

Was that the sentiment in Sister's eyes? She would not be here like this—violated, mutilated, unconscious—if not for my telling Lieutenant Rankin to send around a unit to her neighbor Monaghan's house. And for what puny purpose had I done my policeman's duty—the resolution of a poor man's crime of cadging meals off restaurants? This I added to the sorrows hanging over my head, sorrows heavy as a snow-laden roof.

I bent to kiss Sister's cheek before leaving the hospital and taking to the road. I caught a whiff of her shallow breath: the stinging odor of death.

And then, the guilt of the last night's long talk with Ruby. All night, and into this morning, we talked excitedly of our own good luck and future blessings.

That Monday—the day of the attack on Sister Roberta—had been exceptionally busy for my wife, and long before the performance at Godwin's house. I had merely dealt with Matson at Sex Crimes and Caras at Central Homicide and Rankin at the station house and Quent the actor-trainer. But by ten o'clock that Monday morning, Ruby had come to terms with a buyer for her South Street property. One hour later, she had likely found us the perfect spot in the neighborhood—a whole house for the three of us.

The three of us!

Then by early afternoon, she had delivered a cashier's check to a midtown law firm. This was earnest money, for escrow deposit against a later purchase conditional on approval of civil and structural engineer inspections of the site.

"I'm so sorry I went ahead and did this without you, Irish. But you had so much on your mind. And when you come across a deal like the one I dug up—well, you just don't waste time deliberating."

"You were right to take action. Involving me wouldn't have been any good, I would have slowed things down. What do I know from escrow and property inspection and all that?"

"Nothing, I figured."

I was not entirely sure I enjoyed the vote of no confidence.

"Anyway, where is this perfect house you've found for mama and papa and baby makes three?"

"The place next door to Sister Roberta's shelter." Ruby crossed herself. She is a Southern Baptist. But like many non-Catholics Ruby finds the gesture a comfort at times.

"You mean—?"

"Yes, the Hell's Kitchen house itself. Annie Meath's house. What did I tell you? Perfect, right? Remember on Sunday, we walked past it after dinner at the shelter? Those pretty double windows—?"

"But the stoop is crumbled away."

"Anything can be fixed. I didn't tell you at breakfast, but all night I dreamed about that house, and what we'd do to fix it up."

"But there's a squatter in there."

"Well, there's Mr. Monaghan."

"And God only knows what else is in there!"

"But that's why they call it earnest money, dear. It's conditional on the experts checking it out—to make sure it's basically sound. If it's not, we get the money back. So we're not buying anything blind. See?"

"Wait a minute . . . How did you come by this deal, Ruby?"

"I consulted the expert in anything having to do with the Kitchen."

"Who's that?"

"He knows all, he sees all. Best of all, he's just across the street."

"Eddie the Ear?"

"Who else?"

"You're right. I never would have thought—"

"This time I thought for the both of us."

"So what does Eddie say about the house?"

"That it's part of some old neighborhood estate doing nothing but taking up space in a lawyer's file cabinet."

"Eddie knows who this lawyer is?"

"He's amazing, that Eddie. He knows about the family who owned the property, too. Well, not a real family. Just one old gangster, and his tenants. This landlord was a loan shark, Eddie says. Rosie something."

"Arnold . . . Rosie Rosenbaum?"

"Yes, that's the name."

"What do you know?"

"What a house! Annie Meath lived there, and a gangster called Rosie."

"If the walls could talk."

We talked, about our house. *Our house.* We talked of things nobody but the two of us would care to hear: furniture and wallpaper and rugs for the parlor, and maybe a piano someday; the bedrooms upstairs, and the baby's room; the fireplace—one in the parlor, also one upstairs if we were lucky—and how we could store wood in the basement; a backyard to be cleaned and cultivated, and planted with roses and marigolds and sunflowers.

Also we talked about my dog. How I would finally buy my good big mutt at the pound; how I would come home, and the dog and I would make fools of ourselves on the floor, and Ruby and the baby would laugh.

And after all that talk, it was natural that Ruby and I made love. Among other things, it made us feel safe.

†

"What's happening, I don't know anymore . . . This is all somehow getting away from us."

"Yeah, like we're all slipping under his control."

"I don't mind saying—I, for one, am fucking spooked."

"Oh, what are you talking about?"

"You know how he's always going on—"

"That evil shtick? The guy's wacked, so what?"

"He's using us, that's what."

"Where the hell is he anyways?"

"He's coming."

"Jesus—raping a nun! It's too much."

"You saying he did it?"

"Hey, I don't know any more than you. All I'm saying is, it's the kind of bad crime draws so much attention it throws light on all the unrelated stuff."

"Such as us!"

"Keep your panties dry, pussy."

"Everybody shut up and get a fucking grip! Look—what happened to the nun, it's got nothing to do with any of us."

"Tell it to the judge."

"No man here had any part of it. We're all mustered up, and carded in for that tour. So what's to worry?"

"Hockaday ain't a pushover, that's to worry. Sure, we're all accounted for when the nun got it. But how about when Hockaday starts nosing around and somebody tells him they seen us other times, you know?"

"Nobody seen us."

"So what if they did? It doesn't mean anybody here's a rapist."

"That's not the fucking point, Einstein."

"What is?"

"Getting together like we been doing. That's bad enough."

"Hockaday can't make it out a conspiracy. Neither can any lawyer I ever heard of. Nobody's saying nothing about anybody else, all right? So let's all shut the fuck up about it—right now!"

"One question. What about the guy who ain't here when he's supposed to be here?"

"Yeah, for all we know he could be ratting us out while we're sitting here on our asses."

"It'd be just like him."

"Sure it would. And what's he got to lose? He never did the deeds. He rats us, the DA ain't going to come at him for when he got around to doing the right thing. You better believe he knows how the system works. He's smarter than he lets on, you know?"

"And he's fucking deeply weird. How'd that power thing of his go last time?"

"Power beyond the dominion of heaven and earth!"

"Like that, yeah. Weird shit."

"All right—you ladies about all through with your crying?"

"Fuck you!"

"Yeah, fuck you!"

"I been sitting here waiting patiently for you all to cry your little eyes out over the rough stuff. Now that you done it, I'm having my say. How's that with you ladies?"

"Fuck you!"

"Okay, you're scared. I can respect that. What I don't understand, though, is why you're forgetting what we talked about the last time."

"Talk about what?"

"The sure way out of being scared of big bad Neil Hockaday. You want to neutralize the guy, you go at him through his wife. Remember?"

"By any chance, are you talking pregnant ladies having accidents?"

"Right on the nose, Sherlock."

†

I was no more than ten miles off. Not so far really—and there was no traffic, so I was sailing along ahead of schedule—but still I did not want to wait until reaching the village.

I had to telephone Ruby right then and there. I told myself, If a detective does not trust his own intuition, which is something he works to develop all through his career, then he is stone lost. Not wanting to be lost, I pulled off the roadway into a Mobil gasoline station and found the public phone.

Ruby answered after a dozen rings, just as I was about to hang up.

"It's me, Ruby. The phone rang so long. Are you all right?"

"Well, I'm glad I finally heard the bell. I was running the vacuum in the other room—"

"I said, are you all right?"

"Why wouldn't I be?"

"I don't know. I guess your condition and all."

"Last night, after we talked, you didn't seem to think I was too delicate to handle."

Ruby laughed at me. As usual, she made me like it.

"I want you to do me a favor today," I said. "You can pull it off better than any cop I know."

"Pull off what?"

"There's a bar on West Forty-first, just east of Ninth Avenue. It's called the Savoy—"

"The one Johnny Kay was talking about? You want me to hang out at a gay bar?"

"Yes."

"Well—better me than you I suppose."

"Ruby, what I'm asking, it's not easy."

"Dangerous?"

"No, that's not what I mean. Here's the thing—Joe Kowalski and Johnny Kay, they're father and son."

"No! You asked them?"

"I didn't have to. I saw them together. It connects."

"Not to mention it's pathological."

"That, too, maybe."

"Small wonder John-boy shortened his name. God—so that's why this King Kong Kowalski is a homophobic beast. He's all torn up over having a gay son. He's obese, he's brutal—"

"Too easy, Ruby. There's something more, a lot more. But I don't know what."

"And I'm supposed to find out?"

"There are things I'm not noticing, even though I've seen them all my life. Things I'm not hearing for that matter. I don't understand it, which is why I'm up here in the mountains. So, please—I need you on this with me, Ruby."

†

I was sadly unsurprised by the news waiting for me in the village.

A white-haired man wearing a grim face greeted me as I stepped into the general store. According to Father Declan's instructions, this would be the proprietor—the man who would take me up the mountain in his Jeep to Creepy Morrison's hermitage. The proprietor took one look at me and asked, "You're the detective fellow up from the city?"

"Neil Hockaday."

"Well, you found your way all right. I'm Charlie."

"I've got my car parked out of the way and locked. Is the Jeep ready, Charlie?"

"Sure it is. Who you think's going to steal it?" Charlie sneezed, but otherwise did not move. "Mr. Hockaday, I sure hate to spoil your visit up to Father Morrison, but I got to give you this."

Charlie handed over a sheet of fax paper and I read it.

> URGENT—PLEASE TELEPHONE.
> Dearest Neil:
>
> Peace of Christ!
>
> I'm sorry to inform you that our dear Sister Roberta Lowther passed this morning. She stopped breathing shortly past nine o'clock. You were the last to see her alive, Neil. I'm sure it was a comfort to her in some way that's a mystery to us. In any case, there was nothing more that any of us could do for Sister.

> Please call me soon as you receive this message, Neil.
>
> Most likely, I'll not be in my office. But I'm about just the same. Have somebody fetch me to the phone.
>
> —Yrs in Christ's Love,
> Fr. Declan Byrne

As he expected the case to be, I waited on the line while a secretary—Mrs. Hamill, a parish widow volunteer with her hair in a bun, the sort of woman who works in school offices of every generation—went about fetching Father Declan. I heard her sensible widow shoes clump across the brown-and-white asphalt tile floor. I heard her pick up the old public address speaker horn and blow into it, after which she said (twice), "Father Declan, there's Neil Hockaday on the telephone for you . . . Father Declan . . ."

A minute passed, maybe two . . .

During which time I saw myself as a boy on a hellish cold winter's morning, trudging along Forty-third Street to Holy Cross School. There were pancakes in my pockets, and I was thinking a boy's careless dark thoughts: this is as bad as the world ever gets . . . Someday, I'll take my mum on a big yellow Cirker van, and we'll leave for someplace warm.

"Neil!"

My name fell dully on my ears. As if I were buried in a hole in the ground, and someone was shouting at me from above.

"Yes, Father."

"God bless you, son. I felt I had to tell you straight off."

"Thank you." I felt sweet and sick in the throat, the same as I felt when Kowalski was regaling me with the bad news of the attack on Sister. "She died in a state of grace?"

"We'll trust in the mercy of heaven for that." Poor Father Declan, I thought, not being able to know if Sister comprehended his blessing on her soul through the fog of her pain. “You don’t sound well, Neil.”

“I’m not my best.”

“Don’t be turning around to come back now, Neil. Stay there, talk to Father Gerald. It’s what you need.”

“Yes, all right. I’ll be back tomorrow.”

“Come see me then, Neil, here at the church. I’ll be working Wednesday as usual—the dead table.”

Thirty

"STILL CALLING ME THAT NAME?"

I was standing in the clearing with the hermit. White smoke from his pipe curled around both our heads. Charlie was walking away from us with backward steps, waving good-bye. He turned and headed for the trees and his Jeep beyond, at the edge of the rutty mountain road.

And after all these years, these were the words he chose: *Still calling me that name?* To Charlie, he had said nothing; only the offer of his rough, unpriestly hand, his nod of thanks.

"What name—?"

"You're staying the night, boy." Creepy Morrison was impatient. "We've so little time then to get to the truth you've come seeking. Pity to get bogged down in a lie right off. So don't be pretending you forgot the name."

"I'm still calling you the name, Father."

"Say it out proper, boy."

"Creepy."

"All right then—good for you, you grown-up little shit." The hermit turned, motioning for me to follow him to the house. My shoes grew heavy with cold mountain dew as we walked through the mown grass. He spoke to me over his shoulder. "Now we understand each other, we'll get down to business quick."

"I'm sorry about that name."

"Strange enough, it's like a favorite tune from a long time ago, when I was young."

Creepy Morrison showed me to a small room off the kitchen side of one large central space. There was a cot in my room, and a straight-back chair with a basin for water, and a wooden crucifix draped in rosary beads hanging on the rough plaster wall.

"Settle yourself in here," he said. "I'll make us coffee, unless you'll be wanting tea."

"Coffee, that's fine."

Settling myself took the form of placing my bag on the cot and opening it. Ruby had claimed I would need a sweater in the mountains, whereas I had said, What does a New Orleans girl know from mountains? But she was right, and there was my navy wool sweater in the bag. I pulled it on over my denim shirt and stepped out to the kitchen.

Creepy Morrison was stoking up flames in a stone-manteled fireplace. His ruddy face glowed the same color as the flying sparks. There were two chairs at the fire: one with good leather pads that was clearly for himself, for there was a Holy Bible on the seat, and then a plain oak side chair for me. Two coffee mugs—and bowls with cream and sugar and biscuits—were on a small table between.

I took my chair. Father Morrison said nothing until he was satisfied with his fire, after which it was the coffee brewing on the stove he had to fuss about. I took in the rest of the place. A rolltop desk spilling over with papers was at the window. A long table nearby held a radio, an antique cathedral model. The two other doors off the main room were each open: one was a bedchamber like my own, the other a small bathroom. There were piles of books everywhere in neat stacks, hundreds of books in no particular order.

"All right now, boy," said the priest, bringing the coffee, sinking into his chair. I liked him calling me *boy*. He filled the mugs, then sat back, Bible in hand. "Father Declan tells me you're here on the matter of ghastly crimes. And by the way, did you mention any of the lurid business to Charlie?"

"No. But he might have read about it in the New York papers."

"Charlie's old enough to trust newspapers to get it wrong. It adds years to his life to keep him guessing."

"Father, there's been a rabbi killed, then seven parishioners from Holy Cross . . ." This came out of me in a rush. "And now Sister Roberta Lowther, raped and left bleeding to death. Do you remember Sister?"

The priest's head dropped, as if someone had come up behind him and clouted his neck. "Yes, I remember the dear woman. Please—no further details, boy. They'll only clutter up the understanding of evil, which is the principal thing in need of discussion during this limited time."

His face whitened. He clutched his Bible to his chest with one hand and sipped coffee from his mug with the other.

"Now, why is it I've taken up this Bible?" he asked himself. No response was expected of me. "It makes my hair stand on end when I think of all the time and effort we priests have expended on the elucidation of Holy Scripture. And after all these centuries of priests, what do you think we've gained from our Bible exertions, boy?"

"It's not for me to say."

"Then I'll say what I've come to think. Like all other books, the Bible was written by men. These men were different from you and me, of course; they lived in simpler times, and were more ignorant than even the two of us. And therefore, the book they wrote is quite as ordinary as any other—containing much that's true and much that's false, much that's good and much that's bad . . ." Father Morrison stopped, noticed that I had not put cream in my own coffee. "You're taking your coffee black?"

"I am, yes."

"Only a Prod could drink it that way."

I stirred in cream. Father Morrison set aside his Bible.

"I'm trusting that my little discourse on the Bible remains a confidence between us, boy." I nodded. Creepy Morrison said, "Good, for everything I've said's against my union rules. My remarks run counter to what priests are hired to tell the civilians. But here now—you didn't come all this way after an ordinary priest."

"No."

"So tell me what an aging hermit can do for you. I suppose Father Declan's told you the slander of us Jesuits knowing the sins of the pope?"

"He mentioned that."

"Well, it's true."

"Then help me understand evil, Father . . . I know that sounds crazy . . ." I was again talking in a rush. I took a beat. "I'm an ordinary cop, and chasing more than ordinary sin this time. It's something evil I'm after. Maybe the devil himself."

"If you could shoot old Nick, you would—yes, boy?"

"That's complicated."

"So we're led to believe. Again, the union rules. But I'll tell you true: evil is among God's lesser miracles. Evil has perfect logic, though, which is why we confuse it for being complex."

The priest took a pipe from the breast pocket of his tweed jacket. He filled it with tobacco and struck a match to it, then continued on the simplicities of evil.

"First thing to understand is that if evil did not make its dwelling in man, it would be much more evil than it is. Evil, therefore, cannot be a willful force *because* it is tied to man. Follow?"

"I'm doing my best."

"Because evil's in man, a heavenly watch is kept on evil. God watches all his creations, great and small, good and wicked. Now then, there's the next logical thing to understand. In man—who is, as you know, the image of God—

evil is naturally constricted. Evil's under custody like, as in a prison. And why do you suppose this is?"

"To prevent evil from being more evil than it is?"

"Aye, see here—you're no ordinary copper as you make out. Were evil allowed to roam the earth, alone and free, it would have unlimited destructive power. But it's sheltered, you see, by God's own image."

"Which is how the watch is kept?"

"Good boy."

"The rabbi who was killed—Marvin Paznik by name—told me something along these same lines."

"Did he?"

"He talked about Shabbatai Sevi."

"Oh, and about the Doctrine of Universal Sin? A little help from Satan in the cause of people finding all that's good and just and godly? Bloody fascinating ideas. People called Shabbatai Sevi mad. But who's to say the writings on the walls of madhouses should not be heeded?"

Father Morrison put down his mug. He had drunk little of his coffee, and it had grown cold.

"Look now, I've the animals to tend," he said. "We'll talk later. You must be tired. Why not lie down for a while?"

I took the priest's suggestion. As soon as my head hit the stiff pillow, I began dreaming . . . of the painting by the heretic Petrus Christus that old Glick had described: all of us falling into hell, dropped from the bat wings of something evil that was present even at the assumption of the Virgin Mary, mother of God.

†

It was easier than Ruby had expected. She had simply looked on the problem as a theatrical exercise and decided to play it out in a drop-dead red dress mood.

Easy to play. But, as she would discover, hard to absorb.

"Last time I'll fit in this for a while," she said right out loud as she primped with a lipstick in front of the mirror on the back of the bedroom door, admiring herself all tightly wrapped in Chinese red and uplifted as only a woman in the early blush of pregnancy can be.

Then shortly after two o'clock in the afternoon, Ruby Flagg marched through the leather-paneled door of the Savoy bar, plopped herself on a stool, and made her audience drop dead. Including Johnny Kay, whose mouth flopped open as if it were a pop-top can.

"So," Ruby asked the bartender, "has your boyfriend found his angels yet?"

"You're Ruby Flagg, aren't you? From the play."

"Oh good, you remember."

"Well, how are you?"

"Anxious, Johnny. About angels. Like I asked."

"Stuart's still working on it. It's a process."

"Tell me something I don't know."

"What are you drinking?"

"Orange juice. I've decided to lay off alcohol for a while. Would you believe I'm expecting? As in baby?"

"That would be a historic first for a customer of the Savoy."

Johnny produced a glass of orange juice.

"My husband—you remember him?"

"The famous Detective Hockaday."

"Famous? Do you know what fame is, Johnny?"

"In the conventional sense?"

"You're hardly the conventional type."

"Then tell me something unconventional."

"Fame is proof that people are gullible."

"I like you, Ruby. And I don't say that to all the girls."

"I like you, too. Know why? You're the infamous type."

"If this was the other kind of bar, I'd say you came here in your painted-on dress to . . . How do I put it? Practice your flirtation skills?" Johnny lit up a Camel. "But you know the setup. So, Mrs. Hockaday, what are you doing here today?"

"Being that I'm in a family way, I'm interested in families. All kinds of families. Yours, for instance."

"Stuart and me?"

"You know what I'm talking about."

"Oh, the sacred family you mean. Home of all virtues, where innocent children are tortured into their first falsehoods."

"I'll bet dropping the Kowalski wasn't your maiden falsehood."

"Correct."

"Don't be tight-lipped, Johnny, it's unbecoming."

"What can I tell you? I had a mama and a daddy, my head was properly pulverized by the church, and we lived in Queens." Johnny Kay laughed. It was his father's laugh. *"Queens!"*

"The whole thing must have been as natural to you as a cage to a cockatoo."

"It wasn't the apple pie . . ." Johnny Kay stopped talking. He puffed the last of his cigarette, and mashed it into an ashtray.

"You were about to say?"

"I had a brother."

"Had?"

"James is dead. Jimmy he was called. I suppose you've noticed my old man's about twice the size he ought to be?"

"Yes. I always wonder what secrets a fat man eats."

"That's funny. When I was a little boy Mommy Dearest used to tell me Daddykins got fat because he ate up baby Jimmy."

"What really happened?"

"I think Daddy went fat because he wanted to die about twice as fast as he ought to die."

"That explains your old man. What happened to Jimmy?"

"I only hope it doesn't happen to your baby."

"You want to tell me what that is, Johnny?"

When he finally did, Ruby had to be sick in the bathroom. Afterward, she returned to the bar and forced herself to ask some more questions.

"But how was it squared, Johnny? Legally I mean."

"In those days, there was a doctor working out of a rented room in a shylock's house, here in the neighborhood. The guy had a good business in treating bullet wounds for Westies and keeping his mouth shut about it."

"And the cops knew about this doctor."

"You're a cop wife. What do you think?"

"That your cop father leaned on the doctor to sign a death certificate."

Johnny Kay laughed his father's laugh again, and then said, "As my old man says—whatever needs doctoring, you can always find a doctor."

Ruby left the Savoy, hurrying four blocks home on her high heels. She had to be sick again. But first she paused in the street just outside the apartment building, and stood there thinking for a long moment.

What was it Hock had said?

There are things I'm not noticing, even though I've seen them all my life. Things I'm not hearing for that matter.

Then she hurried upstairs. She was sick.

She telephoned the lawyer holding the escrow account.

"I have to see you," Ruby told him.

†

Father Morrison heated lasagna left from the day before and set this out on the table by the fire, along with corn bread and the last of the peas canned up in Mason jars from last year's garden harvest. There was also milk, fresh from the cow that morning. Being a city hike, I had never in my life tasted milk so direct from the source, milk so thick and butter sweet.

"I couldn't be sorrier for calling you the name," I said. This was about midway through the meal. "We were fool kids."

"Nae, then you was only a bunch of little shits. It's when you was all grown and *still* calling me Creepy that you graduated to fools."

"I thought you said that name was like a favorite tune."

"Ha! You remember that much, do you?"

"Remembering is supposed to be my trade," I said. "By

the way, did I remember to tell you about an old man named Sam Glick?"

"Not yet."

"He was the temple caretaker and sort of Paznik's assistant. The old fellow was devoted to the rabbi. Sam Glick was absolutely paralyzed by Paznik's murder. Afterward he died himself, of natural causes, if you can call a broken heart natural. He left me a message, in Hebrew. Just a single word. *Zachor.* Which reminds me, I still have to find out the meaning in English."

"It's a simple translation you're needing? Who do you suppose you're talking to? I'm a Jesuit, for the love of Christ. I should say I speak the mother tongue of our Lord. *Zachor*—it means *remember.*"

"Remembrance is the message of the play . . ."

"A cliché from the Holy Bible itself—Isaiah, chapter forty-four, verse twenty-one: God saith, 'Never forget Me.' "

"God speaks in clichés?"

"Only when he's preposterously quoted by men writing for the Bible. Come now, are we to believe that God actually told man he'd appreciate being remembered? What possible difference could it make to God and his rather busy schedule if some mortal idiot forgot him? And who but a man—some Bible scribe, some forefather of Robert Waller in the school of mass market literary treacle—entertains the arrogant notion of forgetting God?"

"You would have made an interesting book critic."

"Sorry to be contrarian, boy, but seldom is a critic more interesting than a brusher of noblemen's clothes. Professional critics, simply put, are incapable of writing what they're reviewing."

"I'd like to review some of what we discussed earlier today."

"Query to you first, boy: do you not like cherry pie?"

"Yes . . . No. I mean, I do like cherry pie."

"Good then, I've half a one left. I'll pop it into the oven. We'll have it warm after walking off a bit of dinner."

The wind across the mountains was high that night, as

cutting as any I know that skim across the Hudson River. The windows of the hermit's house rattled. My sweater would hardly do for a walk in the mountain air. So I borrowed one of Father Morrison's heavy jackets, and we set out.

Beyond the clearing that surrounded the house at the crest of the mountain, the hermitage was set up as a rustic campus for a student body of one. There was an adjoining single-room chapel, a small barn and day pen for the animals out back, an aviary, garden, and orchard. Hillside trees were farmed for firewood needs. Woodpiles lined four main walkways cut through the forest. Connecting paths were good for priestly strolls.

Father Morrison led the way down to the west quadrant, and a side path offering us clearest moonlight. Smoke pluming out the chimney from back at the house chased us, wisping through the pines and settling into the wool on our backs like burnt ghosts. Frogs croaked in a brook, owls gabbled in high branches, deer hacked along the stony ground. Father Morrison advised, "Now if a black bear should stumble upon us, just freeze in your tracks, city boy. Let the creature growl, allow him a good sniff at yourself, like he was only a curious dog. He'll likely amble away peaceable."

I missed Ruby and Manhattan.

"You were saying how evil has no will of its own," I said, trying to keep my mind off the idea of something wild and growling in the dark, which is maybe not so much different from city life. "Would that mean it's possible that an evil occurrence is a needed warning?"

"Evil as both Satan and a hapless messenger?" Father Morrison paused. He lit another pipe. We looked up at the constellations in the sky. "That's thinking like a right Jesuit, boy."

"Well—is it possible?"

"I like the idea. An act of evil as warning, the warning being what you could say was good come out as a by-product of bad; or so to speak, the truth versus the lie.

Aye, it's a devilish parallel of the Doctrine of Equivocation—which is positively Talmudic, and therefore thoroughly Jesuitical."

"Doctrine of Equivocation?"

"That goes back to the time of the Society of Jesus needing a way out of heresy examinations, then conducted by their religious enemies who held the power in Rome. If a Jesuit priest was to tell the truth, see, he'd necessarily be placing the lives of followers in mortal danger. Yet according to Society tenets, a priest could not trade off the good of truth telling against the good of saving Catholic lives, for that would be a mortal sin. Well—neither principle would yield."

"The hard question being, How does the priest get a falsehood across without committing a sin?"

"Oh, I tell you—if you hadn't gone and become a copper, you'd be one of us wild-hair Jesuits," Father Morrison said, proud as a papa. "Well, so, the Society came up with the Doctrine of Equivocation, which holds that one can mislead by silence and be free from sin—an aspect of the distinction between action and omission."

"In other words, the Jesuits redefined lying."

"Yes, by way of providing an opening out from the danger of truth to the wondrous safety of the lie." Father Morrison puffed thoughtfully on his pipe. "The heart of any matter—true or false—is found in the opening one gives to the other."

"A middle ground?"

"That's much too certain a place to find. Besides, it's the territory of wee small minds. Lunatics and baseball umpires know certainty."

"So, there is no certainty in the world?"

"Nothing's above suspicion, let us say; no theory, no doctrine. If it's the comfort of certitude you want, I can tell you only this: there is something evil and wild out there, but there is wild goodness, too."

"Do you believe in Satan?"

"The union requires me to propagate such dogma. But

between you and me, boy, I confess to being agnostic on that particular question."

"What are you saying then?"

"I'm saying the devil's boots don't creak. If you can't hear his comings and goings—as you can with the thunder of God, on the other hand—then it's entirely possible to doubt there's a devil at all. On the other hand, if I'm wrong and it turns out the devil's real—well then, I say he doubts in himself, which is why he goes about so quiet like."

"Devil or no, there is something evil and wild out there."

"Aye. And I'm highly persuaded that its name is man."

"A man's boots creak."

"Indeed they do. It's why I take a man serious should he fancy himself the devil. It's a discouraging belief, for history's replete with men dressed up in the devil's mantle. Let's not be forgetting women dressed the same, and even here and there some little shits."

"This is definitely not Catholic dogma as I remember it before falling away."

"Another confidence between us, please: I'm for doubt, and against dogma." Father Morrison had been looking off the mountain, down toward the village. He suddenly turned to me, his face bright with a new idea. "Do you know what I've just this moment come to believe?"

"What?"

"Your dilemma's no dilemma at all. You say you're after something evil, or somebody evil. You wonder if it's in your power to grasp hold of evil, to arrest it same as you'd nab a masked bandit. You wonder if you're man enough. Well now—I say you're the perfect copper for the job. A doubting Catholic is every bit the match of a doubting devil."

"This *opening* you mentioned—"

"Find it, boy, and you've nabbed your Satan."

Thirty-one

FOUR MEN IN KHAKIS and hip boots slapped wet string mops up and down the spongy canvas floor. They had to work fast and furiously inside the big chain-link steel cage. Out there beyond the steam of dry ice and colored lights was an audience of uncompromisingly short attention span—a crowd perfectly capable of overturning an entire parking lot full of cars. No cage in the world was sufficient sanctuary against such sports fans.

In a few minutes, the moppers had nearly got it all, filling their buckets with the sopping remains of two preliminary bouts. A puddle or two remained here and there—blood, mucus, spittle, wet cartilage—but when the sports fans began stamping their feet in earnest, the quick-stepping janitors knew it was time to leave well enough alone and scurry out through the gate.

After which came an uproar of rock music, and the strobed entrance of the first of this night's main card combatants. The music was blasted loud enough at first to distract even Doberman pinschers in heat, but faded down low as a steroid-packed fighter took his place inside the freshly mopped cage.

"Ladeeees and gennulmen!" intoned the tuxedo-clad announcer, perched atop a platform just outside the cage. There were few women among the audience, actually, and no ladies. "This here's the main eeee-vent! Steppin' into the ring now, weighin' two hundred and eighty-six pounds and hailin' from Lackawanna, Pennsylvania—I give you Mighty Joe Fang . . . !"

Sports fans were on their feet, variously shouting encouragements and epithets at Mighty Joe. For his part, Mr. Fang circled the ring flashing the wolf canines he had paid an oral surgeon to implant in his upper jaw.

Johnny Kay remained seated. As did Sergeant Joseph Kowalski, who was a tight fit in three spaces on the bleacher next to his son. It was not King Kong's habit to stand up and sit down too many times in the course of a day. Son leaned to father and said, "I don't believe this is even happening."

"Same thing I think when I'm sitting in your bar full of fairies. So believe it."

"Ladeeees and gennulmen! Now makin' his way up the aisle, the Hawaiian bone crusher—Kimo!" The Doberman pinscher music reached an early crescendo, then quieted for the announcer to say, "Kimo, who has recently undergone a religious transformation, will be happy to autograph your programs, folks!"

Kimo was a barefoot sumo wrestler type with a four-foot tae kwon do black belt wrapped around his belly and an elaborate multicolored crucifix tattooed across his massive back, complete with crown of thorns dripping blood down the beatific face of a Polynesian Christ. He lumbered from one side of the aisle to another signing programs for his adoring fans, always the same message: *All things are possible through Jesus Christ—Aloha, Kimo.*

"What's the act?" Johnny Kay asked King Kong.

"That fat freaking pineapple . . ." Kowalski paused to down a paper cup of beer. There were eight hot dog wrappers at his feet, along with used mustard packets. "One day he's bagging money for Honolulu dope dealers and smoking meth himself, the next day he finds Jesus. Anyways, that's according to his public relations."

Mighty Joe roared and gnashed his fangs with every step Kimo took closer to the cage.

"Who's the champ and who's the challenger?"

"It don't matter."

"No, of course not. Just so long as somebody gets killed or maimed."

"Lighten up. Only once in a blue moon somebody gets croaked out in the cage."

"Sweety, it's moments like these when I'm proud to say I'm ashamed to be a man."

"You call me that again, it'll be the last time you talk. Somebody here's liable to tear out your freaking tongue."

"Speaking of Jesus jumpers, what's Mommy Dearest doing tonight back home in good old Queens?"

"What do you think?"

"No doubt she's with her Sodality ladies. You should bring her here with you sometime."

"I as't her a couple times."

"And what did she say?"

"She says, quote unquote, I abhor the prospect of sudden death. Ain't that some kick in the groin?"

Johnny Kay laughed his father's laugh. Kowalski joined him.

Thirty-two

By ten o'clock on Wednesday morning, I was back on Route 9-W heading south for the city. Charlie had come up the mountain in the Jeep after me, bringing with him a bundle of mail for Father Morrison. No faxes, though.

Charlie had been given a cup of coffee by an utterly silent Father Morrison. He had watched as the priest threw away piece after piece of the mail—the new issue of the *Catholic Messenger,* and all envelopes not addressed to him by hand. That left only notification of a Saturday afternoon softball game in Central Park between Jesuit teams from Holy Cross and St. Ignatius Loyola up on the East Side. Which Father Morrison discarded with a grunt.

My unmarked department car had weathered the night parked in front of the general store in the village. I noticed some scratch marks on the driver's side door, though, and how the window was gooey and smeared.

"The black bears around here get curious about a strange vehicle, same as people get," Charlie had explained. "They have to check it out, you know. I've seen them do it. They hoist themselves up against the side of the car and nuzzle the window glass, staring inside and sniffing all over. Makes an awful snotty mess."

Some of Charlie's pals had come out from the store in a group to check me out, at a distance. They were cracker barrel types, codgers who had spent all their lives in the Catskills; by their expressions, I saw how they harbored general suspicions about folks from down in New York. I overheard one say to the rest, "Looks like he don't sleep the sleep of the good."

True enough. In my hermitage cell the night before, I had fallen to sleep with a montage of faces and voices filling my dreams, confirming what the cracker barrel boys suspected.

God's really pissed off at you . . . Tell me something you remember, besides that I am a guy with one ear missing, which you don't even know how that happened . . . Who can you trust when your back is turned? . . . We need a rodef shalom . . . This killer made a deep incision sideways across the crown of the head, then he sliced down the sides and under the chin and tore off the face . . . These boys, they're the established injustice . . . Charm school makes you think—if you don't hate violent creeps enough, you wind up being just another violent creep . . . If it takes the devil himself to make us remember where we come from, and the promises that brought us to this place—amen, I say, amen!

Now, cruising down the dream of the Hudson River valley, I thought of Creepy Morrison and our talk under the mountain stars. And ringing in my head were the words he whispered to me as I left him, an hour ago: *You can close your eyes to reality, boy, but not to memory.*

I stopped at the same Mobil gasoline station with the public telephone I used the other day to call up Ruby and tell her I was on my way. This time, there was no answer after twelve rings. Not even after twenty.

†

Ruby had arrived shortly before ten o'clock. It was now half-past the hour, and she was still sitting in the diploma-walled client waiting room of the law firm of Ashton,

Baker, Vennum & Vennum. She had walked east across Forty-third Street, entering Grand Central Station and passing on through to the Lexington Avenue side and the Chrysler Building, where the law firm occupied the twenty-eighth floor. Ruby was there to see the last of the quartet of partners—Vennum the younger, who was thirty minutes late and counting.

She thought idly about her baby's name. Patrick if it was a boy, or Patricia if it was a girl? Nathan or Natalie? Francis or Frances?

And what of this attorney's name? In the same way a man named Jeeves is born to be a butler, is a man named Vennum destined for the law?

A tall black woman with a thin waist and expensive clothes glided into the waiting room from behind a mahogany door. She wore a cream-colored silk suit over a yellow-and-green blouse patterned with a Gauguin image of a sloe-eyed island woman and lions slinking under palm trees. She smiled and said to Ruby, "Mr. Vennum can see you now."

Ruby placed both hands on the arms of her chair and pushed herself up. She noticed she was doing this more and more lately, rising out of a chair like a big porker of a pregnant lady; like poor Agnes Gooch in *Auntie Mame,* the movie. Ruby followed the tall woman with the Gauguin blouse down a corridor, watching her glide, wondering if her own buttocks would ever be that firm and high after the baby was born.

Ruby was shown into a roomy corner office containing the standard equipment of a Manhattan lawyer's quarters, including potted palms and stuffed leather animals. She sat down in a chair next to a two-foot-high rhinoceros in waxy oxblood leather, across from the standard teak wood lawyer's desk.

"I'm sorry I couldn't accommodate you yesterday afternoon, Ms. Flagg," said Harvey Vennum Jr.

He rose halfway from his chair and stuck out his hand for a shake. Ruby looked him over, making a comparative appraisal. Vennum had wavy, dark blond hair, whereas Hock's black shock was thinning fast. Vennum was slender and athletic, Hock was built like a peasant. Maybe if Hock kept up at the gym he could look like this lawyer, except for the hair. Hock could never look as dapper in lawyerly charcoal gray worsted, though; a man is either born with a graceful neck, shoulders, and hips, or else he is born like Hock.

"There's really no problem," Ruby said. "I'm sure you've got other clients. Besides which, I was sort of sick yesterday."

"I'm sorry to hear that."

"Anyway, here we are."

"Yes. Ms. Flagg, you aren't backing out of our deal, are you?"

"No, no—it's not that. It *is* about the house, though. Some details I need to know."

"I see."

Vennum swiveled around in his chair and picked up a file from the credenza behind him. He turned again and opened the file on his desk. "Well, here's just about everything we have on the estate of Arnold Rosenbaum, the old house included," he said. Vennum riffled a short stack of old, yellowed papers.

"Did you know," Ruby asked, "that there's a squatter living in the house?"

"Ms. Flagg, I'm not the building superintendent. I'm only the estate lawyer."

"Do you have records on the tenants in your file?"

"Tenants? I suppose so. For what period?"

"About twenty-five years ago."

"That would take us back to"—Vennum riffled some more—"yes, here it is. Mr. Rosenbaum was in residence, until his disappearance late in the year. Let's see now, Mr. Rosenbaum occupied the parlor floor, and also the next floor up. That would leave the garden floor, and the top floor and attic. Now, let's see . . ."

"Was there a doctor in the house?"

"I'm looking for the rental records . . . Ah! Here, there was Mr. and Mrs. Malachy Wollam, and a boy and girl. They were the top floor, plus attic. Pity, there's a notation here. The Wollam girl died of consumption, it says. Isn't that what they used to call tuberculosis?"

"I think so, yes," Ruby said.

"Now, the garden level," Vennum said, reading on through the abstract of legal records. "I suppose it was a doctor's office. Isn't that strange? A girl dies and there's a doctor in the house. Well, anyway, the official tenant name was West Side Family Clinic."

"That's all, just West Side Family Clinic?"

"Are you looking for someone in particular?"

"Not really."

"Because if you are, Ms. Flagg, the principals of this medical clinic would be a matter of public record. I could easily check through the City Health Department."

"I'd appreciate it. Thank you."

"Done. I'll have Eileen get on it right away."

"The lady in the cream suit?"

"Yes. My secretary. Now then, tell me, Ms. Flagg—when will you and your husband be wanting access to the house?"

"Soon. Today if possible, or tomorrow."

"I'll have Eileen ring up the custodian. He's a bit of an eccentric, so it might take a while. But you'll need some days anyway, to line up your civil engineer. Maybe an architect as well at this point?"

"That can all wait for the next time. I think we'd just like to see it for ourselves as soon as possible."

"Very well. I'll arrange it. Eileen will give you a call."

†

I returned the car to the civilian clerk at the police garage on Eleventh Avenue and Forty-first Street, behind the Federal Express office, and walked three blocks back to my apartment house. Eddie the Ear was absent from his post outside Dinny's Lounge, no doubt gone to harvest gossip in the fields of the neighborhood.

The mail in the lobby box was nothing to get excited about: a Lillian Vernon catalogue, a brochure produced at taxpayers' expense giving me a rundown on my congressman's latest heroics, a come-on letter from some health food Ponzi scam—complete with a lapel button reading I EAT FUNGUS, ASK ME WHY. Where do these people come from, and how do they get my address?

I filed these communiqués in the appropriate location, the trash bin under the stairway. Then I climbed up to my place on the third floor.

Ruby had gone somewhere that required some costume preparations. The telltale signs: her side of the clothes closet was standing open, a wire hanger dangled on the knob, her dresser drawers were left pulled out, the lid of her jewelry box was ajar. My wife is as messy as she is good-looking. I spotted Ruby's red dress on the closet floor. And where had she gone in that number?

I closed up the closet and stepped into the parlor.

Wednesday morning's tabloids sat in my chair. The *Daily News* screamed NUN RAPED & MUTILATED AT WOMEN'S SHELTER DIES IN HOSPITAL, whereas Slattery had again somehow won the tip to the tantalizing story behind the story: MOUNTAINTOP HERMIT AIDS COP IN DESPERATE SEARCH FOR KILLER-RAPIST. I skimmed over the reports in each, learning nothing I did not already know except that "sources high in the police department," read Inspector Neglio, had revealed my out-of-town trip.

I did not bother calling Neglio to complain about his leaking to Slattery. With now the dead bodies of a rabbi, seven Catholic martyrs, and a nun, the mayor was no doubt in hysterics. For which I could not entirely blame him. So I understood the inspector's need to make it appear as if some headway were being made, if only a detective consulting with the likes of Creepy Morrison.

Suddenly, an egg salad sandwich and French fries and a chocolate malted seemed like a good idea. So I left the apartment and headed off for the Stardust Dine-O-Mat, with the nagging thought that two hours downtown at the gym would be the cost of my meal.

Halfway between Ninth and Eighth Avenues, I stopped in front of Holy Cross School.

Come see me then, Neil, here at the church. I'll be working Wednesday as usual . . .

As a policeman for all these years, I know of moments that stand outside of time. Untimely moments, I call them. As when a heart stops beating, and a man can be both alive and dead. *The heart of any matter—true or false—is found in the opening one gives to the other.*

Untimely moments are seldom lucky ones. They mostly contain the events of regret and grief that we struggle to forget, only to have them fly back in our faces with the changed wind of some future year.

Standing now at the school entrance, remembering yesterday's brief phone conversation with Father Declan, I felt that what was about to happen—whatever it was, inside Holy Cross and out—had somehow already occurred . . .

. . . Or that both things might have been prevented if only Ruby and I, walking toward each other from opposite ends of the remarkable street where we live, had met in some luckier moment of that Wednesday afternoon.

Thirty-three

"ARE YOU SICK? You've hardly eaten a thing."

Kowalski's plate had an untouched pork chop on it. Another chop was only half gone, still floating in its bed of lettuce and applesauce. Kowalski held a knife and fork over a baked potato filled with sour cream and chives, picking at it listlessly, making a mess.

"Yeah, that's it, I'm sick. Also I am tired. So I am sick and tired."

"Eat up your chops at least. They cost almost six dollars a pound."

"That's the kind of thing I remember you saying to the boy. By which I'm talking about the one of them that survived your sweet motherhood."

"No need for sarcasm and unpleasantness. We're at the table now . . ."

Kowalski's wife wore a housedress, pale green cotton with a cabbage rose print. Thousands of women in Queens, feeding their husbands dinner at the breakfast hour after they had come home by subway from night shift jobs in Manhattan, wore such dresses. In thousands of homely row houses, such meals were quiet moments in workaday Queens, in perfect keeping with ordinary time. Thus had it long been so where King Kong Kowalski and his wife lived with their silent, hated secrets. Until now.

Eva Kowalski banged down her cutlery on the table. Her iron gray eyes went cold and steely as an auto bumper.

"And this is neither the time nor place for ugly disputations."

Ignoring her, Kowalski said, "All these unbearable years since it happened to the little guy, Eva, they been killing me."

"The Lord giveth and the Lord taketh away." Eva said this calmly. Anyone looking at her could tell the temperature was rising, though.

"How come we ain't ever taken a moment to come square about it?" Kowalski asked. "Not even just you and me coming clean to ourselves in this house where nobody ever comes but us."

"Shut up! The Lord giveth, the Lord taketh away."

"All these unbearable years I been thinking about him, you know? What he'd be like and all."

"Don't say the name, it's a stab in the heart."

"That's rich." Kowalski laughed his laugh, mocking her. "A stab in the freaking heart."

"Please, Joe, don't say the name."

"Why don't you say it, Eva? Say *both* their goddamn names. I'd like to hear you say their names. But instead, in all these years since our boys are gone, what do I hear out of you? Bible crapola. You been talking that sanctified shit until I'm gone just about as stupid on Jesus H. Christ as you."

"Wicked, wicked!"

"Not to mention you been cramming me up with food, trying to kill me off early—like it was *my* goddamn fault what happened. Like *I'm* the one needing forgiveness." Kowalski laughed again. "No wonder I'm freaking sick and tired."

"Mind your dirty mouth, Joe dear. For in the Holy Bible,

it saith of the crude man, 'As he knoweth not what to say, he curseth the Lord.' "

"Knock it off already." Kowalski raised himself from the table. He unfastened the checkered cloth napkin tied around his neck and threw it to the floor. "At long last, Eva—can't you find the decency to knock it off with the Bible crap?"

"Joseph Stanley Kowalski, what's wrong with you? You're talking as if you're possessed by Satan."

"Yeah, that's right, I'm freaking Satan." Kowalski laughed. "Sit tight now, Eva, old babe. I'll be back."

Kowalski padded softly out from the dining room to the back hallway. He had taken off his shoes. Being heavy, he wore as little as possible at home, for comfort's sake. He had on his socks, an undershirt, boxer shorts, blue twill sergeant's shirt with a necktie hanging unknotted over his hammy shoulders.

At the back of the modest house, Kowalski opened the door to what he and Eva called the guest room. This was a place where no guest had ever slept. In the gauzy past it had been a bedroom for two boys; one slept in a twin bed under a blanket with pictures of Red Ryder and Little Beaver on it, the other in a crib.

Kowalski pulled a storage box from the dusty guest room closet. It was a wooden steamer trunk with leather straps and an arched top, the kind that smells like mildewed books. It took him fifteen minutes to find what he was after.

He stopped in the kitchen on his way back to the dining room. He picked up the largest knife from a set of six that were sunk into a slotted pine block on the counter. The blade he chose was thick, and heavy enough to butcher a cow. He thought about taking the knife with him to the dining room. Then he thought twice.

Eva had cut her pork chop into ten pieces . . .

She used to tell her elder boy, *"Always ten tiny tidbits. That's the way a lady minds her manners."*

. . . And quartered her potato, after which she quartered

it again. Left hand in lap, ladylike, she forked a crescent of potato into her mouth as Kowalski padded back into the dining room.

He dropped a framed photograph on the table in front of her. The glass over the photo paper cracked.

Eva calmly swallowed her potato, and said, "I haven't my eyeglasses."

"It don't matter. You can see the picture good enough."

"Well, but it's a stab in the heart to see." Eva forked up another piece of potato. She swallowed it, then picked up the photo. She could not resist. "Oh, I remember the year this picture was taken."

"Back when the world was right."

"Yes . . . Look at you, Joe." Eva's eyes had softened to pearl gray. "So young, and fine blond hair."

"Normal size, too."

"Look at your muscles."

"I was beautiful." Kowalski pronounced it *beauty-ful.*

"A dream of a man you were, Joe."

"Our one boy still out there? You were right about him, Eva."

"I was right . . . ?"

"Johnny, he's—"

"Don't speak his name! Homosexuals are an abomination unto God."

"Ain't we all?"

"Ho! Haven't you changed your tune!"

"Charm school, it puts thoughts in a guy's head."

Eva laughed her own laugh, which was remarkably the same as that of her husband. "You can lead a fool to thought, but you can't make him think."

"Anyhow—Johnny, he looks like me in that old picture. Except for the freaking earrings, of course."

"What are you saying? You've seen him?"

"Sure, I been seeing him where he works. In a fairy bar over there in Hell's Kitchen. You remember the Kitchen, Eva. Where the doc helped us out?"

"Shut up!" Eva's hands flew to her ears and covered them. "Shut up! Shut up!"

"Remember?"

"Shut up!"

Eva stamped her feet now. Kowalski spoke louder.

"Only last night I seen him. I picked him up in the Buick. We drove over there to Jersey to catch the fights. Know what I mean?"

"Oh, God . . . !"

"He as't why you never come with me to the fights."

"Those horrible, horrible fights! The very idea. I abhor it!"

"Exactly what I explained, sweety. *Sweety*—that's what your son calls me, by the way."

"Wicked! Abomination!

"Johnny and me, we had us a freaking howler over that one."

"What are you talking about, fool?"

"Your violent nature, sweety."

"What—?"

"You think Johnny doesn't know what you done to his brother?"

"Oh—please, God, don't say the name!"

"You think Johnny and me we ain't talked all about what you did?"

"Jesus, Mary, Joseph, and *God!*"

"Did you say the baby's name when you went and covered his face with the pillow?"

"God!"

"Did you sing all motherly like, Hush little Jimmy now go to sleep?"

"God!"

"Did you, Eva? Did you?"

"Oh—God!"

"To hell with your freaking *God!*"

"Have compassion, have mercy—!"

"Hush little Jimmy now go to sleep . . . That's what you

sung to our baby while I was off to work, right, Eva? Tell me the truth!"

"I can't remember. That's the horrible truth. I was sick! You know it's what the doctor said . . ."

"I know it's the words to a song Johnny can't forget."

"Forget him. Forget the baby, too. It's just you and me now, Joe."

"Strange freaking talk from somebody who says she lives in the past because no place else is fit, leastwise the unbearable here and now."

"Haven't we made the best life we could?"

"There ain't anything *we* about it. It's the life you made for us, Eva. Which is a prison full of wounded inmates. Johnny's wounded, I'm wounded—you're freaking incapacitated. Baby Jimmy, maybe he's lucky to be dead."

"Oh—*God!*"

"How come you can say freaking God but you can't say Jimmy or Johnny?"

"We must forget the boys. We must! Yes, of course, we know what we did—"

"What *you* did, Eva."

"It was you who found the doctor!"

"It was you that tossed out Johnny."

"He wasn't right! He wasn't all boy!"

"That ain't the reason. It never was."

"I was afraid!"

"Afraid Johnny'd remember the song? Afraid he'd tell somebody? Afraid your son the pansy would get you blackballed out of your freaking Sodality?"

"It's a blessing he's what he is. It made him flee this place. It made him flee you!"

"Sure, a guy like Johnny, he had every reason to fear what I become—King Kong Kowalski. I'm sorry as hell about my own kind of fear and what it made me—angry and ugly as sin."

"Joe, how do I make you understand? It's good he left us. I always worried about my nervous spells."

"Mommy the maniac baby killer, she calls it *spells.*"

"I worried I'd harm him, too, Joe. Don't you see? I worried I might kill him, too."

"Say the name. Say *Johnny.*"

"Pray with me!"

Kowalski's face went hamburger red. The veins at his temples bulged and throbbed. He laughed, then snorted, then sang a song of mockery that made his wife draw her hands protectively to her face and head.

"Hush now, Eva, don't you cry . . . Watch all the furniture go bye-bye . . ."

"Stop it, Joe! Pray with me!"

"Hush now, Eva, don't you cry . . ."

Kowalski moved to the dining table, raised a fist, and brought it down against the edge. Cups, saucers, and dishes crashed to the floor. Food spattered the ceiling and the walls. Eva bounced up and down in her chair, hands covering her eyes, screaming. Kowalski reached below the damaged table and ripped away a leg, as if it were merely a drumstick on a baked turkey. He hurled it through the window.

". . . Watch all the furniture go bye-bye!"

"Joe!"

"Want me to freaking pray? Say the freaking names!"

"Please, Joe, don't—!"

"This here's a nice, quiet house in a peaceable street. Know what I mean, Eva? All the time, people get away with murder in the peace and quiet."

Kowalski ripped away another table leg. This one he threw clear into the next room, destroying a television screen.

"No—!"

"You want to hear King Kong pray?" Kowalski moved toward his wife, with his arms raised over his head, the way he held them when he had a braided sap in hand and a cringing perp waiting for his dickprint. "Vengeance is mine, sayeth the Lord."

"No, please—!"

"Johnny . . . Jimmy! Say the freaking names!"

"Joe!"

Thirty-four

By the lights of the usual millionaire presidential candidates of the two branches of the one big party, the only thing poor people have to fear is poverty itself. This is always a winning message. Most people with credit card debt and other such modern inconveniences are trained to believe they are not among the poor and downtrodden. Thus does presidential hectoring seem always to be about Somebody Else. True, we may be indebted up the wazoo, and unemployment may be just around the corner, but we have the saving virtue of being middle-class.

Which is why the dead table at Holy Cross Church—and I suppose dead tables in parishes all over the country, too—has taken on a whole new atmosphere in the space of one generation. When I was a kid, everybody who showed up at the dead table on the second Wednesday of the month knew he was poor. This being neither news nor shame, people were as casual about chatting with one another as they were about trying on clothes for size. Nowadays, nobody chats. Nobody so much as looks at another soul. Everybody slinks around the table in desperate hope of not being spotted.

The changed atmosphere of the dead table I blame on

the success of politicians talking about Somebody Else all the time. Millionaires are good at helping out their friends—appointing them to blue ribbon panels that labor in Washington year after year, luncheon after grueling luncheon, attempting to understand why a poor man does not simply ring the dinner buzzer when he gets hungry—but they have not accomplished squat for friends of mine living on the edge, except to make them feel like pariahs. As a rule, I do not vote because it only encourages them. But I would happily break my rule in the case of a politician who called for a blue ribbon panel to study the pathologies of the rich and recommend ways of improving their behavior.

Anyway, the slinking was in full swing as I walked into the basement dining room of Holy Cross School. People looked like spies in the movies the way they wore hats tipped low to cover their faces. Two women bumped into each other in front of me and were forced into actual eye contact. With a nervous, trilling laugh, one said to the other, "Oh, I'm just looking around for something funky."

I did not see Father Declan anywhere.

Until somebody screamed.

†

Ruby heard the shouting first, then she heard clattering from the floor above. Then she saw the gang of men in ski masks up on the landing. Masks and plastic gloves and socks pulled over their shoes, that much she saw. The rest was a blur.

Approaching the door to our apartment with key in hand, she had a decision to make: dash into the apartment and throw lock and bar, or flee the building entirely. In a moment out of time—too long a moment—Ruby inspected the door, checking to see if a wreath of dead rats was hanging on it.

No wreath.

The clattering was only steps away.

Ruby wheeled around, deciding on a run back down three flights of stairs.

She felt a pain in her back, something that thudded hard against her at waist level . . .

. . . Then the sharp tear in her ankle as she lost her footing, and the bumping and scraping of bone and skin as she tumbled downward on her stomach, all the way to the second-floor landing, where her head rammed into a wall, stopping the descent.

And then the rude kick that sent her tumbling halfway down another flight, this time sliding and bumping on her ribs.

When it was over—it took only seconds—five men jumped over her body on the stairs. She heard them in the lobby, but could not move in her pain to a position where she could see them.

"One at a time out the door," one of them said. "Mask off, socks off, then walk. Different directions. Walk slow."

†

Father Declan Byrne lay on his side beneath a jumble of wool sweaters. The sweaters were not much good, pocked with moth holes and the life stretched out of them long ago. Father Byrne was the same, except that the holes in his back and neck had been made with a knife, and the blood was fresh enough for the killer to have struck within the hour and simply vanished from the crowd of people desperately minding their own poor business.

I had pushed my way through people variously screaming and shoving to get a look at the dead priest—and then scrambling to get out of the basement, up the street, and the hell away from the church. When I reached the sweater bin, I recognized the handiwork of my killer: Father Byrne had been scalped, the blade run down from the top of his head on either side, his face torn away.

I crossed myself, and waited several minutes until a homicide team arrived, along with a uniform squad and forensics unit. None of it would be of any use, and certainly I was no use standing around.

I made my way up the stairs, the same stairs I had climbed up and down as a boy at every lunch period of a winter's day. In the hallway at the top of the stairs, uniforms were herding away the kids and the keening nuns and sobbing brothers. Old Mrs. Hamill with her bun and sensible shoes had fallen to her knees, hands clasped together in weeping prayer. The kids were frightened and hollow-eyed, all of them looking too old to be having such small faces and bodies.

Staggering like a half-blind man up the old street I had walked thousands of times, bumping into posts and fences and people along the way, I had this thought pounding in my head: I am after Satan.

Was I? *A doubting Catholic is every bit the match of a doubting devil.*

Eddie the Ear was standing outside the door to my apartment house when I walked up. Next to him was a uniformed officer I had seen around the station house occasionally.

"What do you hear, Eddie?"

"Bad news, Hock."

I asked the uniform, "What's up?"

"My partner's waiting in your apartment," he said. "He'll tell you."

"What is it, Eddie?"

"They won't tell me exactly neither."

"Have you seen Ruby today?"

"This morning she left for someplace," Eddie said. "I ain't seen her since then. I had things to do. I only just now got back to Dinny's a minute ago."

I ran upstairs.

The uniform in my apartment was a German guy built like a fire hydrant. His name was Haefs, and he was my age, give or take a few years. He had a lot of bags under his eyes, the kind that come from a career of giving out bad news.

"I want you to know, your wife's okay," Haefs said, holding up his hands as if I was about to knock him down. "She's up to Roosevelt. You can go see her right now if you want."

But right now the telephone rang.

"Oh, would this be Mr. Flagg?" a woman wanted to know after I said hello.

"This would be Detective Hockaday. My wife would be Ms. Flagg."

"Detective. I see. My name is Eileen. I work for Mr. Harvey Vennum Junior—of Ashton, Baker, Vennum and Vennum."

I covered the telephone speaker and asked Officer Haefs, "Look, give it to me—how bad is she?"

"She's okay. Really."

"All right, Eileen," I said, back to the phone. "Your boss, he's a lawyer?"

"Yes, we're handling the estate of the late Mr. Arnold Rosenbaum . . ."

"Oh, the house."

"That's right. The West Fortieth Street property. Your wife had some questions for us this morning."

"She's not here right now."

"Well, I can give you the information."

"All right."

"Two things. First, the medical clinic operated in the house for fifteen years—off and on. Don't ask me why. Anyway, Ms. Flagg wanted the doctor's name."

"Yes?"

"I don't know how to pronounce the first name, so I'll spell it: *E-o-i-n.*"

"It's the Irish for Owen."

"I see. The last name is Monaghan."

"You're getting this from where, Eileen—the City Health Department?"

"Yes."

"Any record of where Monaghan keeps his practice these days?"

"Well, I didn't ask that. Is he in trouble, Detective Hockaday?"

"That's an open question. You said this clinic matter was the first thing. What's the second?"

"Oh, yes. I've arranged for the two of you to inspect the property tomorrow morning. Will that be soon enough?"

"How do we get into the place?"

"We have a custodian who takes care of that. Just look for Mr. Mallow in front of the house, at ten o'clock."

"By any chance, would that be Edward Mallow?"

"Yes, that's right."

I rang off with Eileen from the lawyer's office. *Vennum?*

"All right," I said, turning to Haefs, "exactly what happened to my wife?"

"She told the paramedics she fell on the stairs. She's skinned up, but otherwise—"

"Paramedics?"

"One of your neighbors came home, saw her sprawled on the stairs, and called nine-one-one for an ambulance. That's about the whole story, Detective."

"What brings you here?"

"Over at the station house, we heard about an officer's wife having an accident. The desk called your number—but no answer."

"Sergeant Becker phoned?"

"Right. Naturally he sent out a unit."

"Naturally."

"You know, to see if we could help out a tin wife in distress."

"Very thoughtful."

"Go ahead, Detective—go see your wife. I can lock up here."

Eddie the Ear was not outside my building when I got back down to the street. Nor was he sitting in his chair against the wall of Dinny's. Nor was he inside drinking beer.

I legged it up to Roosevelt Hospital, where only yesterday I had held Sister Roberta's hand.

Thirty-five

"So, how was your trip in the country?"

This from Ruby as I barreled into her room. She had bruises on her cheeks the size of tomatoes, a mouse on her left eye, one arm held suspended in the air by a cord hanging from the ceiling, a bandage coiled on her head like a sikh's turban, and a half-dozen electronic monitors hooked up to jelly patches on her side, stomach, chest, throat, and the elbow pulse of her good arm.

She motioned to the doorway, outside of which was standing a courtesy officer, a fresh-faced kid in his twenties rocking on his heels in the hospital corridor. One of Becker's boys, I thought darkly. Obviously, Ruby was thinking her own dark thoughts.

"The kid?" I asked, turning to look at him. He gave me a little salute and turned, allowing us privacy.

"Come here," Ruby said. When I was next to her bed, she whispered, "Pretend you're kissing me."

I leaned down close. Ruby said, "It might have been cops."

The first thing I wanted to do was grab this young kid outside the door—whoever he was, innocent or otherwise—and ram his head against the cinder block wall until it smashed open like a crenshaw melon. Then I wanted to drag the kid down to Midtown South and nail him to somebody's locker—maybe Sergeant Becker's locker, where he keeps his size XXL shirts and his stupid flag pins. After that, I wanted to open a big gash in the heads of the biggest wrong cops I could find and strap their carcasses across the hood of a squad car like they were buck deer I might have bagged up in the mountains. Then I would drive that car about a hundred miles an hour, siren wailing and lights flashing, straight through the door down at Manhattan Sex Crimes, where I would run it over King Kong Kowalski and make him as flat as a sideways Slattery.

My face made no secret of any of this. Which is why Ruby had to be cool for us both.

"Don't let the testosterone get the better of you, Irish. You're too hot, don't say a word. Just listen very carefully." Ruby whispered all this, somehow making it sound like a slap in the face. "We don't know who we can trust, okay? I know I look bad, but I'm going to be all right. Now—can you get rid of the kid posted in the hallway?"

"Sure."

"Take a beat first."

I kissed my wife. Then I walked to the doorway. I thanked the rookie for the professional courtesy of seeing after Ruby and asked him to be sure to extend my thanks to Sergeant Becker. I thought, And Ruby thinks she's the actor in the family.

I watched the rookie walk down the hall. He seemed like a good kid. Which did not matter. I still wanted to smash open his head.

"Okay, give," I said, crossing back to Ruby. She told me what happened and what she saw: five of them, black ski masks, surgical gloves, white gym socks stretched over their shoes. "Two kinds of bad guys know how to make life difficult for the forensics crew: cat burglars and wrong cops."

"It's not about stealing. It's about taking step number two after wreathing. These were cops, I'd bet a thousand dollars." Ruby was right, of course. "Cops waiting on the stairs to jump you, Hock. I came along instead and I saw them, so they beat it out of there."

Or else, I thought darkly, they assaulted my wife as a warning to me. Wrong cops will do that.

"Did you hear any talk?" I asked.

"Just one guy giving the orders after they were all down in the lobby. Short, quick, and to the point. I wouldn't recognize the voice."

"Goddamn Kowalski."

"Same as I thought. Wait until you hear what I've got to tell you about him. I was at Johnny Kay's bar this morning—"

"I'll kill the fat hump."

"No. You can have the city put us up in a hotel until this all gets sorted out, but you can't kill Kowalski."

"They could have killed you."

"Right, but they didn't."

"What's the doctor say?"

"She wants me to stay over tonight for observation. One wrist is bruised, and my ribs hurt. If they hurt worse in the morning, there's breakage. The rest of it's cuts and bruises."

"Jesus, you look terrible."

"I love you, too."

"Sorry . . ." I looked around the hospital room. It was a semiprivate two-bedder with a vacancy. "I'm badging my way into that bed and staying here with you tonight."

"Police protection. Swell."

I sat down in a chair between Ruby's bed and the one I would claim for myself. I suddenly felt as if I weighed about nine hundred pounds. As if what had happened—Marv's slaying, the martyrs cut down below my window, Sister Roberta's murder, and now the murder of Father Declan—was somehow a terrible personal test, making it all somehow my responsibility. *Teach yourself and test yourself.* My face was no more good at hiding guilt than it had been at hiding my rage.

Ruby asked, "You're thinking about Sister Roberta, aren't you?"

"Also some other things."

"Just before you got here, I was thinking about Sister, too. And what's going to happen now with her shelter. I tried to cry, but I couldn't."

"It's the same as me wanting a drink. But knowing I can't take it."

"Maybe that's what it's like being parents. Well—parents of your kid, that's for sure. There'll be so much to do we'll run out of time every day and want to cry. Except there'll be no time for crying."

I was listening to Ruby. But I was thinking of something else: fresh bad news, and how to tell her, so at least she could finally cry. I decided to just blurt it out.

"Father Declan was killed today."

Ruby's hand flew to her mouth. Tears sprang from her eyes.

"He was killed in the dining hall, at Holy Cross School. Where I used to eat lunch out of a brown bag, when I was a kid growing up in this sinkhole. And now I think I have to raise my own kid here. God, what arrogance. God—I need a drink."

"No, you need a clear head." As quick as Ruby's tears had come, her eyes went dry. "Somebody wants you gone, Hock. Which makes me frightened, which makes me need my husband all the more. You need to think, you need to be a detective."

"I don't know what that is anymore."

"A detective is the guy who sees what people are doing, even when he's not there."

"Who told you that?"

"You, Irish. It fits."

I got up from the chair and leaned in close to Ruby again. I kissed her lips, and her tomato cheeks, and the mouse on her left eye, and her chin, and all her fingers.

"I'm sorry, Ruby. I'm so goddamn sorry."

"All right, baby." Ruby stroked my head and neck. "It's all right . . ."

I crept over to the next bed and lay down on top of the stiff sheets and spread-eagled myself. I closed my eyes, I took a few deep breaths and pushed out the air. I set about the business of remembering, of trying to see what people were doing.

Some of the scene was growing clear—*had* been growing clear, ever since leaving Creepy Morrison on the mountain. But so much of the rest was still a blur, like summer heat rising off pavement.

Thirty-six

I TURNED AND LOOKED at Ruby.

"You went to see a lawyer today?"

"Yes, Harvey Vennum. To check through the abstract of the house."

"Abstract?"

"It's the legal history of the house," Ruby said. "Deeds, lease records, miscellaneous notes."

"I've got a message for you. From somebody named Eileen at this guy Vennum's office."

"She called about the doctor?"

"His name was Eoin Monaghan."

"As in Monaghan the squatter?"

"Exactly."

"Dr. Monaghan . . . of the West Side Family Clinic." Ruby said this thoughtfully. I started thinking myself. "So Monaghan was Rosenbaum's downstairs tenant. Upstairs, there was a family. Hock, did you ever know anybody in the neighborhood named Wollam?"

"No."

"Malachy was the husband's name. He and his wife had a boy and a girl. The girl died young, of tuberculosis."

"There was a lot of that."

I remembered no such family. But something in what Ruby said made a great fog of time lift, a fog covering dark possibilities.

"There's something I do remember, though," I said. "There was a doctor who'd take care of things. Embarrassing, inconvenient things that people wanted to keep off the record books."

"Such as what?"

"Gunshots, abortions, social diseases." More fog lifted, and what I saw grew darker and darker. "The nuns used to whisper about it."

"Interesting."

"Are you sure you want to go through with buying this place, Ruby?"

Ruby was quiet for a while. Then she asked, "Do you remember hearing the bells ring on that ice cream truck?"

"You mean the truck rolling along Fortieth Street last Sunday? A street with no kids? At least I didn't see any kids."

"Neither did I. That's the point."

"You believe now in cosmic signs?"

"I believe in little Patrick, or Patricia. I believe in ice cream."

"We can see the place in the morning if they let you out of here, Ruby. Take a wild guess who's going to open up for us?"

"Eddie the Ear."

"How did you know?"

"I didn't. You said take a wild guess."

"Anyway, if you're up to it."

"I'll try my best."

"That's sweet about the ice cream truck, Ruby. This is a good time for sweet. Any other time I might have gagged."

"Speaking of sick . . ."

Ruby told me the story she had heard from Johnny Kay. About a boy waking in his bed in the dark of morning—to the sound of his mother cooing a deadly lullaby over the crib where his baby brother slept. About a dark and shameful thing that happens to some new mothers; something that forever stained the lives of Eva and Joseph Kowalski, and one son who survived; something families hide, and family doctors, too.

"So after she killed the baby . . ." I regretted saying the words straight out like that. How else to say them? "After that, Kowalski squared things by going to this friendly neighborhood gang doctor—Eoin Monaghan? He had Monaghan call it a crib death for the health department?"

"Hyperthyroid, that's what Monaghan certified. It's what the doctors usually said, and probably still do. They used to call it 'crib death' or 'blue baby' syndrome. Now they call it SIDS, for Sudden Infant Death Syndrome."

"It's common, isn't it? I've heard of SIDS."

"Common enough to cover up something you've never heard of. Something I never heard of either, until Johnny told me."

"What's that?"

"Postpartum neurotic depression. Johnny says that's what the doctors these days call his own mother's sickness."

"So what does Johnny know about it?"

"He knows he was a fool." Ruby sighed. "A fool for all the years he tried to forget seeing his mother in the dark that morning, tried to forget seeing what she did with a pillow."

More fog lifted, and more.

"There was a line in the play, Ruby. About blood running in the streets. Can you remember it?"

"Annie Meath says, 'It's a senseless time we're living, ain't it? Shame on people finding comfort in being deaf, dumb, and blind to the sorrows of folks kept down. But I tell you—the last straw's coming. And blood will run in the streets.' "

"That's the one."

"Johnny learned there's no comfort in forgetting."

"And to believe what he witnessed."

We were thinking out the case together now.

"He came to terms with his father, and his father's blind and misdirected rage," Ruby said. "You asked me what Johnny knows. I'd say he knows a lot."

"His mother's sickness, what did he learn about that?"

"That it's something nobody likes talking about. Because it goes against all that sugar and spice we're fed about mothers and motherhood. That this sickness—post-partum neurotic depression—makes a woman weepy and crazy, and makes some of us kill our babies."

Ruby and I lay quiet in our beds for an hour.

I turned to say something to her. But she had fallen asleep. Then so did I, like a dead man.

Thirty-seven

My own sleep was brief, but sound.

For the first time in days, I did not dream of the crime of forgetting. Nor of chilling nuns' tales, nor writers' riddles, nor odd socks in the dusty drawers of Hell's Kitchen, nor of being swallowed into hell under bat wings.

For the first time in days I awoke refreshed; remembering and seeing, thanks to Father Gerald Morrison, and thanks to Ruby.

I felt like a detective in more than name only. For I could now see what people were doing, most of them anyway. One sighting would lead to another, and soon I would see them all. In the cases of some, I could see what they had been doing for years.

In the script of *Grief Street,* here was the opening a hermit told me to seek:

Life, liberty, the pursuit of happiness. Are you forgetting how it was back there in the starving fields of the other side of the ocean . . .

. . . Sure I remember first hearing the promises. But you'd do well to remember this: promises are made to be broken, even American promises.

And here, it struck me like a bolt as I lay atop the hospital bed, was the answer to why an opening is so hard to find: in appearance, it may be the very opposite of open.

Oh, I tell you—if you hadn't gone and become a copper, you be one of us wild-hair Jesuits.

What is life and liberty in the American sense? Or as the mysterious playwright asked in his work, what is it supposed to be? Is it not, in a country of abundance, the promise to all of our daily human needs: food and clothing and shelter—and daily meaning as well as daily bread? And if we should forget this, as a society, what becomes our fate? Streets running in blood?

With his soup kitchen, Rabbi Paznik kept the promise of food.

With their Good Friday pageant, seven marchers remembered for us all the promise and meaning of life-giving sacrifice.

With his dead table, Father Declan promised clothing.

With her refuge for battered women, Sister Roberta promised shelter.

All of them were struck down by something evil and wild out there. *But there is wild goodness, too.* Who but a *rodef shalom* and a doubting Catholic besides to force the devil to doubt in himself?

It was now just going dark. And time was growing short. Lives, too, if I did not act quickly.

I picked up the telephone on the bedside table and dialed the special number. Ruby slept, the best medicine for her.

"Mr. Mayor," I said when he answered in an excited voice. "Listen carefully, here's what I need you to do. First—you find Inspector Neglio, tell him I worked up a hunch thanks to a lunatic imagination. He'll know what that means. Tell him I'll be taking down the so-called Ghost Killer tonight. Got that?"

"Sure do!"

"Tell Neglio to bring some muscle uptown—two or three officers, along with himself. I want these guys on a round-the-clock watch over my wife here at Roosevelt Hospital. You hear me?"

"Yes."

"I want Neglio personally. Along with cops he knows I can trust."

"What's wrong with your wife?"

"She got mugged. By rabid cops."

"Jesus!"

"I'm waiting here at Roosevelt Hospital, room nine-oh-four. I want to see action inside of a half-hour." No sense in dealing with anybody but the top man, I figured.

"You got it," said the top man.

"When you're done scrambling a crew for my wife, then you're going to do it all over again. In this case, you're going to find one more cop I can trust—a rookie by the name of Tyrone Matson, out of the Manhattan Sex Crimes Squad. You give him this special number, tell him to call you back from a secure phone."

"Got it."

"Tell Matson I want him for one-man backup duty. Tell him plainclothes—skelly style."

"Skelly?"

"He'll know what I mean. Tell Matson he should come with a PTP in a bag."

"Pee-tee-pee?"

"Point-to-point radio. He'll know what I mean. Tell him he should keep his mouth shut—especially around King Kong Kowalski and his running buddies."

"Where do you want this Officer Matson to back you up?"

I told the mayor where, and when. Then I rang off.

Twenty-eight minutes later, two big cops I remembered from my days in the bag came clattering up the hallway all out of breath. Kral and Souza were their names, and I remember them being right cops. Both of them were detectives, now assigned to the Nineteenth PDU.

"Hockaday, what the—?"

I hushed Souza. "My wife, she's asleep." Kral wheezed

through the door behind Souza and started to say something. Souza shut him up. I asked, "Where's the inspector?"

"On his way . . . he's right behind us." Souza said this in a low tone, puffing through the words like a cigarette smoker after a hundred-yard dash. Kral stood beside him, with both hands on his banging chest. Souza said, "Neglio pulled us off a Park Avenue burglary follow-up for this. Which you can imagine how that pleased the hell out of the snoots that got hit for a collection of some kind of Chinese dynasty teacups or whatever. Neglio, he told us never mind about the bric-a-brac, we got to triple-time it over here to the West Side. So what's the big goddamn emergency, Hockaday? Say—what the hell happened to your wife?"

Before I could answer, there was more clattering in the hallway. I was warming to the mayor's inspiring style of command.

"Hock—!"

"The lady's sleeping here," Souza rasped, pointing to Ruby, hushing up Neglio. Ruby snorted and turned onto her side. I was afraid she might wake up. But she stayed conked out.

"Jesus, Ruby looks awful," Neglio said. "She going to be all right?"

"That depends," I said. "Is she going to get justice?"

"Don't play around with me, Hock."

"Let me remind you how it's been for me, Inspector." I was now righteously steamed, and about to be insubordinate. And I thought, So be it, I can always put in for early retirement. Not to mention I could cash in on tales told out of school, just as I had threatened in the mayor's office. "I go through channels with an official beef on a rabid cop. What happens? I get wreathed—twice. It's not enough they hang rats on my locker at the station house, these wrong cop creeps bring it to where I live. Then besides, they tell me I should watch my back. Station house crap, you call it. Don't take it serious, you tell me. But today Ruby gets mugged. Is that serious enough for you? You think I'm playing around?"

"Look, Hock—!"

"This is how it's going to be, starting right now tonight—"

"Don't be pushing buttons again."

"Interrupt me again, Tommy, and I'll push the two biggest buttons in town."

"Are you threatening me, Hockaday?"

"That's right, Tommy. If I don't get things my way, the first thing I'll do is ring up your pal, Dick Tracy." I picked up the telephone and held my fingers over the dial. "I'll have to tell him I can't nail this nun-raping killer because you're standing in my way, Tommy. I'll have to tell Hizzoner he should start thinking up some ass-saving comments for when the press calls him. Because the next button I push is this: I phone up Slattery at the *Post* . . ."

I took a breather. Neglio looked at my kneecaps, like he wanted to break them.

"You want me to continue, Inspector? Or you want to waste time?"

"Hang up the goddamn phone, Hockaday."

"As I was saying, gentlemen, here's how it goes." I put the phone down. "The three of you have got two important jobs. First, you're going to take very good care of Ruby until you hear from me. Which means I don't want any cop in the city anywhere near my wife but the three of you. *Capice,* Tommy?"

"Yeah, yeah."

"Also you set up a command post right here for an internal investigation you're going to conduct in a real big hurry. No foot dragging, no charm school, no excuses."

"Anything else?"

"You put the collar on King Kong Kowalski. You remember this Sergeant Becker I told you about?"

"I remember."

"Pick him up, too. Sweat the pig bastards until they give

up the grunts who wreathed me. Also I want the names of the ski masks who did it to my wife."

"Ski masks?"

"Ruby will tell you about that when she wakes up. I want these pigs in particular. I want every rabid cop ass that ever crossed me. *Capice,* Tommy?

"I get it, for crying out loud."

"Just to make sure, on my way out I'll call up Tracy with a memo on what we agreed. Good night, gents. I'll see you later."

"Where are you going, Hock?"

"In pursuit of happiness."

Thirty-eight

THERE WAS I, hunkered down in the dank grit of West Thirty-seventh Street, around the corner from where the late Rosie Rosenbaum was born again as kosher sausage. And this was what it had come to: a stakeout for a rank-smelling shadow come to kill again.

I sat on the bumpy edge of a standpipe, dressed in faded jeans, sweatshirt, a baseball jacket, with the collar torn off, a moth-eaten watch cap, and boots I have owned since Quang Tri province. I drank from a prop bottle of Mogen David fortified wine—Mad Dog as the skells lining the block call the stuff. I took long, slow pulls off the bottle, the way I used to suck down whisky in the darkest of my drinking days. Some things about being a drunk I cannot forget, no more than I have forgot how to ride a bicycle.

A brown paper bag lay at my feet, the kind liquor stores use for wrapping up small, flat bottles. Anybody walking the street would have thought that bag held another pint. Instead, it concealed my department-issue PTP. To kill the foul odor, I had a tin of Vicks chest rub stashed in my jacket pocket. My nine millimeter was clipped to my belt, my .44 Charter Arms Bulldog was holstered under my arm.

The clothes were part of my SCUM patrol wardrobe. The bottle was a prop as well, full of colored tap water. One of the other loiterers on the block—likewise a guy who looked like a skell recently joined up with the crowd that sleeps in Bob's Park; likewise a guy with a paper bag at handy reach—was Officer Tyrone Matson. Matson wore a raincoat a couple of sizes too big, a pair of madras Bermuda shorts strictly from Goodwill, sneakers, and an undershirt.

We had been like this, Matson and me, for better than three hours now. Watching skells taking hits off a shared pipe, or passing around the needle for sweet-dream fixes, or going bottoms-up with a nightcap before heading through the park gates to settle in for another evening. That was Bob Smith's only rule: no drugs or booze inside the gates. Everybody abided, in return for a night of sleep as safe as it gets in the streets of New York.

The Kitchen sky was black and blue, the same as Good Friday, when everything had started. A soft rain began falling. In the gated arms of Bob's Park, where in daylight happiness was pursued, how safe was this night? *About as safe as Christ'd feel right about now.*

I had the cold, sinking-heart moments any cop would have pulling a long stake on a hunch. I consoled myself by thinking that for once I could blame lunatic imagination on somebody else, namely the author of *Grief Street.* But here was I, following a lunatic script, and so what did that say of me? Were my instincts wrong? Would the waiting come to nothing? This time, even worse . . .

. . . Would the devil make me for a cop?

And who knew but that the dark prince might be staking me?

Now coming along the street I spotted my friend Pauly Kerwin the pink-faced midget. He was walking his bow-legged walk, hobbled by the sour sign still hanging around his neck.

Pauly was about a half-block away, weaving drunkenly toward the park, more than ready to lay and pray. A drained bottle of Mad Dog slipped from his stubby midget hand, crashing to the rain-slicked sidewalk.

Then, there it was. Behind Pauly Kerwin, what I was waiting for: a shadow.

I picked up the bag at my feet and whispered into it, "Matson."

A quiet crackle. Then Matson's affirmative, "Yo."

"East of me, less than a block. The midget, and that dark thing closing in behind him. See?"

"Check. What is that—a cape?"

"Looks like it. I'm moving now. Come in for the backup as soon as the cape turns into the gate."

"Check."

I slipped the PTP into a back pocket. I rose from the standpipe and wobbled east toward the park gate, in a rendition of my own boozing days. I let the prop bottle of Mad Dog splinter into the street, just as Pauly Kerwin had. And there was I, just another skell on his way to dreamland.

Pauly walked through the gate, not knowing he was at the head of a deadly parade.

The shadow—face masked, head and body shrouded in a bowel-stinking tent of gray-black wool—followed Pauly like a storm cloud. I came loping after them both, right hand tucked inside my jacket, fingers closed over the hard rubber butt of the Bulldog revolver hanging under my left armpit.

I laughed at myself. *Exceptional clearance . . . Yeah, yeah, as if blowing a hole in a cloud can kill a murdering storm.*

Pauly tripped over his sour sign and fell on his face, rolling into the heap of a brother skell bunked down in damp cardboard and fast asleep. Pauly swore and righted himself. And now stood, looking in my direction, with the shadow between himself and me.

Of all people, at all times, Pauly made me.

"Hock!" he shouted merrily, voice rattling with catarrh. "Hey, hey boyo—how's it hanging?"

The shadow reeled around fiercely. The front of it was the same gauzy gray-black mass as the back, save for one thing: the flash of a long blade, hacking the air.

Silver coming at me was all I could see.

"Hah!" the shadow hissed.

I could have fallen over from the stench of its breath alone.

Then fall I did. But not from stink. There was a slash of heat in my right shoulder, the sound of knife ripping through jacket sleeve. My fingers sprang open, the Bulldog chunked down to damp bare ground.

A shot rang from behind me. Matson's revolver. The bullet went wild, pinging into a low window of the adjacent tenement house. Light popped on in a window, shafting down over the rows of bodies lumped on makeshift bunks. Skells screamed.

"Hah!"

There was the sound of Matson running toward me. And the sound and blur of the shadow, moving to meet the force of Matson. A blur of movement, the ugly sound of knife ripping into limb. Not mine this time. Then Matson, swearing, clutching at himself, twirling and falling.

I pulled the nina from my belt and took an off-kilter aim at the shadow. But it was no good. For there was

Pauly Kerwin jumping up and down in my line of fire, yelling—crazily, drunkenly—as the shadow swept past me and vaulted over Matson's downed body: "Don't be passing me up! *Hey!* For the love of God—talk to me, talk to me!"

I struggled to my feet and moved toward Matson, writhing fifty feet away from me on a patch of muddy ground turning blood red beneath him. I slipped in the mud and fell again, landing on my injured right side. The nina went flying out of my weakened firing hand, somewhere into the crazed movie-house dark. I rolled the rest of the way to Matson, rose to my knees, and knelt over him.

"Take it easy, Matson," I said. The top of his right thigh had been opened. Lucky for him, there was nothing coming out of the leg but blood. But that was bad enough. Matson's rich voice was going faint, so was his color. "Don't be squirming around," I told him. "Save your energy."

"You got to take him down all alone," Matson said, rain spattering a face full of pain. It was hard for him to talk or breathe. His hands were wrapped around his leg, in a death grip. Blood poured thickly over his brown thumbs. "I'm no good to you, Hock. Goddammit, Hock, I'm no good . . . I'm sorry—"

"Save it, Matson. I'll get you help . . ."

Then before I could even stand up, a big shaggy white guy charged out from the house next door, making a lot of noise about it. Besides that noise, there was now a whole park full of screeching skells. Lights popped on in window after window.

The shaggy guy flapped through the rain in pajama bottoms and sneakers and no shirt, stumbling through the gate and into the park. When he reached Matson and me, I recognized him from a photograph in *New York* magazine—one of the pictures that went along with the Pete Benjaminson piece about the right to happiness, even in Hell's Kitchen.

"Bob Smith," he said, kneeling next to me in the mud.

He turned back a torn flap of my jacket, which I saw was soaked in blood. "Can you move your arm?" he asked.

"Yeah, a little." I put my hand on Matson's forehead. "This man's been hurt worse, he's an injured cop."

"A cop? Say, I know you from the papers, don't I?" Smith said. Then he answered himself. "You're Detective Hockaday. How can I help?"

"Call nine-one-one. Tell them you're with an 'officer down.' Exactly those words—*officer down.* Ask for an ambulance, and a mobile blood transfusion crew."

"I saw somebody heading up Eleventh Avenue," Smith said. He rose, and pulled me up with him. Before he flapped back into the house to telephone, he said, "Whoever he was, he was all in black—like a big blanket. Walking along just as calm as could be."

"You can get him," Matson wheezed. "Go on, Hock—take him down!"

I ran west on Thirty-seventh to the corner. It rained from the black-and-blue sky. And from my stiffened right side, it was raining blood.

Following Smith's direction, I turned up the avenue after the shadow. I fumbled into my jacket with my left hand, in search of a gun, only to realize how both had been lost to the mud and black of the park.

So there was I, chasing in the sopping streets after a shadow, having stupidly lost my weapons. I was Sweeney in the play. *Fool blind, too stupid to walk 'round and find the gas wick . . .*

And where else would a fool like me be running this night but to Sweeney's comfort and joy?

Thirty-nine

"HE SHOULD BE COMING right along." The man in the wet cape peering out the grimy window to the street disagreed. "He's stupid, but he ain't entirely stupid."

"Oh, *ain't* he now?"

"Talking proper ain't the point, old man. The point is, Hockaday showed at the park. Which means he went and took the bait tossed to him in the play. So he's probably figured just about all the other bait, too. Which means he's now running smack into my net. Hah! The copper who's going to save the fucking USA!"

"Oh, please—stop it with your disgusting American bloviations," said Eoin Monaghan. He reached a gloved hand across the mahogany table for the whisky decanter. "I mean, really—good God!"

"Shut up then with your fooking God yap."

"I need another drink."

"Aye, go on—you're getting yourself good and smashing pie-eyed. Speaking of fooking godly things—and as you're whisky loose—will you be confessing your crime against the nun to Hockaday?"

"It wasn't I, fiend."

"But you know of it, aye? So in the eyes of the law,

keeping quiet about a horrifying crime's the same as doing it."

"Sister was my neighbor and friend." Monaghan poured whisky into his glass, more than it could hold. He had drunk many prior whiskies, and his sense of proportion was affected accordingly. Whisky trickled from the table to the floor. Monaghan lifted the glass and drank straight back, a good part of it dribbling down the satin lapels of his robe and down over his silk waistcoat. "She was my generation, we shared the same sorrows and infirmities. I could hardly . . . Oh, but I would never—"

"Hah! You're a spry old bastard."

"You're spryer!"

"The state of New York's got a death penalty again, Monaghan. They stick you with a needle now. Did you know that? Aye, they kill you like a decrepit cat. Can't you just see yourself strapped to the prison table, the needle plunging its poison into you?"

"You know I'm not the one!"

"Can you imagine in all New York a lawyer who'd defend a nun-fooking murderer such as yourself?"

"I'm no murderer!"

"As you wish. Let's suppose it wasn't you that grabbed himself a nun and fooked her, Monaghan. Let's suppose it wasn't you hacked off her holy paw, leaving her poor body to the mucking garden worms as blood feast. But what's it matter?"

"Matter?" Monaghan poured another whisky, again overdoing it and becoming all the more slobbery. "Good God—good *God!*"

"Shut up! Shut the fook up!"

"Fiend! Liar! Demon! *Stinking* demon!"

"Aye, like a hundred baboons ailing with the running shits, that's how I stink! And true, I'm the demon you made me. Ain't I, Dr. Monaghan?"

"God—O God!"

"*Ain't* I, dear old Grandfa'r? Or is it Grand-Uncle you truly are?"

"I told you—never call me those names!" Monaghan, roaring and snorting heavily, attempted to stand and throw his glass, only to come crashing back down in his chair. The glass broke in his liquor-soaked hand; crystal splintered through kid glove into palm and wrist, blood flowed into whisky. "Never—never!"

"But here now, it must be so. I see how you're so accustomed to my nauseating whiff you're snorting like a racehorse. Not even bothering to block my stink by breathing through your mouth. Ah, Grandfa'r, how sweet of you to know the rotten scent of your own flesh."

"You're no flesh and blood of mine, you wicked bastard! You're no flesh of any decent soul!"

"Now ain't that a strange and inter-restin' stew of lies and truth and consequences?"

"Wicked . . . !" Monaghan tossed the slur weakly, like an exhausted boxer throwing a lazy punch.

"Sure but I'm yours, and sure I'm a wicked one. But—here you say I'm a bastard? Nae born of any decent mortal? Would you be saying the same of Jesus Christ, who was the right son not of the mortal Joseph but of your amorphous God? Would you be saying then your son of God's a bastard same as me?"

"Truth-twisting fiend!"

"*Fiend.* How easy the word comes to your lips, Monaghan."

"Damn you!"

"And damn you, too, Grandfa'r."

"Never call me that!"

"Shall I call you fiend as well? And shall I call out your own fiendish sins? True sins, Grandfa'r. Aye, cardinal sins we likewise call them in hell—sins that go beyond who gets fooked and who gets birthed."

"Damn you!" Monaghan once again rose, meaning to throw something at the wicked accuser. He fell back to the chair again, but this time his haunches landed hard on the arm, not the seat. Monaghan lost balance and went over the side of the chair, crashing to the floor, where he whimpered now, "Shut up, damn you!"

"There's the sin of a man so shamed of his own he'll even change his name—and run away to bloody America, to prosper as a doctor whilst his own has hardly enough to eat. Ain't that a fiend's sin, Grandfa'r?" The man in the cape turned to the window and looked out to the dark, empty street again. Seeing nothing, he swept from the window to where Monaghan lay sprawled on the floor. He hissed and spit on him, and continued the rant. "And then when the poor ones find him—as children will always find their fleeing pap, if only in their hearts—the fiend doctor takes them in. And they depend on him. Like you're depending on me, see. A lovely irony. The doctor, he even changes *their* name—his own name he's changing yet again! Oh, but watch him cover his tracks! The doctor puts them up in rooms under their false new name, and cuts them off to all but himself. And they grow. And grow terrible lonesome, these two, don't they?"

"I beg of you, please—"

"Lonesome in all ways a man and woman know how to be lonesome, including in the desperation of long nights. Now, Monaghan, you heard how the sins of the father are visited upon the son . . . ?"

Monaghan lay quiet, save for his sobbing.

"And so naturally, they sin. Ain't that true, Grandfa'r?" The man reached beneath his cape, pulling out a long knife still wet with blood. He planted his foot on the small of Monaghan's back. "Answer me, Monaghan, else I'll slit your lungs open like they was toy balloons."

"It's true, it was sin—all of it, *sin.*"

"But now, that ain't the greatest sin inspired by a shameful man. There's much greater crime than fooking the one you shouldn't be fooking. Such as being a drunkard doctor, beholden to despicable patients. A doctor so blind drunk he don't see it when a tiny girl's coughing blood and needing care."

"Oh, God," Monaghan moaned.

"Fook God, I tell you . . . !"

The man in the cape snapped his neck, hearing something at the back of the house. Had he come? No matter, he decided. Let him listen.

"Such as the arrogance of a man who'd conceive of justifying sins he committed when he run away to New York, a man become so bloody American he could no longer distinguish between prejudice and principle. Such a man, what else does he do but become a bloody writer? Here now, the writer justifies his sins—by tricking his audience into believing he's nothing but a mass of noble sentiment!"

"Please . . . Mercy . . . !"

"First tell me, Grandfa'r," said the man in the cape, wheezing now, "what name would you give to such a man as I've described?"

A sprawled drunkard issued his life's last word: "Fiend."

The man in the cape brought down his huge knife. It slashed through the back of Monaghan's elegant satin robe, hacking open one lung and then the other. Then he used the big knife to cut and clip away Monaghan's clothes. He accomplished this job quickly and deftly, like a fisherman putting a fillet knife to a sea bass.

The killer pulled off his gray-black cape. He draped it over the bare skin of the deflated corpse. The remembering woolen fibers of the cape soaked in blood and mucus and liquor and the putrid gases and offal of sudden death. The killer picked up the soiled cape. Before setting it back on his shoulders, he smeared his tongue over the filth, again and again.

Forty

FROM OUTSIDE THE DOOR at the junk-strewn backyard, I had heard the two men arguing loudly; mostly the one not drunk, the one with the wicked voice, the somehow familiar voice. As I listened, I had another cold, sinking-heart moment.

That voice, was it the one . . . ?

I had crept inside the unlocked house and stood in darkness in a back room, absorbing the argument and thereby understanding the truth of rumors whispered by nuns of my youth; realizing the crimes of incest and poverty and isolation that had punished the innocent of this house. Mice skittered over my boots, but I dared not move. Up front, I heard something being dragged across the floor. Then down a stairway.

I moved from the back room toward the front of the house. In the hallway, before I reached the parlor, a door was open beneath a grand staircase. I stepped through the door and found myself at the top of stairs leading downward into pitch black, relieved only by night-gray alley light fogging through cellar windows. There was below the clanking furnace and the dripping ping of cold water, the buzz of flies . . .

Its guttural wheezing. The overpowering odor of excrement and rotting flesh.

Yes, the one. *I take a man serious should he fancy himself the devil.* He spoke in the more natural rhythms of the other side, that was all; the Dublin side of him, and the dark side of him.

I pulled the tin of Vicks from my coat pocket and slathered my nostrils with biting blue menthol.

I heard a shovel spading dirt into a hole. I moved downward, step by step, under cover of this sound. As I crept, I watched it work to bury something in a shallow plot next to a large gray stone.

The shoveling task was finally complete. I listened as it moved over the oily cellar floor. I crossed myself. Here and now was no percentage in being a doubter.

It hissed, and lit a match. The match fueled a candle, which it held beneath its face. Its eyes seemed oval slits of gassy yellow, an alligator's eyes reflecting the moon.

I reached for the Vicks again, and coated my face against its stench.

It moved to light more candles, arranged on a rack of black tapers of different sizes, circled around a chair. Candles lit, it sat down in the chair. Rats were at its feet, staring at me. An enormous rat sat in its ragged lap, worming a fleshy gray tail between its master's thighs. Master stroked the nape of the rat's grease brown neck as casually as someone scratching behind the ears of a collie dog.

My head dropped. I lifted a boot from a lump in the mushy dirt floor. What I thought to be a stone was the remains of a forearm, a wrist, and a small white human hand. A plain gold band encircled the bone of a ring finger. Sister Roberta's hand.

I bent to reach for the ring . . .

Scuttling beetles spooked me, as well as its voice in the refrigerator-humid air, addressing me as if I were an expected guest.

"There's some graves back there, at the bottom of the

stairs. I was putting away the last of my mortal antecedents. Did you happen to notice as you was creeping down on me?"

"Yes."

"There's a tombstone I planted to mark the graves of the dearly departed."

"Including the one you just murdered."

It ignored my accusation. "I'll make you the proverbial Faustian bargain, Detective Hockaday: answer me the riddle of the epitaph, and I'll permit you to live."

"Some choice."

"Did you ever strike a deal with the devil, by the way?"

"I have an ex-wife."

"Such a glorious wit. Let's see if you're as smart about calculating the epitaph. You'll be needing a candle to see. Come here and get it."

I stepped forward slowly, and saw clearly now that I was right, that this was what I was after. I saw, too, what it was wearing: half of Marvin Paznik's skinned-off face, draped over the earless left side of Edward Michael Mallow's own.

"Hah!" It was a laugh and a spray of spittle. "Will you now be asking me, What do you hear, Eddie?"

I fell backward from the wet force of his words and from the stink. And Eddie the Ear laughed and sprayed again. The rats stayed where they were, and seemed to be laughing, too. I picked myself up from muck, and approached the candle rack.

I chose a candle, a thick one with a good long wick, then crossed the cellar floor to the tombstone.

"Fifteen minutes," Eddie the Ear warned me, hissing. "No more. Fifteen minutes before we learn if Neil Hockaday lives, or if he dies."

I crossed myself again and read the chiseled stone:

Here lie
Two grandparents with their two grandchildren
Two husbands with their two wives

Two fathers with their four children
Two mothers each with daughter and son
One maiden with her mother and father
Sister and brother times two.
Yet but six corpses all lie buried here,
Though how this number, 'tis unclear.

"There's nothing unclear about this."

I counted off twelve minutes before saying so, not wanting to give Eddie the impression that his riddle was a simple one, if a guesser knew the key. Which finally I knew—thanks to Ruby's help, and Creepy Morrison's, too; thanks to the brooding pages of *Grief Street,* and thanks just moments ago to my eavesdropping.

"Here now, come to me."

I turned, and crossed back to where Eddie sat with his rats.

"What's the answer then?"

"Incest explains your family tree, Eddie. It starts with a woman bedding down with her brother. This would be your great-grandparents. Great-granny and Pa made this forbidden recreation a habit, and wound up having two kids as the result—a boy and girl. Brother and sister conduct themselves the same as Mom and Dad, and they wind up having two babies of their own—also boy and girl. That's six people all together. The first brother-sister set, that would be your grandparents. The second set are your own parents. Any doctor could predict an eventual birth defect. Too bad it had to be you, Eddie."

"As I was saying only a short time ago, you're not entirely stupid."

"Speaking of doctors, I know that Eoin Monaghan's your grandfather."

"*Was* my grandfa'r. You've seen now I shoveled him under with the rest . . ."

I felt a sourness in my throat and swallowed back.

"Aye, it's a mortal's life I spent in filching accursed family members from their graves and bringing them to where they belong—here, to the lowest room of a house of iniquity what inspired the name of Hell's Kitchen. A ghoul's poetry, wouldn't you say, Detective Hockaday?"

"Speaking of poetry . . ." I was growing sick, I had to keep Eddie from sensing this. "Ruby and I enjoyed your grandfather's play. Too bad you killed a writer of such talent."

"I kil't a drunkard fop, and a liar of the heart. I kil't a self-confessing fiend who tried stealing the grieving truth of others and calling it a made-up story."

"But wasn't it his truth, too, Eddie? His to steal as well as yours? He was a Mallow, wasn't he, Eddie? Mallow being family name on the other side, which he changed to Monaghan when he came here . . ."

There was no response from Eddie. I had thrown him off balance by what he took to be my fine detective work. And good work it was, giving me the strength of second wind.

"Your own dad and mother, they were Malachy Wollam and his sister, weren't they?" I said. "And your grandfather, he took them in, and kept them buried in this house. And renamed them, to renounce them maybe—Wollam being the backward spelling of Mallow."

Eddie hissed.

"Your sister would perish, of consumption."

"How'd you know?"

"But you'd get out, and reclaim the name of Mallow." I paused, allowing Eddie to respond, which he did not. "The tombstone's marked for six bodies, Eddie. But you've buried only five. What about you?"

"Can you not tell by the sight and smell of me?" Eddie stood up from his chair, and slipped off the rabbi's scalp. He threw it to the floor, and jutted out the earless side of his head. He bellowed, "I've a life of being dead! Ain't that just the devil's luck?"

I stumbled backward.

"Yes—I'm the *fiandiu,* the *shooskie,* the *fule tief.* Isn't that so? The *auld sheeld*—the *muckle maister.* Which do you fancy?"

"I'll go with your favorite."

"You can be a king or a street sweeper, but everybody dances with the grim reaper!"

Eddie's laughter at this frightened the rats. They skittered off in a dozen directions. A smog-cloud of his foul breath stung my eyes. I wiped a sleeve over my face, moved back some more, and crouched, feeling around on the gummy floor for the ring I had let slip from my hand.

"Leave that cursed thing be!" Eddie shouted, knowing what I sought. "Leave it lie—for the luck of it, lad! The muck you're kneeling in's like my altar . . . my *memento mori.* It's so nicely shat through-and-through with blood and bone chunks and man-meat and vermin dung. Where there's muck, there's luck!"

I yanked my hand from the floor. Again Eddie laughed, loudly, sourly. I shut my tearing eyes for relief. My feet shifted, my boot heels sank an inch into muck. My head was weaving now; I was swaying on a raft in a nauseous sea, looking hard at some fixed object, praying to God to make the wobbles go away.

Along with this quickly made-up request, I also began reciting the ancient Irish prayer against fear. The one Father Declan had keened for me, reminding me of what now seemed as good a weapon as any gun I was missing.

"God to enfold me, God to surround me, God in my speaking, God in my thinking . . . God in my sleeping, God in my waking, God in my watching, God in my hoping . . . God in my life, God in my lips, God in my soul, God in my heart—"

"Shut up, shut up! You think I'm impressed by your mumbling the *Carmina Gaedelica?* Oh my, yes—I know that bloody old Paddy's supplication. Hah! You thought perhaps I didn't speak the language? I'm really quite erudite, and dead tongues give me particular pleasure."

"God in my sufficing—"

"Shut up, I tell you! Shut up and think! Did your priests

never learn you I'm only that which Holy God allows me to be? That I've no powers but those which Holy God gave to me, including the jurisdiction of life and death—including, in this very instant, *your* life and death?"

"God in my slumber—"

"Shut up! Shut up!"

"God in mine ever-living soul—"

"Fook God!"

Eddie flapped his rat-catcher arms, swooping them down toward the crawling vermin. He raised up a swollen-bellied rat, stretching the she-creature until it shrieked from pain in its womb.

"Fook your God—and fook your saints! The holy fookers all be damned!"

"*Sunt lacrimae rerum et mentem mortalia tangunt*—"

"Shut up with your screaming about the tears of mortal things and your bloody mortal heart! Shut up and behold—a belly full of babies!" Eddie said this softly while twisting the rat some more. "Think careful on this now, Hockaday. Think personal like . . ."

I thought of Ruby, in the hospital.

"After all the horrors I done, ask yourself: how easily might I strangle the innocent life of some she-belly in your world above, or inspire others to do it for me?"

Eddie tossed the shrieking rat full of babies against a wall, then lunged at me.

I saw the huge knife coming at me again . . .

. . . and heard shots ring out from behind.

Forty-one

THE FIRST TWO SHOTS slammed into the low ceiling, scattering bats and dust. A bat flew straight at the candles, and fell, screaming and clicking, its veined black wings on fire.

Another shot to the ceiling, and another. Then the unmistakable sound of somebody racking up a Remington twelve-gauge riot gun, the department-issue short-barrel sweeper that rides up front in every squad car in the city.

"Drop to the freaking floor, Hockaday!"

When I did, a final volley of shots went sailing over my head. They caught Edward Michael Mallow in the chest and stomach, blowing him back against his chair in two pieces.

"Did I nail that sick wacko, or did I nail him?"

King Kong Kowalski was standing over me now in the muck. He had a smoking Remington in one hand, and a smoking Te-Amo in the other. He stuck the cigar in his mouth and offered me a hand up from the floor.

"When did you get down here, Sergeant—and how . . . ?" There was nothing I could say for a few seconds. I was as disoriented as the burned bat.

"In the freaking nick of time, that's when. How come? Well, that's a long and weird story."

"Which has to do, in part, with this house," I said, pulling myself to my feet with Kowalski's help. "Your son, Johnny, he had a talk with my wife . . ."

"Did he now?"

"Yes. I understand. Part of you anyway."

"Must be nice. I wish I understood." Kowalski screwed his face, and puffed furiously on the Te-Amo, the stink of which I had never appreciated until now. "I think we got all the business done that needs doing in this goddamn hole. Come on, let's go."

Kowalski led the way, plodding past the tombstone and the graves of the Mallows and the Wollams and a Monaghan, then up the stairs and out the back corridor to the fresh air of a trash-strewn garden plot.

There was a high yellow moon in a sky that had cleared of rain.

"Look, Kowalski—"

"You don't got to thank me, Hockaday. I seen the wacko with the knife coming down on you, I seen my own rabid self." Kowalski tossed his cigar to the ground, and jammed a pinky up one of his nostrils. "I wonder if I'm ever going to get the freaking stink of this place out of my nose hairs."

"How do you mean you saw yourself?"

Kowalski said nothing and neither did I. The two of us just stood there in the dark.

"This morning I thought about dicing my old lady with a butcher knife," Kowalski finally said. "Which I eventually did not do."

"Lucky for your wife."

"She don't look at it that way. She's looking at the house I busted up. Which is lucky for Eva, because I almost creamed her, like I was a freaking contender at an ultimate fighting match."

"Now what's the problem? Eva doesn't think of herself as the lucky type?"

"The problem . . ."

Kowalski went silent for a few seconds. I heard him snort. Or was he laughing?

"Problem is, Hockaday, I'm trying to decide something of a religious nature."

"Such as what?" I had to ask.

"Ain't you heard what I said? I almost canceled out my wife. Then I almost beat the crap out of her. So how come I didn't go through with neither one?"

"I give up, Sergeant."

"Maybe on account of an intervention by God. Maybe something else. Guess what else?"

"I'm tired of guessing."

"Something I seen on a chalkboard at charm school, where I'm going on account of your beef."

"What was that?"

"Lesson of the day. 'Where there is yet shame, there may in time be virtue.' See my meaning?" Kowalski stepped close and looked me up and down. "By the way, you look like shit."

"My apartment's a few blocks away from here. I want a shower and I want to burn these clothes."

"Any beer at your place?"

"No beer."

"Well, that's all right. Probably you got a phone though. I should go by the book and call in a deadly force report on that wacko almost took off your head. Let the body boys do their mop-up without us, what do you say?"

King Kong Kowalski in my apartment. What could I say? We walked around the side of the house, and up Tenth Avenue toward my tenement on Forty-third Street. I walked slowly with the big man who had had a big day.

"Incidentally," I said, remembering how Neglio, Kral, and Souza were supposed to be conducting an investigation, "have you seen Inspector Neglio tonight?"

"He's up there to Roosevelt with your wife. Neglio was

looking for me, I hear. So I went to him—and brought him what else he was looking for."

"What was that?"

"A list of Becker's wrong cops, the ones that wreathed you. That's right, I knew about this gang out to scare you off the beef. Sorry, Hockaday. I'm ashamed of myself for that, too. Anyway, about this gang—I never knew exactly who was in it. I didn't want to know. When I got virtue, though, I went and persuaded Becker to give up the names."

"How did you accomplish the persuasion?"

"That you don't want to know."

"Maybe not."

"So Becker also told me how the wreathers would all hang out in this Eddie Mallow's dump, which I know from this other time in my life I'm ashamed about . . ."

Kowalski lost his voice again. He spent a couple of seconds taking a walk along some personal street of grief. And I thought, meanwhile, Of course—it was Eddie all along; Eddie who organized the rabid cops, Eddie who lured me to his hell on earth.

"So anyways, I ratted out everybody to the inspector. Then I went on a personal hunt until I found every last one of the bastards. After which I went after Mallow. Who I sure freaking found. Along with you, Hockaday. In the nick of time."

"Thanks."

"I know from penance. So don't mention it."

"Becker's gang assaulted my wife. She's pregnant."

"Yeah, it's what Neglio says. Honest to God, Hockaday, I never knew about that part of it with your wife. You got to believe me."

"I believe you."

"So you want to know where the wrong cops are, right now as we speak?"

"Where?"

"Wearing leg irons in the cage at the station house.

We're waiting for the morning before we take them down to Central Booking."

"Why tomorrow?"

"The inspector, he wants the press corps all nice and rested for the perp walk. Which he wants on the prime time news."

Forty-two

RUBY'S DOCTOR ORDERED HER TO STAY on for a second night at the hospital.

"Don't worry, Irish," she told me. "Some of the tests didn't pan out, that's all. They have to run them all over again. Call up the lawyer, tell him we'll see the house later."

I lied to Ruby, by not telling her right away what had happened since leaving the hospital room, in pursuit of happiness. Some happiness.

Ruby knew I was lying. As I knew she was lying to me. For one thing, she never asked what Neglio and two other cops she had never seen before were doing in her room when she woke up. For another, she never let on to me how much her insides hurt.

I wanted to sleep over in the hospital again, but Ruby shooed me away. I tried sleeping at home, but failed.

Ruby's second overnight at Roosevelt came and went.

There was a third night.

Then finally the news, which was not good.

We lost our baby.

Epilogue

A COUPLE OF WEEKS BEFORE Independence Day, on the Saturday afternoon of a perfect blue and sunny day in June, a man by the name of Mike Taylor telephoned Ruby and me.

"All right," he said, "I've got enough done so that I want you over here to see what a genius I am."

Mike Taylor the genius was the general contractor we had hired to overhaul the house on West Fortieth Street. He started this work of his only after I had arranged for three other jobs to be done.

First, I paid a lot of money to have the basement dug up, drained, cleared, and cemented over. Next, I hired an exterminator to fumigate the place from top to bottom. And lastly, I persuaded a hermit priest to come down off the mountain and into the city to perform an exorcism of the house.

Many people in this day and age believe an exorcism is a big deal. Which it is not, usually. Certainly not in the case of a house, which involves only a little holy water being tossed about and a lot of "I cast thee out, Satans" hollered by a priest duly authorized by some mortal higher-ups. Creepy Morrison was happy to do the hollering. And I was the genius—no, Ruby said, merely the just-in-case type of Catholic—who figured that an exorcism at our new house was good medicine for the whole neighborhood.

That sunny day in June, we entered the house by walking up Mike Taylor's sturdily rebuilt stoop and through the grand front door. Taylor the genius had personally repaired the ceiling, buttressing the crossbeams and replacing delicate plaster. The front windows were being fitted with new oak frames, inside and out, by a fine carpenter named Roger Padgett. New lath work was being installed in the corridors and parlor, and in the walls of the sweeping central staircase. Both fireplaces had new brick and marble foundations ready for mantelpieces.

Taylor had hired a gang of women from the church-sponsored shelter next door and put them to work, too. This was all Ruby's idea: her newest project, on-the-job training for an all-female architectural restoration crew. Two women were busy replacing rosettas and cherubs in the parlor mouldings when we arrived. Four more were at work in the back of the house, tiling the kitchen counters, and painting the walls a lacquered green and yellow. They had put up a sign outside the kitchen entrance that read SINNERS REPAINT!

Home.

"When can we move in?" Ruby asked Taylor.

"A little more time, a little more money—well, a lot more money—and your genius contractor will have you all tucked in by Labor Day, give or take a few weeks. Let's hope, anyway."

Hope.

When we were back in the parlor, standing around admiring the future, I said to Ruby, "Remember my telling you about Tyrone Matson, the young cop who backed me up that terrible night?"

"He's recovered?"

"Yes, he was lucky. He asked me once, Is there any hope?"

"What did you say?"

"I laughed it off then. But I've been thinking about hope ever since."

"And now?"

"I think this neighborhood of ours is the meaning of hope. People who don't know the place, they'll look at Hell's Kitchen and say there's no hope. But people like us who live here, we just keep trying."

Printed in the United States
By Bookmasters